I0688841

DESTINY

Book Three in the Legends of Ralladin

Gunner Long

Copyright © 2025 by Gunner Long

All rights reserved.

No part of this publication may be reproduced, distributed, or transmitted in any form or by any means, including photocopying, recording, or other electronic or mechanical methods, without the prior written permission of the publisher, except as permitted by U.S. copyright law. For permission requests, contact contact@gunnerlong.com.

The story, all names, characters, and incidents portrayed in this production are fictitious. No identification with actual persons (living or deceased), places, buildings, and products is intended or should be inferred.

Dedicated to Cody, Henry, and Samuel West, for being so helpful in my writing as beta readers and friends.

I T IS YEAR 321. One year has passed since the annexation and takeover of Faldon by Elara, ending the three-sided war that waged for almost three hundred years.

Faldon is no more. The proud kingdom that served as a beacon of hope, the last kingdom of the United Empire, is nothing more than a memory. Although they fought valiantly and strategically, it wasn't enough. Now, the land once called Faldon is occupied by Elarian troops and only serves as an extension of Elara's territory. Loronis, the former capital of Faldon, is left in ruin, with no survivors escaping the siege made on the night of its demise – save two.

Elara has won. After three centuries of struggle, and countless battles fought, Elara has completed the mission it determined to achieve when rebelling from the United Empire. The land of Faldon now in their hands, they need only to tighten the grip to solidify their dominance, a process which is well underway.

In Kallary, the days of the city-states are at an end. Under the banner of several powerful kings, each city gathers in groups to be led by who they believe to be the most powerful. The kings on the border watch Elara, leery of an attack at any moment. So far, however, the Kingdom of Shadow has made no move.

And so Ralladin waits, in fearful expectation. The war has ended; the victors are decided. But after so long a conflict, how will the world alter when there is none?

PROLOGUE

C osgroc couldn't believe that this man thought he was smarter than him. Any other time, this would have amused him. He wasn't amused now.

"After we tricked them, it was simple: my men rushed them from either side of the bridge, all eight of us. The looks on their faces when they realized what was happening were priceless. They put up a stout fight, to be sure; I can see them causing a fair bit of trouble for you. Luckily, our numbers worked to our advantage, and we took care of them without any losses."

The bandit leader spoke to Cosgroc in an even tone. He tried not to notice how much taller Cosgroc was than him. The brigand was usually the intimidating one in conversations, but in this case, the dark knight was far more imposing. The bandit tried not to let it bother him, although he found it a little unnerving, the way the dark knight stared at him through the black eyeholes in his helmet.

Both of them stood in a tent, one of the many that made up the brigand's camp. It was midmorning, and outside the tent the men just finished breakfast, and were lazily puttering around the camp.

About five minutes ago, the leader was doing the same, before the knight walked into the camp without warning. The men were all frightened when they saw him, and started to grab their weapons, but the leader stood them down and explained that this was their contractor, the warrior who agreed to pay them for getting rid of the two men on the bridge. The leader then led the warrior into his tent to talk business.

Once there, the tall warrior spoke for the first time since arriving, asking for the leader to explain exactly how he went about getting rid of the two men on the bridge. The leader was surprised. How did he know they had taken care of it? The leader didn't send out any word of their success to them; after all, it was only two days ago that the confrontation on the bridge occurred. The leader pushed the thought out of mind, deciding that the warrior must have made a lucky guess.

"We dumped their bodies in the river," the leader continued, ignoring the way the warrior stared at him. It annoyed him that the knight was wearing a helmet, so he couldn't see his face and his expression. "We made sure to leave no trace that anything happened. They've probably floated miles away by now, if not already eaten by vultures."

The warrior didn't respond or make any move. In fact, there was a possibility that the warrior had turned to stone with how still he was. The leader was a little uneasy. He knew that, technically speaking, he was lying to this giant knight's face. Although words like 'we took care of them' didn't exactly mean that they killed both of them, it was close enough. Their order was strict that they were to make sure the targets were dead, but what did that matter?

All that really mattered was the fact that they were never going to be seen again. And if one drowned in a river and another was a slave, then it was the same as if they were dead.

After a long and uneasy silence, the warrior spoke. He made absolutely no movement when he did, which startled the leader and made it seem as if the voice was coming from nowhere. "Both of them are dead?"

The leader hesitated. He was faced with a choice. He could go with the truth. It would be the right thing to do. But, as it turns out, honesty doesn't pay. "Yes. There is no way that they are still alive."

Another period of silence. The dark knight stood as still as a statue, staring down at the brigand chief. The chief, trying his best not to look intimidated, stared back up at him. The empty gaze of the knight stared holes into his soul, but the leader didn't let his gaze waver, even if it caused fear to gnaw at his heart.

The leader spoke, partly to break the silence, partly because if he didn't, he was afraid the fear might get the best of him. "Now, about you holding up your side of your agreement?"

The dark knight chuckled, a chilling laugh that was as warm and friendly as the wind in a snowstorm. He finally moved, lifting his head slightly to amplify his laugh. "And what about it, may I ask?"

The voice was sarcastically innocent. Cold fear gripped the leader's heart. He had the feeling that this knight was toying with him, like a cat toyed with its prey. The leader did everything in his power not to show how panicked he was on the inside. "Don't banter with me! We agreed on the price to be paid for my work. I assume you brought it, unless you planned on dropping in just to have tea and chat?" The bandit's voice faltered slightly at the end, because even he knew that the last comment was a little too much.

"Oh, that!" Once again, the warrior's voice was mockingly naïve. "Pardon me, but I did not come with the money. See, it's an aggravating trait of mine to only reward those who actually do their work, not people who halfway complete their job, then lie to my face about it!"

Another gust of cold wind in the leader's heart. "What do you mean?"

And just like that, all pretense of the friendly and sarcastic attitude dropped. The dark knight's voice lashed out at the bandit like a wild animal. "You fool!" Cosgroc screamed, his words brimming with pure rage. "You think I don't know? You must consider me stupid to think that I wouldn't know, that there wouldn't be consequences!"

Startled, the leader stepped back a few paces, cowering like cornered prey. He dropped his gaze from the warrior and stared at the floor. His cracked voice testified to his fear. "Wouldn't know what?"

"That you failed!" Cosgroc yelled. He chuckled sardonically when the leader looked bewildered. "Don't act so surprised. I have eyes and ears everywhere, and it's hard not to notice when the two men I specifically ordered to kill are still running wild. Even I am capable of that!"

The leader cringed. "But one of them is dead! I mean... the first one drowned! And – and the second one, he's a slave, so you'll never see him again! It isn't any different than if they were dead."

"It is different. Very different." Cosgroc said slowly but heavily. "For your information, they are *both* still breathing. They are more dangerous than you realize, more dangerous than your vain little head could ever comprehend. I hired you to do only one thing, one simple little task, and you failed." The knight chuckled again. "Do you know what happens to people who fail us?"

The bandit knew all too well. "Please, just give us another chance! I – I can make sure of it this time! I won't fail you again. You have my word!" The brigand spoke quickly, his voice choppy.

The warrior shook his head slowly. "I don't make the same mistake twice. Now, neither will you."

***

The men all noticed when the dark warrior left the leader's tent, but said nothing. They all pretended to be occupied, fixing their eyes on something else as the dark knight walked through the camp, afraid that he might notice them. Everyone breathed a sigh of relief when the knight disappeared into the woods.

For a long time, they waited for their captain to emerge from the tent. They were expecting money, but didn't see the knight carrying any. They had questions, but knew better than to barge into the tent without invitation. So, they waited.

And waited. And waited. Finally, after almost an hour, they suspected that something was wrong. By the time they worked up the courage to enter the tent and saw what happened, the knight was long gone.

I

*H*ow far away could *they be?* Jayfor wondered as he walked quickly down the road. He didn't know how long he had been walking, but it felt like too long. Then again, he didn't know how long he had been unconscious after falling in the river, so he couldn't gage very well how much farther he had to go.

He looked ahead. In about fifty yards, the woods started to fade into an open plain. The trees that currently lined the roadside became sparser, and instead of underbrush, grass became the lawn of the ground.

As he was walking out of the woods and into the plain, Jayfor started to second guess what the man at the riverside said – the hooded, mysterious man that seemed to know everything about both Jayfor and Trenson. He said that Trenson was enslaved, and currently heading to a city – what was the name? Talikan? Something like that – to be auctioned. Jayfor, still a little light-headed from being knocked out, accepted the man's words as truth. But now, his head a little clearer, he wondered if it was a good idea, trusting the man. Could he?

The man denied that he was a Senver. Could Senver lie? Was that possible? Or maybe this man was just a normal person and it was all a coincidence.

Jayfor decided not to think too hard about it. He had something far more important that he needed to focus on: find Trenson.

The road became wider under his feet, and as Jayfor noticed this, he saw something that caught his attention on the ground. He stopped walking and kneeled to get a closer look. He wasn't an expert on tracking, but he recognized the two lines in the road as being wheel tracks, the type that would be made from caravans.

While he had a closer look, he also took note of the fresh footprints that lined the ground as well. These markings had to be fresh. It had rained a few days ago, and any markings made before that would have been washed away.

Jayfor got to his feet again and started walking with new vigor. Maybe the man at the river wasn't crazy after all.

As Jayfor made more progress, his thoughts drifted to the last words of the riverside man, about Trenson being enslaved and taken to be auctioned. In his mind, he pieced together what happened after falling into the river. He fell in, and Trenson kept fighting, but had lost in some way. The bandits found a slave caravan, and sold him to them on the spot.

Jayfor frowned. Slave caravan? What were slaves doing in Faldon? Jayfor remembered putting in more strict penalties than there originally had been for those dealing with slaves. It was a practice that, while common in Elara and Kallary, was unheard of here. It had been illegal in Faldon before the division of the United Empire.

Well, this isn't Faldon anymore, Jayfor thought, *and so there is no law. Who is there to enforce it? No one,* he dolefully answered his own question. There was nobody in charge, nobody honored

Va'ar like they used to, when the world was at least a little better place.

Far ahead, he saw something that halted his thoughts. There it was! Or at least, it probably was. It was a caravan. It was still too far away to make out any details, let alone Trenson, but the outline of it lifted Jayfor's spirits. He needed to get closer before he started celebrating.

Something dawned on him: He shouldn't follow the train from behind. If he just walked and followed it behind – and he didn't know how he was going to free Trenson, and so it might take days to find a way – they might get suspicious.

He looked around for a way to follow more inconspicuously. The sides of the road were a little higher than the road itself, forming little hills on either side of the path. An idea presented itself. Jayfor walked to the side of the road and started to walk slowly up the incline, grunting under the weight of his equipment. Thankfully, the hill wasn't too tall, and he made it to the top.

From his view at the top, beside the plains that lay before him, Jayfor noticed something else: the hill slowly declined until the ground became the same level as the road. After congratulating himself for this discovery, Jayfor resumed walking, this time on the opposite side of the hill as the road and the cart. Now he could follow them without their knowledge.

He kept checking over the hill as he walked, never allowing himself more than a few moments of looking over before retreating down and out of sight. Slowly, the caravan started coming closer, the outline becoming clearer. Before long, he could make out a few shapes moving around the wagon, which he assumed were people.

Leading the convoy was the wagon itself. It was a fairly large wagon, larger than the one Jayfor and Trenson defended in the woods, but not by much. An older man with a sour face was driving the cart from a stool in the front.

Lining the convoy on either side were guards, all of them with spears and wearing plain leather armor – mercenaries, Jayfor guessed. They looked like they were paid to be there. There were nine of them, and they walked on either side of the convoy.

What attracted Jayfor's attention the most was the human cargo that was being forced to walk in time with the squeaking wheels of the cart: slaves. Jayfor spotted Trenson immediately. It was easy to do so because he looked the freshest, the most well-fed, and the least depressed. Everyone else in front of him, chained together in a single line, was walking with their backs hunched over, their skin tight against their bones, and bearing empty expressions. Jayfor shuddered at seeing how animal people could become when they were treated like one.

Now he had his target, and knew the dangers. Trenson really was a slave, and really was chained and being taken to be sold.

There was no way Jayfor was about to let that happen. He had to find a way to free Trenson before they reached the city he was to be sold at.

Jayfor looked up at the sky. It was late afternoon. He had a few more hours until nightfall. If he was to attempt anything, it best be done under the cover of darkness. Methodically, he devised a plan: when the convoy stopped for the night, he would sneak into the camp, search for the keys to Trenson's chains, and find a way to set him free. It was a skeleton plan, he knew, but it was the best one he could think of.

Jayfor had no idea how far away the next town was – the map that he used was in Trenson's pack, which was now in the hands of the slavers. They could reach the town tomorrow, or in a month. It was the uncertainty of time that forced Jayfor to act quickly. And once he freed him, they could continue on their mission – who knew how much farther they had to go to reach the end of that.

In any case, he would free Trenson tonight. Jayfor's stomach grumbled. *I can't wait to eat and get warm by a fire tonight,* he thought. Then he realized that Trenson wouldn't be able to start the fire for him. He sighed. *Minus the fire.*

II

TRENSON STARED DOWN AT the cakey, bubbling, steaming soup in his bowl. He shook it, watching the pieces of who knows what shake and gurgle. A few hours ago, he had been starving, convinced that he could eat almost anything. Now, not so much.

The slave that was sitting next to him, a young man by the name of Colly, grinned at Trenson knowingly and nudged him in the ribs. "I had the chef make this batch special, you know, to welcome you here. It's his secret recipe."

Trenson huffed, still staring down at the bowl. "It's no secret that even the vultures would find this inedible."

"Aw, it's not that bad! Sometimes, I pinch my nose, and if I think hard enough, it almost tastes like runny eggs." Colly never stopped grinning.

"You like runny eggs?" Trenson asked skeptically.

"Well, no, not really, but it sure tastes better than this soup. Maybe that's one of the ingredients."

Trenson didn't respond. He knew that any type of response would only make Colly talk more, and talking was one thing Trenson didn't want to do.

He didn't understand how Colly could be so cheerful. Earlier that day, when Trenson was chained to the others, Colly was the slave in front of him. Trenson soon found out he was talkative – very talkative. In a matter of minutes, Trenson knew where Colly was born, how old he was, that his favorite place to fish was near here, and that he had a dog named Chips he wished he had brought with him. Trenson had no idea how Colly managed to treat this like it was a vacation, but he did. Trenson was already dying to leave, not just to continue the mission, but so he wouldn't have to deal with this man who was even more talkative than Jayfor.

"I asked the man who cooks it, I asked him what he puts in it," Colly started again after Trenson didn't respond. "He wouldn't tell me, though. I would tell you what he said, but they weren't very nice words. Anyway, he didn't tell me."

Colly stopped talking for a precious second as he lifted the bowl up and tipped the contents into his mouth, drinking the soup slowly. He wiped his mouth with his arm and licked his lips slowly, as if savoring a famous delicacy. "I think I taste a hint of turnips in there. Maybe that's what the chunks are."

"Sure," Trenson replied evenly.

"I like turnips," Colly continued. "We used to have contests back home to see who could grow the biggest turnip in the town. I tried to enter once or twice, but I always lost to farmer McDan, who could grow some as large as your arm. I don't understand how he did it!"

Trenson gave Colly the side eye. Either Trenson wasn't doing a good job sending the unspoken message that he didn't want to talk, or Colly was just ignoring him. "I don't know."

Colly shrugged and took another sip of the soup. He looked around him, and Trenson knew that he was looking for something else to talk about. Unfortunately, he found something. "Hey Aquila, do you think anything is wrong with this soup?"

Trenson followed Colly's gaze to a man – a very large man, at that – sitting across from them on the other side of the fire. Aquila had already finished his soup – he had literally poured it down his throat as soon as he received it from the guard. With a smile that showed the wide gaps in his teeth, Aquila shook his head.

Trenson looked up from the soup. Normally he wasn't one to start a conversation, but his interest was piqued at the man's name. "Aquila? Your name is Aquila? Like in the story?"

Aquila's smile slowly faded. He stared at Trenson a few seconds, then looked at Colly. Colly turned to Trenson.

"You'll have to excuse him. He can't talk."

Trenson was taken aback. "Oh..."

"It's OK, he's used to it. Don't get me wrong, he's every bit as smart, if not more, than the rest of us. But when he was born he never could make as much as a noise. He can lift just about anything you ask him to, and wouldn't hurt a fly, but... don't try to start a conversation, 'cause it would be pretty one sided."

And you know all about one-sided conversations, Trenson thought. He glanced apologetically at Aquila. "Sorry."

Aquila smiled again and waved his hand in a dismissive gesture. Then he looked him in the eye, looked at the bowl of soup in Trenson's hands, then looked at Trenson again, still smiling.

Trenson caught the unspoken message. "You want this?"

Aquila nodded vigorously.

Trenson's stomach rumbled. He was hungry, very hungry. But looking down at the gray-colored goop in his bowl, he knew that someone else would enjoy it much more. He stood up and started walking around the fire, but he forgot about the chain around his right ankle. The chain grew taunt and rattled, and Trenson hobbled forward on his free leg before regaining balance, almost spilling the soup in the process.

Colly chuckled. "I was wondering if you would forget!" Trenson sighed and looked down at the cuff that circled his right ankle. He had forgotten; he wished he could forget again. It was bad enough that he was chained, but even worse was the fact that everyone was chained together in one long line. If he wanted to escape, he would either have to break his chain, or take everyone with him. Two not-so-great options.

"Here," Colly offered, holding out his hand. "I'll pass it around the circle."

Trenson handed the bowl to him and returned to his seat on the ground. Colly passed the bowl to the slave next to him, telling him to pass it around to Aquila. The slave, without so much as batting an eye, took the bowl and handed it to the next man, who handed it to the next, and so on until the bowl finally reached Aquila.

Aquila hungrily watched the bowl as it was passed around, rubbing his hands together. When it came around, he snatched it from the last man's hand and started chugging it down, drinking it like it was water in a desert.

Trenson let a rare smile cress his face. It was good to see someone enjoying themself. Trenson spoke in a low tone to Colly. "His name is Aquila, you said?"

"To be honest, I don't know. He was in this caravan longer than me, and when I first met him I immediately thought of the hero from the story, you know? The hero Aquila, who could lift trees out of the ground like it was nothing? That's who I thought of when I first saw him. I asked his name, but of course he couldn't tell me, so I started saying all the names I could think of, but he shook his head at all of them. I eventually gave up and told him I would call him Aquila, since he reminds me of the story. He liked that, so I don't think he minds."

Trenson looked at Aquila again. He didn't remember much of the old story, but from what he remembered about the hero, this man seemed to fit the description pretty well.

Shockingly, Colly didn't start another conversation. Trenson looked over, figuring that something had to be wrong, but surprisingly, Colly was silent. Colly was sipping his soup very slowly with a philosophical look on his face, trying to decide on what ingredients were in it. Trenson was relieved; maybe now he could have some peace.

He surveyed the camp as a whole. It was split into two groups: the slaves, and then everyone else. The slaves' area was a fire. That was about all there was to it. The guards had made a fire, instructed that the slaves stay around it and that this where they'd spend the night, and that was it. No tents, no blankets, nothing. It would be a long night in the cold.

Trenson shivered in the cool breeze that suddenly blew through the camp. The air had turned much colder recently, and Trenson wasn't dressed for it. He longed for his woolen vest that he wore at Loronis when it was cold. He tried to sit as close to the fire as possible, but was cautious not to get too close in case the wind suddenly changed direction.

Trenson looked at everyone that was huddled around the fire. The rest of the slaves wore more threadbare clothing – *they must be freezing,* Trenson thought – and looked defeated. That was the word that Trenson thought best described them; they had given up on everything and now simply did as they were told, without a word. Trenson hadn't heard one of them speak since he joined the caravan. They also looked starved, their skin drawn tight against thin bones. Although Colly and Aquila looked a little hungry as well, it wasn't near as much as the others. Trenson concluded that they must be new to the caravan as well. Was this what they would look like in time? The thought chilled Trenson's heart.

The guards and the cart driver didn't seem cold or hungry. Trenson could see them in their group to the side, their tents in a neat circle around a fire. Trenson could also smell the slab of meat that was cooking over the fire, and it sent his mouth watering and his stomach rumbling even more. *Must be nice,* Trenson thought as another gust of wind came and chilled him to the bone.

He needed to escape. The thought came to him again. He looked down at the chain. Maybe he could break the chain in some way? But this looked like reinforced steel, not at all like the light steel used in common utensils. His eyes landed on a key hole on the cuffs. Key holes mean keys. If anyone was to have a key, it would be the cart driver. Maybe he could ask for the rest of the slaves help in retrieving the key from the driver's tent while he was sleeping, so that he could move around without being held back. His reason dismissed it – too many moving pieces, and far too likely to go wrong.

As he sat in thought, Colly decided that it had been silent for too long. "I wonder what breed that dog is," he said suddenly.

Trenson snapped out of his trance. "What?"

"That dog. I wonder what breed that dog is."

Trenson followed Colly's gaze to a medium-sized dog that was covered in thick gray hair, curled up in a ball by the slaver's fire sleeping. It had a snout that was longer than usual, and rested it on the ground beside his bushy tail that acted as an extra blanket. *I wish I had a bushy tail I could use as a blanket right now*, Trenson wished dolefully.

"I don't know," Trenson replied.

Colly looked harder at the dog, as if squinting would make its breed apparent. "He looks too hairy to be a Southern Sheperd, but he has the build to be one. Maybe he is one? No, he can't be. Or maybe he's a mutt and has some Southern Sheperd in him. That's probably right."

"Probably." Trenson tried to act like he was listening, when in reality he was walking the line between awake and asleep, trying to resist, but failing miserably. He had to stay awake, he told himself. Even if it meant he had to stay up all night, he would wait for an opportunity to escape, no matter what. He wouldn't – he let out a gigantic yawn, so large that he thought he would dislocate his jaw – he wouldn't fall asleep.

"If that's true, then maybe he's nice. Southern Shepherds are usually nice, I never knew a mean one. Well, there was one that was mean, but that's only because I forgot to feed it when my friend asked me to one day, but it stopped chasing me the next day. I can't blame him for being mad at me after forgetting to feed him. But I had a lot of friends that had them, and they were the nicest animals you ever saw."

"That's great." Trenson still wasn't listening.

"So he's probably nice."

"Probably."

"I used to have a dog. Did I already tell you that? But it wasn't a Southern Sheperd. I can't remember what breed it was. It was probably just a mutt, but it was the nicest dog you ever saw. He was also the craziest dog I ever saw. He could probably run laps for days and never run out of energy. He was big, much bigger than that dog there, and so people were sometimes afraid of him. Chips was his name. I found him all alone in the rain, he looked so cold and miserable, I couldn't help myself and fed him. After that he would follow me anywhere, but he had a bad habit of chewing on my extra boots when I was gone, but he would only do that if I was..."

The rest of the words became faint to Trenson's fuzzy mind. Like a blanket, the warm feeling of sleep came over him, and its embrace seduced Trenson. His head hung low, and sitting on the cold ground, his ears tuning out the buzzing noise of Colly's chatter, he fell asleep.

III

HIS EYES ADJUSTED TO the darkness, Jayfor clipped his sword onto his belt before swinging his satchel over his shoulder. Then he climbed up the hill and peered over the top. He saw the caravan on the other side, sitting as far over on the side of the road as it could without leaning against the other hill. A circle of torches surrounded a smaller circle of tents, most likely where the overseer and his guards were sleeping.

Jayfor could see much more than what was illuminated by the torches with his night-vision eyes. He could see the two horses that pulled the cart still attached to the cart, but instead of being harnessed to the front, they were tied by their halter to hitches that stuck out of the side of the cart, and were sleeping peacefully, standing straight with their legs locked.

He could also see a guard standing by one of the tents, holding a spear in his left hand and looking extremely bored. Jayfor frowned. He hoped that there wouldn't be sentries posted, or if there were, that they would be asleep. He would have to do this carefully.

His eyes eventually landed on what he wanted to see: the slaves, sleeping in an uneven circle around a dying fire. He spotted Trenson, who he could make out even in the dark by his attire.

So now he knew where Trenson was. All he needed to do now was find the key. Simple, but not easy.

He descended the hill and started heading towards the camp, staying low to the ground as he walked. How would he get the key? It was a detail that eluded him. There was no other way to break the chains. Iron chains were almost impossible to break. Well, on second thought, he had read that sometimes sword blows could break chains.

Sword blows! Maybe that was the solution. After all, he had a special sword. If he got to Trenson, his sword might be able to cut through the chains. This was a sword that held the power of a Senver's blade, possibly even greater.

But. . . what if it didn't work? What if the blade didn't cut Trenson's chains? Then that would be it. He wouldn't free Trenson, and he would most likely be discovered, ending the entire rescue mission. It was a risk, but the question was, is it too great a risk? Could he trust the sword to do its work and not go for the key?

He debated for a few moments, then reached a conclusion. *No. It's too risky, not having the key. I don't know if this sword has the potential. I'll try to find the key instead.* Jayfor didn't know if he was making a right or wrong decision, and felt a little guilty at not having total faith in his weapon. He pushed the feeling away.

The closest object was the cart, so that was what he hid behind. The horses were directly across from him, attached to the other side of the cart. He would have to go around them without waking them. Could horses hear very well? Jayfor didn't know. He wondered if he should take off his gear so he wouldn't be so loud. It seemed like a good idea, but he dismissed it after recognizing that he would have to make a quick getaway after freeing Trenson.

Holding his satchel tight against himself to prevent it from making noise, he slowly tiptoed around the wagon. He didn't stop when he went around the horses. He saw their ears twitch slightly in his direction. The sound of his footsteps made a soft crunching noise on the grass, and he wanted to stop, but he forced himself to keep going. The horses didn't make any more movement, and Jayfor was now near the campsite. He silently congratulated himself.

Now to find the key. But where would the key be? Most likely in the cart driver's tent. But where was the cart driver's tent? Jayfor realized that he should have figured that out earlier. Now he was on the edge of the ring of torches, and if anyone looked in his direction, they would easily see him in the orange light. He needed to act quickly. The overseer's tent would most likely have something different about it. He scanned the tents until his eyes landed on one that he guessed was it. The only evidence he had that this was the one was that it looked more carefully set up than the others. Jayfor didn't know if it was just him or not, but it was the only lead he had. Once again, he held his gear close as he snuck around the dead campfire in the center of the tents, toward the tent he hoped was the overseer's.

That's when he heard the noise. At first it was so low and deep that Jayfor thought he was imagining it. But it slowly grew in volume, a constant, steady growl. Jayfor turned around and realized with a sick feeling where it was coming from.

It was a dog. It was a medium-sized, gray dog covered in thick hair and with a bushy tail. But most importantly, it was a medium-sized, gray dog covered in thick hair and with a bushy tail that was standing a few yards from Jayfor with its teeth bared and looking like it wanted to pounce on Jayfor.

Jayfor panicked. "Shhhh," he tried whispering to the dog, as if it would listen. Either the dog was a bad listener or didn't understand the language. In any case, the dog only crept a few inches closer and started to growl louder, too loud.

Jayfor was trapped. He had to do something before the dog started barking. He recalled that he had some cured pork strips in his satchel. Maybe that would keep him quiet? He moved slightly as he reached his hand around and toward his bag.

It must have been too much movement, because the dog suddenly let out a torrent of barks, shattering the peaceful silence with the sharp staccato. The dog lowered its head and front legs almost to the ground as it exploded into a fury.

All hope Jayfor had of rescuing Trenson crashed to the ground. He saw a guard emerge from behind a tent directly in front of him, and enter the light of the torches. His first expression was aggravation, then confusion, then realization as he caught sight of Jayfor. He started yelling in a foreign language and running towards Jayfor, evidently trying to wake his comrades.

The dog stopped its baying and turned its head to the side when the guard started making noise, and that was the opportunity Jayfor needed. Not caring which way he was going, he broke into a mad dash, his legs carrying him as fast as they possibly could out of the circle of tents and torches, and down the road. The guard started chasing him, yelling either curses or wake-up calls. Jayfor couldn't tell.

The dog was faster than the guard and Jayfor. Even after Jayfor made it outside the area of the campsite, the dog kept pursuing him, swiftly gaining ground until it jumped and landed on Jayfor's back. Jayfor wasn't expecting it and fell forward to the ground, landing hard. He quickly rolled on his back, just in time to see the dog in the air again, its jaw open wide revealing yellow and black teeth, its eyes orange in the little torchlight that remained, its front paws and claws ready to land on Jayfor.

Jayfor kicked hard with his foot. He hit the dog in the face and, with a yelp, it was knocked backward. For a brief second, Jayfor was free, and swiftly drew a dagger from his satchel. It was all the time he had before the animal rushed at him again. Jayfor let the dog land on him this time, and it almost knocked the breath out of him. The dog reached for his throat with its long snout. Jayfor could smell the pungent breath of the dog. Before the jaws locked onto him, Jayfor thrust his knife up and into the chest of the dog.

The blade found its mark. The dog immediately went limp, and its jaws halted just inches from Jayfor's throat. Jayfor withdrew the knife. The dog fell to the ground beside Jayfor, lifeless.

Jayfor was shaking. He wanted to just lay there, but he heard more sounds from the campsite. Quickly, he rose to his feet, and, not looking back at the tents, he ran.

IV

"I CAN'T BELIEVE YOU slept through it! It was so loud, and everyone else woke up. How in the world did you sleep through it?"

Trenson shrugged. "I'm a heavy sleeper, I guess."

Colly, who was walking in front of Trenson, shook his head. "So am I! But I still heard it, and so did everyone else. Aquila! Hey, Aquila!" Colly called forward to the giant man a few slaves ahead. The guards walking beside the slaves looked witheringly at Colly. Trenson felt somewhat comforted that he wasn't the only one that wished Colly would talk less.

Aquila turned around and raised an eyebrow at Colly. Colly quickly said, "Did you hear the raid last night? Did it wake you up?"

Still looking a little confused, Aquila nodded, then resumed looking forward and keeping pace with the slave in front of him.

Colly looked back at Trenson with a proud smile. "I knew I didn't imagine it! Everyone was in an uproar. I don't know how many of them there were, they won't tell me. It had to be quite a few to cause so much trouble. And they even killed the dog! The same dog that I was talking about last night!"

"I know," Trenson replied evenly. "You've told me that. Three times, now."

Colly shrugged, not ashamed in the slightest. "I just want to make sure you remember."

Honestly, Trenson wasn't sure how he had slept through it, either. It sounded like a lot had happened while he dozed. Of course, Colly was probably exaggerating about some details. But even then, Aquila agreed it happened, so it most likely did.

Raids were common, especially on lonely roads. Years ago, when Trenson would march out to battle with the army of Faldon, a raid would be attempted on their supply wagons at least once a week. It was a common thing to happen, but the raiders seldom made off with anything of value. So the fact that they had been raided didn't interest Trenson as much as it did Colly.

Instead, Trenson focused on the road moving beneath his feet. He was miserable. For one, he was freezing. The air was bitterly cold, and there was no sunshine, thanks to the clouds that covered the sky. And he was also a slave, chained right behind a chinwag and forced to march in a caravan to be sold like an animal. These were reasons for his depression, but not the biggest.

His best friend was dead.

Of course, there was a chance that Jayfor was still alive. There was a chance that Jayfor had merely been knocked out, not struck dead by a sword. But his reason was louder than the voice. Even if that was the case, his reason replied, Jayfor couldn't swim. So why hold on to hope when it was hopeless? Why expect the unexpected? And let's say Jayfor is indeed alive. How would he find Trenson now? Would he go looking for him? Or continue the mission?

It didn't matter. What mattered was that Trenson had failed. Jayfor was dead, and he was a slave. For years, Trenson thought that maybe there was still some good in the world. His former life as a thief was without purpose. The life he had lived serving Jayfor and accomplishing all that he had, Trenson knew that had purpose. It was a reason to keep living. But that was taken from him now. Now he was nothing.

Why, Va'ar? Why have you done this? Why do you do this to us? I know you're out there. I know you're listening. Why do you put me through this? Is this really what it takes to be someone worth remembering, to be the person I always wanted to be? If it is, please take it from me. I don't want to do this anymore!

But there was no answer.

"I wonder," Colly lowered his voice slightly, as if talking over his shoulder in a hushed voice would prevent the guards standing a few feet away from hearing him, "why the thief killed the dog. It looked nice. It never caused me any trouble, and always sat on the cart next to our driver, peacefully enjoying life."

"I don't know," Trenson mumbled.

"Although, maybe it was a guard dog. I always assumed that it was a pet of the cart driver, but it could have been trained to protect the camp. Oh, maybe it was even trained to look friendly, so it could trick everyone! The thief was probably fooled."

"Evidently, he wasn't fooled enough."

"Well, obviously, but still. It must have been a skilled thief. Or maybe it was more than one thief? Now that I think about it, there was probably more than one. How many do you think?"

Trenson wished so badly that he was somewhere else. Anywhere else. "How many what?"

"How many of them do you think raided us last night?"

"I don't care."

For a second, Colly was silent. He looked over his shoulder at Trenson, one eyebrow raised. Colly was starting to get a hint. "Is everything OK?"

Trenson didn't raise his head, but looked up just enough to meet Colly's eyes. He kept his voice even and his face expressionless. "No."

Colly let the silence hang for a second, waiting to see if Trenson said anything else, but he didn't, instead glaring into Colly's eyes, daring him to continue. "Is there... I mean, is there anything I can do to help?"

Trenson shook his head slowly. "Just leave me alone."

Colly opened his mouth to say something, then met eyes with Trenson's cold stare, and closed it. He was silent.

***

Jayfor decided he didn't like dogs as much as he used to.

He walked on the other side of the hill from the caravan, alone with his thoughts. It was another dreary day, with gray clouds blotting out the sun. Jayfor had his arms tucked under his armpits, trying to use his own body heat to warm himself. He needed warmer clothes.

The dog had ruined everything. If the tent that he chose was indeed the overseer's, then he might have stolen the key, then freed Trenson, then been on their mission. A lot of ifs, but it could have worked. If the dog wouldn't have been there, that is.

Jayfor sighed, his breath coming out in a vapor. Now he would have to try again to free Trenson, before he reached a city. Once the caravan reached a city, Trenson would likely be auctioned away. And Jayfor didn't know how auctions worked, which added an unknown element.

He would try again to free Trenson tonight. Now there was no guard dog. Although he had raised the suspicions of the caravan, making a second attempt more difficult, there was no choice. He had to risk it. If he didn't, then Trenson might reach a city.

Jayfor blew another breath of hot air in front of him, watching the air turn cold and visible, then float away. As the fog cleared away, Jayfor saw something in the distance, a small speck. It took Jayfor a second to register it, but once he did, he groaned.

It was a city.

V

"Ah, Kallary! There's nothing quite like getting back to the homeland," one of the guards beside Trenson said, elation in his voice.

Another guard, who was walking a few paces ahead of the other soldier, replied, "Is Talikan in Kallary? I always thought it was on the border."

"The border of Faldon, yes, but there's no more of that."

"Hm. Good point."

Trenson's spirits immediately dropped when the city came into sight; he knew that this was where he would be sold. How he would be sold, he had no idea. But the chances that he would be were high, if what he heard about slave trades were true.

Kallary... Is this Kallary? He thought about it. Politically, it probably wasn't. If anything, the borders were probably hazy and not exact, and Faldon territory was likely left alone, with the old borders remaining the same as before Loronis' destruction.

Nonetheless, Trenson might as well consider himself in Kallary now. He was bound to enemy lands, lands that, if they found out his true identity, would not take kindly to his presence. Not that Kallary was unified enough to do anything serious if they did discover him. Still, he would have to be cautious.

The city in the distance growing closer, Trenson spotted a line of people, animals, and caravans waiting to be admitted into the city. The city walls were reddish in color, made from a material that was different from the rock used in the walls commonly protecting Faldon's castles and fiefs. Trenson wondered if it was any stronger or weaker than the walls back home.

As they approached the crowd, Trenson could make out what was happening. Three other caravans were already waiting at the entrance. Two of them were ordinary merchants, with normal wagons and a pair of horses carrying the driver and a wagon filled with supplies. The wagon in front, however, was another slave caravan. Trenson couldn't make out much of it, but he caught enough glimpses now and then and saw the human cargo chained to the back of the caravan, and recognized their empty faces and slouched posture.

This must be a busy city for three caravans to try to enter it at once.

The overseer stopped the caravan a few feet from the rear of the wagon in front of them, bringing the convoy to a halt. Most of the slaves weren't paying attention, and ran into the slave in front of them or simply kept walking until they hit the back of the wagon. The guards scowled as they ordered everyone back into an orderly line, and their scowling must have worked, because within a few minutes, everything was settled and the slaves were in order.

Colly, scanning the walls on either side of the entrance, ventured to make a comment to Trenson. "These walls are a different color than anything I've ever seen," he said, a hint of caution in his voice. Since Trenson's harsh warning earlier that day, Colly was more timid about talking, only saying something every now and then. He now knew that Trenson was like a sleeping bear, one that disliked noises and would lash out if someone angered it. But Trenson was quiet and said little after that, so Colly was gradually gaining his confidence to speak to him again.

Trenson looked up at the walls. "I noticed," he said, but without as much animosity as he usually spoke with. He felt guilty that he had said what he did, realizing that although he got the silence he wanted, the guilt he felt afterward wasn't a fair price to pay. He was too ashamed to apologize and instead tried to make up for it by seeming more friendly.

"It must be a different material used in making it," Trenson added. "Where I come from, the walls are always made of stone. These look more like sand."

Colly nodded. "That's what I was thinking. Maybe they are made of sand. I guess that in large enough quantities, sand can be as strong as rock."

"I doubt that," Trenson replied. "It probably isn't actually made of sand. But it looks like it."

"It sure does."

Before Colly could say anything else, the caravan at the front of the line was admitted into the city. This, in turn, made the second wagon move to the front, which made the third one move, which eventually gave the overseer enough room to resume the procession forward. Again, some of the slaves weren't paying attention, and were yanked forward by their chains as they grew taut.

There wasn't a gate at the entrance of the city. It was a simple arch-shaped hole in the wall, with a guard standing before it, granting people admittance. Trenson was surprised. This wasn't a very defensive design; anyone could easily overpower the guard to get inside. Either the leaders of the city didn't suspect an attack, and so left themselves open to one, or they were just lazy. Or both.

The second caravan and third caravans were allowed through, and finally, it was their turn.

"Business?" The guard said in the exact tone and manner as he had the previous merchant.

"You know my business," the overseer replied curtly. "Only a blind man couldn't guess my occupation."

Trenson couldn't help but be surprised. The overseer must have some courage talking to someone that decided whether or not to let them through. Arrogance, Trenson corrected, not courage.

The guard eyed the overseer, but made no comment. "Pass?" he said, as if the overseer had said nothing. The guard was clearly no nonsense, and didn't especially care if he was insulted or not, so long as he got people out of his way.

The overseer mumbled something under his breath as he pulled something out of his pocket. It was a small, rectangular piece of wood, with words and numbers written on it. Trenson had never seen anything like it. It must be an identification card of some kind, but why everyone, including a random slave driver, was required to carry one, was beyond Trenson's understanding.

Just like he had done to the cart before them, the guard glanced at the pass before handing it back. "Move along," he said uniform-ly.

With a quick flick of the reins, the cart started back with the creaking of wheels, and the slaves started walking to the jingling of chains. They passed under the arch and into the city of Talikan.

***

Jayfor waited a few minutes after he saw Trenson's caravan enter the city to join the line to get in, letting a few wagons go through to increase the distance between him and the cart. Jayfor knew that the longer he waited, the less likely his chance of being caught by the caravan was, but it would also make it harder to track, especially in the city.

While waiting in line, he took in the walls of the city and the way they were built. Obviously, they were a different material than what the walls of Loronis were made of. This looked almost like sand. The strangest thing about it was that there was no sand around. The ground was rock hard, standing in stark contrast to the wall, which had a hint of red color to it. Maybe it wasn't sand.

Jayfor stopped thinking about the walls and instead focused on the guard that would admit him. Jayfor noticed that the guard was making people give him something before letting them in. Did you have to pay to gain entrance? Jayfor frowned. He had money, and plenty of it, but why in the world would a city charge people to enter? It made no sense.

The line shifted forward; he was the next one to be admitted.

"Pass?" The guard said mechanically.

The man in front of Jayfor pulled something out of his pocket and handed it to the guard, who grabbed it for a few seconds before handing it back. "Move along."

Jayfor was confused. Was it not money that you needed to get in? He wasn't sure what to do, but before he could think it through, the guard was staring at him. "Business?"

Jayfor cleared his throat. "Visiting family," he said, hoping his voice was convincing.

It must have been, because the guard moved on. "Pass?"

Jayfor reached into his satchel and grabbed a handful of coins, dropping them into the guard's outstretched hand. "I think this should suffice."

The guard looked down at his hand, surprised. He shifted the gold in his hand, making it clink together. He seemed to be caught between turning Jayfor in or letting him through. Jayfor held his breath and didn't make a sound.

The guard suddenly closed his hand around the coins. "Move along," he said, putting his hand by his side and nodding to Jayfor.

Jayfor breathed a sigh of relief and, without waiting another second, walked briskly past the guard and into the city.

VI

"IT'S REALLY COLD IN here," Colly said, hugging himself with his hands on his shoulders.

Trenson nodded with chattering teeth. He was cold, but not enough to hug himself. He doubted he would ever be that cold.

To keep himself distracted, Trenson looked out of the window of the barn and watched as some of the slaves were being sold. It wasn't a pleasant sight, but it focused his attention on something other than the cold. Trenson had never seen slaves being sold, so he watched the proceedings with interest.

"Come now, don't be shy! We've got a fine selection here today, stuff from all over Kallary, and even beyond! Will you not at least take a look?"

The loud voice of the overseer rang over the previous stillness of the day. Trenson watched from inside the holding building, peering out from the window to watch the fate of so many men be decided with the jangle of coin and sold like cargo.

"I can't watch it," Colly said. His usual cheerful voice and expression were gone. Now he was sitting staring at the ground, fingering a piece of hay. Trenson had never seen him like this. Of course, he hadn't known him for long, but long enough to know that this wasn't the normal Colly.

"You don't have to," Trenson replied without looking away from the scene. "But don't you want to see how it's going to happen? How we're going to be sold, I mean."

Colly shook his head, still looking at the ground. "No, I don't. I can't. It's just so wrong. I don't understand how this is allowed to happen."

"Because men decided they were smart enough to rule the world without Va'ar," Trenson replied dryly. "And this is the result."

The inside of the building that they were being kept in was about as dry, dark and empty as the hearts of the men holding them here. It was obvious that this used to be a barn, perhaps a stable, in former times. This was evident by the high roof, small stalls on either sides of the wall, and pieces of old hay on the floor. The slaves weren't kept in the stalls, but in the middle aisle and were chained together. For the most part, all the slaves sat in a circle in the aisle, shivering from the cold, but without making a sound or expression. There was just enough slack in the chains for Trenson to stand and look out a shuddered window and view the scene outside – if Colly let him, because wherever he went Colly was forced to go, being chained next to each other.

The scene outside was not much better than that of the inside. The podium that Trenson noticed on his way in now displayed twelve men, all in chains, proudly to the world. They stood shoulder to shoulder, shaking in the cold with their threadbare clothing as the overseer paced back and forth in front of them, calling out to customers and onlookers.

"Who here isn't in need of a farm hand? Or perhaps a servant, maybe a housekeeper? What better way to fulfill your needs than with another pair of arms and legs to keep your business intact? These are hard times on all of us, and assurance of quality labor is hard to come by. So please, have a look! Is there anything to lose?"

With his squawking, the cart driver was drawing a crowd of a few dozen, all peering at the slaves and looking over and around each other, as if each man on the stage would look better if looked at from a different angle.

Then one man, presumably a farmer by his attire, raised his hand. "Forty crescents for the two on the left!" He pointed his finger at the two men on the leftmost line of slaves. It was clear why he chose them: they were both larger and stronger looking than any of the other men. Trenson's heart leaped, then sank when he caught a glimpse of one of the men: Aquila.

Aquila had been among the lucky few that were chosen first to be sold. He stood tall on the stage – literally, his height making everyone else on the podium seem small. He stood out, but this was not a good time to do so.

"Fine choice, fine choice!" The overseer's voice became faster and faster. "Now can I see one for fifty? Fifty-five? Or perhaps twenty-five for one of them? Come now, forty crescents the current bid!"

Trenson's heartbeat quickened. He couldn't explain it, but during the two days with Aquila, he had grown attached to him in a way. Unlike many people, he didn't see a man that was mute, but a kind soul that was undervalued by the world. Trenson felt a responsibility to protect the man, and even though he couldn't protect him in this moment, he could plead to Va'ar in his heart that Aquila would at least be sold to someone that would treat him well. Which was exactly what he was doing.

"Fifty!" The speaker was a different farmer, with a large straw hat not on his head, but in his hands, as the wind was blowing too hard for it to stay on.

"Fifty for both, fifty for both! Fifty is the new bid. Now do I hear fifty-five, sixty? Sixty, sixty, fifty-five? Fifty going once, going twice..."

Just before the bid closed, another person, a woman, cried out, "Thirty for the one on the far left!"

Since previously, the two men were being bought as a pair, the price would be split among the two slaves; so in essence, each one was going as twenty-five when the man bid fifty. But thirty for one of them, which is less than the previous bid, would still be allowed since she was only bidding on one of them.

Trenson felt a small wave of relief. The one on the far left wasn't Aquila. Maybe Aquila wouldn't be sold today, maybe nobody would want him. It was doubtful, but hope was all Trenson had. Aquila was relieved that he wasn't being sold either, and his shoulders relaxed slightly. The slave on the far left didn't show any expression, not even as his future was being decided. He was emotionless, looking blankly into the distance.

"Thirty for the farthest one on the left! New bid thirty, thirty, do I hear thirty-five? Forty? Or perhaps a new bid for both as a pair, sixty-five? Thirty going once!"

Nobody spoke.

"Thirty going twice!"

Nobody spoke.

"Sold!" With a flourish of the hand, the overseer pointed at the woman who had bought the slave. "A good choice, miss, a fine choice! Meet my man along the side of the podium and he'll get you worked out." He turned behind him and motioned for one of the guards. The guard knew what to do, and pulled a key out of his pocket. He walked up to the slave that had been sold and quickly unlocked the chain holding the slave to Aquila. The chain connecting the two slaves together came loose and reached the ground, dangling while attached to Aquila's wrists. The wrist cuffs weren't removed from the slave. The guard grabbed the slave, who was a full head taller than him, and led him down the stage to the side, where the lady was waiting to take her prize. And still, the slave was expressionless.

"Now then, we still have many to choose from here! The sale isn't over yet! Come now and take a look, yes, you there, you look in need of a good hand! Why not see if we have just what you need?"

Trenson backed away from the window. He had seen all he needed to see – all he wanted to see, anyway. He had a fair idea of how the process worked when he arrived, and his assumptions were correct: auctioned off like animals. That was cruel. But did the overseer and the people buying slaves care? Evidently not, for they purchased and used them like any other animal. People's lives thrown left and right, sold here, bought here, no control or free will, all decided by coins. For shiny, round pieces of metal that people valued more than souls.

Trenson turned away from the window and sat down. He needed to be thinking about freedom, how to escape this mess.

Colly, now sitting beside him, spoke. "Who is he?"

Trenson was confused at first. He looked around the room, trying to spot who Colly was talking about. "Who?"

"I don't remember how you said his name, but it sounded like Vay... Vay something." Colly saw Trenson's eyebrows knit together. "When you talked about slavery a little while ago. You said that this is what happens when people let themselves and not Vay rule their world. Who is Vay?"

"You mean Va'ar? You've never heard of Him?"

Colly shook his head.

Trenson opened his mouth to reply, then stopped short. Here was an opportunity: to share the message of Va'ar to someone who didn't know, and to provide them with the same hope he had. But now that he had the opportunity, how would he explain it? It was simple, yet vastly complicated at the same time. He would be trying to explain the unexplainable. Words couldn't do it justice. How could he make it simple enough that Colly understood and not think him a madman? Trenson had faced problems the size of mountains and overcame them, but this innocent question made him pause. This might be one of the biggest mountains yet.

"Va'ar is... well, it might be better to say what Va'ar isn't. Va'ar isn't a person like you and me. He doesn't live in the world like us either, although He is in it. He's not physical." Trenson sighed. This was already hard. He remembered when he had asked Jayfor this same question years ago, and Jayfor was only able to give a mixed answer. "He is a being. That's a very general answer, I know, but it's true. He is a being who has no other beside Him, and who isn't just powerful, and wise, and sovereign, but is all-powerful, all-wise, and all-sovereign. He doesn't have a physical form, because He can see everything and is in control."

Colly stared at the ground for a few seconds, his lips moving silently, as was his habit when trying to understand something new. "So... He's like a spirit?"

"In a way, yes, but not exactly a spirit like you're thinking of. He's not limited to one place, but He's everywhere and can control everything, and there's nothing He doesn't see. He's the only all-powerful being in the world. There are none beside Him or above Him. He sees us here right now, in fact, and He has put us here for a reason."

Colly nodded slowly. He looked like he had a dozen questions to ask, but wasn't sure how to ask them. "I-It's confusing," he admitted. His teeth were still chattering from the cold.

Trenson nodded, understanding completely that he wasn't doing a good job at explaining. *I'm probably making this a million times more confusing than it should be.* Maybe he should come at this from a different angle. An idea formed in his mind, and he asked, "I've got a question for you: how do you think the world was created?"

Colly looked Trenson in the eye with the same confused look. "I thought you were explaining who Va'ar was to me?"

"I am. I'm just doing it differently that might be easier to understand."

"Oh. OK, well... I haven't really thought about it. I mean, I guess I've wondered once or twice about it, but I never really thought it through. Let's see... I don't really have an explanation. I always figured that the world always existed, and that things have always been going at the same rate they are now."

Trenson nodded. "I see. That's the view a lot of people have. But if that's true, then there are a few problems. First of all, there has to be a beginning at some point. There's no such thing as something just being there, and always being there, without first being made."

"But is there a chance that there could be? Is there a chance that maybe the universe has been going on forever with no beginning?"

Trenson shook his head. "Not really. Like I said, everything that is mortal or that can be destroyed has to be created at one point or another."

Colly thought about this for a few more seconds. He didn't seem as depressed anymore, now that he had something else to think about. "What about Va'ar, then? If everything has to be created, would that mean that Va'ar has to be created to?"

Trenson already knew this question would come. "Anything that is *mortal* or *can be destroyed* has to be created. Everything in this world is mortal and can be destroyed, from people to plants to animals to even the ground we walk on. It would take an outside force, something greater than all of this, something that was immortal and indestructible, to create all of this, but that outside force would have to be uncreatable."

The confusion seemed to lift slightly from Colly's face, like a curtain pulled slowly back. "I think I see what you mean." His voice was soft and light, the tone of which people spoke when they discovered something incredible for the first time. "It would take something more than the world to create everything in it. And this... being, is Va'ar?"

Trenson nodded, relief and happiness filling him as Colly grasped the truth. Trenson said nothing; Colly was doing his own work of putting the piece in the puzzle. It would better to let him discover the details himself.

It only took a few moments for Colly to speak yet again and ask another question. "Is He good? I mean, is He a good person? I guess He isn't a person though..." It wasn't easy trying to reference something that was beyond human understanding. Even for Trenson, it was difficult, and he had spoken to Senver and seen their power.

"That's the best part: He is good. In fact, He's perfect. After all, we each have an innate sense of morality, about what is right and wrong. He put that in our hearts, because we were created in His image. When we do what we know is right, we're serving Him, and He rewards that, and the opposite goes for people who don't."

"So... If he rewards good deeds, and punishes bad ones, why does he not deal with people who do bad things every day? Those people seem to get off free. And – why is there any bad in the world, anyway? Why wouldn't Va'ar create the world perfect, instead of making it so bad?" Colly looked around the shambled barn where they were huddled, shivering in the cold, latched together with chains. It wasn't a pretty picture, and would make anyone doubt that there was someone out there who rewarded good and punished evil.

For a brief second, Trenson asked the same question to himself: why didn't He? Why didn't Va'ar smite these people holding them captive and selling people as merchandise? That would be the right thing to do, right?

"It was created perfect," Trenson replied in a voice that reflected the gloom in the barn. "That's how it was intended to be. There was no pain, no sadness, no death, no regrets. Everything was perfect..." Trenson's voice trailed off.

"Did it stay that way for long?"

"Not long enough. See, Va'ar wanted to give the people a choice. He didn't want to use them as pawns under His thumb. So he put the Mountain of Power, far to the east, in Elara, where there was a giant gate leading into the mountain. Va'ar warned the people to never open the gate, because it would release darkness over the world, and they would die."

"And they opened it? But why?"

"They did. Well, how were they supposed to know what darkness and death was if they had never experienced it? It would be like trying to explain cold to someone who has no idea what it was. The people let their curiosity get the best of them. So Va'ar let them do it because He gave them free will. That's how we're here now."

Colly still twisted the stalk of hay in his fingers mechanically. "So, the world's not perfect today because the Mountain of Power was opened a long time ago. But why do we have to suffer for what they did? We may live in the same world as they did, but I would never want to open that gate. Why do I have to suffer for their mistake?"

"I used to wonder the same thing," Trenson replied. "But the more you think about it, the more you see that it was more than just their mistake; it was everybody's. Everybody wanted that gate to be opened, and to feel the power that was said to come from it. They didn't know any better, but that's still no excuse. It's everybody's nature to do things that they're told not to do. If I were in that situation, I would open that gate at one point or another. I know it. And so would you, if you were being honest."

Colly looked down at the floor. "I probably would."

Trenson wondered if he should tell Colly the truth: that Va'ar sent him on a mission, that he had witnessed the power of Va'ar and battled alongside Senver. It was easy for him to believe, after everything he saw. Trenson remembered that he himself didn't fully believe until Agrond revealed himself in the throne room. But that was a special instance – almost everybody else in the world would have to trust Va'ar without the miraculous signs. But Trenson didn't think it was a good idea to reveal all that he had been through. A person needed to believe on their own, and Trenson doubted that his testimony would have much of an impact on Colly's belief.

"So that's it?" Colly asked out of the blue, continuing the conversation. "Va'ar has just left us here, alone?"

It took Trenson a second to get back into the conversation mindset once he had stood up. A faint smile touched his lips as he shook his head. "No, not at all. Va'ar isn't like most kings – cross him once and that's it. He is merciful and gives us second chances, even when we mess up or break his commands again and again. Those who choose to follow Him have his protection, and while it might not make your life perfect, it gives you a sense of... truth, and contentment, I guess. Does that make sense? It almost feels like your soul says, 'this is what I was made for.'" He saw Colly staring at him blankly. "I'm sure the way I explained it didn't make sense."

"No, I – I think I understand." A new tone was in Colly's voice, one that Trenson had never heard before. "It makes sense. It's too big for me to grasp the whole picture, but I think... I think I understand. I know. I know it's true. I have done some terrible things in my life, and I need forgiveness." Colly looked at Trenson, and that's when Trenson saw a faint spark in his eyes. "Would Va'ar really take someone like me?"

Trenson kneeled on his knees and placed a hand on Colly's shoulder. "It's not a matter of if you're good enough for Him, or if He'll take you. Va'ar wants everybody, even the worst criminals, even – even the people holding us here, to find truth in Him. There's no initiation ceremony or anything. All you have to do is believe."

Colly looked Trenson in the eye, and Trenson saw what he hadn't seen before in his eyes: a spark of hope. He saw it in every follower of Va'ar. Colly was silent for a few moments, then resolutely, firmly, without hesitation, he said, "Yes."

It was a joyous and monumental occasion. Nobody else in the room could see it, but in that dusty barn where people were sold into slavery, one soul had been saved and seen the light.

But there was no time for celebrating. At that moment, one of the large doors of the barn was pushed open, allowing sunlight to pour in. A guard entered and barked orders at the other soldiers in the room. "Need more kindling for the pyre. Bring some more of 'em out! And be quick about it!"

VII

T HE TEMPERAMENT OF THE people inside the city matched the current temperature: cold.

After making it past the gatekeeper, Jayfor stopped a few paces inside the walls to take in his surroundings. The city wasn't as different as he thought it would be. He didn't know why he had expectations of something being different about the city, but he did. He felt that towns that sold slaves should differ from normal towns.

Years ago, he had spoken of Kallary as an enemy, a hostile nation filled with hostile people. But rarely did he speak of the inhabitants as people, as husbands, wives, fathers, mothers, children... he had thought of them as entities, not humans. Things were different now that he was equal to them.

He saw an old lady sweeping the street with a willow broom. There wasn't much dirt on the stone-paved road, but the woman nonetheless moved the tool back and forth, getting what little dirt there was into a pile. Jayfor approached her. "Excuse me, but I'm looking to buy a slave. Do you know where I might find a place that sells them?"

The old lady scowled and responded with a few words in a foreign language, and it was probably a good thing Jayfor didn't understand them, as they didn't sound nice. She then returned to sweeping, acting like Jayfor wasn't there.

Jayfor shrugged and resumed walking down the road. He should find somebody who spoke the common tongue to give him directions.

"Ahem," he directed to a man walking out of a shop that lined the road. "I need a slave. I've heard there's a place here that sells them?"

"Ha! You must mean the auction. I'd take your coin elsewhere, unless you plan on selling an arm and leg for what's left of a man."

With that, the man turned and began walking away, apparently deciding that the conversation was over.

"And where can I find it?" Jayfor called.

Without turning his head, the man yelled back, "Follow the road further down and you can't miss it."

It didn't seem like Jayfor was going to get any more information than that. With a shrug, he continued down the main road.

How was he supposed to free Trenson when he did reach the auction? Well, that would depend on whether Trenson was being sold at that moment, or if he was being held somewhere. If he was being held somewhere, that would make it easier. He would just spring the bars – if it was a prison-style holding area – and then he'd be free. Simple. But if Trenson was being sold at that moment, Jayfor would have to buy him like anyone else to stay incognito. He hoped he had enough money in case that ended up happening. He had a fair amount in his satchel, but he didn't know how much slaves went for.

His thinking was cut short by a sound that immediately caught his attention: a scream. Not the playful hollers of children, but a cry for help. It made Jayfor stop and listen, his senses now alert. Then he heard another one: a shrill, loud scream that pierced not only the air but Jayfor's soul. It came from his left. He changed his course, briskly jogging toward a passage between two houses.

He went down an alleyway and came out into an open street. Well, it was open to a certain point. About a hundred yards away, a large crowd of people were gathered, pressed against each other so close that an impenetrable human wall was formed. Jayfor couldn't tell exactly what was going on over there, but he saw the crowd was gathered in front of a large building.

Maybe this is the auction! The thought hit Jayfor's mind, along with a wave of relief. He had found what he was looking for after all. He started towards it, and as he was walking, another thought entered his head, this one more troubling: why had there been a scream? Surely not from the auction. No, it must have been from somewhere else. He forced himself to believe it, to stop his mind from racing through the possibilities and imagining Trenson suffering. He quickened his pace.

He pushed his way through the crowd, which wasn't easy as space was premium, with everyone trying to make it up to the front. As he squeezed his way forward, he felt an atmosphere that he didn't expect. He caught on by the troubled looks on people's faces to the unintelligible whispers that there wasn't the feeling of community expected from an auction.

He heard a loud voice from the front of the crowd. He wasn't close enough to the front to see who was speaking or what was going on, but the voice was deep and full of confidence.

"Now see here. I don't want to do that again. For one, it's a hassle, and two, it leaves a mess, not just on the ground but all over our blades. An annoying inconvenience. And another thing, it pains my heart that you would be so selfish as to throw away her life like that. We told you our terms: leave us be as we do our business, and we'll see that none of these folks are harmed. Simple. I thought you had more heart than that. But one of you had to charge us and play hero, so we simply held up our part of the bargain. Tell me, did that do anyone good?"

Jayfor made it to the front. The sight that met his eyes was one of the last things he expected. He only stared for the first few seconds. It made sense now, the scream and the uneasiness in the crowd.

This was no auction. This was a robbery. A large building, bigger than the other houses on the street and clearly of some importance, was before him. Men casually entered and exited the building through the large front doors, most carrying sacks on their way out and tossing them onto a growing pile of bags, the bags jingling as they landed. All the men wore the same dull gray outfit, marking them as a gang.

Five men were separate from the others. Out of these, four were standing together, each one holding a citizen with one arm and holding a dagger in the other. A farmer, a wife, a merchant, and a little boy were the souls trapped in their grip, their eyes wide and filled with fear. Hostages, Jayfor thought scornfully, to prevent anyone from charging in to stop them.

Apparently, it didn't work. On the ground lay two bodies. One had the look of a normal citizen from the crowd, and judging by how he was closer to the crowd than the guards, Jayfor guessed it was someone who tried to make a rescue attempt. Another body lay on the ground, much closer to the guard, which must have been the hostage they killed as a result. It was a little girl, no older than ten. Both bodies lay in a puddle of red.

After dumping yet another sack into the pile, a rogue came forward and spoke to the fifth man standing there. "Almost finished, sir. Just a few more and we'll be out of here."

The boss maintained an oily look of confidence for the crowd and replied in a hushed tone, but Jayfor caught the words. "For pity's sake hurry up! They'll find us before long – a miracle they haven't already."

The man nodded and returned to his work. The leader, meanwhile, crossed his arms and smiled at the crowd. His arrogant expression said it all: *I have the upper hand, and no matter what you do, someone is going to die.*

Jayfor had already started scanning the area, searching for an avenue, any avenue, that may give him an opportunity to help. He couldn't just stand here and watch this happen. But the leader was right to be confident. They had the higher ground, and there was no way that he could rush in alone without someone innocent being killed.

But he wouldn't have to work alone.

<u>VIII</u>

"COME ON, NOW, THERE'S still plenty to choose from! Take a look at what we have in stock today! Is it a crime to at least see if there's anything of value here?"

Trenson was painfully aware of the fact that there *was* something of value here, or at least something that he considered valuable: his freedom. He wished he could buy himself – that would make this whole thing much less of a headache. Actually, before he was sold into this and his money given to the overseer, he *did* have enough money for the price the overseer was selling most of the slaves for. He could have bought himself easily, maybe even twice, and probably had enough money to free another slave while he was at it. Yet another reason Trenson wished he wasn't the slave in this situation.

It was a strange feeling, being presented in front of all these people. In reality, the scene wasn't that different from when he used to give speeches at Loronis – he was standing on a stage, and the people were all looking at him, or at least in his general direction. He had given speeches and been the center of attention countless times before, but in this case, he would have given his left arm to have the people's eye off him. Unlike his speeches, he wasn't the one talking. The overseer did most of that.

"We'll start the bidding on this fellow here." The overseer held up the arm of an older man, three slaves away from where Trenson was. "He's a little well into his years, but I assure you he'd outwork the young ones in his sleep. Or maybe you would use his experience in setting him as a manager of affairs? See, the possibilities on this one are well-nigh limitless. Asking price starting at twenty-five crescents, twenty-five, anyone?"

"Here!"

"There's the man I was looking for! Twenty-five it is. Now who will raise? Thirty, is anybody asking thirty?"

"Thirty!"

"And thirty it is, to the man with the big hat! Will anyone challenge that, I repeat, will anyone challenge that?"

Most of the time, Trenson was enamored by the system of auctioning. Sometimes in his strolls through town back in Loronis, he would stop and listen to the livestock auctions just for fun, even though he had no intention of buying anything. The simple and fair way in which it worked intrigued him. He liked to hear the sellers calling out new numbers and raising the price. At this point, however, he had heard the overseer chatter on for so long his ears hurt.

He looked to his left. Aquila stood right beside him, his giant stature making everyone else on the stage feel small. Trenson wondered if it was such a good idea putting Aquila on stage beside everyone else. After all, Aquila made everyone seem much smaller than they were, so, logically, that would make the other slaves less appealing. Trenson inwardly shrugged. Why should he care?

Aquila didn't show any fear as he stood on the platform. In fact, he had grinned good-humoredly at Trenson and Colly when they had been brought out. *I'm glad Aquila's spirits haven't been dampened,* Trenson mused. Then he realized what he had just thought, and countered it with, *it was Colly and Aquila's spirits that made the slave trip so miserable. Now you're just being soft.* Trenson ignored it and looked to his right.

There stood Colly. It was the same Colly he had known for the entire slave trip, the same cheeky and through-the-roof-with-optimism person. Of course, Colly's optimism had faded a little once they arrived at the auction, but anybody's would. But Colly didn't look downhearted now. He looked confident and – solemn? It was a strange look that Trenson had never seen in him, and it surprised him. But he knew why it was so. Va'ar can change the hearts of anyone, and once that change had been made, it gave the person renewed hope and the fortitude to resist armies. It had happened to Trenson, and now Trenson couldn't help but smile seeing it happen in someone else.

You're being soft again, his inner voice told him again. This time, however, he spoke back in his mind. *I don't care. I can be happy for my friend.*

He was again aware of the overseer beside him, conducting his bidding. "Forty was the last call, will anybody challenge? Forty, going once... Forty going twice... and... sold! Thank you sir, for your business. My man over here will settle the exchange. A pleasure, sir."

Snap went the key as it turned the slave's locked hands. The overseer's voice rose again, "Alright, now we've got here another fine example of a man, fit for just about any type of work you please. Starting bid is…"

But the overseer's voice died away. Trenson looked over, confused, and his confusion remained despite what he saw. A man in expensive attire, emerald and gold colored, was on the stage beside the overseer, and the man was talking to the overseer in a hushed voice. The man was obviously an official of some type; if not for his clothes, then for the golden brooch on his right chest, which depicted a swooping eagle barring down on its prey.

After a few minutes of hushed conversation, the man backed away a few paces from the overseer. The overseer, who had clearly been instructed in what to say, spoke in a loud voice, "The captain of the guard of our majesty the king, has requested an order of slaves be brought to him. As such, I will let his proxy here choose from our options before the bidding commences."

Now it made sense, thought Trenson. High-ranking officials obviously got first choice over any type of spoils, and with slaves, it wouldn't be any different.

The bumble of the crowd grew silent as the official started walking across the platform, slowly. He was smaller than average, and so he had to look up to see into the faces of most of the men, but even then, he maintained a look of pride and confidence. Whether he was experienced and rightfully confident, or he was just arrogant, Trenson couldn't tell.

Trenson still didn't know if he wanted this man to take him or not. If he was taken, then it would likely be to a wealthy place, maybe even a fief. But the question was, would he be treated better and given more avenues to escape at a fief, or a farm?

He didn't have the time to think about it. The official walked across the line and assessed each man quickly. When he saw a slave he liked, he pointed at him and nodded at the guards, never stopping his slow pace. A guard undid the chains of each man the official chose, while another guard led that slave off the platform. The richly clad man didn't need to look long at Aquila – he had to look almost straight up to meet eyes with the giant – before nodding at him.

Now he was in front of Trenson. Again, he scanned him mechanically, then nodded again, before moving on.

So he had been chosen. Trenson felt mixed emotions, not sure whether to be glad or anxious. After leading Aquila off the stage, the guard slid the key into Trenson's cuffs and let the chains attached to them fall, then grabbed his forearm and walked him toward the stairs leading down.

Trenson looked over his shoulder, and Colly's light blue eyes met his own. Trenson could read a message in his face: *I'm glad we met, thank you for all you have shown me.* Sadness mixed with gratitude mixed with remorse that they had to meet and depart in such a way all surfaced on his countenance.

Trenson nodded back and offered him a rare smile. Then Colly was out of sight as Trenson was forced down the wooden stairs to stand with the other slaves that were chosen.

The slaves that the official picked were chained back together until they formed a line. There was a special slit in the cuffs that Trenson recently noticed that allowed chains to be slid through and locked into place along a line, and this made grouping the half-dozen slaves easier.

The official was finished. A few minutes after Trenson walked off the stage, the proxy stepped eloquently down the stairs and settled the price for the slaves with the man taking payment. The proxy dropped the appropriate amount of coins into the man's hand, and then turned to the guard in charge of keeping the slaves in order.

"Hold them until I fetch my caravan," he instructed the soldier. Then without another word, he turned and strode down the street. His long, brown cape flapped in the wind, a faint symbol of the swooping hawk visible on the back.

Trenson looked at Aquila, and gave him a reassuring nod. Aquila returned the nod. Both men said without words, *here we go again.*

IX

J AYFOR SENSED IT BEFORE he saw it – the feeling that someone was watching; that something was about to happen. He looked up and saw what was going to happen a split second before it did.

Four men stood on top of the building. The sun was at their back, hiding their faces in their own shadow. They stood on the edge of the rooftop. There was one man for every hostage-holding thief, and each was standing directly behind and above each of these criminals.

Then they jumped. Drawing out knives while they fell, each one landed directly behind a hostage-holder and, before the thieves could turn around, plunged their knives into their backs.

It happened in seconds. One moment, the criminals had the upper hand, with four people imprisoned to guarantee their safety; the next, all four criminals were dead and on the ground, and the captives, after figuring out what happened, ran back into the crowd and reunited with friends and family.

The leader of the heist, who a few seconds ago was standing smugly with complete confidence, now lost that confidence to disbelief as he stumbled backward a few steps and stared at the men who had just turned the tables on him. He finally found his voice. "They're here, they're here! Help, I need help!"

One assassin smiled at the leader. "Yes, you do."

Jayfor quickly assessed the men who had freed the captives. All four of them wore leather armor, not unlike the bandits, except they wore metal spaulders on their shoulders. To Jayfor's surprise, they didn't sheath their knives before drawing the swords at their hips; they simply unsheathed the weapon with their free hand and stood in a ready position, holding a knife in one hand and a sword in the other.

Bandits emerged from the building at their master's calling, and once they saw the assassins standing there, their expressions changed from confusion to anger. With a cry of defiance, the leader of the robbery and his accomplices charged at the ones that had ruined his plans. The assassins stood their guard, preparing for the onslaught with firm faces of determination. The two sides smashed together in a collision of swords, and the fight begun.

Screams came from the crowd at the fight, and the people watching the scene didn't know what to do. Some people ran away, but most of them just stood there, spellbound by the bladework and the piercing yet musical sound of battle.

Jayfor was caught between action and inaction, unsure of what to do. He needed to find Trenson. But these four assassins needed help. More thieves emerged from the building and joined the fray, stacking the odds even more in the criminals favor. The assassins would be overwhelmed and defeated – it was inevitable. Although they were extremely skilled, they didn't have the numbers to oppose the criminals. But if Jayfor joined to fight, they had a chance. The numbers would be more balanced.

Jayfor inwardly sighed and stepped forward from the crowd, drawing his sword. His sense of justice wouldn't let him leave these men to die, no matter how pressing it was to find Trenson. He jogged forward, unnoticed by either side.

He chose a criminal who was engaged in a furious duel with an assassin. Both blades flashed back and forth, the assassin meeting each slash of the opponent's blade with his own, but despite his efforts, he was being pushed back by the powerful blows. Sweat was already forming on the foreheads of both attackers. Jayfor pulled his blade back to begin a finishing thrust to the criminal's back, but he hesitated for a split second. Technically, he would be killing a man in cold blood. But this man had probably done worse things and killed countless people in much more brutal ways. Still, Jayfor didn't want to lower himself to that. To justify it, he yelled, "Look out!"

The bandit stopped his attack and glanced over his shoulder, but he only caught sight of the young man before he felt the cold steel of a blade pierce his midsection. He screamed in pain before falling to the ground.

Jayfor withdrew his blade and looked the assassin he had saved in the eye. Actually, now that he was paying attention, he realized the assassin was a woman. Black hair, cut just below her shoulders, flowed around her brown eyes in the cold breeze. Her face was firm, and she nodded a thanks to Jayfor, looking a little confused. "Who are you?"

Jayfor opened his mouth to answer, then closed it as he realized that more men were coming out of the building, and some of them had identified him as another enemy. "I'm a friend," he said quickly.

The woman still looked confused, but knew that there were more important things to do now than ask questions. Facing the three ruffians that emerged from the building, Jayfor and the woman both took a ready stance to face them.

For the rest of the battle, Jayfor and the woman worked together, an unspoken pact forming between them after Jayfor saved her life. They faced the three men together, fighting close to one another as a team. They assisted each other, swapping around who was fighting who, which confused the brigands and took away their advantage in numbers. Jayfor was surprised at her skill. She had superb footwork and moved effortlessly around her opponents as she fought. Jayfor felt his sword doing most of the work, feeling it's power flow through him and guiding his movements.

After a few close calls, Jayfor and the woman defeated the three brigands, and just in time, since the rest of the brigands had either fallen or fled. After pulling his blade out of the last brigand to fight, Jayfor saw the leader and a few of his soldiers fleeing the scene. The crowd parted to let them through, and booed them as they fled the scene, but did nothing to stop them from leaving. They left without any of the money they retrieved from the building.

After the last of the brigands left, the crowd let out a cheer for the men who had saved the hostages and the treasury – Jayfor guessed that was what the building was. Jayfor let out a sigh of relief, glad that it was over, and turned to the woman, but she had walked away a few paces to talk with some of the other assassins, who were all staring at him as the woman talked.

Jayfor couldn't tell if their stares were friendly or not, but he felt like he should give them an explanation. He sheathed his sword – he knew his sword was filthy now, and should be cleaned before put back in a sheath, but did it mainly to show the other warriors that he wasn't hostile – and approached them.

The woman stopped talking and looked at Jayfor, then back at the man who she had been talking to. The assassin stared at Jayfor and crossed his arms. This wasn't someone that Jayfor would want to make an enemy of. He was a heavily built man that was agile despite his size and deft with the sword and knife on his belt, the silver blades which matched the color of his eyes and somehow complimented his short, dark hair. Oddly enough, the man didn't look very old; in fact, he looked a few years older than Jayfor.

"She tells me that you saved her, and helped her." The man spoke in a voice that was calm and not as menacing as Jayfor expected.

Jayfor didn't know exactly how to respond, but he found himself saying, "Yes, sir." Even though technically he was the former king of the kingdom of Faldon, he felt small before the man, and decided it would be wise to be respectful.

The man smiled. "Thank you. She's my wife." He looked at his wife, and they smiled at each other. "I don't know what I would do without her." He met eyes with Jayfor again, and his smile was replaced with a look of curiosity. "Who are you?"

Jayfor didn't know how to answer. "I-"

An unfamiliar voice shouted, "You there!"

Jayfor whirled around to see the crowd had silenced, and the joy on everyone's faces was gone. Peacekeepers. Or the Kallary versions of peacekeepers, at least. They wore furs, which not only kept them warm as much as displayed their rank, as fur coats were expensive items. The crowd parted to let the dozen peacekeepers through. The peacekeepers stopped about ten feet away from the warriors, and the two groups stared at each other. There were a dozen officers, compared to the five warriors.

A decorated man who Jayfor guessed was the leader drew his schiavona from his scabbard with a flourish and pointed in at Jayfor's feet. "Drop your weapons."

They think we're the criminals. Jayfor glanced behind him. Neither the woman, nor her husband, nor the other two warriors said a word. One of the other assassins said quietly to the woman's husband, "Ernest, now's a good time."

Ernest frowned, but didn't avert his eyes from the peacekeepers. "No, Novak."

"We can't just run, there's too many of them," Novak argued.

The leader of the peacekeepers was getting impatient. "I said, drop your weapons!"

"He's right," Ernest's wife said. "It's the only way out."

Jayfor looked at Ernest. "What?"

"This is the last warning! Drop your weapons before they fall out of your limp hands!"

"I'm going to do it," Novak said decidedly. He reached into a pocket in his coat and pulled out a small, round object that Jayfor couldn't identify.

"Don't do it," Ernest warned.

The captain was done waiting. "Suit yourself! Men, do your work."

What happened next, Jayfor would never forget. In the moment, it seemed to happen so fast, but later, Jayfor slowed down his memory to relive it in the order that it happened.

Novak threw the object in his hand to the ground, hard. It didn't bounce like Jayfor expected. It exploded. The second it hit the ground, there was a bang. Then, out of nowhere, a cloud of smoke suddenly slammed into Jayfor's eyes and nose. He choked, his vision blurred by the tears that flooded his eyes. He tried to force his eyes to open, but they wouldn't. Choking on the smoke, he gagged, causing more coughing as his lungs filled with smoke. He couldn't see anything.

A hand suddenly grabbed his wrist, and he felt himself being pulled. Not knowing if it was a peacekeeper or a warrior, he allowed himself to be dragged forward. He could hear sounds around him, but didn't register them, as he was still in a dazed state of mind.

When the air lost some of it's smokey taste, Jayfor managed to crack his eye open and see through the tears. To his relief, he saw that it was Ernest who was holding his wrist and guiding him. They were in a narrow alley, and Ernest's wife and the other two warriors were running in front of them.

"I think this is far enough," Ernest said, slowing his running and, after seeing that Jayfor's eyes were open, letting go of his wrist.

Jayfor stopped and started a series of gags and coughs, his throat burning as he tried to expel the smoke from his lungs. He leaned forward and put his hands on his knees. After he finally caught his breath, he wiped the tears from his eyes and looked up. Everyone was staring at him. Surprisingly, even though everyone had soot on their faces, none of them looked as crippled by the smoke as he was.

Jayfor cleared his throat and stood upright. "What..." he cleared his throat again. "What was that?"

Ernest's face was stern. "That is what happens when someone doesn't obey orders." He turned and glared at Novak.

Novak put his palms up in an innocent gesture. "I was only doing what I thought was necessary! They would have caught us had I not acted so quickly. You should all be thanking me."

Ernest shook his head. "It did, but we have costed ourselves more than what our capture would have. We talked about this, Novak."

Jayfor interrupted. "What? What was that?" He looked around at the faces staring at him, all of them solemn. "Who are you?"

Ernest's wife looked at the ground for a second, thinking, then looked Jayfor in the eye. "We are—"

"Tindra, no." Ernest cut her off.

Tindra turned and looked at her husband, her hair swishing around her shoulders. "He just saved us, saved me. I think we can trust him."

Ernest glanced at Jayfor. "How do we know?" He spoke like Jayfor wasn't standing right there, listening to them. "We've misplaced our trust in the past."

Tindra looked at Ernest resolutely. "I trust him. Is your trust in me misplaced?"

Ernest opened his mouth to say something, but Novak cut him off. "Sorry to interrupt, but we really need to leave. It's getting late."

Ernest closed his mouth. "You're right." Jayfor couldn't read his expression. Was it anxiety, or anger, or uncertainty? Ernest remained quiet for a second, evidently deciding what to do about Jayfor. "Face the wall," he said suddenly.

Jayfor was confused. "What?"

"Face the wall." Ernests nodded calmy at one wall of the alley.

Jayfor frowned, not sure where this was going. He could make a dash for it, but something told him that it would be wise to listen. Slowly, he turned to face the wall.

"Now walk close to it, until your forehead touches it."

Jayfor did as he was told. The wall was cold.

"Good. Now, I want you to count, slowly. Don't move or look away from the wall until you reach one hundred." There was a pause. "Start."

Jayfor once again considered making a break for it, but once again decided against it. He counted out loud. "One. Two. Three…"

He heard the sounds of them leaving, the thudding of their boots as they left the alley. Once he reached ten, he couldn't hear the noises anymore. By the time he reached twenty, he knew they had gone, and all was quiet, beside the sound of his own voice. They were gone now; he could turn around without any consequences – probably. But he wasn't willing to take the risk.

The seconds seemed to get longer the closer he got to the end, but finally, "One hundred," rolled off his tongue, and the second it did he whirled around.

Just as he expected, he was alone.

X

FTER THE AUCTION ENDED and night fell upon the city, the overseer asked Philon, one of his hired guards, to assist him with some tasks before joining the others to relax. Unwillingly, Philon complied. He knew the faster they got the work done, the better.

A few minutes later, Philon didn't know why he thought "they" would get the job done; he was the only one moving the supplies from the wagon, and the overseer just stood watching. The boxes of supplies weren't even that heavy, and all he had to do was unload them from the wagon and place them in a stack in the barn. It was the same barn they used to hold the slaves in, but now it was empty, and so they used it to hold the horses and supplies.

The overseer instructed Philon to finish unloading the supplies, then unhitch the horses and see they were tended to for the night, before heading towards the inn. This miffed Philon – why was he the only one that was called to stay and help? He could use some of the other soldiers' help with this. It didn't make a difference at this point, though.

He finished unloading the wagon, then unhitched the horses from the wagon and took off their harnesses. After tying the two horses to a hitching post and pouring some oats and water for each of them, he was finally done. With ale on his mind, he opened the door to the barn and came out.

What he saw, he wasn't expecting.

In the little light that remained before nightfall, was a man, a young man at that, holding the overseer by the collar of his coat, and talking to him with his face close to the overseer's. The overseer was almost off the ground, terror written on his face. The threatener was calmly talking to him in a voice that wasn't loud enough to hear. Both men were a stone's throw away, and neither of them saw Philon.

Philon took a second to register surprise. This wasn't something he saw every day. Then, the realization that his contractor was in danger hit him. Well, in reality, the realization that the person who paid him was in danger hit him. He took off toward the two men.

He could hear the overseer's voice now, at a higher pitch than what he had ever heard. "I don't know! Please, is it money? I have money, take my money." His voice was on the verge of breaking down.

"I don't want your money," the man said, in a voice that was calm and low, and had a foreign accent to it. "I want an answer."

Philon slowed to a stop a few yards from both men. "What's going on?" he demanded. He realized at this moment that he was unarmed. The threatener had a sword on his hip, which meant that Philon and the overseer were now totally harmless to the man.

At the noise, both the overseer and the man looked at Philon, one with relief, one with panic. The man changed his position so that he was behind the overseer and using him as a shield. The overseer whimpered and continued gripping at the hand around his shirt.

Philon yelled, "Let him go!" He tried to sound intimidating.

"Listen," the man said, "I don't want any trouble."

"Too late," Philon said.

The man rolled his eyes. "I don't want any *more* trouble. All I want is for him," he looked at the overseer, who he was still calmly holding by the collar, "to tell me where he is."

Now Philon was confused. This man wasn't looking for money? That was a first. Who was he looking for?

Before he could answer, the overseer finally gave in. "OK, OK, I'll tell you, I'll tell you! Just let me go!"

The man looked relieved, and suddenly let go of the overseer's collar. The overseer fell on the ground in a heap. He made no movement to get up. The man stepped back a few paces and waited awkwardly until, finally, the overseer rose to his feet. He was breathing heavy, and staring at the man who had just threatened him.

The man said impatiently, "Well?"

The overseer couldn't bear the thought of being in that iron grip once again, and quickly replied, "A regal official came to the auction. He was buying slaves to take to Augustria. He bought your friend."

"Augustria? Where is that?" The man demanded.

"It's east of here. Take the main eastern exit of the city, and you'll reach it in a few days."

The man didn't respond. Instead, he seemed to be thinking. Philon was unsure about what to do. He didn't have any affection towards the overseer, other than he was his boss and paid him. He was also unarmed and was more concerned about his own safety than his boss's. Not wanting to make a wrong move, he stood still, watching what was happening and ready to act at any moment.

When the man didn't respond immediately, the overseer started begging, "I swear, that's all I know! I haven't done anything wrong, I'm just trying to—"

"Nothing wrong?!" The man's demeanor suddenly changed from calm to fuming. He took a step closer to the overseer. He said in a low tone, "I would think about all the lives you have ruined, all the souls of men you have traded for coin, the way you barter away the lives of husbands, wives, and children, before I started talking."

The overseer started shuddering with fear and cowered. He didn't reply, not just because fear stole his voice, but because he had no answer. Philon took a step forward, ready to act if this interaction turned violent.

The man looked down at the trembling overseer, his fists clenched, jaw set, fierce rage in his features. Philon was about to react to stop what was going to be his contractor's certain death. Then the man's features suddenly changed. His wrath softened, and his features relaxed, and he took a step back, like he was surprised at what he had just said.

He looked at Philon, then at the overseer. Now there was pity on his face, and sadness that shocked Philon. The man said a few words before turning and leaving Philon and the overseer alone in the night.

"Why... Why do people like you choose to be so bad?"

XI

I N A FEW DAYS, Trenson found himself in the barracks of the captain of the guard in the city of Augustria.

"If I hear any trouble, or there's commotion of any kind, everyone involved will be hanged." One of the guards warned as Trenson and the other slaves were ushered into their barracks. "And I mean everyone. You think you're special? Get over yourself, you're easily replaceable."

If the guard was expecting a reaction from the slaves, he was sorely disappointed. Although there was no doubt that everyone in the small room heard him, nobody trembled in fear.

After seeing that there would be no reaction, the guard huffed and closed the reinforced door. It hit the reinforced walls with a clang, and the reinforced latch and lock fell into place. The guard looked through the barred window of the cell for a moment, then turned and left.

Trenson surveyed the room they were just forced into. Homely is one word he wouldn't use, but he could see this being a nice place – if only one person was living here, rather than six. Trenson was actually glad that it was cramped, since the more people occupied a room, the more body heat was released and the warmer it would be. There was another barred window high on the wall, allowing bone-chilling air to seep in.

There were no cots or designated sleeping areas. Instead, the welcoming sight of a dirt floor was before them, and that was all there was to the room. Well, there was one thing that made everyone's spirits soar: a pile of blankets in the corner.

In less than a minute, everyone in the cell was wrapped in a blanket of their own. The blankets were large enough to wrap around your ankles, all the way up to your head. Everyone threw the top of the blanket over their head to create a little hood. Even though the material was rather thin, to Trenson, who had spent many nights in the cold without protection, it was the second-best thing to freedom.

"This isn't so bad," Trenson commented to Aquila.

Aquila nodded heartily with a smile. Trenson couldn't help but smile faintly when he saw that, while the blankets covered everyone else from head to toe, for Aquila, that meant waist to toe. Aquila made up for it by sitting with his back against the wall and pulling his knees in, which turned him into a small enough ball that the blanket could cover the whole of him. The rest of the slaves did the same, but so they could rest, not to get more use out of their blanket like Aquila. As always, they didn't say a word to each other or make eye contact.

Trenson found his thoughts wandering to Colly. He wondered where he was, who he was sold to. Trenson also wondered if Colly would continue to believe in Va'ar. He told Trenson that he believed, but time would tell if he could hold on to it. All Trenson could do was hope that Colly would keep believing.

It was getting darker, the light from the window above turning orange in preparation for sunset. Trenson yawned. He was tired enough now that maybe he wouldn't wait for night to sleep. Although his mind wanted to plan, to think about what might happen tomorrow, to devise ways to escape, exhaustion pulled him into sleep like a riptide, and it wasn't long before he lay on the ground and sank into its warm embrace.

***

"I'm going to tell all of you right now: Each one of you is the unluckiest slave I have ever bought."

Trenson stood at attention. Slaves stood on either side of Trenson; some were from Trenson's original group of six, others from different auctions, totaling about a dozen.

" 'Why', do you ask?" The speaker walked slowly, only a few feet from everyone's face, as he looked into their eyes with his own gray ones. "Because I didn't ask him to find men who can cook or clean, who can tend to cattle or work in fields. No, those skills are easy. There's no risk, no need to worry about your safety, because your profession won't kill you." The man stopped walking and looked up and down the line.

"Starting today... your job is to kill each other."

For the first time, Trenson saw a reaction from the emotionless slaves he had known the entire journey. They looked left and right, confused, looking at each other to see if they had heard correctly.

A small grin touched the speaker's lips at the bewilderment. Trenson assessed the man. He was obviously the captain of wherever they were. Tall and broad chested, he stood taller than most of the men, although still dwarfed in height by Aquila. His face had scars, and his nose was slightly crooked, a sign that he broke his nose in the past. Long hair that almost reached his shoulders was tied back in a braid. He had two weapons that surprised Trenson: hatchets. The small axes were on either side of his hip, mostly hidden by the sheaths they were in, and by the way he occasionally stroked their handles, Trenson guessed the warrior was fond of his weapons.

They were in a small room, barely long enough to allow the slaves to stand shoulder to shoulder in a line. Wooden beams held up the wooden roof. After Trenson woke up and ate the measly breakfast that was offered to everyone in their cell, they were taken to this room, following their guard through multiple hallways until Trenson lost his sense of direction. A few turns later, they were here.

After waiting a moment for the room to settle down, the warrior let his voice, which easily carried itself to each corner of the room, bring everyone to attention again. "But I think it best not to overwhelm your small, fragile minds at the moment. I need those minds intact, at least for now. I shall start with who I am. Although my name is Wulfric, captain of the regal guard of Augustria and protector of His Majesty the King, you are not to address me as such. If any of you call me anything other than, 'sir,' or 'my lord,' you will be happily flogged. Understand?"

He swept his gaze across the group. Nobody responded, and everyone avoided eye contact. Wulfric chuckled once and said in a low voice, only intended for himself, and yet everyone could hear, "And still some will disobey, knowing full well the whip is for them."

Wulfric then continued in his usual loud voice. "Soldiers are what I'm looking for. That is the only reason I sent my proxy out in the first place. In a few days' time, it will become clear to me which of you can fight, and which of you can't. How?"

Here Wulfric stopped pacing and turned to face the group. His features, which remained stoic and passive this entire time, now started to light up. A broad smile crested his face, and he said with a light in his eye and pronouncing it with a flourish, "The arena."

An arena? Why... Then it clicked, and immediately dread grabbed his heart. That was why everyone was going to try to kill each other. That was why Wulfric called them the unluckiest slaves he bought.

Trenson looked at the rows of people standing beside him. Already they were glancing at each other, Most of them were horrified and made no attempt to hide it, either because they were no good with weapons, or they couldn't stand the thought of killing each other, or both. Aquila was one of these. Trenson met eyes with him, standing further down the line, and they could read each other's fear perfectly.

Wulfric decided he had let his words hang in the air long enough. "Today, you will be showed around the arena and the training grounds. Familiarize yourself with everything; you only get one chance. After that, you will be asked to choose a weapon, and this weapon you shall use in the upcoming fights. For the rest of today, you shall use the training grounds to practice what little to no skill you have. It's tomorrow that the fun begins.

"The previous captain of the guard loved to do large scale mock battles. And they were impressive, much more impressive, most would say, than one-on-one tournament style. I have to agree with him; nothing draws a crowd more than twelve people trying to stop all eleven other hearts from beating." Wulfric was genuinely excited as he talked, which sent chills down Trenson's spine.

"But clearly, he was weak and frivolous, which is why I am here today. What I want, rather than a day of entertainment ending with a lucky few still standing, is men who can lock onto their opponent, who have the skill and tenacity to bait them in, to get them to let their guard down, and the potency to capitalize on this." Wulfric continued his slow pacing, looking ahead and not directly at any of them.

"Tournament style is therefore my mode of determining which few are worth it. But all these details are worth nothing to you. What you need to know is this: Today, you train. Tomorrow, you will fight, and if you are the one who survived, you will move on to the next fight the next day, on and on and on, until the last few will be chosen to train for my services. The rest I have no use for." Wulfric once again stopped pacing and turned to his audience. He stood in the middle of the two lines, and his eyes scanned the group, making brief eye contact with everyone. "Understood?"

Everyone nodded.

"Good, then. That is all. Either you meet me again at the tournaments end, or you will see me in the afterlife. Your choice."

***

The arena was diamond shaped – or a square depending on how you looked at it, but from where the judges box was situated overlooking the arena, it made more sense for it to be a diamond. Trenson guessed it was about fifty yards from each wall to the opposite wall, making it fairly small.

A twenty-foot-high wall drew the outline of the arena, made of smooth, gray stone that would be impossible to climb out of. No seats were situated above the wall for spectators to watch from. Trenson was surprised by this at first, then remembered that these tournaments were done for a purpose, not to entertain a crowd. There was, however, a sort of balcony that jutted out slightly over the wall, with a thatch roof and three-sided walls. Trenson couldn't make out any details inside the room from where he was standing, but he assumed it was where Wulfric would sit to watch the fighters. *It must be nice,* Trenson mused bitterly, *watching life and death dealt from safety.*

Another thing Trenson took note of was the ground: it was sand, and not packed sand at that. Trenson's feet sunk a little into it with each step. A shifting surface meant he couldn't move his feet as much, and since so much of sword fighting was in the footwork, it placed him at a disadvantage against weapons that required less footwork.

After they left the arena, guards escorted them to a small training yard, barely large enough for everyone to train comfortably. As soon as they entered the area, a servant took tally of what weapon they wanted. When it was Trenson's turn, he obviously chose a sword, and the servant nodded and added an extra sword to the list.

Aquila had a difficult time asking for a weapon. Unable to tell the servant what he wanted, he had to use hand gestures to try to portray the weapon, which didn't go well, as the servant had to scribble out an axe, a hatchet, and a spear after writing each one thinking that was the weapon he was trying to ask for. Finally, the servant guessed a staff, and Aquila nodded, relieved that he had finally chosen his weapon.

After all the slaves' weapon choices were tallied, the servant left the grounds for a few minutes. Then a few guards came in, each one holding an armful of weapons. Trenson was disappointed to find that they weren't real weapons, only wooden training ones, but he should have expected that.

For the rest of the day, Trenson trained. Looking around at the competition as they trained, Trenson could tell that pretty much everyone had little to no expertise in combat. Trenson was both encouraged and saddened by this. He could win this tournament easily, but the path to winning was only achievable through killing his opponent, and his opponent might as well be defenseless for all the skill these men possessed. Was he willing to sacrifice other people's lives to save his own? But wasn't his life more important than theirs, so would it be justified?

It would be justified legally, Trenson decided, but he could never justify it to himself. He wouldn't kill anyone. He would disable or unarm his opponent, but he wouldn't kill them. Trenson didn't know how Wulfric would respond to that, but it was a risk he was willing to take.

Trenson was painfully aware of the absence of his own sword as he warmed up with this feeble wooden one. He missed traveling with Jayfor. He would never experience those days again. Grief tried to overtake him once again, but he pushed it away and focused on training. He reminded himself of his mission: he had to escape. He had to find some way to get his real sword back. And then, after accomplishing two impossible tasks, then he would continue on his journey to the Tree of Ramadas, a tree which he had no idea of its location.

But he wouldn't think about that. First, he would focus on surviving the tournament.

Trenson spent some time with Aquila and trained with him a little during their time here. Although he knew that giving advice to a potential opponent wasn't smart, Trenson wanted Aquila to get through this tournament alive. He was the closest thing he had to a friend. Hopefully they were on opposite sides of the bracket, and wouldn't meet until the end.

Aquila had never held a staff before, so Trenson, whose primary weapon used to be one, showed him a few basic techniques, such as blocking and positioning himself favorably. Most of the other slaves chose a staff as their weapon as well, so Trenson gave him some advice about countering other staffs. Aquila took in the information and learned quickly, and although he couldn't speak his gratitude, Trenson could see it in his eyes.

XII

IT WAS WHEN HE saw the person in front of him get arrested that Jayfor started to have doubts.

Jayfor had joined the line for admittance into Augustria around half an hour ago. The line was much larger than the one he stood in to get into Talikan. This made sense, considering that this city was so much larger than the last one.

While Jayfor waited behind a tall man who had a suspiciously bulging satchel at his side, he contemplated what his course of action would be when he got inside. Unlike the last time he went into the city, he didn't know what Trenson's master looked like, so he couldn't search the crowd for a face, or know exactly where he should start looking. The overseer told Jayfor that the Captain of the Guard of Augustria had bought him. This wasn't very helpful, but it gave Jayfor a starting point for his search.

Jayfor was now closer to the end of the line. He wasn't worried this time; he figured that since the last gatekeeper he encountered was so easy to bribe, it would be no different with this one. When he was the second-to-last one in the line, he was already holding a decent amount of gold in his hand.

The person in front of him stepped before the guard. Unlike in Talikan, there were half a dozen warriors standing watch at the gate, while one of them admitted people.

"*Doma-cartel?*" the guard said, his accent complementing the word.

The man standing in front of Jayfor was confused and didn't respond immediately. Jayfor wondered what in the world the gate-keeper was saying. He was deeper into Kallary now, so naturally, the Kallarian language was more widely spoken.

After the realization came dread: how was he supposed to find Trenson and survive in this city for days if he couldn't understand a word of the city? He was trying to come up with solutions to this problem when the guard, seeing as he wasn't getting a response from the man, spoke again.

"Business?"

Both Jayfor and the man in front of him were relieved to hear that the guard was bilingual. The man quickly responded, "I need some tools and equipment that can only be bought here."

The guard nodded once. "Pass?"

The man reached into his pocket, as if to pull out his pass, but when he pulled his hand out, Jayfor could see that his fist was filled with coins. This piqued Jayfor's curiosity; it was a good test to see if bribery would work.

The man poured the gold into the guard's open palm, doing it discreetly so that only he and the guard – or so he thought – could see the gold. The guard looked at the shimmering gold in his hand, but kept a straight face, so that neither Trenson nor the man could tell what he was thinking. Finally, the guard put the gold in his pocket, which made both of them sigh with relief.

"You are under arrest."

It was a jaw-dropping moment for Jayfor, but even more so for the man who tried to bribe. "W-what?"

"You heard me. Okala!" The guard yelled over his shoulder. One of the watchers at the gate snapped to attention and started walking towards the scene, spear in hand.

"Please," the man begged, putting his hands together in a gesture of appeal. "I have more! Just let me through!"

The guard coldly shook his head. "No pass, no admittance. Okala, take this man to be searched and examined."

Okala saluted. "Yes, sir." He then roughly grabbed the man by the arm and pulled him through the gate. He had gained admittance into the city all right, but not the way he intended. The man still tried to reason and offered incredibly large sums to the guard, but it was to no avail. Soon, the man's voice could no longer be heard, and the fiasco was over.

The guard then turned, expecting to see the shorter, sandy-haired man that was behind the last man, but to his surprise he was gone, and a different person was in his place. The guard shrugged and continued. "*Doma-Cartel?*"

***

It was too much of a risk to take. Jayfor wasn't about to try the same thing that the man in front of him tried and expect a different

result. Although maybe if he put even more money into his hand...
no, that probably wouldn't work. And plus, the gatekeeper took
the money before arresting the man, so no matter how much
money he gave him, Jayfor would still get arrested.

After the imprisonment at the gate, Jayfor snuck away from
the line while the guard's attention was distracted. Now he stood
about twenty yards away from the gate. He made a point to stand
close to the wall so that the guards standing directly under the
archway of the gate couldn't see him. Now all he had to do was
figure out another way in.

"I knew it." A voice calmly said.

Almost as fast as the shock wave of surprise hit him, Jayfor
jumped, the hair on the back of his neck standing straight up. He
spun on his heel and looked behind him, where he thought the
voice came from. He was already in a ready position, adrenaline
pumping through him.

He didn't see anything at first. Then something stirred in the
shadows of the columns that stuck out of the wall. A hooded figure
emerged from the small shadow. He stepped forward a few paces,
then stopped. He wore a dark-colored outfit with a separate hood,
which was draped over his head. He was tall and stout.

Jayfor backed up a few paces. "Who are you?"

Slowly, the man grabbed the edges of his hood and pulled it
back, his face finally revealed. "I didn't expect you to forget me so
quickly."

Jayfor furrowed his eyebrows. "Are you... Ernest? The assassin?"

The man's eyes dimmed from the silver gleam they held a few
seconds ago. "An assassin isn't a term I would like to describe

myself, but yes, I am he." He crossed his arms. "You weren't even supposed to know my name."

"One of the other men called you by it."

Ernest sighed. "Leave it to Novak to cause more trouble."

Jayfor relaxed, but only slightly. Now that he recognized this man, he was a little more at ease, but only slightly. "What are you doing here?"

Ernest kept a stoic expression. "You didn't let me finish. Let me continue: I knew it. You're not friends with the law either, are you?"

Jayfor didn't know how to respond. If he said no, he would be lying, since he was technically a criminal in Kallary. But if he said yes, then he would imply that he enjoyed criminal activity, which was not the case. And the way Ernest said *either* was enough for Jayfor to be suspicious. "It depends."

Ernest let out a single chuckle. "On what?"

"On what law."

"Ah, but that is my point. You're a criminal by the world's law, an outcast under their standards."

Jayfor frowned. Where was this going? "But aren't we all?"

For once, Ernest smiled. "See, you understand."

"Understand what?"

"That it's not supposed to be this way." Ernest looked over Jayfor's head and around the horizon, as if he was surveying the world. "The world is broken, fractured. It never was intended to be this way." He looked Jayfor in the eye. "You know this."

Jayfor nodded apprehensively. "Yes."

"And you also know that although the world is fallen, the Creator still cares about us, and will restore it."

Jayfor perked at hearing the term *Creator.* "And what do you mean by 'Creator?'"

"I mean exactly what I said. You didn't think you were the last believer in Ralladin, did you?" Ernest said with a smirk.

"Well, actually... I did," Jayfor admitted.

Ernest uncrossed his arms. "Well, unfortunately for Elara, destroying a capital city doesn't grant them victory."

Jayfor now felt like he could relax. This man was a believer, and that was enough to put most of his apprehensions at ease. But it didn't answer all his questions. "Who are you really?"

Ernest smiled. "Do you really want to know? If I tell you who I really am, what I am fighting for, then your life will never be the same. You will live in blissful ignorance no more."

Ernest took a few steps closer to Jayfor and peered closer into his face, as if he was looking for something. Jayfor was puzzled and took a step back. Ernest continued staring at him, then he said, "I followed you here, because I sensed something different about you. Even after you helped us, I knew you were no ordinary person." Ernest looked him in the eye. "The better question is, who are you?"

Jayfor paused. Who was he, really? An exiled king of a kingdom that no longer exists? A follower of Va'ar, once on a mission from Him, but now interrupted as he tried to free his friend? He was both. But what should he tell Ernest? Could he trust him that much?

He decided that he couldn't. "We both have our secrets."

Ernest frowned. "So it seems." He stopped staring at Jayfor and instead looked behind him at the walls of the city. It seemed that he had moved on from his questioning. "So it seems."

Jayfor opened his mouth to reply, but Ernest wasn't done. "I saw you leave the line after the arrest. I take it you don't have a pass?"

Jayfor gave Ernest the side eye, still unsure how much he could trust him. "I wasn't aware I needed one to travel in Kallary."

Ernest huffed. "Passes have been around for almost a hundred years, and they still enforce them now as much as they did then," he said bitterly. Then he glanced quickly to his left, then his right, as if checking to make sure no one was listening. "It seems you're in luck, because I happen to know that there's more than one way into the city."

Now Jayfor was interested. For the past few minutes, he had tried to figure out what Ernest's motives were. He had verbally danced around the subject instead of asking directly, not wanting to make any wrong assumptions. But if this man was offering him another way into the city, then he was interested. "There's another way?"

"There's always another way. And no, I'm not talking about one of the other main gates. You'll have no better luck there." Ernest checked around him once more, scanning the surrounding area. "Follow me."

Ernest started walking away from the walls, and toward the plains that lay all around the city. Jayfor was confused. Shouldn't the alternate exit be close to the town? Curiously, he followed close behind Ernest.

They walked for a few minutes. With each step, Jayfor was painfully aware that he was losing ground, but he reminded himself that it wasn't losing ground if Ernest was right. Jayfor wanted to ask questions but thought it better to keep silent. Ernest didn't say anything either, or even look behind him to see if Jayfor was following.

After what felt like a long time, the main road to the city about half a mile to his right, Jayfor saw something ahead of them. It was an old well, and about as standard as you could get. As he approached it, Jayfor saw that not only was it ordinary, but it was extremely old. Built out of rock, it was a simple circle that gave way to an inky black hole, at the bottom of which was most likely water, but there was no way to tell.

Ernest stopped at the edge of the rock. He looked over the edge for a moment, perhaps seeing something that Jayfor couldn't. Then he turned to Jayfor. "If you want to be part of something bigger and know who I truly am… then you'll have to fall."

As soon as he said the last word, Ernest leaned his back against the stone of the well and, without a sound, flipped backward over the edge and disappeared into the darkness.

Jayfor was shocked. He heard a violent splash from the well as Ernest hit the water at the bottom. He peered over the edge, but couldn't see anything. The sounds of the splash stopped as soon as they began, and Jayfor was left alone. Ernest was gone.

He realized he had a choice. Ernest wanted to show him the whole picture, but Jayfor had to decide whether he would take the risk of seeing it. Jumping into a well? Definitely not the scariest thing he had done, but still, could he trust him?

He looked down into the well again and took a deep breath. *I mean, what do I have to lose?*

At first, he couldn't think of anything. Then, his mind started creating a massive list of ways this was crazy and what he was risking. Fortunately, this list didn't start forming until after he jumped over the edge.

XIII

WULFRIC WOKE UP IN his cushioned bed with the happy prospect of watching carnage before him. He did not have to worry about organizing the affair; servants had already been up for hours, making sure everything was in order. They would handle almost everything, from preparing the arena to checking the weapons, to making sure the slaves were ready for combat. So Wulfric took his time getting ready.

At breakfast, which this morning was ham and potatoes mixed with cheese dressing, Wulfric had the rare experience of sharing the meal with his son, Geoffrey.

"You're back," Wulfric said emotionlessly.

Geoffrey, who was a stout twenty-year-old with short, auburn hair, replied with the same enthusiasm, "Brigid was boring. All that is in that ancient city, beside beggars and rats, are scrolls and tombs. I hardly see any benefit of my journey."

Wulfric nodded with a mouth full of food. After taking a few moments to swallow and wipe his lips with a napkin, he replied, "You shall get benefit out of it, regardless. I didn't send you on a vacation; I sent you on a mission to become more acquainted with the world. You will find a use for what you learned."

Geoffrey looked as though he wanted to say more, but knew better. "Yes, father." A ring of sarcasm was in his tone, but Wulfric didn't notice, being occupied with his meal.

Wulfric didn't have a relationship with his son that most fathers did. When Geoffrey's mother died in childbirth, Wulfric always viewed Geoffrey as responsible. As soon as he was born, he was whisked away by tutors and teachers who taught him everything from swordplay to politics to chess to other languages. Throughout his career, Wulfric had a private conversation with Geoffrey only a few times in his life. It wasn't that he was bitter. It was simply that he didn't share any bond at all with his son, viewing him instead as someone that was in his charge.

That didn't mean that Wulfric neglected any aspect of Geoffrey's education – far from it. Although having no affection toward his son, he knew that his title of Captain of the Guard would be passed down to his son, and he wanted his family's good name to be preserved. Also, when Geoffrey spoke at important meetings or was engaged in some political activity, Wulfric would be respected for his son's achievements.

Now, however, Geoffrey was almost old enough to choose a profession to do before being the next captain. Although the title would be passed down upon Wulfric's death, Geoffrey still needed something to do in the meantime. Wulfric had no idea what he would choose; he didn't have those sort of conversations with his son. If he had to guess, he would say Geoffrey would choose being a proxy – traveling to communities and meetings in the steed of politicians or other officials.

After a long period of silence, Geoffrey said casually while spooning more breakfast, "I hear you're holding a tournament of slaves to determine new soldiers?" He said it as a question instead of a statement.

"Indeed," Wulfric replied.

"I don't see the point. There are plenty of other methods to attain soldiers, and strong, disciplined ones at that. Why, in Brigid, soldiers are trained from birth, and they are raised in buildings where they are taught everything they need. If we instigated something similar, not only could we maintain a healthy amount of soldiers and breed them in the way we saw fit, but this whole process of searching for skilled fighters would be eliminated."

Wulfric frowned. "Perhaps in a city that has been practicing it for a long time. But to start such a process would take months, even years. Besides, I rather enjoy the tournaments."

Geoffrey scoffed. "A waste of time. Even the strongest slave will prove to be the weakest soldier."

"We shall see," Wulfric replied coldly.

There was no more conversation after that. Both Wulfric and Geoffrey finished their meal and, without a word to each other, left the room. Geoffrey went to finish overseeing the slaves unpacking his bags from his trip, while Wulfric went to his seat in the arena. Although the competition didn't start for almost an hour, he wanted to be ready and make sure everything was ready. He couldn't wait.

Although most would not have guessed it, Wulfric liked putting on a show, even if it was only for himself. Accordingly, he placed trumpeters on the walls above the opposite gates of the arena, with instructions to herald the arrival of combatants and the end of the fight. It added to the excitement of the event, in Wulfric's eyes.

Sitting on his chair on his shaded balcony, Wulfric ate grapes from a table beside him. In a few moments, the trumpets would sound, the gates would raise, and two armed men would walk into the battlefield, intent on killing each other. Wulfric couldn't deny his excitement. He didn't get to hold events like this very often.

Finally, just when he was about to inquire his managers as to why it was taking so long, the long-awaited bugle pierced the air. They held the same note for a few seconds, then let it stop, allowing the silence to fall back over the ring. Wulfric tensed and let his eyes wander to the arena entrances.

Then, slowly, the gates of the entrances started to rise. The barred gates went straight up into the roof of the walls with the clanging of metal gears. When the gates were halfway up, high enough to allow someone to walk under, the gladiators made their entrance.

Both men were wearing very thin leather armor, more for clothing than for protection. The man on the right had a staff and walked cautiously into the arena like he had never held one before. The man on the left also had a staff, and didn't look any more skilled than the first one.

A few guards, wearing much more formidable gear, jogged into the arena after the slaves and took positions at intervals along the wall.

The slaves took a few more steps into the arena, then stopped. They first looked at each other, then around them at the ring they were trapped in, the guards who were ready to force them to fight, and last, their master, who sat above on his balcony, looking down on them, enjoying the game of life and death before him.

Although suppressed fear was evident in their countenance, the slaves locked eyes with fierce determination. They knew that only one of them was leaving the ring today. Animalistic instinct took over. Although they each had no skill in fighting, they would use tooth and claw to win the battle – or fall prey to the same weapons of the enemy.

The slave on the left side made the first move. Without a word, he rushed at his opponent, holding his staff in an amateur grip. His opponent, seeing his adversary coming closer, brandished his spear in a no better fashion and sprinted to clash into in his opponent. The empty space between them quickly diminished.

The guards in the ring started cheering. They had bets placed, hoping to add more excitement – and profit – to their day.

Wulfric leaned forward in his chair. This was it: the first fight of the day.

After a few drawn-out seconds, the slaves crashed violently into each other. Upon getting within a staff's reach of the other, both men started swinging and spinning their staff, almost blinded by fear and their own recklessness. It was a fury of long wooden poles.

It only lasted a few seconds. The staffs clonked against each other twice, each hit brutal and bone-rattling. It was the third swing, however, of one of the slaves that found its mark on the other's leg. The wounded man screamed in pain before falling to the ground, causing the dry sand to swirl into the air. Before the man on the ground could beg for mercy, the other slave gripped the end of his staff, and with one, brutal swing, followed by a sickening crack, shattered the skull of the man on the ground.

The victor had been decided in a matter of moments.

A hushed silence fell over the battlefield. As the dust settled and the gruesome scene became more clear, Wulfric rose to his feet, a grin on his face and clapping his hands. "We have a victor!"

A few guards cheered, presumably the ones that won their bets. They were the only ones in good spirits. The slave who won the fight looked broken. He was staring down at the mutilated remains of his fellow brethren. He had killed him. This realization hit him hard. He was shaking and looked on the verge of sobbing.

It must be his first kill, Wulfric mused. He motioned for the guards to clean up the mess and prepare the next fight. He didn't want to witness a breakdown from the victor; he wanted this to be entertaining and exciting, at least for himself.

"Congratulations on surviving the first round," Wulfric said to the slave in the arena. "Let's see if your luck holds until the next round."

The slave didn't respond. He kept his gaze fixed on his fallen enemy. The guards came and picked up the carcass of the dead slave and removed it from the arena, while others escorted the dazed victor out of the gates.

Wulfric clapped his hands together with a smile. "Now then, let the next round of warriors enter!"

***

Trenson could hear muffled sounds from the arena, but couldn't discern them. He was in the holding area, an enclosed room with two doors: one leading to the hallways where their quarters were, and one leading to the arena. Darkness lurked around the corners of the room, kept at bay only by the torches on the wall. There were no windows.

Trenson, sitting on the dirt floor with his back against the wall, surveyed the faces of his fellow slaves. Like pale ovals, their faces stood out in the torchlight, but the leather armor they wore blended into the shadows, causing the illusion that their faces were floating in midair.

Trenson shivered. Although the thin padding he wore provided some protection, the outfit couldn't shield him from the piercing cold. On top of that, the leather was scratchy, making his wait even more unbearable.

He turned to talk to Aquila, then realized he wasn't there. Aquila was on the opposite side of the arena, and so was in a different holding area. He wondered if Aquila was suffering from the cold like he was.

Since Trenson first learned about the gladiator tournament, the possibility that he might have to fight his only friend here haunted him. He had done his best to push it out of his mind, but it lingered. He knew that worrying about it would accomplish nothing; he should focus his mind on things that he could control, such as prioritizing disarming his opponent but not killing him. Things that he could actually do. That didn't stop him from worrying nonetheless.

But even if he wasn't pared against Aquila, surely Aquila would face a different opponent, one who would try to kill him. So no matter what, unless Aquila was some master at combat – which he wasn't, Trenson could tell by how he fought in the training yard – Aquila wouldn't see Trenson again.

The door leading to the arena squeaked open, and a guard emerged. He said something in a foreign tongue that Trenson didn't understand, but whatever he said, it meant that it was time to bring out another slave. And when the guard grabbed Trenson by the arm, pulled him to his feet, and started walking him to the door, it was clear who was to fight next.

Trenson didn't resist, knowing that it would be futile. He let himself be walked through the door, stopping briefly as his captor released his grip and locked the door behind him. He was in another dark hallway, where the only light came from torches, but far away at the end, he could see a little circle of natural light. *The light at the end of the tunnel,* he thought to himself. Funny how his light at the end of the tunnel was an arena and fight to the death.

The guard wasn't finished with Trenson. He walked to the side of the wall, where various weapons leaned against the stone, from staffs to swords to hatchets. The guard pointed to the row of swords and looked questioningly at Trenson. Trenson nodded. The guard promptly grabbed a sword at random and handed it hilt first to him. Trenson grabbed it, then immediately froze.

It wasn't possible.

He looked down at the sword in his hand. There it was. Were this any other sword, he would have said, *no, it's impossible. This must be a different one that looks the same.* But he knew by the overwhelming feeling of power and peace that came over him, that this wasn't just any sword.

This was his sword.

The guard grew impatient. Thinking that Trenson's gawking was from never holding a weapon before, he said some curt words in his native tongue before shoving Trenson towards the light at the end of the hallway. He couldn't follow Trenson out; he was given orders to stand guard at the door. Slaves would make their way by themself to the arena.

Trenson was snapped out his daze by the push, but only momentarily. He started walking to the end of the tunnel, his eyes still fixed on his sword. How did it get here? Did Wulfric's proxy buy his sword, and Trenson happened to choose the one that belonged to him? That had to be it: the slave driver must have sold him the proxy the sword along with the slaves.

Running his fingers over the simple and modest design of the weapon, he knew the only way he was holding this was because of Va'ar. He closed his eyes. *Thank you... Thank you!*

He opened his eyes and looked forward. He could feel the power of his king coursing through him, sublime peace and power flowing from his sword into him. He walked forward, getting closer to the end of the hall. Now he was confident. Now he could face anything, and no matter what came his way, he would overcome.

XIV

IT DIDN'T OCCUR TO Jayfor that the water at the bottom of the well would be freezing, but when he slammed through the face of the almost iced-over water, it hit him – literally. He almost gasped in surprise, but stopped himself from inhaling water. It felt like raw ice was burning into his skin from all angles. He opened his eyes, but couldn't see anything.

He struggled for a few seconds before feeling the stone bottom of the well hit his feet. He stood up, his head bursting through the top of the water. He gasped, freezing cold air replacing the freezing cold water. The water only came up to his shoulders. Wiping the water away from his eyes, he looked around.

"Invigorating, isn't it?"

Jayfor turned around and saw Ernest, who was also dripping wet, but wasn't shivering. He was standing on a ledge right above the water, a torch-lit passage behind him. He was smiling, evidently enjoying Jayfor's discomfort.

His body numb but still moving, Jayfor shuffled forward in the water towards the ledge. Ernest leaned down and offered him a hand. Jayfor took it, and with a grunt, Ernest pulled him out of the water.

Jayfor's knees hit the stone floor. The freezing air hit him like a second shock. He tried to regulate his out-of-control breathing. He felt more awake than he had ever been in his life.

"The first time is always the worst," Ernest said. Jayfor didn't know if he was trying to be comforting, or just stating a fact. "After you do it a couple of times, it gets easier. In fact, I know some people who do it almost daily." Ernest held out his hand once again. "The faster we're through here, the faster you can get warm."

Warm! Jayfor grabbed Ernest's forearm and rose to his feet. The thought of warmth alone was enough to energize him. His voice shaky, he said through chattering teeth, "Before that, I was starting to like you."

Ernest chuckled. "Welcome to the underground, my friend."

Jayfor, trying to find something to focus his mind on, looked around. The ledge they were on extended for a few yards, before narrowing to a small hallway that burrowed deep into the stone walls. The ceiling of the passage was very high, almost halfway up the well, but only a few feet wide, making it a tight fit. *Good thing I'm skinny,* Jayfor thought to himself. *Well, skinny enough.*

"Well," Ernest said, "let's get going." And with that, he started walking toward the corridor, Jayfor close behind him.

"Who built these tunnels?" Jayfor asked as they squeezed and weaved through the snaking passage, guided by torches placed high on the wall.

"Nobody really knows," Ernest replied. "There are different theories, but I personally think that there used to be other groups that needed ways into the city, and so they made a network of tunnels to go into hiding and travel faster."

"Network?" Jayfor asked, wincing as he scraped his shoulder against a sharp edge of the wall. "Are you saying that there are more of these tunnels?"

"Oh yes, dozens. I don't even think I've been through all of them. They are all over the city, some even outside – like this one."

Ernest stopped suddenly and put his hand against the wall. "You can feel it, the walls vibrating."

Jayfor curiously put his hand on the cold stone wall and realized he was right: he felt tremors, almost unperceivable, running through the stone. "Does that mean we're under the city?"

"That is exactly what it means." Ernest let his hand fall from the wall and resumed walking at a quicker pace. Jayfor followed behind him, amazed at the amount of work this would have taken. How did Ernest know about these? What group was he a part of, that required him to travel under the city in secret? He had so many questions.

A few times, they would come to intersections, where the passage branched out to two or three different ways. There were never any signs that indicated which one was which, but Ernest always chose one with confidence. *He must use these tunnels a lot, to know them so well.*

Jayfor lost track of time, but he guessed they had walked for about thirty minutes, when Jayfor peered over Ernest's shoulder and saw something strange: a curtain, hanging from the high ceiling and reaching down to the floor. Before he could ask, Ernest answered his question. "That's to act as a sort of wall between the cellar and the tunnel, and to keep the cave bugs out."

Jayfor almost asked what he meant by cellar, but he realized that it was pointless since he was about to find out. Without slowing his stride, Ernest pushed aside the curtain, and Jayfor did the same behind him.

Now he understood: it was a cellar. The walls were appropriately far apart now, and the roof was average height as well. Boxes and crates and bags and everything you would see in an everyday cellar were in here. There were even more curtains on the other walls, so that the one disguising the entrance to the cave didn't look suspicious. Everything looked normal.

A ladder stood against the wall, leading up and to a trapdoor on the roof. Ernest approached it and put one hand and one foot on a rung, before turning to Jayfor. "This is it." He said the words without expression. Jayfor waited for more, but instead, Ernest climbed up the ladder and opened the trapdoor above, then disappearing through the hole in the roof. The trapdoor was left open.

Jayfor took a deep breath, unsure about what he was about to see. It was all very suspicious, this whole elaborate setup. What if this was a trap? Maybe Elara was onto them and found out where he was. He shrugged. He was too deep in it now to think of backing out.

As he started climbing the ladder, he had another chill sent down his spine, but this time, it wasn't from the cold. He didn't know why, but he suddenly had an innate feeling that wherever he was, Trenson was in danger.

XV

WULFRIC RECLINED COMFORTABLY IN his chair as the next pair of slaves entered the arena. The gates on either side opened once again with mechanical clangs, and other than the red stain on the sand from the last fight, the stage was set. He hoped that this battle would last a little longer; maybe something interesting would happen this time. He doubted it, as these were simple slaves, but a man could hope.

The gates reached their pinnacle of height and stopped. Once again, two slaves exited the arena, looking almost identical in their leather armor, the only difference being that one man had a sword, and the other a staff. Both men faced each other as the morning sun cast their tall shadows on the ground. The guards watching and who had placed bets were restless. The gates behind the slaves started to close.

Who would make the first move? There was no forcing move; the slaves decided when to start the fight. One could argue that might lead to a stalemate, with neither man wanting to fight. But it never did. Since only one man could leave the arena alive, it was either fight, or die at the other man's hand.

The gates continued to slide down, closer to the ground. Still, no one moved. The air was electrifying. Neither man moved so much as an inch.

The sound of the gate lowering ended with the last clank of the gears and the bar frame hitting the sand. Almost as if that was his cue, the slave with the staff suddenly broke into a sprint. The guards who had bets on him cheered him on as he shortened the distance between him and the swordsman.

So it begins, Wulfric thought with a smile. Here is a brash, inexperienced staff wielder. And here... Wait.

Wulfric was so surprised that he rose from his chair and stepped to the edge of the balcony. His eyes were locked on the slave with the sword. In a few moments, Wulfric went from thinking these were two weaklings flailing at each other, to wondering how the swordsman was even here in the first place.

It was the stance of the swordsman that enthralled Wulfric. He was standing sideways to his opponent, but he held his sword beside his face, with his hands gripping the handle slightly behind his head, the tip of the blade aiming at the other slave. Not only was this technique, known as *Semptarius*, a style only utilized by masters of the blade, but the stance was executed flawlessly by the slave.

The swordsman kept a stoic face as the other slave came closer and closer, completely unaware of how skilled his opponent was. Wulfric gripped the edge of the balcony in excitement. In a flash, the two men collided in the arena...

And the battle was over.

It happened so fast, Wulfric had to rewatch it slowly in his mind to realize what had happened. As the slave met with the swordman, he brought his staff above his head, intending to bring it crashing down on the swordsman's head. But the swordsman had other plans. As the staff came down, the master of the *Semptarius* form stepped to the side while simultaneously swinging his sword up in the air where he used to be. The staff came down, and the sword came up to meet it. The staff shattered in the center as the blade exploded through it.

But the swordman wasn't done. Using his opponent's exposed position to his advantage, he stuck his leg out in the path of the slave. The shattered staff wielder couldn't stop himself. He fell facedown on the sand. He only had time to realize what had happened before feeling the point of a blade touching his exposed neck.

Silence. The guards stared. Even Wulfric, who considered himself a master in all forms of combat, was taken aback. This slave had just executed a move that was used by masters. Who was this man?

Everyone waited for the swordsman to finish his opponent off. The swordsman had already won the battle; only a gory conclusion remained. Would he behead him? Or thrust into his chest? So many ways, and with the display of skill so far, the victor was sure to make it interesting. The seconds felt like minutes as the swordsman stood, poised with his blade ready.

The swordsman made an interesting finish all right, but not the way Wulfric expected. Without a warning, the victor stepped back a few paces from the fallen man. Then he turned to face the balcony on which Wulfric sat. "This man surrenders. The fight is over."

Wulfric, realizing that this man was from Faldon by the language he spoke, was shocked, and for numerous reasons. One, this man is a master of the sword. Two, he chose to not kill, but instead risk reasoning with his captor. Third, he was declaring what was to happen, even though he was a slave.

Wulfric's jawline tightened. Should he punish this insolence? Usually that wasn't a question, but then again, this man had skills, skills that could be an asset... Should he throw them away? But then again, the Faldian was showing that he had little respect for authority, so would he be more of a threat than an advantage?

It's just a game, the captain's mind reasoned. *This man may be defeated by the end of the tournament, anyway. And even if he does survive, he wouldn't become a threat so great we couldn't handle. We know where he sleeps.*

The fallen slave on the ground had his eyes shut tight, but once he realized he might survive, he opened them and slowly stood to his feet, still holding the stubby end of his staff. He didn't take his eyes off the Faldian.

The guards waited patiently for their master's order.

Wulfric finalized a decision, then rose to his feet. "Very well. The fight is over. Congratulations to the winner. Get both of them out of here." He said these words with little enthusiasm, as he was still deep in thought.

As the swordsman and slave were being escorted out of the arena, an overseer came to Wulfric. "Sir, what about the loser? What should we do with him?"

"Sell him. If we cannot get entertainment out of him, we might as well get coin."

"Yes, sir."

The overseer left, leaving Wulfric alone with his thoughts. He didn't pay much attention to the next combatants entering the arena. *Who was that man?*

XVI

"WHAT IS THIS PLACE?"

That was the first question Jayfor asked when he scrambled out of the trapdoor and into a new room. Well, to be accurate, he paused for a moment, staring at everyone in the room as they stared back, while Ernest closed the trapdoor in the floor. Then he asked the question.

"This is our hideout," Ernest replied.

It was an obvious answer. The lack of windows and other sources of outside light necessitated placing many oil lamps throughout the room. These pools of light let Jayfor see the bookshelves across the wall, the weapon racks and armor stands set in the corner, and the large table in the center of the room with a dozen chairs around it. In half of these chairs sat people, all staring back at him. Jayfor recognized Ernest's wife as a familiar face in the group. He raised an eyebrow at her in question, but she just smiled at him, then Ernest.

Ernest smiled back, then turned to Jayfor. "Do you know who we are?"

Jayfor thought about it for a second. "Believers," he said.

"True, but that's not all. You could say we're a special task force of believers, trained to protect the faithful and spread the news to the world. We work in the shadows, to serve the light. Although few in number, our strength comes not from ourselves, but from the True Ruler of Ralladin. We are the Willing."

Jayfor still wasn't satisfied. "The Willing?"

Ernest nodded. "We get our name from our calling. In this time of darkness, it seems that only a few will answer a higher calling and accept the light. Not only that, but for this cause, we are willing to sacrifice everything we have in this world to serve Him. Material things will fade away, but we don't put our worth in them."

Jayfor tried to understand. He was still soaked in icy water, and so his mind worked at a considerably slower pace. "So... You are a group of believers who work in secret to fight the Dark Order?" Jayfor said, trying to summarize what Ernest said.

"That's exactly what we are," another man sitting the table said. Jayfor was surprised to see that he recognized the man as Novak. He was the one that somehow created the smoke explosion during the bandit fight. Novak grinned at him. "You'll have to pardon our captain. He has a habit of dramatizing things."

"Novak." Ernest shot him a stern glare.

Novak shrugged. "What? I was just translating what you said for our friend here!"

The conversation likely would have continued, but Tindra – at least, that's what he thought the name of Ernest's wife was – interrupted. "Do you think we should be a little more thoughtful and save this conversation until *after* he's in dry clothes?"

Jayfor wanted to voice his agreement, but his teeth were chattering at the speed of a woodpecker, so instead he nodded enthusiastically.

"Now that I agree with," Ernest replied.

***

Jayfor was given a simple outfit to wear until his clothes were properly dried. As he changed in private, he counted the days since he had worn a different pair of clothes. *Months,* he finally decided. He hadn't even worn a different tunic since they started the journey. It felt nice to get into something fresh.

He frowned when he went through his satchel at all the items that weren't supposed to be wet, but currently were. A map, rations, salt... everything was soaked. He sighed, but wasn't too worried. He had a feeling that his journey would take a turn now. Not that Jayfor was expecting help from these people, but... *OK,* he admitted to himself, *I guess I am expecting some help.*

After emerging from the room in a clean, dry outfit, Jayfor spotted everyone at the meeting table. With attentive faces, they discussed something that was presumably important. When Jayfor approached their table, the conversation died as everyone hushed to look at him.

Jayfor didn't know what to say next. *Thanks for showing me your secret group, but I've got to go,* seemed a little out of place. So he just stood there awkwardly, not meeting the eyes that stared at him, until Ernest came to his rescue.

"What's your name?"

Jayfor opened his mouth, then shut it. Did they need to know? He would be lying to another believer. But would the information that he used to be the king of Faldon change the way they looked at him? There was no doubt it would. And besides, the Jayfor of old was no more. He died when his kingdom was destroyed. Now he had a new identity.

"Conrad," Jayfor replied.

Ernest nodded. "Tell us about yourself, Conrad."

Jayfor quickly thought up a story. "I was born in Faldon, or what was once Faldon. My father was not only a magistrate, but a skilled swordsman, and he taught me everything I know. I was to follow in his footsteps as a politician, and he thought it would be good for me to travel and see the world before I continued my education. So I took one of my closest friends with me, and we set out on the journey. After traveling for a few months, we decided to return home. But slavers had other plans."

Jayfor took a deep breath. He knew it was a cover-up story, but he still felt inner turmoil when thinking about Trenson's enslavement. "As we were separated one day, slavers caught and imprisoned my friend. I vowed not to return home until I freed him. Since then, I have followed the caravan, looking for ways to free him. The last place I saw him was in chains, being led into this city. That's why I need to get in."

When Jayfor finished, everyone took a moment to consider what he said. Jayfor's palms started to sweat. He had just lied to his only allies left. What if they found out? But did it really matter? That was the question. It didn't matter if they knew he was the king of Faldon or not, because Faldon was gone. And since everything about his past was gone now too, it didn't make a difference whether he was Conrad, or Jayfor.

"You're an awful long way from Faldon to be on an excursion," Novak commented.

There was no ill will behind the remark, but it left Jayfor scrambling to find a reply. "Our fiefdom is near the border, so it's not too far."

"Fiefdom?" Tindra asked. "Your father is a baron?"

Jayfor simply nodded, afraid that he might give away too much information, either through his words or tone.

Ernest, satisfied with Jayfor's story, changed the subject. "I suppose you were expecting this, but I feel the need to explain it nonetheless."

"As always," Novak said with a smirk. This brought a few chuckles from the others around the table.

Ernest masterfully ignored him. "We are all believers here. Although you may not be initiated into our company, we share common knowledge of the truth, and the goal to share it and protect it. I saw you fight. You fight with a blade made with the same unworldly steel as ours."

Seeing Jayfor's eyebrows rise, Ernest smiled. "You didn't think you were the only one in Ralladin with a special sword? Every true believer receives their own at one point or another. When you fight for another world, you notice things people of this one don't."

Jayfor wasn't currently wearing his sword – he left it by his clothes to dry – but he looked up at the weapon racks on the wall, and noticed there *was* something about them that was familiar.

Swords, axes, even bows hung on pegs, and while there wasn't anything visually striking about them, Jayfor could vaguely tell that they weren't ordinary weapons.

"The fact that you wear such a blade," continued Ernest, "is further proof we are mutual allies. I know you're only here to rescue your friend. But you don't have to do it alone."

He jerked a thumb behind him toward an oak door, latched and bolted. "You can walk out that door at this moment and forget this ever happened. You'll continue searching for him and maybe even find him by yourself. Or you can stay, and join us, and agree that we will help each other. For us, that means lending us your skills. For you, that means having a team to help you locate and find your friend."

Ernest leaned back in his chair, finished with his monologue, and giving Jayfor time to think. And think he did. The other members of the Willing stared at Jayfor, waiting to hear his answer. Inwardly, they all already knew what he would decide.

Their hunch proved right. "I'm in."

XVII

"WE HAVE A WINNER!"

Wulfric found himself saying these words over and over again to the same person: the mysterious swordsman whom no one knew anything about.

The guards had stopped placing bets on his fights, because no one would bet against him. It was a guaranteed loss for anyone pitted against the swordsman, but they need not fear their life, since he would disarm them or force them to resign, but never draw blood.

Every other fight Wulfric witnessed in the arena was child's play. The two combatants would simply rush at each other, swinging their weapons wildly, until someone managed to land a fatal blow. Sure, a few slaves were more skilled than others, but no one was actually trained. Except one man.

After two more rounds of seeing his skill on display, Wulfric decided to question his manager about the man.

"Where did he come from?" He asked.

The manager scanned through the list of names on his paper. The manager kept meticulous care that his records were in order, although his desk was rather a mess. "He was purchased by one of our proxy's in Talikan, in a standard auction."

"Standard, you say? There is nothing standard about the way that man fights. The way his sword moves through the air, his timing and footwork, it's flawless!" Wulfric found himself praising a random slave in front of his manager, something that did not happen often.

The secretary shrugged. "Perhaps he's of noble blood, the son of a knight?"

Wulfric frowned deeper, the scowl lines on his face deepening. "But why would he be sold at an auction, of all places?"

The manager didn't have an answer for this. "It may be wise to ask him in person."

"Me?! Ridiculous! I've never once conversed with a slave as an equal, and I will certainly not treat him as though he is special!" Wulfric retorted.

"Then ask a guard to question him?" The secretary suggested.

"No, no, it would be best that he is not interfered with. He must not come up with the notion that he is better than anyone else, or he will start feeling rebellious. Is there really no more information? No habits or anything noticeable about him?"

The secretary thought about this for a moment. "The only piece of information that I know about him, is that he always requests to use the same sword in every fight."

Wulfric, who was expecting the answer to his question to be negative, showed renewed interest. "The same sword?"

"Yes, my lord."

"What type of sword? Is there anything unique about it?"

"I wondered the same thing, my lord, and so I had it inspected by numerous captains and blacksmiths for any foul play. But there was nothing extraordinary about it. In fact, most of the swords used by the other slaves in the arena are actually superior to it, according to the chief of weaponry. The only thing that is worth noticing is that the blacksmith couldn't identify what metal was used to craft it, but he admitted that it was likely an alloy."

Wulfric didn't reply. Instead, he stood rigid, thinking, his eyes resting on the manager's messy desk. He wondered why the man would keep asking for the same sword. Superstition, most likely.

The secretary was uncomfortable with Wulfric standing above him, and so he broke the silence. "I can easily deny his request to use the same sword, if you wish."

"No, no, let him do what he pleases. He's superstitious, and that's a flaw in itself, but I don't see the harm in letting him continue. Let him keep his good luck charm, and we'll see if it holds out."

The manager nodded. "Yes, my lord."

***

The "good luck charm" did hold out, because the swordsman effortlessly made it through another round. In truth, it was the swordsman's knowledge of *Semptarius* that ensured his survival. Patiently, he would wait for his opponent to make the first move, and once he did, the counterattack was quick, finishing, but always non-lethal.

This puzzled Wulfric. The swordsman would never kill or even injure his opponent, instead disarming him or making him yield. Did he have an intolerance to blood? Or maybe he was soft? Both of these were unheard of from masters of the blade. Regardless, Wulfric always allowed the swordsman to spare his opponent, while he sold the slave that lost.

After a few days, the final match of the tournament came. Wulfric knew both combatants: the swordsman – obviously – and a very large man whom the guards had nicknamed "The Mountain." Everyone had their bets placed on the swordsman, and so did Wulfric. The Mountain was clumsy, but his staff swings were deadly, and he had more smarts than most slaves.

But the swordsman would win without a doubt. Wulfric was already debating on what position to bestow on him when he won the tournament. Lieutenant, or secondary general? He would decide later. Right now, he wanted to enjoy the final fight of the tournament.

The guards were more rowdy than usual, as instead of merely guards being stationed atop the arena walls, soldiers and even captains came to see the event. Of course, it was a good excuse to not train, and Wulfric knew this, but he still allowed it. The winner of the fight would join their ranks, and so it was best they saw their future comrade in action.

Wulfric sat once more on his balcony, once more looking over the battlefield. The sand, although looking clean and smooth, had been fixed at the end of each day of the tournament. He would sit here for the last time, until the next gladiator fight was arranged.

He smiled. The battle would only last a few moments, as usual, before the swordsman emerged victorious. The rank of secondary general would be given to him – he would reduce the current one to a brigadier – and the games would be over. He was unusually excited, so much that he almost forgot about the frigid cold wind that blew through the air and made his breath visible. Almost.

Wulfric's thoughts were interrupted by the high, piercing note of the trumpets. The guards all quieted, all eyes turned to one of the two gates. Slowly, with the clanging of gears, the bars started to raise. Wulfric himself didn't know which slave would exit which gate, and so he switched his focus from one to the other.

Once the gates reached their pinnacle and the trumpets ceased their note, everyone waited in suspense for two seconds. Then the swordsman emerged from the gate on Wulfric's left.

Cheers immediately rose in honor of the man who made fighting look as simple as breathing. His reputation had spread among the ranks of the soldiers. Everyone had heard about him. And everyone wanted to see how much of the rumors were true.

But after he stopped a few paces into the arena, everyone focused their attention on the slave that exited the other gate: The Mountain.

He certainly lives up to his name, Wulfric mused as the slave walked into the arena, brandishing a staff that looked like a mere twig in his massive hands. Cheers followed his entrance; some guards had money on him. Although not many people had placed money on The Mountain, a few soldiers decided to make a gamble, knowing their wins would be exponentially higher if they were correct.

The Mountain stopped a few paces into the arena as well. The gates started to close behind them. The crowd cheered. A cold wind swirled through the arena. The final fight had begun.

Neither man moved. Wulfric couldn't see their expressions from the angle they stood at, and also because of their leather helmets. A few seconds passed. The crowd continued cheering, encouraging either man.

Wulfric was confused. *Why isn't the swordsman assuming the* Semptarius *stance? Is he planning on something different? But he isn't moving, he's just standing there. And so is the other man!*

But at that moment, the swordsman did move. With purpose, he walked into the center of the arena, turned to face Wulfric in his balcony, held his sword high in the air, thrust it down into the ground, deep into the sand, then stepped back a few paces, letting his signature sword stand alone.

The cheering stopped. Wulfric raised an eyebrow, as did everyone else watching. Silence pervaded the battleground. Even the swordsman's opponent seemed confused.

Speaking in the Faldon tongue, the swordsman said five simple words, loud enough for everyone to hear. "I will not fight him."

Most of the crowd had no idea what he was saying, their only language being the local variation of Kallary's common speech. They looked at each other in confusion, whispering the same question to each other. However, Wulfric understood, and didn't, at the same time.

Wulfric rose from his seat and walked to the edge of the terrace, staring back at the defiant eyes of the swordsman. He could see the features on his face now that the slave wasn't facing another direction, and Wulfric frowned. The slave's expression gave an unspoken message: *You heard what I said, and no matter what you say, that's the way it's going to be.*

Wulfric was now angered and confused; a combination that made him dangerous. "What do you think you are doing?" Wulfric demanded the swordsman, speaking Faldian.

"I don't *think*, I *know* what I'm doing. This man is my friend, the only person that has cared about me in this wretched imitation of a mansion. I will not kill him for the sake of your amusement."

Wulfric and everyone else who spoke Faldian – which amounted to no more than a dozen – gasped. They couldn't believe what they had just heard. No one had spoke that way to the captain of the regal guard of Augustria!

After having a few seconds to realize what was just said, Wulfric scowled so hard that the creases in his face became more like valleys than wrinkles. Any respect he had for the swordsman prior to the match was gone; he was seething with rage. "You will do as you are told, you loudmouth fool!"

The swordsman simply crossed his arms and looked Wulfric in the eye, unamused.

Wulfric turned away from the balcony. He chuckled a few times, a sadistic chuckle. He faced one of his managers. "Kill them both."

The manager was confused. "My lord?"

"Kill them both!" Wulfric screamed.

Stumbling backward a few steps, the manager didn't ask any more questions, and started to head to the door, when one of Wulfric's advisors, who had decided to watch the arena fight, motioned for him to wait. The manager stopped mid-step, and could hear the conversation between the advisor and Wulfric.

"My lord, I understand that this is treason."

"Treason?! It is worse than that! I respected him for his abilities, even considering making him second general! And *this* is how he repays me?"

"I understand, my lord, but please, let's take a moment and look at this from a different point of view."

Wulfric glared at his advisor, but said nothing.

The advisor took this as a sign to continue. "My lord," he resumed – he used that phrase a lot when he was trying to convince his master of something, "this man possesses astonishing skill. In fact, call me a fool if he could be smarted in a sparing match by any of our elite soldiers. He is one of those rare people who has massive talent in something, and has not only discovered this, but reinforced it with hard work and training."

Wulfric kept staring at his advisor like he was babbling on about something worthless – which is exactly what he was doing, in Wulfric's opinion. "And?"

"And, while he has skill, he is still young. Youths are brash, not yet knowing wisdom. There is no way to instill talent in someone... but you can instill fear and loyalty."

When the advisor paused, Wulfric considered the words, so much so that he dropped his death stare and looked back toward the arena. He walked toward the edge of the balcony once more.

There stood the swordsman, still staring in his direction, and there stood his opponent, still looking confused and unsure of himself. And there was the crowd, looking at the swordsman and

The Mountain and Wulfric, whispering to each other, wondering what would happen next.

Wulfric's anger had diminished significantly in the last few seconds, and so he was able to look at the slave in a more rational mindset. He scratched his chin thoughtfully. Could he break this man, and turn his skills into an asset?

After a few more moments of thinking, Wulfric turned back to the manager, and gave him his order. The manager nodded his confirmation and left the balcony to execute it.

XVIII

"Conrad, I can't let you use carry one of these yet! I've told you before, these can be dangerous if misused."

Ernest chimed in. "What do you know about 'misusing' a smoke bomb?"

Novak glared daggers at the captain. "You still haven't thanked me for saving our hides that day, you know."

Ernest smiled. "I think we would have been fine, although it was courteous of you to provide us with eye irritation."

All three men were sitting peacefully around the table of the hideout, talking to pass the time before they turned in for the night. A fire crackled in the corner, kept alive even after it was used to cook supper for the group. The other members of The Willing were occupied cleaning weapons or doing some type of chore in other parts of the room. Some men had already fallen asleep on their cots. Jayfor almost followed suit, but when Novak offered to explain to him what had caused the enormous cloud of smoke at the raid, all thought of sleep left Jayfor's mind.

Novak skillfully ignored Ernest's comeback. He ran his thumb across the terracotta shell of the bomb in his hand. "Anyway, this is something we only use at certain times, and only in the most dire situations. The recipe is top-secret; it's given us a huge advantage over our enemies."

Jayfor nodded. "So in essence, it's a volatile solution that, when broken, creates a huge cloud of smoke?"

Novak chuckled. "I have no idea what 'volatile' means, but that is correct. It's just like you saw during the raid. I've been experimenting with different ingredients and combinations, testing out different colors and amounts of smoke. What you saw there was a medium-class bomb, but I've made bigger – much bigger." Novak tossed the bomb into the air and caught it without looking. Ernest watched the bomb as it came up and down, his lack of confidence in Novak's abilities evident.

"I've never seen anything like it," Jayfor said. "How long have you been using this?"

It was Ernest who answered. "A few months, at most. We recruited a few chemists who were obviously very good at their craft, and it was their ingenuity that led to what you see in Novak's hand. As far as I know, the world doesn't know what these are. Our secret stays a secret, because we only use them in life-or-death situations."

"Truth be told," Novak commented, "it's still a wonder how our enemies haven't picked up on it."

Jayfor didn't respond, instead thinking about the bomb. It was incredible! Not even the smartest people in Loronis had developed something like this. A shell the size of a palm that could create a massive smoke cloud for cover and escape? He needed to learn the recipe. Imagine how much Faldon could benefit from this!

Then it hit him: Faldon was gone. Once again, he had fantazed and forgotten that his homeland was no more. The rush he felt from discovering the explosive diminished as the memory of Loronis burning like a giant bonfire surfaced in his mind. He forgot what he was going to say in reply to Novak, so instead he sat in silence, staring at the floor, his grin replaced by a forced, calm countenance.

Whether he knew it or not, Novak diminished the depression in Jayfor's mind with his cheerful voice. "So Conrad, this may seem like a strange question, but how many languages do you know?"

Jayfor snapped out of his trance and stared at Novak dumbly before he realized that he had been asked a question. "Oh... um, just traditional Faldian."

"Well, obviously, that's the language we all speak as well. But what about others?"

"I don't know any others."

"What?!" Novak was shocked, so shocked that Jayfor was trying to figure out what he said that was so bewildering.

Ernest came to Jayfor's rescue. "He's from Faldon, Novak. They don't have many languages there."

"Evidently not!" Novak said. "Unlike you," he directed the statement to Jayfor, "I have spent most of my life here, and in order to even live in the city, it's almost a requirement to know at least three languages. The culture is so diverse, with so many dialects and tongues." he shook his head. "Have you not had any trouble with that?"

"No, not really. I haven't been here long."

"Well, if you intend to stay here any amount of time, it is paramount you know at least the basics. Someday soon, I'll teach you some basic things, so you don't get lost in a sea of foreign speeches."

Jayfor nodded his thanks. Truth be told, now that he thought about it, he was surprised his vocabulary was so limited. It's not like Faldon had only one language; with its size, there were a least a half-dozen variations of speech within the borders. But he had never been in a situation requiring knowledge of another language. That's what translators were for. But he didn't have his translators anymore. Although he planned to only stay in the city long enough to free Trenson, it wouldn't hurt to pick up some new knowledge. It might be helpful later on.

A few moments later, Tindra approached the table, holding a folded piece of yellow parchment. "This came today," she said to Ernest. "I think you need to see it."

Ernest frowned. Jayfor guessed that whenever something like this came, it wasn't good. Ernest took the paper and unfolded it, his eyes tracking from right to left as he took in the message. Novak glanced at Jayfor, thinking the same thing he was. Tindra returned to her spot by the fire, where she was sharpening her blade.

Without a change of expression, Ernest calmly folded the note back into its original size and set it on the table. He then slouched deeper into his chair, crossed his arms, and closed his eyes, like he was about to fall asleep in the chair. He certainly looked comfortable enough to do so.

Jayfor was confused. "Well? What did it say?"

Ernest didn't open his eyes. "Nothing that can't wait until to-morrow. I'll address the group about it in the morning."

Jayfor sighed. *Guess I'll have to wait.*

Novak, however, had different plans. Nimbly, he stood up from his chair, leaned so far over the table that his feet went up into the air, snatched the note from the opposite side of the table, and then rocked backwards to land on his feet before pulling his chair back into place and resuming his previous sitting position. He accomplished this all in a matter of seconds.

Ernest didn't react at all, and said with a tone of mild indifference, "I knew you would do that."

Novak didn't respond. He had already unfolded the note and was swiftly reading the contents. Jayfor sat erect, ready to hear the news.

Novak's expression gave away the message before he spoke. "The parchment says..." he paused, looking up from it, "...that a few of our members have been taken hostage by the Scorned?" He spoke as if it were a question, as if he hadn't just read it from the paper in his hand.

"Congratulations, you can read." Ernest replied mundanely.

Novak wasn't finished, however. "The Scorned?"

Ernest nodded, his eyes still closed and his arms still crossed.

Jayfor tilted his head. "The Scorned?"

"That's our primary enemy," Novak explained. "We are The Willing, they are The Scorned. It's a nice play on words, is it not? We have many enemies, of course, most of them petty thief guilds. But The Scorned work for Elara, and they want nothing more than to spread its border to every corner of the world. They're a lot like us in terms of how they operate: working in the shadows, and so most people don't know they exist, but they are very real, and their influence is more powerful than any political or philosophical ideology. We fought them during the raid on the treasury. They must be getting low on funds," he commented.

"Their strength lies in their numbers," Ernest added, opening his eyes and looking at Jayfor. "We may win most of the battles we fight, but they have more members, more influence, and more strongholds. As a result, they don't even have to fight battles to win. Unlike most cities in Kallary, Augustria is quite large, so it's naturally a very important city to hold. The fight has been going on for some time, but we're currently balanced."

Novak shook his head bitterly. "Not balanced anymore. This report lists five initiates captured by The Scorned. And I know one of them." His voice dropped even further in gloom. "He knows the recipe for the smoke bombs."

Ernest's indifferent attitude suddenly changed. He shot a concerned look at Novak. "Are you certain?"

"Positive. I doubt they know that, but if they question them, and if they find a bomb in his pack..." Novak's voice trailed off.

Even Jayfor, who had only known about the bombs for a few minutes, understood how dangerous the situation was. "If he was carrying a bomb," Jayfor continued, "then they could analyze it and figure out how it was made."

"And if they do," Ernest followed suit, "then they could steal our advantage." He sighed, a mix of frustration and exhaustion.

There was a period of silence. The fire snapping and popping in the background was the only sound, providing a nice accompaniment to the grinding noise of Tindra running a stone down the length of her sword, working the edge.

Then Novak rose from his seat and clapped his hands together with a smile. "Well, I'm turning in. We quite possibly have a dire situation on our hands, but not as dire as my need for sleep. Sweet dreams!"

<u>XIX</u>

"**Y**OU'RE NOT LIKE THE others, are you?"

Wulfric took a swig of coffee from the cup on his desk – he must be one of those people who drink coffee all day, Trenson mused – before setting the steaming mug back on the table. Wulfric's expression was the usual: stoic and calm. But Trenson could see a hint of curiosity. The scowl lines hid it well, but it was there nonetheless.

Trenson answered, "It depends."

Wulfric leaned back in his seat, choosing to remain silent. He stared at Trenson, and Trenson stared back. Trenson knew this was all part of a mind game. The captain wanted Trenson to feel intimidated, scared. It was easier to get people to tell the truth when they were nervous. Trenson had used the technique himself on multiple occasions.

He wasn't falling into the trap, however. "What do you want?" he asked. He could have said, *why have you brought me here?* Or *Why are you doing this?* But that would have shown submission. What he said showed that he wasn't the one who needed answers.

Wulfric didn't answer the question, instead motioning with a slight wave of his hand to the surroundings of the room. "Do you like my office? It's rather a mess at the moment, but it serves its purpose well. Honestly, I think it needs repainting. What say you?"

Trenson took a moment to take in the room. Truth be told, there was nothing messy about it. Although it was small, everything had a place. A few wolfskin coats hung on a rack along one wall, a collection of trophies and trinkets were organized on a shelf against the other wall. The desk, behind which Wulfric was sitting, held only an inkwell, a feather pen, and the cup of inky black coffee.

Since Trenson knew it wasn't a genuine question, he didn't answer. Although, in his opinion, the walls were a little dull and could use a fresh coat.

"You're not much for words, are you? Good." Wulfric nodded his approval. "I don't like to waste my time. You don't either, as I saw in the arena. I've seen quick battles before, but to end a duel within a few seconds is a feat not many men can accomplish."

Wulfric stood up from his desk. "Please don't burden me with your life story about how you grew up an only child or were taught the art of the sword from your father. I couldn't care less. The reason I brought you here isn't to hear you gush over your childhood. I only want to ask you a simple question."

He leaned forward and placed his hands on the table, staring hard at Trenson. "Why wouldn't you fight the only man standing between you and the end of it all?"

So that's the reason he brought me here. Trenson had suspected it was the case. This probably wasn't something that usually happened in gladiator fights.

"He's my friend," Trenson said evenly.

Wulfric huffed. "That man couldn't be more different from you. He's built like an ox and has the coordination of one as well. He fights like he's being chased by a swarm of bees. There is nothing about him that benefits you."

Trenson looked into his steely gray eyes. "There's more to life than seeking the advantage."

"Ha! And you are one to lecture me? Look at our beliefs and look at our positions. Not similar, are they? Fine. Believe what you want. I am not out to change what you believe."

Wulfric slowly sat back down in his chair. He cleared his throat and placed his arms along the intricately carved armrests by his side. "You've wasted enough of my time already, and I haven't even gotten an answer from you." His tone had a hint of frustration.

"Answer to what?" Trenson said, confidence continuing to build inside of him. Wulfric's last words showed him that he possessed knowledge that the captain wanted, which allowed him to ask the somewhat snarky question without fear.

Wulfric's face twitched at the sarcasm in his voice, but remained stone cold. "Oh, I suppose that my question has changed. A few moments ago, I wanted to know why you spared your opponent, but after sickening me with your cute friendship, I lost all interest in any further questioning." Wulfric sighed. "By the way, congratulations on winning the tournament. You've spared yourself of a quick end and granted yourself a spot in my guard. You know, I was considering giving you a high position, like second general or something. But I changed my mind. You'll have to prove your competence a little more than that. From now on, you work for me."

Wulfric leaned forward, his voice turning cold and dangerous. "But mark my words, if you ever dare to defy my orders, or speak to me like you are above me, I will not hesitate to cut your throat. Your skills with the blade are the only thing that have carried you thus far. Am I clear?"

Trenson nodded once, not breaking eye contact. He showed no signs of fear or cowardice. Hiding his emotions was a natural skill he had used many times, and it was easy to do so now. He had used his skill to hide pain from his friends; it was easy to hide fear from his captor.

Wulfric intended that to be the last thing that was said between them, but Trenson wasn't finished. "And what about my friend?"

Wulfric raised an eyebrow. "What?"

"My opponent. What will happen to him?"

"Oh, him. I was planning to keep him. Technically speaking, your fight ended in a draw, and so both of you shall become soldiers. He needs a little more work than you do, but with a stature like his, he'll make a fine axe-wielding warrior."

Trenson breathed an inward sigh of relief. He had feared that he wouldn't see Aquila after the fight. The mountain of a man would fetch a good price at an auction, which is where Trenson thought he would go. At least he wouldn't be alone here.

Wulfric resumed his relaxed, calmed demeanor once more as he let a faint hint of a smile touch his lips. "Excellent! Then you are no longer needed here. My secretary should be waiting outside for you; he will show you your new room and give you further instructions. And your name was...?"

"Trenson."

"Trenson! Well, get some rest, Trenson. The easy part of being here is over."

XX

"Is it necessary for us to be on the roof?" Jayfor whispered.

"No, it's not necessary," Ernest replied, also in a hushed voice, "but it decreases our chances of being spotted. They have guards on the roof, and their focus will be the streets. In our attire, we blend in with the rooftops. The streets are also busy, which makes espionage difficult."

"Wouldn't we blend in with the crowd, though?"

"In a sense, but if we're the only ones staring at the building, we're more likely to be noticed than if we're in hiding."

Jayfor saw the reasoning in this. He continued peering over the pinnacle of the roofs triangle, trying to find a balance between seeing as much of the building as possible and concealing himself.

"It looks like an old forge," Jayfor whispered. There was really no need to whisper; there definitely wasn't anyone else on the roof with them, and the buzz of the street crowd was enough to drown out a voice at normal volume. But they did it anyway. Maybe it added to the mood. In Jayfor's case, it certainly did.

"That's because it is. I knew the man who owned it. He was a good fellow, but he and his family disappeared a few weeks ago. I suspect they were evicted for avoiding taxes. Anyway, the blacksmith was closed down. I expected it to be bought by the smithy guild, but apparently The Scorned occupied it before they could."

The building in question was everything Jayfor expected out of a forge: A squat building that had a shorter roof than the other houses that pressed against its side, but was more than double their width. The roof had two chimneys, one on each side—more chimneys meant more fires, enabling faster weapon production. There was a wooden door in the middle of the wall facing the street. Two large windows, one on each side of the door, would have provided people the chance to look inside the building, except both windows were barred with oak planks.

The cheerful and cozy aroma the shop would have earlier possessed was gone.

"Are you certain this is the right place?" Jayfor asked.

"Positive. One of our men tracked the group here and saw them bring the hostages inside." Ernest frowned. "They most likely want to torture them here, since if they brought them back to their hideout and they escaped, their base would be compromised. They are quite crafty," he added.

That much is true, Jayfor inwardly agreed. "So, how do we get in?"

"I..." For the first time, Jayfor heard uncertainty in Ernest's voice. "I am still working on that."

This left Jayfor somewhat shocked. He didn't know the captain was capable of not planning something all the way through. Luckily, he had an idea that he was excited to share. "What if we –"

Ernest cut him off. "—Use a smoke bomb? I'm afraid the situation isn't quite dire enough. I only use them in the most life-threatening moments."

Jayfor's spirits dropped when he heard this. He was hoping to see the device in action again. Now that he knew how it worked, he wanted to see it again, so that he could watch it unfold and understand the process. Earlier today, he was elated when he saw Ernest pack the small, palm-shaped shell. Shortly afterward, those feelings were slightly dampened when he was told he couldn't carry one. Now, seeing as all hope was lost, he gave up. Perhaps he would get lucky and they would be in a life-or-death situation.

OK, he wasn't actually hoping for that, but still.

"Have you rescued hostages in the past?" Jayfor asked.

Ernest nodded. "A few."

"What did you do in those instances?"

"Well, what we do most of the time is send a few men in to pretend to be new members of their group. Usually, they make it inside without any hassle, and once inside, they try to release the prisoners and escape secretly. If that fails, we have another team waiting outside to rush in and attack. If we can get the prisoners outside and in the clear, we throw a bomb and escape."

Ernest sighed irritably. "They're less gullible now, and won't let anyone they don't recognize inside. The last two extractions failed for that reason."

Jayfor pondered the information. He now saw that sneaking in would be impossible. In addition, they didn't have any backup. It was just the two of them. Jayfor almost asked Ernest why he hadn't brought more people, but then he remembered earlier that morning, when Ernest was giving orders to everyone else in the group. The Willing were stretched thin across multiple lines; they would have to do it alone.

An idea suddenly appeared in Jayfor's mind. "What about our swords! You said yourself that you were also given a special blade by the Senver."

Ernest smiled sadly. "I know what you're thinking: why don't we rush in and trust our blades? If this was a petty thief's guild, I would, because our blades have the power to easily defeat powers of this world. But Va'ar isn't the only one who grants his followers special weapons."

Jayfor's jaw dropped slightly as the realization hit him. "Are you saying... Do they have weapons like ours?"

"Not exactly, but in a way, yes. They don't glow the same color; they have a darker tint to them. But believe me when I say they are nothing to joke about. The severity of wounds inflicted by the weapons are deadly." He pulled the sleeve on his right arm back, revealing a scar about three inches long across his forearm. But strangely, the scar was a gray color, not red. "I would know. This small cut almost killed me."

Jayfor wasn't sure how to respond. He was digesting what Ernest had said. He had a habit of instantly diving deep into thought when something interesting was brought up, and this would cause him to forget that he needed to respond. After a few seconds, when Ernest realized that his partner wasn't going to reply, he pushed his sleeve back over his arm.

"Anyway, we still need a plan. We've been sitting on this roof chatting for ten minutes," Ernest said, a hint of annoyance in his voice. It didn't seem to occur to him that the reason it was taking forever, was because his explanations were lengthy.

Jayfor snapped out of his trance and focused on the building once more.

Before he could say anything, Ernest whispered softly to himself, "This shop had two doors, one of which is on the opposite side of the building. The doors aren't barred. It's soft wood. No, it's risky. But it would work... maybe. Well..."

Jayfor looked at him quizzically. "What?"

"Nothing, nevermind. Well, actually..."

"What?" he asked again.

"I'm just thinking."

"Thinking what?"

"About how to break in. And I think it's the most ridiculous idea I've ever come up with."

Jayfor grinned. "Those are my favorites."

Ernest rolled his eyes. "I'm sure." He sat in silence for a few more moments, turning his mysterious idea over in his head, before sighing. "Well, it's my only idea, so unless you have any suggestions, that's what we're doing."

Jayfor shook his head. "You're supposed to be the genius here."

Ernest used his skills at ignoring Novak to ignore Jayfor. "This smithy has two doors; one on our side of the road, and other on the other side of the building, facing another road. The doors are directly across from each other, and the material is old. I'll run through this door, through the building, and out the other door as fast as possible, and –"

"You'll what?!" Jayfor asked, bewildered. "Crash through the doors, run through the building, and then what?"

"I was getting to that part," Ernest said coldly. "After that, I'll continue running down the street, hopefully drawing some of The Scorned inside to follow me. If they do, then there should only be a few left inside, which you can handle much easier. After that –"

"So I have to do all the hard work and rescue them?" Jayfor asked.

"No, because you won't risk breaking your ribs – twice – and having to run from probably six armed men."

Jayfor nodded. "Fair enough. But this plan is still ridiculous."

Ernest shrugged. "I'm the genius here, aren't I?"

***

To be exact, there were actually eight men inside the smithy – not including the five hostages.

"Please. . . Please stop."

"Ah!" one of The Scorned said with satisfaction. "So you can speak!"

"You killed him – you killed him! What information can he give you now?" Tears ran down the face of The Willing, taking the same path down his face as so many had before.

The Scorned flipped his knife around in his hand. "Nothing. But I don't need him to speak. All I need is for one of you to." He pointed the knife at the four men, bound to chairs pressed against the wall. The Scorned, both the one handling the torture and those who stood behind him, were smiling. The Willing, all with bruised faces and bloodshot eyes, were not.

"It's a simple matter. You know the location of certain things that we don't. Tell us the location of your rat holes, and we might let you free." He turned to his comrades. "I knew our enemy was stupid, but this is something else entirely!" This brought a round of laughter from The Scorned.

The Willing initiate who was being questioned shook his head. "I won't tell you anything."

The torturer smiled. "That's what they all say. But pain has a way of changing a person's convictions." He walked close to the man's chair and looked down at him. "Unless you're foolish like your friend." He nodded toward the dead body, still tied to the chair.

The Willing initiate's lower lip quivered, and he looked down at the ground.

"Aww, did I hurt your feelings?" The torturer put the point of his knife under the initiate's chin, forcing his head up. "I'm truly sorry. But sometimes you have to face consequences when you don't listen. Now talk." The last two words were said in a dark, warning tone.

The Willing said nothing.

The torturer looked up at the other initiates, who stared back at him blankly. "If nobody decides to wake up and be reasonable, well..." He chuckled. "Bad things will start to happen."

CRASH!

It all happened so fast, all anyone could do in the room was spin their head around and watch, dumbstruck, as the door exploded into six pieces of wooden planks. The boards scattered across the floor, and a stocky figure ran through the open doorframe. He covered the distance of the shop in three seconds, too fast for anyone to catch a good look at him. He didn't stop or slow his pace. Instead, he barreled through the other door of the smithy, causing another explosion of wood. Then, just like that, the man was gone, and it was over.

Beside the blinding light that entered the room from the gaping doorframes and the timbers strewn across the floor, nothing had changed.

Both The Willing and The Scorned stared blankly. They looked at the doorways. Then they looked at each other. What had just happened?

The torturer was the first to gather his senses. "What are you doing?" he yelled at his posse. "Go after him! We're under attack!"

The other Scorned were snapped out of their daze. They scrambled to their feet, checking to make sure they had their weapons. Then they all started sprinting toward the door.

"Not all of you! Three of you stay here!"

All of the men stopped and turned around, each one thinking they were doing their captain a favor. Once they realized they were all volunteering, they all looked at each other, unsure of how to divide the five of them into two groups in the fastest way possible.

The torturer was red in the face, furious at the incompetence of his soldiers. "Are you kidding me?! You three, stay here!" He pointed at the three closest men.

The two men who weren't chosen dashed out the door. The torturer hoped that the man who had broken through the doors wasn't too far gone; they had wasted enough time sorting things out that he could be halfway across the city now. The remaining three jogged to the center of the room, beside their commander. They brandished their weapons. The captain drew a sword from his hip. Two of the other Scorned had swords, while the third had a hatchet. They cautiously looked around, ready for another break-in at any moment.

The Willing, although still helpless and at the mercy of their captor, looked at each other with hope. They knew what was happening. Their brothers had come to rescue them!

The captain of the Scorned didn't want to be on the defensive. "You, stand guard outside that door!" He didn't know the names of his troops; he didn't care to learn them.

The man nodded and walked to the door. He stepped outside and immediately felt the cold wind on his face. He sighed, briefly enjoying the moment, before turning to look to his left.

It was a fatal mistake. Had he turned to his right, he would have seen Jayfor, sword in one hand, sneaking along the outside wall of the smithy. When he saw this, the man would have had time to alert the others and engage, taking the offensive immediately.

But he didn't. Instead, he looked to his left and saw nothing. Then he turned to his right and saw something: the pommel of a sword rushing toward his head. After that, he saw stars and then darkness as he crumpled to the ground.

This didn't go unseen by the captain of the Scorned. "He's there!" He screamed, pointing at Jayfor. "Get him!"

Jayfor gripped his sword tighter and stood about a foot away from the doorframe. He did this so his enemies would have to engage him one at a time.

The first man approached, brandishing a sword and already preparing for a swing. Jayfor glanced at the blade. The sword certainly looked nicer than his own, with intricate carvings up the blade and fine patterns. He had expected a plain sword, like his own. But what interested him more was the fact that he could see it: the dark tint of the blades. In fact, he could *feel* it, as he blocked the first blow. He felt a slight chill in his heart as the weapons crossed. This wasn't a weapon of this world.

Sparks flew, more than two regular blades would have produced. Jayfor reset his position and pulled the sword back, preparing for a forward thrust. His opponent saw it coming and parried the thrust to the side, leaving Jayfor exposed.

Now on the defensive, Jayfor blocked the next few hacks designed to weaken his defense. He was letting the sword take over, and so his instinct and speed increased. But his enemy seemed to have the same ability. Jayfor felt sweat build on his forehead, despite the cold.

After a few more strikes, Jayfor saw his enemy recover slightly late, and that was all he needed. He swung his sword from right to left, and his opponent blocked the attack and prepared to deflect the blade as it came the other way, from left to right. However, Jayfor didn't follow the traditional method. Instead, he followed through with his blade over his head and swung – with even more force – from right to left again. His opponent was caught off guard, and barely deflected it, leaving him open to a deadly thrust.

And this time, Jayfor followed the traditional method and ended the fight swiftly.

His second challenge was a hatchet-wielding brute who stood at least six inches above Jayfor in height. The weapons surprised Jayfor. *Does Elara give their warriors weapons besides swords? Apparently so.* In any case, Jayfor felt the same chill and saw the same shade in the hatchets edge.

Unlike a sword, the hatchet had a much smaller blade, and so parrying it would be much more difficult. Keeping this in mind, Jayfor backed up to give himself more room. The Scorned initiate was enraged that his comrade had been killed. Stepping over him, he lunged at Jayfor.

Jayfor sidestepped the path of the swing. The man didn't anticipate it well, and his weight carried him forward. Now Jayfor was behind the man. With a quick backhand slice, he ended the battle. His opponent's eyes widened, and he dropped the hatchet to the ground before falling beside the weapon.

Jayfor didn't savor his victory. He ran inside the building, his bloodied sword in hand. He only made it a few steps, his eyes quickly adjusting to the dark interior, before he saw who he guessed was the leader of The Scorned. The captain gritted his teeth in anger and fingered the grip on his sword, which was also richly decorated.

"You won't take them alive!" he cried. Then he turned to face the hostages.

It seemed to happen in slow motion to Jayfor. A sick feeling wrenched his gut as the realization hit him. He was too far away to stop it. Jayfor cried, "No!" but it did nothing. The Scorned captain pulled his sword back, preparing to thrust forward and end the life of the helpless Willing in the chair.

In the moment before the sword ended his life, the Willing locked eyes with Jayfor. They had never met each other, but the convictions they held, the freedom they fought for, made them brothers. With a sad smile and acceptance of what was to come, The Willing initiate nodded. *You tried your best. My mission is over. I'm going to a better place now.*

And then it was over. The sword went in and out with uncanny speed. The light left The Willing's eyes, and he slowly lowered his head.

"You monster!" Jayfor screamed. He sprinted forward with all his speed. The captain was about to kill yet another captive, whose eyes were wide in terror as the burly Scorned approached him. The captain attempted another thrust, but Jayfor managed to reach the chair in time and swing his sword out, pushing the thrust away. The sword of The Scorned embedded itself in the wooden wall of the smithy.

Jayfor didn't think about what he did next. All he felt was rage. As soon as he recovered his balance and backed up, the captain had wrenched his weapon from the wall and turned to Jayfor, equally, if not more infuriated, that he hadn't finished the job.

Jayfor wasn't a violent person, and he didn't get angry often. He always had control of his emotions, and could calm himself down before he made foolish decisions. Oftentimes, he had to talk Trenson out of reacting from his impulses, or clean up the aftermath.

But watching a defenseless person, fighting for a greater cause, have his life taken in revenge by another man... it was too much.

Jayfor swung his blade, holding nothing back. The captain blocked it and pushed it to the side. Jayfor didn't even pause, but hurled another strike, strike after strike, building a combination that he kept adding to. The captain's sword flashed with a dark hue as it met Jayfor's blade, which was glowing with a faint white light.

The captain was used to tough opponents, opponents tougher than Jayfor. He had seen his share of fights with the Willing, enough to be promoted to the rank he currently was. In normal combat, it would have been a close match. But he was being pushed back by this young man, each blow weakening his defense. Killing the initiate hadn't discouraged the man; instead, it fueled him.

Jayfor didn't notice it, but as the fight progressed, his sword grew brighter and brighter. At the start of the battle, a faint light enshrouded the blade. But the light was growing stronger and more brilliant. Blueish-white light started to fill the room, slowly at first, but increasing as the fight progressed and the light grew brighter. And as the light grew brighter, more sparks flew from the weapons as they clashed.

Jayfor didn't notice this, but The Willing, tied to their chairs, did. And their jaws dropped slightly in awe. They knew what was happening: they had experienced it before. When someone fighting for Va'ar gave himself fully into the sword's power and fought for true justice, it was like a supernatural force came over the user. It put a spark in the person's eyes and gave them agility and reflexes that far surpassed an average human.

Jayfor's blade grew even brighter; now it was impossible to look at anything other than the streaks of light left behind with each swing. The captain felt something he hadn't felt in a long time: fear. He continued stumbling backward, blocking each swing, the sparks from each collision searing his skin and face.

Then, in one fell swoop, with devastating ease, Jayfor's imbued blade cut clean through the Scorned captain's richly decorated sword.

For the first time, Jayfor stopped his advance on the captain. The Scorned stumbled backward, dazed. He didn't realize what had happened at first, and repositioned his sword in front of him. That's when he noticed that that top half of the sword was severed clean off and lying on the ground. His face slowly filled with dread.

The steel of the sword, both the part on the ground and in the captain's hand, started turning dark, an even darker shade than it was. It became like a pile of gray dust, and even though there was no wind in the room, it disintegrated and blew away quickly, like sand in a gale. It disappeared, leaving no trace except the pommel, which the captain was blankly staring at, his mouth agape.

Jayfor stared at the Scorned captain. He stood tall. His sword was still glowing vibrantly, but it began to diminish. Jayfor blinked a few times, the fire slowly leaving eyes. Within a few seconds, the light from the sword faded until it was gone, the room now barely lit from the two open doors. Jayfor returned to his normal self. He looked down with wonder at his sword. *What just happened?*

He looked up and met eyes with the Scorned captain. His face was a mix of fear, rage, and amazement. Jayfor set his jaw and pointed his sword at the captain. "Your day of judgement is not today. Leave."

The captain gritted his teeth so hard Jayfor thought they would break. "I hate you!" he screamed. Then, his dignity and his sword lost, he ran out the closest door.

XXI

"**I**T'S NOT HOPEFUL FOR the city."

Three men stood together in a small clearing in the woods. All three were about the same height; that is to say, over six feet tall. Their build was similar too, each man possessing a muscular frame and a broad build, which looked even larger with the steel plate armor they were wearing. Even their faces held something in common, although there were really no physical similarities.

If anyone could see these men – which they couldn't, even if they looked directly at the spot where the men stood – they would assume that these men were related. And in a sense, they were. They weren't related by blood. But they were brothers nonetheless.

"That's a great way to start the meeting, Reginold. Way to be positive." One of the men said with a toothy grin, a grin that set him apart from his comrades, who both wore faces of stone.

Reginold grunted. "I do not see any reason to delay the point of our conversation. We came here to discuss important business."

The other man, who hadn't spoken yet, said, "Then why don't we do this in the Homeland? Our enemy lives here, his spies are everywhere."

Reginold replied, "Because there's no time. This is a precious moment of time when we all aren't urgently occupied with our duties. We are too strained to return home. We need to keep this meeting quick."

"Well said, although I think Erador addressed his question to me, the senior officer here." The man who had spoken second said, good nature in his tone.

Reginold looked slightly ashamed of himself, but since his expression was already stoic, his features didn't change much. "Forgive me, Agrond."

Agrond smiled. "I shall consider it, since you committed such a grave crime against me."

Reginold and Erador looked at each other. As warriors, they tried to hide their emotions. It wasn't that they thought they were evil; they simply didn't see it necessary that they show how they were feeling. Business was business. Most of the Senver had the same attitude.

Agrond couldn't have been more different. There were few Senver that could match his unique personality and even less that could smile as wide as he did. Nothing seemed to bring the lieutenant down. It puzzled Erador sometimes as to why Agrond was like this. The lieutenant could easily save the trouble of being so lively and stick to his command.

But secretly, both Reginold and Erador appreciated Agrond's good humor. He proved that there was a bright side in any situation. He could be optimistic to a fault sometimes, but generally, his humor – which usually was funny only to himself – provided much needed morale in grim times. And times were certainly grim at the moment.

"Is our position in the south holding?" Erador asked Agrond. That was where the lieutenant was usually stationed, ever since Faldon's destruction. Elara had swept through what was left of Faldon and claimed the land with little to no resistance – who was there to resist them? For months, the Senver had been fighting to establish a line of defense against the Krenors. Ever since Faldon fell, Elara had rushed forward, like an unstoppable tidal wave. All they could do was try to hold it back.

" 'Holding' is a generous word, but yes, we are gaining some ground. Va'ar be praised, we even won a few battles near the Great Desert. Perhaps we'll establish a firmer hold on a few more territories and make some real progress."

"That would be ideal," Reginold agreed.

"And you two?" Agrond asked. "I have heard little about you in the last few weeks. What missions were you assigned?"

Agrond referred to them both as *you*. Reginold and Erador were like brothers, always engaged in missions together or accomplishing tasks side by side. *Twin brothers,* Agrond mentally corrected; not only did they work well together, they acted similar, looked similar, and frowned similar.

Reginold answered. "Mostly espionage, along with some hit and run attacks. Nothing complicated."

"Our mission was to monitor the progress in Augustria," Erador continued. "The Willing have a large presence there, but so do The Scorned. Both sides are struggling for the advantage."

Agrond nodded, his face turning serious for once in the conversation. "I see. And Trenson and Jayfor?"

Erador and Reginold looked at each other. They weren't sure how the lieutenant would react to the report. "Trenson is still a slave, just in a different name," Reginold answered. "He has been introduced into the regal soldiers by Wulfric, the captain of the guard. His status is uncertain, but he isn't in any danger at present."

Agrond nodded again. "And Jayfor?"

"Jayfor joined The Willing, just as anticipated. Although he is still actively searching for clues to Trenson's whereabouts, he has lent time helping The Willing free hostages and accomplish other goals. We are not sure if Ernest has learned Jayfor's true identity."

Agrond scratched his chin and looked at the ground, deep in thought. This surprised the two Senver; the lieutenant usually had an answer ready for any situation.

"We didn't engage with them or anything related to them. We were only told to monitor them and sabotage any Krenor activity, which we followed. Anything that happened to them had nothing to do with us," Reginold said. He added the last sentence out of uneasiness. Agrond's unusual attitude was making him worried. He ran through his briefing in his mind, making sure he hadn't forgotten anything.

Erador didn't want to wait any longer for Agrond's response. "Have we failed in any way?"

Agrond looked up and met eyes with each of the Senver. "No, you haven't. You've done exactly as you were told. I was worried that you might have intervened with their mission in some way, so I'm glad to hear there was none of that."

"The mission?" Reginold asked, "Do they know that their quest isn't just to find the Tree of Ramadus, but to upheave the entire social structure of Augustria and change the city?"

"No, but they will. They just don't know it yet. They don't know that their presence will have a ripple effect on the city. And it's best that they not know. In fact," Agrond straightened his posture, "that's the reason we're meeting here today."

Erador raised an eyebrow. He wasn't sure what Agrond was talking about. Did he mean that the reason they were meeting was to give them more instruction? It had to be.

"I decided to drop by to check on your progress. A lot hangs in balance on your mission, so I wanted to make sure everything was running smoothly."

There was a pause. *That's it?* Agrond had abandoned his post and called for a meeting in the middle of a war – just to catch up? "Is that it? You risked your life and your men, just to chat?" Erador said, before he could stop himself.

Agrond stared at Erador, not with anger or frustration, like Erador expected, but with confusion. "No. I risked my life coming across enemy lines to make sure my friends were safe and there was nothing wrong. Nobody ever came to see me when I was on a dangerous mission," Agrond said, a hint of sadness in his voice. "I thought meeting with you might give you some encouragement."

Both Erador and Reginold looked at each other, not sure of what they just heard. Did Agrond come all this way – just to make sure they were all right? That was... strange. They didn't know how to react to this.

"Oh... Thank you." Reginold said, rather flatly. He wasn't sure how to take this. Was this another one of Agrond's jokes? It was a possibility, but there was no hint of humor in the lieutenant's face now.

That didn't last long, however, as the familiar grin eventually returned to Agrond's face. "Don't worry about it. We need to go the extra mile for each other if we are going to make a difference in the war. But anyway, you're doing great. Just keep an eye on Trenson and Jayfor, and whatever you do, don't engage unless absolutely necessary. I was told that last part so many times by my general, I don't think I'll ever forget it."

Reginold relaxed, now that the mood was defined. "They aren't making recon easy. At least, Jayfor isn't. He's always on the move."

Agrond laughed. "That sounds like Jayfor to me. I could never quite convince him to settle down when I was with him. But you're doing good; even my general told me so."

Erador raised an eyebrow. Compliments from their general were rare, if not unheard of.

"Well, I need to get back to my men. They probably miss me so much," Agrond joked, but Erador and Reginold didn't doubt it. Agrond was a popular general. "You two are in charge of two of the most influential men in Ralladin." He smirked. "No pressure."

XXII

WULFRIC WASN'T KIDDING WHEN he said the easy days were over. Trenson thought being a slave was hard enough. The truth was, it was an easier life than what he had to do as a guard.

Trenson painfully realized that he had lost much of his strength in the past few months. He hadn't trained while traveling. He used to train every day, back when he lived in the palace at Loronis, when the world was easier. But after it all burned down, he had simply walked every day. It was his endurance that suffered, which resulted in him burning out quickly while training in Wulfric's yards. This angered him, and he worked hard to rebuild what he had lost.

On the other hand, his living accommodations were a lot better than they were before. Although he was still sleeping in the same room as other people, at least he had his own cot – even if it was small. The warm blanket that gave Trenson a little comfort from the cold nights became his new best friend. Not only that, but he was properly fed in the hall with the other guards. Trenson devoured the food until he felt he could eat no more; it wasn't gourmet compared to his previous life, but now, it was heaven.

The rest of the guard immediately received Trenson with respect. He was taller than most of them, even though he was younger – people in Augustria seemed shorter than average – which helped, but what made the biggest difference was his skill. Most of them had seen him in action in the arena, and those who hadn't, heard the stories, which may have been a little dramatized. As a result, many of them wanted to spar with him during his training sessions. Trenson was relieved that the other guards didn't scorn him for being an outsider, and so was more than willing to spar with anyone who wished to.

Another thing that added to his aura of greatness was that he didn't speak the variation of Kallarian that everyone else spoke, so he couldn't understand what anyone was saying. He expected this to only make his position worse, but it actually made him seem all the more intriguing in everyone's eyes. He was the master swordsman from afar, whom no one could best in battle, and could not impart his knowledge to others. Trenson tried not to let it get to his head.

It was a relief to him when he found out that Aquila was staying in the same dorm as him. Although he wasn't much for conversation, Trenson didn't mind; in fact, he actually liked the peace and quiet. It was just comforting to know someone in a land where he was the foreigner. Surprisingly, Aquila wasn't picked on because of his height. Trenson had expected him to have a harder time, because he was mute and the size of two ordinary guards. But he was Trenson's friend, and so whenever Trenson was around, they treated the giant with respect.

Their days were fairly easy: they woke up early, hours before the sun came up, and headed to the hall for their breakfast, which was always eggs, bread and some type of meat, along with a small glass of mead each. They were given thirty minutes to eat. After that, it was off to the training yard.

They were split into groups depending on what weapon they fought with. Trenson was surprised to find out that a staff was considered a knightly weapon and was wielded by a number of soldiers. Back in Loronis, this wasn't the case, and staffs were frowned upon because they had no lethal edge to them. But here, they were made of light metal, which meant that they wouldn't shatter easily. Plus, each end of the staff had a short blade attached to it, so it basically became a double-edged spear.

The design of such a weapon intrigued Trenson. He wondered why he had never thought of it. *Maybe I should have stuck to my staff after all.* But that was ridiculous. He had a sword given to him by Va'ar Himself. That was far better than any weapon mankind could make.

Trenson never found out how exactly his sword ended up in Wulfric's inventory. He found out later that weapons were bought in bulk, large shipments from blacksmiths, and, on occasion, secondhand. It must have been that as soon as he was auctioned off, his sword was lumped together with a load bound for Augustria.

"Thank you, Va'ar," Trenson whispered to himself one night, lying under the blanket on his cot, thinking about how it could have happened.

The morning training was split into two parts. During the first half, everyone was led together in basic attacks and group exercises.

After that, everyone dispersed and did their own thing. Trenson usually ended up sparring with Aquila, or taking turns practicing with the other guards. In any case, there was always someone that wanted to train with him, and so he was always exhausted coming out of training. *Not for long,* he told himself.

After the morning was over, they were given a list of chores to do, and had the rest of the day to complete them. Technically, they could lounge around and not do them, since they were allowed to go about the areas of the barracks and do whatever. But if you didn't do your job, you were whipped and given no supper. At least, that's what Trenson was told. He had never seen it happen, but nobody dared finish their assigned jobs late, so Trenson assumed it was true.

The jobs they were assigned ranged from sweeping the floors to sharpening the weapons to cleaning the cooking supplies. Trenson's tasks one day would be swapped with another guard's another day. Trenson found out quickly that cleaning the pots and pans in the kitchen was one of the most desirable jobs; it was inside, away from the cold, and required the least amount of effort.

Despite his condition not being so bad, Trenson didn't stop looking for ways to escape. He still had a mission to complete. His friend may be gone, and he may be wildly off track, but his quest remained the same. He had to get out.

***

Geoffrey hated Trenson. And he had a good reason to.

Throughout Geoffrey's stay at his father's house, he had secretly craved attention from his father. If anyone who knew him knew this information, they would be shocked. Geoffrey was twenty. He was a self-sustained adult with a viable career in front of him. Why would he want attention from his father, who did a very impersonal job of raising him?

It was because he never saw himself as important in his father's eyes. He was definitely an important person compared to most people in Augustria. But all that attention didn't mean anything when his father overlooked him, or treated him as an asset. He had never been what most would call a "well-behaved child." Far from it, he was often getting in trouble. But he didn't get into scrapes because he wanted to be bad – at least, that wasn't the whole reason. It was mainly because if he did something bad enough, it would get his father's attention. And while his father was terrifying while mad, it was better than no attention at all.

Although he was now older and knew that angering his father wasn't a good method of getting attention, he still wanted the same recognition. He had returned home after his long trip, hoping his father would be at least somewhat interested. Brigid was a long way from Augustria; maybe Wulfric would be curious on how the city was doing.

But he wasn't. His attention was riveted on the foolish tournament he had planned. *No matter,* Geoffrey had thought to himself. *When it ends, he will return to reason.* And so he had waited until the tournament concluded to expect anything out of his father.

Unfortunately, his father's attention wasn't focused on him after the games were over. It was focused on someone else.

"I'm watching him closely," Geoffrey overheard Wulfric say to one of the secretaries. "You could say I'm testing him. He has enough skill with the sword to easily become my second-in-command. But being able to swing a sharp stick around isn't enough. He must have intelligence, wisdom, and a quick wit."

"And that's why you decided against promoting him immediately?" the secretary asked.

"Correct. If I see that he has what it takes, I'll consider it. Until then, I'm keeping an eye on him. He seems different from the others. Most slaves are nothing more than animals when they come in. They simply do what you tell them to do. Which is great for infantry, but leaders need to have something else, a certain creativity, if they are to be any good. It's hard to come across free thinkers nowadays, but he strikes me as one – and possibly more."

The secretary nodded. "I see what you mean. I have heard about him. What's his name?"

"Trenson is what he told me."

"Ah, Trenson. That's an eastern name. Perhaps that's where he's from."

"Possibly. In any case, make sure to monitor his doings, and check on him regularly. I would rather promote him sooner, than later."

And so it turned out that Wulfric had more interest in a random slave who won a tournament than his own son. Geoffrey realized this bitterly, and since then, he hated Trenson. It wouldn't have bothered him as much if Wulfric wasn't always discussing it with his officials. Geoffrey couldn't share a single meal with his father without Wulfric mentioning the subject. "He has potential," the captain would say, sitting across from his son. "I can see him becoming a tactician. He has a certain air to him that would fit the role perfectly. The other guards exalt him and are afraid to even speak to him, and so he commands respect even when he is not ranked above them."

Geoffrey was sick and tired of hearing the praise. "Is he really that important? Barely a month ago, he was a lowly slave. Not much has changed."

Wulfric frowned. "You're correct, not much has. But that is beside the point. He is in one of the lowest positions on the guard, but he carries himself like he is a general. Even the other guards hold him in respect. I'm beginning to think that he used to be a soldier at some point. There's no other logical reason that explains it."

Geoffrey didn't say anything, but inwardly, he groaned. Why was his father like this? The only time he saw him was during dinner, and Wulfric was more interested in talking about his new favorite soldier, than his son? Geoffrey's tutors kept him busy during the day, and he had no choice but to devote his time to finishing his *very* extensive education. He was studying to become a proxy – to speak on behalf of officials during meetings they couldn't attend. It was a job that required lots of knowledge and public speaking, but also gave the proxy – and his family – high status.

So Geoffrey had a few interests: studying, eating, sleeping, and wishing Trenson would fall down a well or get run over by a horse. Those were pretty much all he thought about.

***

Trenson wasn't expecting it so early, but he wasn't completely caught by surprise when a secretary approached him in the kitchen when he was putting the freshly washed pans on the rack.

"Trenson?" The secretary asked. Trenson recognized the man's occupation because of the quill-shaped brooch on his right chest. Brooches seemed to be a popular thing in Kallary.

Trenson nodded.

The secretary nodded back, now knowing that he would have to speak Faldian to the man. "You have been given a promotion."

Trenson raised an eyebrow. He wasn't completely surprised, but this was earlier than he expected. "To what exactly?"

"To sergeant. You've displayed traits that would be beneficial in command. You must present yourself to my office once you finish todays work, where we will discuss what changes shall be made."

The secretary said it in a monotone voice, so Trenson guessed he said the exact same thing to everyone who got a promotion.

"Thank you," Trenson said.

The secretary nodded and walked away, leaving Trenson to his work. As he quickly put the rest of the dishes away, he thought about what this meant for him. A promotion was useless; he wasn't planning on staying here. But it would probably give him greater freedom, and with greater freedom came a greater chance that he could escape.

XXIII

"You did well, Conrad. There was nothing you could have done that would save them," Ernest said comfortingly.

Jayfor looked up at him mirthlessly, without a trace of a smile on his lips. "You weren't there. You don't know."

"Oh, I think I do. This isn't the first time we've lost men. It hurts, but we have to work through it. Their lives weren't lost in vain."

Jayfor stared at him. "You talk about them as if they are not people. They had fathers, mothers, siblings, people who loved them – and they loved them back. But now they are gone, and those people will never see them again in this life."

"No amount of wishing or pitying will get them back," Ernest said quietly.

"I know!" Jayfor said, louder than he intended. "It seems like you just don't care. They are people – like you and me! What if that was you in that chair, who watched as I wasn't fast enough to save you. I don't think you would treat your own life as lightly."

Ernest looked into the fireplace, the logs crackling sparks into the air and smoldering a light orange color. His face revealed he didn't think he needed to explain this. "You have to realize that death isn't the end. If we give our lives to Va'ar and sacrifice our-selves to give Him glory, then is there a better way to die?"

Jayfor thought about this, turning the idea over in his mind. Truth be told, he knew all of this perfectly well, but he was venting because he was mad at himself. What Ernest was telling him wasn't new information, or things he hadn't thought of before. He knew all of this. He was just suppressing it.

"I know it's hard," Ernest continued, "to move on. But those men were courageous. They didn't give any information or betray their beliefs, even if they knew there was no way out. Death claims all men eventually. How we choose to receive it, in honor or not, is our choice. And they chose honor. There is nothing about their character that should cause us to be sad."

Jayfor looked down and said nothing.

Ernest leaned back in his chair and sighed. "Maybe it gets easier, dealing with this, the more it happens."

No, it doesn't, Jayfor responded in his mind. He had been the king of Faldon, and was responsible for the death of thousands, if not millions, of people. If he let that realization sink in, it would crush him. No, it never got easier.

Ernest changed the subject. "On the other hand, you saved three of our men from further torture and brought down some Scorned in the process. I would call that a victory."

"I guess that is true," Jayfor said admittedly.

"What are we talking about?" Novak, in his signature way, walked in and interrupted the conversation. He glanced at both men, sitting in front of the fireplace, and decided that he should grace them with his presence. He plopped down on the last chair by the fire and stretched his arms above his head before crossing them.

" 'We' weren't talking about anything," Ernest replied, "but me and Conrad were discussing how he saved the hostages."

"Oh yeah! Great job, by the way," he nodded to Jayfor with a smile. "I actually talked to one of the men you rescued. You should have seen the happy tears rolling down his face when he came home to his family and held his children in his arms again. His entire family lives at a different base, and they thought they had seen the last of him. But you proved them wrong."

Jayfor shrugged, but couldn't help but smile, himself. It was a reminder that he didn't fail, that the mission was still a success. "I did my job."

"Is there any better job out there?" Novak asked no one in particular. After no one responded, he answered his own question. "Call me a liar if there is. It's a job that has a purpose that is literally out of this world. I guess The Scorned have a similar calling, but we're the good guys!" He chuckled, as if it were a great joke.

Jayfor barely heard any of it. He was staring into the fire, the orange light reflecting from his face and eyes and making his sandy hair seem even more blonde. He was in his analytical stage again, where he was lost in his own mind.

Even though Ernest didn't know him that well, he could read the look on Jayfor's face. "You have something on your mind?"

Jayfor nodded. "It's just..." he looked at Ernest. "I am trying to figure out the end here, of our 'job,' as he put it. We can fight against Elara all day long, and they can fight back. This war has gone on for centuries. We recruit more followers, but so do they. Is there ever going to be an end? Or is it just a vicious circle?"

There was a period of silence. After he said the words, Jayfor wondered if he had overstepped. He wasn't really close enough to them to start asking deep questions like that. *Why did I say that out loud?* It had always pestered him, whether or not there was going to be an end. If everything was just futile, and no matter what, it would be a supernatural power struggle... was there any point in fighting?

"Technically speaking, Faldon lost the war," Novak pointed out. "But I see what you mean. Just because the kingdom is destroyed doesn't mean those who believed in it will stop fighting. But to answer your question, well, of course we believe we're going to win," Novak said. Even he seemed to put some thought into it. "Who would fight for something unless they thought they would win? We know that Va'ar is supreme and, even if Elara takes over Ralladin, it will only be temporary. I don't know exactly how it will work, but I have a feeling that, one day, He will recreate the world, and make it what it used to be."

That made sense, Jayfor inwardly agreed.

"Until then, we fight with everything we've got," Novak continued. "If I live, then I give my life to serve Va'ar. If I die, I return to Him. So I never really lose, do I?" He sighed contently, shifting in his chair to get into the most comfortable position possible. "Maybe if we're lucky, we'll live to see the Prophecy unfold."

The Prophecy? The word stuck in Jayfor's mind. "The Prophecy?" He asked, raising an eyebrow. "What's that?"

Novak looked shocked. He glanced at Ernest, expecting the captain to look equally shocked, but the captain kept the same face of stone as he stared blankly back at Novak. Novak returned his gaze to Jayfor. "You mean you don't know what the Prophecy is?" he asked slowly.

Jayfor tried to search his memory, but came up with nothing. With a bold name like that, he would have remembered it had he heard it before. "I don't think so."

Novak looked at Ernest again with the same look of surprise. Again, Ernest showed no response. Novak's surprise slowly turning into an excited smile, he rubbed his hands together. "Well then, I think you deserve to know."

Ernest sighed. "Here we go."

"The Prophecy," Novak began, his voice turning more formal, "is a promise that was given to King Mada, the first king of Faldon and of the world, right after he opened the gates of the Mountain of Power. I'm sure you know that story, right?"

Jayfor nodded. The story of how Ralladin was created by Va'ar and how the three kingdoms were originally united, was a story that Jayfor had heard countless times growing up in Loronis. He knew it by heart: After creating the world, Va'ar created people to govern the land, and they established the Empire of Ralladin, which in those days encompassed the entire world. Everything was perfect, and there was no pain or suffering or toil or wars. It was paradise. Until Mada became unsatisfied with his power and decided to release the force within the Mountain of Power in hopes of gaining more. After that, the world erupted into war as darkness entered the world and corruption took hold of every man and woman. The world had not been at peace since then. "Yes, of course I know the story."

The firelight reflected off of Novak's face, illuminating his eager expression. "What most people don't know is that Va'ar said some words to Mada right after he opened the gate. I don't know the exact words He used, but I know the summary of it. Most versions of the story don't have this. I guess you can say that it's overlooked, or not paid attention to. Some deny that Va'ar even said them. But I believe them."

Jayfor leaned forward in his chair and rested his elbows on his knees, waiting for Novak to get to the point.

After allowing a short period of silence to emphasize the moment, Novak continued. "Va'ar basically said what the consequences of Mada's action were: death and everything else. But right at the end, there were a few words that He said that make up the Prophecy. I can't quote the words, but as close as I can remember, he said: 'And although you have bound yourself to your own shackles, there will come one who will break your chains. The captivator will wound Him, but He will end his Reign.'"

The captivator... That must be Tar-Raw, or the Dark Order. Jayfor's mind was like a clock, all the gears turning, taking in this new piece of evidence and fitting it into what he already knew. *I never heard this part of the story before. I would remember something like this. I've even read the original story myself from the archives of Loronis. But those were written down from oral stories...*

"It's a little different from what you were told, I assume," Novak said with a knowing grin.

Jayfor had to agree. "Definitely. How do you know that this is true?"

"Well, how do you know that the story itself is true?"

"There are professional archives where the story was written down, in the palace in Loronis. I read them myself." Jayfor got a sideways look from Novak, then realized why. He hastily added, "My father took me to visit it sometimes – he was a close friend of the king."

Ernest didn't look satisfied with the answer, like he didn't believe him. Jayfor felt his neck grow hot from guilt. Novak, however, believed him completely. Either that, or he hid his doubt remarkably well.

Ernest spoke up. He had remained quiet for so long, his voice scared Jayfor a little. "It's not in the records because the author of those records took pieces of information from multiple eyewitnesses, then boiled it down to the important information. Most people don't know that Mada had a diary."

Jayfor's jaw dropped slightly. Why didn't he know about this? "A diary? Why isn't it in the archive?"

The right side of Ernest's lip curved upward in a smile. "Because it was stolen. After Mada's death, there was a fire at the palace archives. All the artifacts and ancient technology that engineers and scholars created burned. A few thieves used it as cover to raid the archive. One of them carried away the journal of the first king of Ralladin."

Jayfor immediately doubted it. "No, that's not true. There was a fire in the palace, but almost everything in there burned except a few relics. There was never any journal."

Ernest continued as if Jayfor had said nothing. "A thief bundled it with the rest of his things and took it to the black market, where it circled around for many years – centuries, to be exact. Then, four years ago, in one of our raids, we took over what used to be a hideout for criminals. And there, in a carefully covered case, was the journal.

"Of course, we thought it was a fraud to begin with. If someone could fool others into thinking they had something written by one of the first men on Ralladin, he could sell it for a fortune. So we had our historians check it. They examined it, and – to our shock – unanimously agreed that it could very well be what it claimed to be."

He sighed. "Since then, there have been many who think it is trustworthy, and others who don't. If you believe it's actually his diary, then you believe in the Prophecy, since he writes about it."

Jayfor couldn't believe it. He opened his mouth, then realized he had no idea what to say. He closed it. Then he thought of something, so he opened it again. "Wow."

Novak jumped back into the conversation. "I wasn't here at the time, but Ernest was, and he remembers when they first found it. I've seen it. It's kept in our main headquarters, which is closer to the center of Augustria, under heavy surveillance."

Jayfor shook his head. "That is something I am going to have to see someday. I had no idea."

Jayfor wanted to say more, to tell them he knew as a fact that there had been absolutely no mention of any journal in any records, or any evidence suggesting that there was one. But if he said that, then they might ask him how he knew that. And the only reason he knew it was because he used to be a king. So he kept his external mouth closed, but the voice in his head was bombarded with arguments and new ideas.

If the Prophecy is true... then there would be an end to it all. The Willing would be fighting for an end, an end that would come once the One the Prophecy spoke of arrived. There was hope for the world. But was it true?

One thing is for sure, Jayfor made up his mind. *I need to see this for myself.*

XXIV

WITH GREATER RANK CAME great privileges. Trenson wasn't required to sleep in the cold dorms the rest of the soldiers slept in. He didn't even have to sleep in the same room as other men – which was a relief, as those "other men" didn't bathe often. He was given his own room – his very own room.

When he first walked into it, something felt off. He looked around at the small room. On one side of the room was a cot, with a window along the same wall. The other wall had a crude dresser, which was more like a shelf, to hold his clothes and garments. On the opposite side of the wall was where he could store his armor – there was a basket with divided sections for it. It was a small room, and the amount of space for him to store things was even smaller. But he wasn't exactly burdened with a lots of stuff, so that wouldn't be a problem.

So why did he feel something was different? He had a strange feeling when he looked at the room. Then it hit him, and he felt the urge to chuckle at first, then drop his head in sadness. He did neither.

This room was set up the same as his room back at the palace in Loronis.

Of course, this was far more minimal. He didn't have lots of outfits to wear, he didn't have luxury bedding, he didn't have a bookshelf or a nightstand or anything like that. But the few things that the two rooms shared, were in the exact same place.

Déjà vu, he murmured to himself. He shook the feeling off. This was his room, for now, until he escaped. He wouldn't be getting comfortable here.

"As sergeant," the brigadier said formally, "you'll be expected to lead the men in basic drills during training sessions. You will be briefed on what exercises to teach them the night before."

Trenson nodded. "Yes, sir."

"Some days you will not be assigned to instruct. In that case, you shall also be told of your duties the night before. Your days will operate much in the same way as they did when you were a normal soldier, except you'll have more privileges. But those privileges can be taken away at any moment. Understand?"

"Yes sir," Trenson answered. "What sort of privileges, sir?" He knew he might be overstepping, asking the question, but he was curious.

Thankfully, the brigadier didn't seem upset. "You'll be dining with commanders in the officer's hall, your labor will not be as strenuous as that of an average soldier, and, most importantly, you'll have respect."

Trenson nodded. "Yes sir, thank you, sir."

***

A few days later, Trenson ran into Wulfric.

"Ah, the popular one!" Wulfric turned the corner just to see Trenson a few yards in front of him, walking the opposite direction. The captain smiled and held his arms open as if Trenson were an age-old friend. "I was wondering how you would take the rather quick promotion, but you seem to fit into your role well."

Trenson put his fist to his chest – a gesture he noticed other guards did when they encountered someone with authority. "Yes, sir, thank you. I have to admit, I was not expecting anything this early." He spoke a little more truthfully around Wulfric than he did most people. Some people had an uncanny ability to see other people's true intentions. Wulfric was one of those people. And since Trenson didn't want his true intention – escape – to be noticed, he was a little more honest around the captain than he liked.

"But you were expecting it, no?" Wulfric asked. His tone was casual, but there was a serious question beneath it, which he hid with a smile.

Trenson hesitated. It sounded selfish, but he had expected to be noticed for his skills. He couldn't hide the fact that nobody else in the training yard could beat him. Of course, that was mainly because of the sword's power, not his own, but Wulfric didn't need to know that.

He waited too long to reply. "I see," Wulfric said knowingly. "You are lucky and your abilities match your expectations." He started walking again, but as he passed Trenson, his tone suddenly became serious. "Don't get cocky."

Trenson turned his head to see Wulfric's smile gone, replaced with a steel scowl. Trenson was surprised at first, but then inwardly shrugged. *That's Wulfric for you.*

***

Both Trenson and Wulfric didn't know it, but Geoffrey heard the entire conversation. He was following his father, trying to catch up to him to ask what should be done about his horse – she had done something wrong to her ankle and was unable to walk, and he was wondering if he should put her down. He immediately forgot about it as soon as his father turned the corner ahead and started talking in a way that could only be to one person: Trenson.

A bitter taste wallowed in Geoffrey's mouth. He stopped walking and listened as his father talked to Trenson with more thought and care than he had to him since he arrived home. It wasn't so much the words he said as the way he said them.

Different emotions hit Geoffrey throughout the exchange. Initially, he harbored rage for his father, then at Trenson. After that, he wondered why he wasn't good enough for his father's attention. He quickly replaced it with the conclusion that his father was too bullheaded to notice anything of value. Wulfric was only interested in Trenson because Trenson could elevate the status of the army. Once Trenson failed Wulfric, it was all over.

Geoffrey smiled at the possibility. It would only take one little slip-up from Trenson to knock down all the hope Wulfric had in him.

If I could prove to father that I'm better than this slave, then maybe he shall stop idolizing him.

That's what gave him an idea.

He could hear Trenson's footsteps coming closer. He swiftly backed up a few paces, and when Trenson rounded the corner, it looked like he just happened to be walking the opposite direction.

"Ah, you must be the one father talked about!" Geoffrey said cheerfully, with a smile. He made sure to talk in the Faldian language. "Trenson, is it?"

The man seemed suspicious of Geoffrey, but he held out his arm in greeting. "Yes, sir, at your service. And your name is?"

"Geoffrey. I have heard good things about you, Trenson. It's a pleasure to finally meet you." He shook his hand. He wanted to twist his wrist and break his arm, but he resisted the impulse and assumed a friendly demeanor.

Trenson didn't look like he was buying it. "The pleasure is mine."

Without a pause, Geoffrey continued in his persuasive tone. "Pardon me if this seems a little upfront, seeing as we just met, but I was wondering if you would allow me to see your abilities in action."

Trenson raised an eyebrow. "Abilities?"

Geoffrey laughed. "Everyone says you have the instincts of a cat and the agility of one, too. I saw a few of your arena fights, which were enough to convince me that there was some truth to this." There was a small, almost unnoticeable amount of ill-will in the last comment. "I know you can wield a sword. But what do you know about other weapons?"

Trenson shrugged. "I've used my share of arms."

Geoffrey nodded. "I have no doubt. I would like to see what else you can do. And there is a perfect opportunity for a demonstration next week. I shall be hosting a party, of sorts. There will be games and challenges, from boxing to archery to ninepins. It is intended only for people of higher rank, but I think I can make an exception." He forced a smile. "It will be a great time to familiarize yourself with the generals, and show us what else you can do."

Trenson nodded and smiled slightly, but even Geoffrey could tell the smile was fake. "That sounds great, I appreciate the offer."

Geoffrey didn't miss a beat. "So, I have your word that you shall attend?" Although he intended the words to be friendly, they came out as more of a threat. He wanted to know as a fact that Trenson would show. He was bordering on the thin veil of goodwill, but he didn't care. He would make Trenson come.

It was clear on Trenson's face that he didn't want to go, and that he knew Geoffrey wasn't offering this to him out of the kindness of his heart, but he had no other choice. "Of course. I will be there."

Geoffrey clapped his hands together and grinned. "Excellent! I shall tell the managers to make room for one more. I hope you look forward to it as much as I do."

Trenson nodded. "I do." Looking into Geoffrey's eyes, seeing through his act and knowing that something wasn't right, he meant those words.

XXV

Thirty minutes may seem like a long time to wait on something, but to the Scorned captain, it passed by much too fast.

He leaned his back against the wall and took a deep breath, watching as the warm air diffused from his mouth and became a gray cloud. He shivered. Although he was dressed to combat the harsh cold, wearing a tight-fitting vest and even a fur hat, that didn't stop the occasional gust from getting through some opening and making him shiver.

He looked out at the streets. People walking by. All oblivious. He smiled. Don't judge a book by its cover, as the saying goes. From the cover, it looked like another day in Augustria. Cold, cloudy, and somewhat monotonous. For the past week, gray clouds blanketed the sky, not threatening rain, but simply blocking what little warmth came from the sun.

The people dressed appropriately. Fur caps and long, burly coats that went down to the knees were what everyone sported, and from there, it depended on how fortunate they were. The captain could spot a rich person from almost a mile away from the lavish colors and extra clothing they wore.

He was watching one such person in the distance when he heard a deep voice behind him. "Well?"

The captain's heart leaped, and he broke into a cold sweat as he spun around. There he stood: the Mentor. "*Intekalin,*" The captain said, using the Kallarian word for teacher.

"You're fortunate I had the time to acquire this." As he spoke, the Mentor offered him a sword in a leather sheath. The hilt of the sword was decorated with traces of silver and gemstones. Much like the captain's last sword. The sword that was shattered by that insufferable follower of the Willing.

The captain's eyes lit up. "Thank you, master, thank you. I promise, this will not happen again." He said the words quickly. He wanted to get this whole thing over with. It was embarrassing that his sword had broke. For beginners just entering the system, such things weren't uncommon, but it was almost unheard of for a captain.

He grabbed the sheath with his right hand and tugged, but the Mentor didn't release his grip. The captain now realized, with bitterness, that he wasn't going to just take his sword and leave. Now there would be a speech.

"I am disappointed that this happened to someone of your standing," the Mentor said slowly. That was the defining trait of the Mentor: he always talked slowly, giving you the time to take in each word to its fullest.

The captain didn't respond, or look the Mentor in the eye. He tugged on the sword. It still didn't come free of the man's iron grip.

"When you are placed above others, you must be better than others. After what has happened, you proved that you are not better than others. Your conviction is weak."

The words cut into the captain, and he turned to his master, looking him in the eye. "My conviction is not weak!" He protested. He tried to hold eye contact, but failed, the steel gaze of the Mentor withering his courage.

His master didn't say anything for a few seconds, letting the suspense eat away at the captain's consciousness. Then he said, in the same low, articulated tone, "Then prove it."

He let go of the sword. The captain, who had been pulling against it the entire time, stumbled backward a few paces in surprise. When he regained his balance, he looked down at the sword in his hands – exactly the same as his last one.

He didn't feel gratitude to his Mentor, or his new weapon. All he felt was wrath, wrath towards himself, for not being strong enough to prove he was worthy. He wasn't worthy. He lashed out at himself silently.

When he looked up, the Mentor was staring at him with the same cold glare. Cowardice mixed with resentment, and he turned and walked down the street without another word, clipping his new sword to his belt, not bothering to look behind him to see if his master was watching him.

XXVI

Trenson told Aquila about his experience with Geoffrey that night.

"I don't trust him," Trenson got right to the point, after he finished telling the story.

Aquila shook his head in agreement.

Since Trenson was promoted to sergeant, he technically had no reason to be talking to Aquila, who was inferior to him in rank. Technically. But Trenson found himself missing the presence of "The Mountain." It was unusual for Trenson to want company with anyone, but after a few days of working with the other sergeants, and only a few of them knowing how to speak Faldian, he started to feel lonely.

Lonely. That was a feeling that lingered with him more than usual. He knew exactly why he was feeling this way – he was an expert at analyzing his emotions – but he wasn't proud of the reason.

It was because he had lost Jayfor. He no longer had the companion that had been by his side for six years. And –

No. He wasn't going to think about it anymore. It was finished; he needed to focus on what was ahead.

"I don't know how this 'party' of his is going to go," Trenson continued. "There were a few gatherings at the palace, where games and all sorts of things were done. Maybe it will be similar to that."

Aquila raised an eyebrow questioningly. Trenson paused and tried to figure out what he said wrong, then realized he had slipped and said *at the palace.* "I only heard about them," he added, "from some friends of mine. I used to know some people who were influential in my city, and we used to call the regal meeting hall the 'palace.'"

Aquila seemed satisfied with this response. Trenson breathed a silent sigh of relief. *That was close.*

Aquila gave Trenson a look that said, *what are you going to do now?*

Trenson shrugged, as if the question had been voiced out loud. "I guess I don't have a choice but to go. If I don't, Geoffrey will find a way to cause a stir about it, which will probably lead to me facing consequences. My only option is to go, and hope that nothing bad happens."

Aquila shook his head in a way that seemed to say, *I hope, but I wouldn't count on it.*

***

Next week, as expected, Trenson was informed at breakfast by a servant about the party. He was told that, once he finished his work, he was to go to the baths, where he could shower and give himself "a good washing." After that, the party started at seven – he would be led to the grounds by another servant. And, the servant added, he was to wear his best attire.

After the servant left, Trenson huffed. First of all, the way the servant wrinkled his nose when he said "a good washing" was a little dramatic. Secondly, as for his best attire, he only had a few outfits, and all of them were exactly the same. *How will I ever choose what to wear?*

Regardless, he would try to make an effort. At the end of the day, he did exactly as he was instructed: he went to the baths and gave himself as close to "a good washing" as he could. After that, he put on his "best attire."

As soon as he finished strapping on his belt, it must have struck seven, because there was a crisp knock on his door. Opening it, he found the same servant that had talked to him that morning standing there, his arms behind his back in a very formal posture. "Are you ready, sir?"

Trenson inhaled through his teeth. "Ready as I'll ever be," he said, stepping through the doorway.

***

The grounds where the party was hosted had an antique feel to it. It wasn't just the fact that the stone that paved the floor was old and weathered, or that there were no fancy decorations or carvings like other parts of the property.

It was because it was built like the entertainment grounds of old: it was shaped like a square, and the center of the grounds was where the entertainment happened, all the activities and action. This space was out in the open; there was no roof over this section. However, along the edges of the square, there was a roof supported by pillars. This was where the conversation happened, and also where the eating and drinking were held.

He was one of the first to arrive. As he took a moment to take in his environment, Geoffrey spotted him and walked over. He was richly decorated, adorned in a dark blue coat with red patterns on it, contrasting each other in a way that made it hard not to look at it. He also wore a golden necklace that shimmered in what little light remained from the sunset.

"Trenson, my friend!" He spread his arms in greeting. "It's good to see you. I am glad you came!"

Like I had a choice, Trenson thought to himself. He forced a half-smile. "Likewise." He kept his response short. He didn't want his true feelings to leak through the tone of his voice.

Geoffrey smiled broadly. "You are one of the first to arrive! I was just talking with the administrator of spices over there." He motioned with his arm to a short but large man who was standing by one of the many tables filled with food. He had a large bowl in one hand and a ladle in the other, and he repeatably scooped the contents from a steaming pot into his bowl.

Trenson raised an eyebrow. "The administrator of spice?" He had never heard of such a job.

Geoffrey nodded. "Yes." He must not have noticed the surprised look on Trenson's face, or else he would have been equally surprised to know that there was no such chief in Faldon. "I was telling him about your reputation, and how good you are with a sword. He said he was interested in meeting you. Until more guests arrive and the fun truly begins, I advise you to introduce yourself."

Realizing that this was an order, not a suggestion, Trenson nodded. "I will." He tried to search Geoffrey's face for any ill intentions, but he found none. He inwardly shrugged. The so-called administrator of spice didn't look intimidating.

Geoffrey looked over Trenson's shoulder and saw other guests entering the grounds. "Ah, welcome!" he said cheerfully, walking around Trenson and heading to greet them.

Now Trenson was left alone, with no other option than to meet with the "administrator of spice." But priorities came first, and right now, the food at the table looked tempting. He had already eaten supper with the other sergeants in the dining hall. But that didn't mean he didn't have room for more.

After making a plate, he walked to the table where the "administrator of spice" sat. Trenson couldn't help but feel bad for the chair the chief was sitting on. It looked like it would break at any moment, the legs bowing out slightly at the enormous amount of weight it was supporting.

"I heard from Geoffrey that you're the administrator of spice?" Trenson started as he grabbed the chair on the opposite side of the table.

The man, who was leaning over his bowl of soup, looked up to see Trenson sitting in front of him. Bits of the soup dribbled down his first chin, then his second. He professionally wiped this away with his napkin. "And you are the man George spoke about? Trevor?"

"Trenson," he corrected. He was a little surprised that the chief called Goeffrey by his informal name, and a little miffed that he had ignored his question.

The man waved his hand in a gesture of dismissal. "All the same." He said. He had another spoonful of soup, half of which made it onto his chin rather than his mouth, but he wiped this away again with his napkin. He took a bite from a slice of bread and, still chewing, said, "So, what do you know about spices?"

Trenson looked up from his plate. This was a question he hadn't anticipated. "Well, I didn't know it was a bigger industry in Kallary," he offered.

"Ha!" Bits of food flew across the table as the chief spoke. "A bigger industry indeed. How is it that you, who is held in such high esteem by George, are unaware of the importance of my trade in Augustria?"

Although this was more of an insult than a question, Trenson decided to interpret it as the latter. "Where I come from, spice wasn't as essential."

"As essential!" The chief repeated, with a horrified expression. "My, where is it that you come from? A cave? I can't imagine a civilization so depraved!"

Trenson felt his neck grow hot in anger, but he stifled the impulse to throw the contents of the plate at the man's face. "Faldon. Near the capital, Loronis."

"Ah!" he nodded, as if it all made sense now. Having just now finished swallowing the last of his bread, he proceeded to stuff another slice into his mouth. "I should have known."

Trenson scowled and stared at the man. Maybe this was Geoffrey's grand plan: to force him into a conversation with this man who had the character of a brick until he cracked and did something that would get him in trouble. If that was the case, then it was almost working.

"Allow me to expand upon what little knowledge you have," the administrator of spice began, as if someone had asked him to give a speech. "Spices, although it seems like a trifle, are an important part of not only cuisine, but trade. Like salt, it can give food flavor and preserve it. I do not carry out the trade on salt – that is conducted by the minister of salt."

The minister of salt? How many ministers and administrators are there? Trenson mused.

"Augustria is a booming economy for spices. In fact, twenty percent of the royal income comes from this simple source. Our men are hard at work in the fields, sowing and reaping the precious commodity. Without them, Augustria would not be what it is today."

Trenson nodded to show that he was still awake – barely. If there was one thing that made him doze off, it was a lecture on economy. He wasn't a numbers person – or a letters person, for that matter. He was an action person. In Loronis, he left that job to Jayfor.

The minister continued talking, but Trenson wasn't listening. After a few minutes, he discovered that the man didn't care if he didn't keep eye contact – he was talking to himself as much as he was Trenson. So Trenson turned around in his seat to watch the party.

There were a lot more people here now; the grounds were almost full. Like a giant sea of colorful outfits, everyone was laughing and moving and chatting. There were tall men, short men, fat men, skinny men, all sorts of men. There were women too, in long flowing dresses no less colorful, likely accompanying their husbands.

Each man had a brooch on his chest, and each brooch was different. The shape of the brooch often correlated with the status of its owner. For example, one brooch was the shape of an anvil, and judging by the wearer's barrel chest and big hands, Trenson would bet his life that the man was a blacksmith.

It's too bad I can't understand a word these people are saying, Trenson thought to himself. He was sure that there were so many things he could discover about this place by listening to the people's conversations.

Trenson turned to see Geoffrey and three other men approaching the table. All three of the men were young, probably the same age as Geoffrey. Judging by the clumsy way they all walked, it was clear that they had already started drinking the wine.

With a cheerful voice, Geoffrey motioned to Trenson and said a few words to his friends in Kallarian. The three young men laughed as if it were the funniest thing in the world. If Trenson was dramatic, he would have rolled his eyes, but since he wasn't, he just huffed in disgust.

The administer of spices stopped talking – a true miracle! – as he saw the three men approaching. He let his words drift into silence as he mumbled the last words of his sentence. He looked miffed that people would walk up and interrupt him, so he resumed eating his soup rather indignantly.

Geoffrey, with his suspiciously present grin, said a few words to Trenson – in Kallarian. As a result, Trenson hadn't the slightest clue what he was talking about. Trenson stared blankly at Geoffrey.

Geoffrey quickly realized his mistake. "Oh, that's right, you don't know the basic language!" He said, in Faldian. "Pardon me. Anyway, what was I doing? Oh yes, we wanted to invite you to partake in some games with us."

"Games?" Trenson asked.

"Ah, so you have ears, after all! Yes, games. After all, everyone else is having fun. Why not us? My friends and I, we want to see your skills in action. We have heard plenty about you. Now it's time for you to deliver!"

Trenson shifted uncomfortably in his seat. This wasn't what he had in mind. But did he have a choice? "What type of games?"

Geoffrey knew he had Trenson right where he wanted him. "Anything we choose! Come, join us!"

Trenson had no choice. Rising from his seat, he was led by Goeffrey and his friends into the crowd of people, his plain outfit soon lost in the swarm of colors.

The chief of spices wiped some soup off his mouth. "Hm. Rude."

***

Now it was Geoffrey's moment. Father was here, along with everyone else in the building. It was time to humiliate Trenson. That would teach him for taking father's attention.

Geoffrey was one of those people who was smart and immature at the same time. Meaning, he could recite math formulas all day. He had a knack for geometry that wowed his professors, and could recite poems in the ancient languages all day long. This was his "smart" side. However, he had a tendency to pout and complain, much like a young child. He had never outgrown his childish phase. He craved attention, and whatever he wanted, he usually got. Because of this, there was little punishment, and little reason for him to realize that acting immature wouldn't get him what he wanted – at least, not in the real world.

And so, because of this, it seemed perfectly logical to him that if he beat Trenson in a competition in front of Wulfric, Wulfric would then praise him and ignore Trenson. Obviously, these were high officials. They didn't hold one mistake over someone like that.

But Geoffrey did.

And so, with a cheery heart, he put his arm around Trenson's shoulder and led him into the crowd where people chatted, music played, and a riotous yet pleasant atmosphere hung over the area. Geoffrey had convinced his friends that he could beat Trenson in anything; they would serve as the witnesses.

So many options! There is juggling, ninepins, archery... I'm not sure what to choose! So many ways to beat him! It never crossed his mind that he could lose. It also didn't seem odd to Geoffrey that most of the time, his opponents would let him win so as to avoid Geoffrey's inevitable wrath.

It must be something not too hard, but not too easy. Something that requires a moderate level of skill. Juggling is out of the question – I doubt Trenson knows how to do it. Ninepins is a frivolous game; it needs to be more manly. Archery is a good option, but I do not want to wait in line that long.

Things were starting to get awkward. Geoffrey was leading all of them in a straight line with no clear direction, and his friends were starting to figure it out. He needed to choose something fast.

Then he saw it: the perfect activity.

It was relatively difficult, but not so much that someone with no experience couldn't do it. It was slightly out of the ordinary. It was considered a masculine ability to do. Finally, it was close to Wulfric, who was talking with several other officials nearby, in perfect view of the game that Geoffrey was certain he could crush Trenson in.

Knife throwing.

Already grinning in anticipation of his victory, Geoffrey led his friends and Trenson to the throwing area. No one else was here, which made things all the better. A table stood about eight yards away from the target, a circular tree stump. A three-sided box around the target, with the walls extending from the stump to the table, ensured that nobody behind or around the game would be hurt.

On the table were an assortment of knives, arranged in stacks, making a few dozen in total. They were rather cheap, Geoffrey thought, but they would do the job.

"Tell me, Trenson, have you ever thrown knives before?" Geoffrey asked casually, picking up a knife and flipping it in the air before catching it again. It was a trick designed to intimidate Trenson.

Surprisingly, Trenson didn't seem intimidated at all. "A few times," he said.

"Are you good?" one of Geoffrey's friends asked.

Trenson shrugged. "I don't know who to compare myself to."

Which just means he's scared to admit he stinks. "Let's see for ourselves. I shall go first. We will go in order, first me, then Trenson, and so on. Three throws each. The highest score wins."

As everyone else backed up a few paces, Geoffrey grabbed a knife. Rather light, and heavy in the blade. But it would manage. The stump had many circles painted on it, getting smaller as they came closer to the center. Inside each circle was a number from one to ten. The symbol for ten was written directly on the bullseye. That was where he aimed.

Taking deep breaths to steady himself, he preformed several mock throws, pulling the knife back each time. Narrowing his eyes, he pulled his arm back, then slung it forward, whipping his wrist forward and sending the knife cartwheeling through the air...

It stuck itself into the number three circle.

His neck turned red. Embarrassment. He heard a few snickers from behind him. He whipped his head around and tried to locate the source of it, but his friends conveniently looked away at the same time, probably hiding their smiles. Except Trenson. He was smirking while staring back at Geoffrey.

Geoffrey gritted his teeth and uttered an oath under his breath. Then he looked behind Trenson and noticed that his father was watching him. Geoffrey's heart sank. Wulfric looked at him, then at the target. His father frowned deeper as he looked back at him, then continued talking to his official.

Great job making an impression.

He wouldn't let it happen again. Grabbing another knife, he quickly threw it forward without any preparation. His reasoning was that if he didn't pause, there would be no time to overthink it.

And it must have worked, for his next knife sunk into the wood within the number 8 circle.

The embarrassment slowly fading, he picked up another knife and threw it the same way, adjusting from how he had thrown it last time. A 9. A final score of 20.

Not bad. Not as impressive as he had hoped, but he hadn't thrown knives in a while, so it was still good. It was better than everyone else would do. He heard the groans of his friends behind him when he threw the 9, which caused him to smirk as he turned around to face them. He shrugged good-naturedly.

"Not bad; it's better than nothing. It's your turn now, Trenson."

Not bothering to go retrieve his knives, Geoffrey stepped back from the table and motioned with his arms that the table was all his.

Silently, Trenson walked up to the table and picked up one of the knives. He looked up at the target and performed a few mock throws, just like Geoffrey did. Geoffrey was slightly impressed with the practice throws; his form was better than he anticipated. *Still, that doesn't mean he can hit the target.*

Trenson cocked his arm back and, calmly, smoothly, like poetry in motion, his arm came forward, the knife somersaulted toward the stump, striking the target and embedding itself in the wood.

Nine points. Right next to Geoffrey's highest scoring knife.

Geoffrey was shocked. How in the world did a former slave manage to hit so close to the bullseye? *No, no, don't overthink it. He simply got lucky. Even a blind squirrel finds a nut every once in a while. We will see how his luck holds out.* Calming himself down, he instead attempted to show enthusiasm. "Great throw, Trenson!"

His friends uttered wows and amazement. Geoffrey currently wanted to punch them in the face and knock their smile off, but resisted the urge.

Trenson didn't seem too impressed with himself. He grabbed another knife from the table and did several more practice throws. *Let's see if he's lucky enough to hit the target.* Geoffrey had no idea that Trenson had spent the last several days practicing his knife throwing at this exact range.

Thunk! Bullseye.

Now Geoffrey was really stunned. Blind squirrels rarely, if ever, find two nuts at the same time. This was starting to become worrisome. Geoffrey felt the back of his neck turn red again. This could be bad. Really bad. He was starting to kick himself for not choosing another activity. He gritted his teeth and didn't even attempt a smile. Luckily, his friends were too busy gawking at Trenson's throw to notice.

Trenson didn't seem surprised at his throw. Instead, he simply grabbed another knife from the table. He didn't need to practice throw this time. With the same calm demeanor, he sent the knife toward the target.

Instead of the solid bass noise of the knife hitting the wood, the knife made a sharp crack when it hit its target. That was because it hit the bullseye again, but since there was no room for the knife to go, it struck the back of the knife already there. The blade fell to the ground.

There was a stunned silence. Geoffrey's friends looked at Trenson in amazement. One point away from a perfect score was unheard of. Not even the best in the army could do that. And Trenson turned around and met them with a gaze that said: *yes, I did that. And I can do it again if you would like.*

"Trenson, that's incredible!" one of Geoffrey's friends broke the silence.

"Where did you learn to do that?" another asked.

Trenson shrugged. "An old friend taught me."

"With skills like that, why aren't you in a higher position?"

Geoffrey's fists tightened. He was about to say something – something he probably would have regretted – when he heard a voice approaching from behind that made his freeze.

"I say, that was rather uncalled for, wasn't it?" Wulfric.

Trenson met eyes with his captain and bowed respectfully, but didn't respond. Geoffrey's friends all bowed low at the sudden appearance of their lord. Geoffrey didn't bow.

Wulfric continued. His outfit, a blend of rustic and modern, combining animal furs with fine material, was much more interesting to look at than his face. "I had no idea you were also deft with knives." He looked at the target again. "I saw you hit the bullseye. Twice." He looked back at Trenson. "That is something I have not seen before. Not at that range, anyway."

"I practice daily," Trenson said plainly.

Wulfric nodded. "I have no doubt. Well, don't let me interrupt your frivolities. Consider me an impressed onlooker who merely gave his opinion. Carry on." And with that, along with bows from everyone, he turned and walked away, merging into the crowd.

The eyes of Geoffrey's friends soon landed back on Trenson. "Even our lord sees your skill!" one said.

"He does not speak often, let alone show praise for a sergeant!" another said.

Trenson simply shrugged again. There was faint grin on his lips, which showed that even though he kept a stony appearance, he was inwardly proud. "I think I just got lucky."

All three of them shook their heads. "I think not. I have a feeling that lord Wulfric will promote you after this!"

Trenson shook his head. "I don't think so."

"Don't doubt yourself! Anyway, whose turn is it now?" one of the friends asked. Then, looking around, he said, "Hey, where is Geoffrey?"

XXVII

THE NEXT FEW DAYS seemed normal. Nothing out of the ordinary happened, and Trenson went along with his usual routine. It was almost like the party never happened. He was a little worried that his coworkers would resent him, since he was the only one invited to the party, but thankfully, they either didn't know, or didn't show their knowledge.

Trenson was always watching his back, though. He knew that Geoffrey was probably plotting something.

He hadn't seen Geoffrey for the rest of the party, or the next few days, for that matter. He realized that he didn't have any real reason to suspect Geoffrey of anything. Although he had his suspicions, Geoffrey was nothing but friendly to Trenson. Trenson sensed it was all guise – his intuition told him. *Stay clear of Wulfric's son,* the inward voice said. There was no justification for this, but Trenson trusted his gut more than his reason.

Presumably, Geoffrey was pretty upset about losing. That was the only explanation for his sudden departure. Or maybe he had eaten some bad soup and had to use the outhouse at that exact moment? Unlikely.

But would Geoffrey retaliate from his embarrassing loss? That remained to be seen.

The first few days passed. Nothing. Trenson got up early, did his usual routine including breakfast, chores, and training – during which he talked little, if any, to anyone else. He didn't see anyone from the party, or Aquila, or Wulfric, and thankfully not the "chief of spice" he met at the table. It was peaceful.

It remained that way for only three days.

***

It was the almost evening on the third day. Trenson was doing one of his least favorite activities, washing dishes. After submerging the dishes in a bucket of water, he took a brush and scrubbed the insides of the pan, attacking the stains until they finally came off. After he finished one pan, he moved on to the next. The water soon had crusty pieces floating in it that had been brushed off.

The sound of footsteps behind him broke his rhythm. He was surprised. These weren't the light footsteps of a chef, nor the quick steps of a servant. These were heavy, brisk. A heavy boot must be making the noise. The boot of a soldier.

Trenson turned around to see three sergeants, people that he worked alongside but never spoke to, entering the kitchen. They stopped and locked eyes with Trenson. Trenson stopped his work and raised an eyebrow at them. What were they doing here?

Their expressionless faces gave no answer. Then Trenson saw that each of them had a small knife in their right hand.

Trenson jumped up from his stool and backed away a few paces, still holding the dripping pan in his hand. Was he being attacked? What was going on?

The men glanced at each other. Then one of them spoke, in Faldian. His accent heavily infected his words. "You are under arrest, Trenson. Please do not resist. You will learn more later."

The words were clunky. Obviously, this man had not been learning Faldian for long.

Trenson still didn't know what to make of this. "Arrested? For what?"

"You can appall when you are brought to our master." The same man said.

Trenson frowned. "Appall?"

"Um, er... What is the word? Apple?"

"I think you mean appeal."

"Ah yes, thank you, appeal. You can appeal when you are brought to our master. Until then, do not resist, or you will face more problems."

With that, all three men started walking to Trenson. Trenson's first instinct was to fight. He could probably do some serious damage with the pan in his hand. But that would be futile. More would come. He couldn't fight every soldier here, much less escape.

And he didn't do anything wrong. Maybe they had the wrong person? In any case, it was useless to act guilty when he didn't even know what the charges were.

So he let one of the men place a hand on his shoulder and, one man in front of him while the other two were behind him, lead him out of the kitchen. The men didn't sheath their knives.

Trenson had a feeling he knew where he was being taken, and his suspicions proved correct. When they stopped in front of the door, one of the men knocked three times.

"Enter."

The man pushed the door open, and Trenson was led into the room. It was exactly the same as when Trenson was here a few months ago: the wall were still a dull color, the wolf skins still hung on the wall, trophies and trinkets were still arranged on a shelf against one wall. And the same steaming pot of coffee was on the desk, beside the mug.

And the same stoic, frowning captain was sitting behind the desk.

Trenson made it a few paces into the office, still held in the iron grip of the sergeant, before everyone stopped before the desk. Wulfric sat there. He had his right foot propped up against his left knee. He didn't look happy.

"There he is, the man of the hour."

His voice wasn't happy either.

Trenson didn't speak. He didn't know what to say. One wrong word and he could be convicted of something he didn't do. He just kept his eyes on Wulfric, and maintained a calm expression.

"Pride is a funny thing, isn't it?" Wulfric said, in a casual tone – a forced casual tone. "Is it not? You would know. You act like you don't know. But you do. Pride isn't a vice, despite what people say. Pride is like a sword. It is a tool, a tool of either purpose, or downfall. It depends on which side of the sword you're standing."

How inspirational, Trenson thought.

Wulfric continued. "We make a choice which side to stand on. Is there a wrong side to stand on? Depends."

Wulfric paused. Trenson waited for him to resume, but Wulfric kept waiting, kept staring at Trenson. Trenson realized that the captain was prompting him to contribute to the conversation. Trenson inwardly sighed. "Depends on what?"

"Depends on how ambitious you are. What you want to achieve. How wise you are. Like I said, pride is neither vice nor virtue. It is simply a tool, and a powerful one at that. Pride leads to ambition, ambition leads to action."

He picked his right foot off his knee and set it on the floor, then crossed his arms. "Something like a promotion gives someone more pride. Attention. Admiration. Whatever you call it, that pride can have an effect on them. Sometimes, that pride can encourage them to work harder. To be encouraged in what they do. Or... it can give them, as the phrase goes, a big head. They start to think they are better than everyone else. They get ahead of themselves. Their ambition doesn't fuel them, it blinds them. That is when you are on the downfall side of the sword."

Trenson was tired of this verbal sparring. "What is your point?" He wished the sergeant would loosen his grip on his arm. His fingers were starting to tingle from lack of circulation.

"You would know better than the rest of us," Wulfric answered smoothly. He uncrossed his arms and reached under his desk and set something on the table. Trenson frowned when he saw it.

It was a pack. The type that travelers would carry when on long journeys. It was different from a satchel in the fact that it held more and was strapped to the wearer's back. This was a nice backpack, with leather straps and multiple pockets lining the back. This was for someone that was traveling a long way.

Strangely, the bag looked full.

Trenson eyed Wulfric, curious as to what this bag had to do with anything.

"Yesterday, a few things were missing around the place. It's not unusual for things to go unaccounted for around here, but the qualifications of the items were no coincidence. Food, specifically non-perishable; cooking utensils; maps and compasses; enough money to survive for months – all these items stolen last night."

Wulfric shook his head. He was mad. That much Trenson could tell. His tone never showed it, though. "I honestly have no idea how you pulled it off. Our security must be worse than I thought. I need to remedy that."

It didn't take a genius to piece together what Trenson was being accused of. "You think I did it," he concluded.

Wulfric spread his arms apart. "Well, unless someone decided to stash the supplies under your bed for safekeeping, yes, that is exactly what I think. And you stand before me guilty, caught red-handed. There isn't even anything you could say that would convince me otherwise."

Wulfric slowly rose from his seat. His mouth was set in a firm line. "What say you to that?"

Trenson stared back. "You want me to tell the truth?"

"I will not accept anything else."

"Then I will: I do not know why that was there."

"And still, you lie to my face."

"You don't trust me?"

"Why should I?"

"Because it's the truth."

"Truth is relative," Wulfric said. "But this is beside the point. Realize, now, that I am putting more effort into your case than I do most people. Few are given the courtesy of speaking their case, and most of them are higher ranked than you. I am giving you the chance to defend yourself. And all you can give me are dim-witted excuses."

Trenson was already running through the possible explanations in his mind about why this had happened. The first thing that entered his mind was Geoffrey. He was the only one that would have held a grudge against him and had access to the cellar. It was the only explanation.

"Well?" Wulfric asked, his tone soft but dangerous.

He couldn't just plead guilty. That wouldn't help him, he would receive the same fate. He had already tried the truth. That worked great. So what else could he say? They found the bag stashed under his cot, so what excuse could he give that they would believe?

Nothing. There was nothing he could say that would help his case. So he remained silent.

Wulfric took that as the final evidence needed. He cleared his throat and straightened his posture. The angry body language that was like a boiling kettle, just waiting to explode, slowly fizzled out. His formal attitude regained, he looked at the guard holding Trenson by the wrist.

"It's the prison for him. And I don't mean the detention areas for prisoners here – we use those for people who will eventually return to work here. This man isn't returning. Take him to the local jail. Tell the warden I sent him. Tell him that he was found guilty of thievery and attempted rebellion. He shouldn't ask questions. He knows you."

The guard nodded and, without emotion, turned and forced Trenson towards the exit. Wulfric called after to the guard, "And when you're finished, return here. A higher position just opened up, one that I think you would be perfect for."

XXVIII

"So, this is the place?"

"This is the place."

"It's not what I was expecting."

"And what were you expecting?"

"Well... I'm not exactly sure. Nothing like this, though. Nothing so simple."

"In case you haven't noticed, we aren't exactly overflowing in resources here. We had to make do with what we had."

The two speakers were Ernest and Jayfor. They stood in a dimly lit room, with light coming only from small candles on the walls. It was chilly that night, and even though they were inside, Jayfor couldn't keep out the occasional chill that sent shivers down his spine.

This place is as dark as every other hideout of The Willing, Jayfor thought, noting the scanty amount of candles that hung on the walls. *I guess Ernest was being serious when he said they worked in the shadows.*

"It's usually closed and locked," Ernest said, referring to the small metal box open on the table in front of them. The box was small, about as long as his forearm. Inside was something small wrapped in a brown cloth. "As you can see, there are three keyholes. Three separate keys are needed to open it. On top of that, the box won't burn, and the metal is extremely durable and long lasting."

"I guess there's more security to this journal than I thought."

Ernest huffed. "Indeed." He approached the table and, taking great care, lifted the brown cloth from the box. Jayfor watched. When the cloth was lifted, a small journal was revealed. It was simple. Leather bound. Primitive, but complex at the same time. Almost like the creators of it knew how to make it more elaborate and fancier, but chose not to. The withering force of time only had a small effect on it, darkening the brown cover of the book and making the edges crispy.

"This is it?" Jayfor asked.

Ernest slowly turned and looked at Jayfor, blankly. That was one of the dumbest questions he had ever heard. Jayfor realized this all too late. His face reddened – good thing it was dark in here – and he cleared his throat. "Sorry."

Thankfully, Ernest forgave him. "Yes, this is it. This is the journal that was stolen from the archives during the great fire of Loronis. This is the diary that tells of the prophecy – if you believe it is indeed reliable."

Jayfor, who had seen his fair share of ancient artifacts, had to nod his head. "It's appearance certainly fits it claims. But just because something looks old, doesn't mean it is."

"Definitely. I mean, just look at me." Ernest said. Jayfor looked at him questioningly, wondering if he had just made a joke. Ernest's face didn't show any hint of mirth. Even his tone was even.

"Was that a joke?" Jayfor asked.

"No."

Well, there's my answer.

"Anyway, after we figured out what it was, we made sure to keep it a secret. Most of my comrades don't even know about this. Only a few of us know this secret, and even fewer have seen it.

Ernest sighed. "Novak wasn't supposed to know it either. If he hadn't been nosing around this base, he wouldn't have found out at all. The others were so mad, they said we should kick him out. But I defended him, like I have so many other times. I honestly don't know why I keep sticking up for him."

Jayfor didn't know if he was supposed to respond to this or not. Judging by the period of silence that followed, he assumed he was. "I don't know why either," he supplied, saying the only thing he could think of saying.

"He's a good man," Ernest responded. He seemed to be lost in his own thoughts. "He's as loyal and caring as any man I've ever had. Although we have our differences, he has heart. And heart is something that cannot be taught." Ernest frowned. "Why am I telling you this anyway?"

Jayfor shrugged. "You tell me." Judging by the embarrassment on Ernest's face, he saw that that leader didn't intend to open up like this. Jayfor broke the awkward silence by saying, "Can I read it?"

Ernest inhaled sharply through his teeth. "I don't know if even I have the authority to do that."

"Authority? You mean you're not the leader of this whole thing?"

"Of course not. The Willing have been fighting for longer than you've been alive. I simply joined the scene later."

"Huh. I always assumed you were the leader of the whole thing."

" 'Leader' is not exactly a rank in our group. We don't have a system for who is in charge. That doesn't mean that nobody is in control; it simply means that everyone listens to the person who is the most courageous, the most intelligent, and the wisest."

"And that isn't you?" Jayfor asked, sincerely.

Ernest huffed. "No."

The finality of the word made it clear that the topic was over.

"So to answer your question," Ernest said, "I could take it out. But I don't know if it's respectful to do so."

"Respectful to who, exactly?"

"My superiors."

"But you just said you don't have superiors. That everyone respects each other."

"I respect the more intelligent of our group *as if* they were my superiors."

"And you don't think they would let you open it?"

"No."

"Why?"

"Because they said we should avoid opening it, or else it could fall apart. It's an old book."

"I've handled old books. I've never broke one before."

"There's always a first time for everything." Ernest said.

"How about we compromise?" Jayfor proposed. "I'll just read it as it is, without taking it out."

Ernest looked like he was about to say no, then rethought it, then decided the answer was still no, then finally gave up. "Fine. Just be careful." He thought to himself, *he's starting to become all too much like Novak.*

With extreme care, knowing Ernest was right beside him ready to chastise him, Jayfor opened the cover of the book to the first page. The binding protested.

E tarth Mada posision.

Ancient letters leapt out of the pages. Jayfor recognized them at once: Origin. The original language of the world. All other languages derived from it. Today, it was a dead language. Only a few people could read it.

"Do you understand what it says?" Ernest asked.

If Jayfor wasn't so caught up in his own thoughts, he would have answered negative. Only scholars and some royalty knew how to read this language, and so it wouldn't make sense in his fabricated backstory for him to understand it. But he wasn't thinking about that, and automatically answered. "Yes. It's the original language of Ralladin. *The possession of Mada,* it reads. The writing style and the ink definitely check out with the time period of the early 50s. It's strange that he wouldn't put his title before his name."

If Ernest was surprised, he didn't show it. "Indeed. I wondered that myself. I assume it was because this was for his eyes only, and as such, there was no need for any regality."

Jayfor heard the words as if they were a long distance away. He turned a few more pages, being careful to listen for the sharp popping sound that would alert him if a page was coming out of its binding.

The writing was so neat – perfect, even. The letters spaced themselves evenly from each other, the construction of each letter was so fine that Jayfor guessed it would take him several hours just to churn out one paragraph. He had seen writing like this before; in the ancient textbooks in Loronis.

"The writing," Jayfor said, not thinking about feigning ignorance, "it matches with real documents from that time. See how each letter is evenly spaced, and the care that went into each word. It must have taken him days to write a single entry!"

"Ah, but in those days, the world was perfect. Mistakes were extremely rare, if not unheard of. Mada probably wrote even faster than you and I."

"I didn't even consider that. But it makes sense. Look at the date on this entry: *Year 47.* The translation doesn't quite do the text justice, but it roughly says, *"And so today, at the advice of Fanor, a shipment of apples from the orchards were delivered from Loronis to Tarsen, in exchange for iron and other metals, for although we are still abundant in such materials, our scientists are experimenting with the properties of such, to determine what abilities it may grant us. For the secrets of the world lay as a pearl on the shore, waiting to be discovered, drawing those who understand its true value."*

Ernest smiled, not asking the obvious question about how Jayfor was able to read the words so easily. "Poetry, is it not?"

Jayfor nodded. "The rest of this journal is just like it." He flipped more pages, spent a few moments pouring over them, then turned a few more. "Simple things, such as trade and festivals. Parties. New inventions." He sighed. "How different the world is today."

Ernest didn't reply.

Jayfor continued turning pages, the words of Mada flowing through his mind. His reading only quickened as his knowledge of the ancient language began to came back to him. He wanted to stay on one page and pour over its words, soaking in everything. On the other hand, he wanted to keep turning pages, to not miss out on anything. He settled somewhere in the middle.

It read like poetry – and Jayfor didn't even like poetry. So smooth. So easy to read. So simple. It was a record of people living normal lives. Happy lives. Nothing seemed to go wrong. But it wasn't boring, it was... pure. Suddenly Jayfor felt a longing to be in this world. It didn't seem real, that the world was once like this. But the names were real, the places were real, and the dates were real.

Then Jayfor turned another page...

And everything changed.

It was such a shock that Jayfor was thrown out of his trance, back into the real world. "What?"

Ernest's usual frown deepened. "That is the turning point. That's when everything got worse, after he opened the gates to the Mountain of power, and the world experienced pain."

Jayfor almost didn't want to read it. He knew what had happened, why the writing was distorted, wild, and raving. He knew why the tone of the journal suddenly changed. He knew why this was the end of the happy journal entries he had previously read.

Jayfor took a deep breath, and, steeling himself started reading.

Mad. Madness. That is what I'm going. I am going mad. Madness! I knew not this word existed until that day! THAT DAY!! Understand this – understand? What is there to understand? Noth-

ing! We are nothing! It is done! Finished! Understand that we, we fleeting piles of dust, us filthy piles of rotting flesh, rotting on our very bones! WE ARE NOTHING!

If the earlier entries in this journal were day, these were night. A dark night. Once the words had been flawlessly written; now they were ugly, in wild shapes. The tone of the words reminded Jayfor of a madman.

Then Jayfor realized that these *were* the words of a madman.

"This is…" Jayfor didn't know exactly how to describe it. "Sad."

"Sad? In what way?"

"It's ruined," Jayfor said softly. "This doesn't even sound like the same person. The writing is different. And look at these pages." He lightly ran his finger over the paper. "It's old, but I can tell that at one point, this paper was wet. Very wet. Maybe this was dropped in water at one point? But the pages before this are crisp, like nothing happened."

Jayfor turned the problem over in his mind. The entire page didn't show signs of being wet, it was only in a few spots. Maybe…

Then it dawned on him: Tears. Tears had fallen on the page.

"You've realized tears were on these pages, correct?" Once again, Ernest seemed to read his mind.

Jayfor silently nodded, at a loss for words.

There wasn't much left of the journal, only a few dozen more pages. Jayfor skimmed through them. Each sentence brought another level of despair and hopelessness. If this truly was Mada's journal, he lived the remainder of his life unhappily.

The handwriting only became worse, so bad that Jayfor had a hard time distinguishing the words. At this point, Mada was raving. Each entry was another three pages of Mada unleashing despair. He wrote of turmoil. Turmoil between the empire, which was now on the brink of civil war. Turmoil between the people, how they conspired against him and made attempts at his life. And the turmoil between him and his wife, how their relationship had deteriorated and worsened...

Then Jayfor flipped a page, and in much neater handwriting and more collected tone of writing, a few lines were written. Jayfor realized that it was a poem. This momentarily surprised him, but he kept reading.

Now, King of Shadows, proud and tall,
See the land which harkens to your call.
By treachery and deceit, through honey-soaked lies,
The land that was perfect has met its demise.
All life fades, the light grows dim,
Mired and trodden are the hearts of men,

Now, King of Shadows, proud and tall,
See the land which harkens to your call
And know, despite the power in your hold,
The torment we suffer, you shall suffer tenfold.
Bounding is your end, closer than you realize,
For coming a day, not far away, a Hero shall arise,

An offspring of mortals, He will enter our world
A beacon of light; Justice as his sword.
In vain you fight, King of shadows, proud and tall,

In vain to keep this land which harkens to your call,
The Hero falters, his flesh weary and tasting death,
But on you the jaws shall snap, you who meets doom.

On the day which tells of your fall
Many will rise and heed the call
To return to the light and leave the past,
For the world is renewed, at long last.

Now, King of Shadows, proud and tall,
See the land which harkens to your call,
Prepare your hosts, for approaching soon,
The Hero Himself, and with Him your doom.

Here the journal ended.

Jayfor flipped the page, expecting to find more, but there was nothing. Confused, he flipped another one, then another one, being more rough on the worn book than he should have. The pages were empty. There were twenty pages of blank paper.

No explanation for what happened later, what happened to the kingdom, anything. It was empty.

"We still don't know what happened in the later part of Mada's life."

Ernest's voice was like a clap of thunder in Jayfor's ears, shocking him from his trance. He shook his head, clearing the misty thoughts that gathered in his mind after reading the poem. He cleared his throat. "I don't think anyone does. Various theories exist. Some say Mada continued to rule Faldon until he died peacefully. Others say he went mad and fled the capital in a rage. Some even say he joined Elara and aligned himself with the darkness. There is so little information about that time that it's impossible to know for sure."

Ernest nodded. "He did end it on a rather abrupt note, didn't he? It's almost as if one day, he suddenly felt the need to write a song, and then get rid of the journal and think about it no more."

It seemed that way to Jayfor as well. "Speaking of the song, I see the mentions of the Hero. I assume that's where you get the prophecy?"

"Yes."

A blanket of silence settled over the two men. There wasn't much to say. Ernest wasn't much of a talker, so if anyone were to break the silence, it would be Jayfor. But Jayfor was deep in thought, thinking about what he had read. This certainly changed his perception of the old records. Now he had no doubt that this was, indeed, Mada's journal. No amount of forgery could make something that accurate. *Call me a fool, but this diary checks all the boxes.*

Jayfor took a few steps back. "I'm ready. I have seen enough."

XXIX

THE STRANGE PART ABOUT this dream was the fact that Trenson knew he was dreaming.

He knew immediately when he suddenly appeared on the edge of a forest. It was so obvious. He was young. Eight years old. Or was he nine? He couldn't remember. Not like it mattered.

In any case, he knew he was dreaming because he was looking at his house. His old house. The house he grew up in. The old cabin that his great-great-grandfather had made decades ago. It was old, and some parts of the outside were rotting – mainly the corners.

There was a faint breeze blowing, causing the leaves above him to rustle. He hadn't heard that sound in a long time. He realized that he could actually feel the wind on his skin, which was unusual for a dream. Beyond the house, he saw the hundreds of rows of barley and other crops, growing diligently and swaying in time.

It's so peaceful.

Then he heard the scream, and his heart dropped. His heart rate quickened. His breath became shallow. Beads of sweat built on his forehead – sweat? Could he feel sweat in a dream?

He knew what was happening. This was no dream. It was a nightmare.

His family was about to be slaughtered.

He didn't want to be in this dream. He shook his head, wondering how he could wake up. He slapped himself in the face. Instead of waking up, pain shot through his cheek – pain that was all too real. He tried pinching himself on his right forearm. Once again, the sharp sting of pain shot jolted him, but he didn't wake up.

Why isn't this working?! He was in a frenzy now. He knew what was about to unfold in front of him. He had replayed it in his mind thousands of times. He had spent years pushing those memories and those emotions into the farthest corner of his mind.

A man exited the front door of the cabin. It was one of the criminals. Although most aspects of this dream were crystal clear, the features and general appearance of this man were blurry. Trenson wondered why this was, then realized it was because he didn't remember exactly what the bandits looked like.

A few more men came out of the cabin. All of them were blurry as well. Another scream came from inside the house. The pain already beginning to come down him, he tried to run forward, to knock out some of the ruffians, to save his family, to do *something*. But he found his feet wouldn't move. He was stuck to the ground.

More men emerged from the house, and they dragged people out with them. People that Trenson instantly recognized, who weren't indistinct or hard to see at all. These people were some of the clearest things that Trenson could see. He wanted to close his eyes, but he couldn't. Not even his eyes would do what he wanted.

He saw his mother, her short and slim figure dominated by the man dragging her on the ground by her wrist. She was crying. Trenson saw his father, although a sizeable man, bruised and battered, the black and blue patches on his face covering where his dark beard wasn't. His expression was broken. He saw his brother, his frail form and short brown hair. He was crying.

Trenson wouldn't allow his brain to process what he was seeing. It was his last line of defense. He had no choice but to watch the scene before him, but he tried with all his will to not focus on it. He tried to let his mind wander, his eyes go out of focus.

It didn't help.

The men held his family while more men emerged from the house, carrying various items. An expensive plate of pewter. A necklace. Agriculture tools in good condition. Anything that was worth anything was taken outside.

His mother and brother were still crying, but Trenson's father decided he had enough. With renewed strength, he shook off the grip of the men holding him. He kicked one man in the knee, knocking the man down with a cry of pain. He turned to the other and brought a savage right hook into his jaw, spinning him to the ground.

Now the group was angry. Cursing, they gathered around him. Trenson's mother and brother screamed at him to run, while he had the chance, to go get help. But Trenson's father was in a rage, and could think of nothing else besides avenging this crime and freeing his family. A brave course of action.

But also foolish.

He had no sooner broken free from his captors and recovered his balance, that a spear came from behind.

It went through his chest without a sound.

"*NO!*" Trenson screamed. Time froze. He tried to move, but couldn't. The gaping faces of his brother and mother screamed, but no sound came out. They were frozen, as was everything else, suspended in this pivotal moment which would go on the haunt Trenson for the rest of his life.

The sky started to turn red. Everything grew darker. Trenson felt the ground start to shake, and he stumble to recover his balance, then realized he could move. Before he could run forward to his family, the ground crumbled underneath his feet.

He fell backwards, backwards in nothingness. He screamed in anger and terror, and his own voice rang in his ears. He kept falling and falling and falling, the world around him becoming darker and darker, the wind around him swirling harder and harder until –

He woke from the terrible nightmare, still screaming.

"Shut up! If you don't, I'll sew it shut! Shut up!"

When Trenson jolted back to reality, the first thing he noticed was that he was still screaming. He quickly closed his mouth, but then opened it again as he started panting. He was covered in sweat. His heart pounded in his ears.

"Thank the sun he's stopped. I'll personally break his jaw if that nonsense ever starts again."

The voice of one of the prison guards was loud enough to be heard over his throbbing heart. Trenson stared up at the stone room overhead. He tried taking deep breaths. Now that his heart rate started to lower, he realized that his blanket was now soaked in sweat, and he was freezing cold.

His teeth starting to chatter, Trenson sat up on his bed – bed? There was no bed. He was sleeping on the floor. The ground was made of stone as well, and as he sat up, he felt his back cracked. He inhaled sharply and stretched his arms above his head. His back continued popping. *I must be getting old.*

He looked around. Everything was dark, but his night vision allowed him to see most things in the room. Not that there was much to see. A square room with three walls, each wall containing a window. Two windows allowed him to hear his fellow inmates snoring in the cells beside his own. One showed a barred view of the outside street and city, although the window was currently covered by a curtain to keep the cold out.

There was no fourth wall. It was simply bars, with a door made of the same in the middle. It was through these bars that Trenson saw one of the guards, who was cursing him, walk out of sight. He was carrying a lantern, and the light grew fainter and eventually disappeared as he left.

He's certainly a cheerful fellow, Trenson mumbled.

He had no idea what time it was, but he did know it was late. Moonlight illuminated the curtain that draped over the window. It did a pitiful job of retaining the warmth in the room. It was freezing outside, and Trenson would have preferred that there be no window. At least there wouldn't be that chilly breeze that made his bones feel like ice.

He slowly pushed the blanket off him and stood up. He was surprised at how tired his legs were. He felt fatigued as though he had just finished running for miles. That was a strange side effect for a dream.

He walked over to the window. He was just tall enough that he could peer over the bottom once he had lifted the thin curtain. Immediately a bone-chilling breeze whirled in his face, making his teeth chatter. Strangely, he was glad for the cold, and it gave him something to focus on.

He saw the streets of Augustria. Barren. It was empty. The roads finally had a break from being trampled on all day. Squares of light shone on the ground, cast from the windows of adjacent houses. These houses had glass windows. In some places Trenson had been, glass was considered a luxury. For it to be common enough to be used as windows testified of the richness of the city.

Trenson noticed a large, dark shape over the roofs of the houses. Curious, he focused on the dark shape and tried to adjust his eyes to see better in the shadows. *Mountains,* he finally concluded. There were mountains far in the distance, beyond the city walls. He wondered why he didn't notice them before.

Not that it mattered.

His nose was beginning to feel like an icicle. He decided he had seen enough of the outside. He let the curtain fall back down and stepped back from the window.

Now that his heart rate was lower, he realized how cold he was, mainly his feet – apparently shoes were too deadly for prisoners to wear. His sweat, which his body released in an effort to keep him cool, was now freezing and sucked the warmth out of him. The plain prison clothes he was given weren't enough to keep him warm.

He shivered. Grabbing the blanket, he laid down on the ground once again. Covering himself with the inadequate cloth, he pulled his feet in close and tried to retain his body warmth. He was dead tired now and wanted to sleep again, but the cold was making it difficult.

What should I do now? I wanted to rid myself of Wulfric's guard anyway, but this isn't what I planned. This is much harder to escape. I guess Geoffrey did help a little, but I'm not sure I'm better off.

Geoffrey. Now that was someone Trenson could easily hate. Trenson couldn't stand that Geoffrey was pitiful enough to frame him for a crime just because Trenson threatened his image. That boy wouldn't get anywhere in life. What a sorry excuse for a son.

Anger wouldn't help him here. Trenson shifted his focus to escape once again. How long ago was it that he had been made a slave? How long ago was it that Jayfor had died, and those bandits sold him? Months?

It didn't matter. He needed to escape. He would need to find his way out of the prison, to attain some gear and supplies fit for travel, make it out of the city, and head north. He needed to continue the mission. Head north to the great tree of Ramadus. His quest hadn't changed.

Then another thought hit him: his sword. He would also need to get his sword back. He was lucky enough that it ended up at Wulfric's, but he would need it back before he left the city. Did that mean he would have to break into Wulfric's barracks to retrieve it? That would make things even more difficult.

He sighed. As the heavy hand of sleep started to overtake him, he wondered what caused him to have such a violent nightmare. He had not dreamed of his family in years. And certainly, the dreams had never been that dark and realistic.

I wonder what would have been different if that didn't happen. I wondered if I would inherit the property, farm the land, and raise a family like my father. I wonder... if I would have been happy.

<u>XXX</u>

*T*HREE WEEKS LATER.

Before Thrance screamed that morning, everything was normal.

Thrance, the king of Augustria, had a tendency to sleep in, and so even before he screamed, all the staff and attendants were already up and starting their day. The chefs that prepared everyone's breakfasts were awake even before them. The secretaries had already sorted out their work and planned the day's schedule, determining what civil service works needed to be addressed. In fact, today was another ordinary day. Augustria wasn't exactly an "exciting" city – that is, there weren't many riots or dangerous criminals to worry about.

It wasn't until Thrance yelled – with much more gusto than most had ever heard in his voice – that everyone in earshot snapped to attention.

The guards outside the doors were the first to react, since they were the closest. Startled by the sudden noise, they looked at each other, making sure they weren't imagining it. Then they quickly opened the door to the room, expecting the worst.

What they expected to find inside, wasn't there. It was simply Thrance, standing in his sleeping garbs – his silk and very expensive sleeping garbs – his mouth agape as he stared at the wall.

It was a nice room, without a doubt. And the king of Augustria would have expected nothing less. There were a few paintings hung on the wall – the king had a strong taste in paintings, especially abstract works of art that didn't look much like anything. A desk was in the room, a rather large one, with various papers and inkwells strewn across it. The bed took up a large part of the room, the largest part in fact. The wood was imported from a city that was a hundred miles away. It was likely the most expensive as well.

It was beside this bed, with its rumpled sheets, that king Thrance stood, in his sleeping attire. Thrance was tall and skinny, with a beard that came down to a point a few inches below his chin. He wasn't muscular, but he had an air of importance about him that commanded authority. He was in his later years, causing his hair, which was always unkempt and wavy, to have streaks of gray through the otherwise blonde strands.

The guards forsook the usual bow they had to do when entering the king's presence, instead scanning the room for threats.

"My Lord! We heard your scream! What is the matter?"

Thrance snapped out of his coma and looked at the guards. "Someone has been in my room! Look!"

He pointed at the wall. The guards looked and saw what caused all the commotion: There was something written on the wall. Although too far to read, the guards clearly saw neatly written words in the middle of the freshly painted wall. Like someone had come in the middle of the night and written on it with ink.

The guards, realizing that nothing dire was happening, relaxed. "My Lord, we feared for your life."

Thrance waved his hand. "Nothing of that sort. But I may have to fear for my life now."

"Have you inspected these words? What do they say?"

"I have not," Thrance replied, growing more relaxed. "I only woke up a few moments ago. I saw the words and called for help before taking further action."

Before thinking it through, one guard asked, "You screamed when you saw words?" He instantly realized how insulting this sounded and cringed.

Thrance frowned and stared at the soldier, who refused to look him in the eye. "I didn't scream. I called for help," he said firmly.

Not exactly, the other guard thought. He broke the tension in the room by saying, "We should take a look."

The friction somewhat resolved, all three men walked to the wall. Thrance made sure to stay a few paces behind the guards, figuring it safer that they inspect it first – it might be a trap.

"What under the sun is this?" one guard said when he stopped a few paces from the wall and squinted at the words.

At this point, more soldiers and personnel were entering the room – Thrance had screamed loud enough for quite a few people to hear. Six knights, three servants and one chef, who had no reason to be there except curiosity, soon rushed into the room, expecting the worst. But they all stopped short when they saw the king, safe and sound, staring at something on the wall.

Thrance didn't notice the arrival of more people in the room. "Is it in Kallarian? I can't read it."

One of the guards shook his head. "No, I don't think so. These are letters I have never seen before." The guard noticed the people standing uncertainly at the door. "It's a message," he said, "written on the wall."

Before long, everyone was gathered around, staring at the symbols on the wall. It was a message of some type, written in a few sentences. But the letters were a peculiar shape that no one had seen before.

"It's not that it's a different language," one servant said. "It's that this is an entirely different writing system!"

Everyone else nodded their agreement.

"I have been told that some languages use a different form of writing," Thrance said.

A secretary answered, "Yes, my Lord, there are a few that do. Perhaps that is the reason."

"Well then, get a translator or someone in here! I want to know what it says!" Thrance snapped.

The next few moments were a flurry of activity. Some people rushed out in search of the translator, while others, realizing they weren't supposed to be there, uncomfortably left the room. Some people stayed, however, spending time trying to decipher the words. Thrance thought about dismissing them, since they were annoying. But he might as well give them the chance. After giving them a few minutes, he got fed up with them and kicked them out.

"Get out of here! Make yourselves useful and search the place. The person who wrote this might still be here!"

Most everyone cleared out of the room. Some guards stayed and proceeded to look in the closets and under the bed, searching for more clues or, maybe if they were lucky, the culprit.

"My Lord," one soldier said, "it's possible that the criminal might be one of our own. In which case, we're not going to find him."

Thrance quickly answered, "I know," even though he didn't. He just wanted to seem like there was no possibility he hadn't thought of. "But who has access to my room?"

"Well, I believe that since your room is guarded at night, it wouldn't make a difference. You're the only one that bears the key to your own room, anyway."

"I wasn't asking you, fool! I was simply thinking out loud. Of course my room is guarded, and I'm the only one that has the key. Perhaps someone snuck in during the day to hide? And perhaps they are deft with lock picks. Either way, I want everyone questioned. Everyone."

The soldier nodded. "Yes, my lord." He thought it wise not to point out the fact that there were thousands of people employed in the palace. *He can address this himself later,* he mused as he ran out of the room to give the order to someone of higher rank.

Finally, the translator arrived. A bald man with a beard and a tendency to overeat, he wore glasses that he insisted were made by the craftsmen of lower Faldon. "My lord, I was told something unusual has happened?" he said as he walked through the door, adjusting his glasses.

"Indeed. Get over here and tell me what this says," he snapped.

Puzzled, the translator approached the wall where Thrance stood and immediately noticed the writing on the wall. "Oh my."

"What?" Thrance said, fear leaking through his words. "Is it a death threat?"

The translator leaned forward to get a closer look and squinted. There was really no need to do so, however, since the words were rather large. "No, no, nothing of that sort. I just don't recognize these words." He quickly added, "Of course, I can probably decipher them if I have enough time."

Thrance relaxed. "How much time will you need to analyze before figuring it out?"

The translator straightened, then shrugged. "Probably half an hour, at least."

"Well then, this can wait. I need to don some appropriate clothes before we go any further. And the rest of you, get out of here while I change!" the king addressed the knights, who were still searching the room. "Hey, don't you dare touch that sculpture. I don't care if anyone is hiding behind it, it has more value than your life!"

After Thrance changed, he let the translator come back in and take another look at it.

"Well? You've spent enough time fidgeting with them, you should at least have an idea of what it says?" Thrance snapped.

The translator took off his glasses and wiped them on his coat, letting out an exasperated breath through his teeth. "I have learned a lot, to be certain. But I still have not the slightest clue what it says."

Thrance wasn't happy. "I appreciate you wasting an hour of my time! And here I thought you knew every language under the sun. Turns out I was wrong!"

"That is impossible, my Lord. Anyone who claims such a thing is trying to sell something," the translator replied smoothly. "I was able to gather some information about the words, however, based on their shape and structure."

Thrance calmed down and listened.

"You see, systems of writing are very similar to family trees and generational traits. You can trace the origins of someone through their family tree, all connecting to common roots. The traits become muddled as time goes on, making things more difficult, but not impossible. Likewise, writing systems develop changes over time, colliding with others and changing. I have studied the origin of writing systems as well as the languages they belong to, and well... I believe that this is something else entirely."

"What do you mean by that?"

"I mean that this may be a completely different tree. All writing systems and languages derive from the singular "common," which was used at the beginning of the world. We can trace the patterns and style of different cultures' alphabet to this common language. Only this writing seems to bear no connection at all to anything, either modern or ancient."

Thrance stared at the words and thought about it for a few moments. *So basically, it's too complicated for him.* Now that he thought about it, it was strange how the symbols were written. Some were connected to each other, while others were larger or smaller. Some were even on top of each other.

"Nonetheless," Thrance retorted, "it is your *only* job to be able to understand this." He walked away from the wall, trying to act indifferent to the situation. "I shall give you a few more hours while I attend to some business. If you can't figure it out by then, I don't see why you should feel qualified to bear a role in my house."

The translator smiled and bowed. "There's no need to wait, for I can confidently say I will not be able to decipher it."

Thrance stopped and turned on his heel, struck by the old man's boldness. He made sure not to show any signs of it. "Then leave."

<u>XXXI</u>

J AYFOR TOOK A DEEP breath, feeling the icy air churn in his lungs, causing him to shiver. He let it out and watched the mist as it was swept quickly away by the breeze. The forecast today was much like it had been for the past weeks: cold, cloudy, and windy. Was winter always like this in Augustria? It was the definition of gloom.

He sat on a bench by the road. At least Augustria had one good thing about it: they built benches along the sidewalks at intervals. Jayfor wondered why they did this. What good do they do? You can sit on them and... then what? Watch people walk down the street? When he was the king, he was always looking for innovative ways to improve. But he couldn't see the benefit of benches lining the street.

And yet, here I am, using one.

It was a nice bench, comfortable to sit on. It made it more enjoyable to watch the people as they passed by. People in Augustria were shorter than most people in Faldon. Jayfor wasn't tall, and so he felt a sense of pride finally seeing people shorter than him. He wondered if this is what it felt like to be tall. It was a nice feeling.

He then remembered Trenson, and the nice feeling went away. Trenson. A day didn't go by that he didn't think about him. He wondered where he was, how he was doing. If he was still alive. Was he still a slave? Or even still in the city? Time and time again he had asked Ernest about it, but the captain of the Willing simply shrugged.

"I'm doing my best, Conrad. We're stretched short, and I don't have the time to send many men on scouting patrols."

Jayfor frowned, clenching his fists. "You know the only reason I agreed to help you was to find my friend. That was the deal. You get me into Augustria and find him, and I'll do whatever I can to help your cause in exchange. But time is passing quickly, and while I've taken many risks for you, you can't seem to turn up a single clue. It's been weeks, Ernest! I don't have time to waste!"

For a long time Jayfor had held back, fearing that saying something would destroy the finely held alliance between them. But he was getting tired of waiting.

He still had to get to the Tree of Ramadas – is that what the Senver called it? It was so long ago Jayfor had a hard time remembering it. He had trouble recalling the name, but he remembered the instructions well: travel north until you reach it. You'll know when you get there.

Well, Jayfor had traveled north a good bit to begin with. But after their run-in with the brigands, he had chased Trenson to the west for a while, and now he was going nowhere. He had stopped making progress in the journey. He probably could have made it to the tree by now.

Was it important that he reach the tree soon? Did the tree carry some secret?

He wouldn't know until he found it. But first, he had to free Trenson!

"I know what we agreed to," Ernest replied calmly, "and I promise you I have been doing my best."

"Well, your promises haven't done anything to free him, or even get a general direction on where he is. In fact, it's possible that he could have left the city, and that I have no need to be here anymore!"

"Highly unlikely. I have men set at all entrances of the city, watching everyone who enters and leave. They haven't seen anyone, including slaves, who matches your description of your friend."

"Men make mistakes," Jayfor shot back.

"True. But your friend is a foreigner around here. He would stand out, based on his appearance."

Jayfor sighed and ran his fingers through his sand-colored hair. "Listen, Ernest, I know what you do is good, and don't get me wrong, I have helped many people by joining you. But I have my own agenda. Helping you isn't my goal. I have my own. And my friend is required for that goal. So, unless you start gathering some evidence in the next few weeks, I'm finding him myself, and you'll need someone else to play as your sidekick."

While Ernest simply gave a nod in reply, Jayfor noticed that he seemed to take the words more seriously this time. After that, Jayfor caught glimpses of him talking to people from different hideouts, and asking if they had seen anyone that matched Trenson's description. This comforted Jayfor to some degree, but not much.

Every day he wasted, was a day that something terrible could happen to Trenson. He was torn between using their help in numbers for scouting but risking them passing over Trenson, or trying to find him on his own but without covering much ground.

"Someone is deep in the thought."

Jayfor knew the cheery voice before he looked up and knew it belonged to Novak. The Willing was standing beside the bench with his head to one side, as if he had been studying Jayfor for some time. He probably had, knowing Novak. And, of course, he had that ever-present grin on his face.

"And someone has been spying on me," Jayfor replied, not mirroring the smile.

" 'Spying' is a rather strong word, don't you think? Reserved for the enemy. I was casually observing you without your knowledge."

Jayfor grunted, then realized that by doing so, he had used one of Trenson's favorite replies. This didn't put him in any better of a mood.

"Well, let's get to work!" Novak declared, slapping his gloved hands together. "Off your lazy bum. Time to go meet our contact."

"Who are you calling lazy? I'm the one that had to sit here and wait for you – thanks for being late, by the way." As he stood up, he grabbed his sword, which was sealed in its scabbard and leaning against the bench. Jayfor had taken it off to get more comfortable. He felt a strange sense of calm strapping it back onto his belt, but this was countered by the fact that his left leg had fallen asleep from sitting.

"I lost track of time!" Novak retorted, not looking ashamed in any way. "It's not like I have a magical instrument on my wrist that I can look at, which tells me the exact time."

"If one ever gets invented, you need to be first in line," Jayfor said, massaging his leg to try to get feeling back in it. When the tingling finally became manageable, he straightened his back and stood tall. He was ready to go. He wanted to get this job over with.

Novak understood the unspoken urgency in Jayfor's demeanor and nodded. "Just follow me. I know these roads well."

As they entered the street and merged with the sparse crowd, Jayfor remarked, "I can not keep track of these roads. The names are so strange. They all sound the same."

"Well, welcome to Augustria. I guess the people who named these weren't trying to make it easy for you to pronounce."

"The least they could do is name them something easy to remember. I mean, look at that one." Jayfor pointed at a sign at an intersection, with painted arrows on it pointing to different streets and naming them.

Novak's grin widened. "For me, those names make perfect sense. For example, *Floredium-medalim-navi* means "Maple Leaf Street." A bit of a mouthful for outsiders, but it rolls off the tongue nicely when you know what you're doing."

Jayfor shook his head. Nothing about the name seemed to roll off his tongue. "In Faldon, we don't name roads. Or put signs up. Personally, I think it's a waste of wood to put a sign up everywhere."

Novak raised an eyebrow. "Then how do you figure out directions to places? If someone needs to know how to get somewhere, how do you tell them without using street names?"

"Easy, you just tell them to take a left at the fourth intersection, or follow this road until you see an inn, then take a right. It's more basic and much simpler."

"Or," Novak countered, "you could just say 'take *Floredium-medalim-navi*, then turn onto *Didectumarum-navi* and follow it all the way to your destination."

Jayfor threw his hands up. "You prove my point! It's easier my way!"

Novak laughed. "Maybe when you're used to it. Trust me, though, in a city this big, street names are helpful."

" I grew up in a big city and never needed them." Jayfor was in an arguable mood, where he would disagree with everything just for the sake of doing so.

"Then you must have lost your way many times," Novak replied. He lost none of the mirth in his voice.

"No I didn't! My point is, it is entirely possible to not have street names, or signs which designate them. Therefore, it is useless to waste so much time on them when they aren't necessary."

Novak nodded. "And, pray, what shall we do with all of this extra time we will suddenly gain from not naming roads?" He said it in an airy tone, probably to annoy Jayfor.

"Lots of things! There are probably a million different projects going on at the same time. In Faldon, they were always building things and working on new developments. I assume it's the same here. With all the extra time, they could focus on these things instead of wasting their time with roads."

Novak nodded and stroked his chin poetically. He looked like a philosopher. "But who shall name the roads?"

"Nobody! Nobody will need to!" Jayfor yelled.

Novak continued gazing stoically into the future, as if he were some old sage with many years of wisdom. "But then, if the roads don't need names, how will people know what to call them?"

Jayfor was infuriated that Novak would defend such a useless point. Novak just wanted to argue. Jayfor was about to respond, when he realized that this was a conversation that he and Trenson could have. It reminded him of their old banters when they were traveling on the road. Novak was responding in almost the exact same way Trenson would.

"You went quiet all of a sudden," Novak commented.

Jayfor shook his head, trying to clear the thoughts. "I'm fine. I just have a lot on my mind."

Novak shrugged. "I don't think I'll ever understand you and Ernest. Always deep in thought, pondering all the *what if*'s and stressing about things that you can't change. I don't see the point. Just enjoy your time here while in this world! You only get one go at life, why waste it?"

That's definitely not something Trenson would say, Jayfor thought. He changed the subject. "So, what is the story with this contact we're meeting?"

"He used to be a part of the Scorned, but he says that after what he's seen, he doesn't want to be a part of it anymore and will do anything to stop them. He claims that he has some inside intel about the Scorned that we would benefit from."

Jayfor frowned. "You don't seem convinced."

"That's because I'm not. We have been ambushed before by people like this, claiming to have switched sides, only to stab us in the back later. Fool me once, shame on me, but fool me twice, shame on you."

"That's... not how the saying goes."

"Really?"

" 'Fool me once, shame on you; fool me twice, shame on me.' "

"Why would I be ashamed if you fooled me though? You should be ashamed for fooling me twice! I'll be ashamed the first time, but not the second time. Disappointed, but not ashamed."

Jayfor sighed much in the same way he would if Trenson had said something similar. "Just continue."

"Anyway, I've heard more bad stories about supposed 'converted' Scorned than good. So keep your guard up. He's pleaded that he speak to one of our leaders to tell us the information he has. He said he wouldn't tell it to any of our normal warriors because the information was too vital and dangerous. Pfft. More like he wants to get close to our leaders to assassinate them."

Jayfor blinked rapidly to try and warm his eyes up, the cold wind drying them. "Ernest mentioned that there would be some role-playing involved. He didn't explain what that meant, though."

Novak sighed. "Leave it to Ernest to throw everything on me. Basically I'm going to pretend that I'm one of the leaders of the

Willing, and you're acting as my bodyguard. My deaf bodyguard, at that."

"Your what?"

"Deaf bodyguard. Now hear me out," Novak put his hands up in a defensive gesture when he saw Jayfor's raised eyebrows. "He told us that he would only give his intel to one of our leaders. If that's true, then he won't let you listen. Unless we convince him that you're deaf. If he is who he says he is, he shouldn't have a problem with that. But if he does, that's a big red flag that he wanted one of us to come alone. It's far easier to ambush one person than it is two."

Jayfor thought about it. It didn't make a whole lot of sense. Pretending to be deaf? Then it hit him. "Ernest didn't make that part of the plan, did he?"

"Well... no, but I think it's better that way. Just trust me! You can look deaf, right? I mean, you pretend not to hear me all the time, so you have plenty of practice."

Jayfor snorted. "It's much easier when I don't care about the conversation. But for something like this, I think I'll be more interested."

"In any case, we'll pretend like you're deaf. Hopefully it doesn't get brought up, and he will just let you hear this 'secret intel' with me. But if not, you have an excuse." He sighed. "To be honest, we usually don't risk things like this anymore. After we fell for the bait the first few times, we stopped making time to meet these 'converts' who had some 'secret intel.' But the contact we're meeting today mentioned that the intel he has relates to the Mentor, and, well, we need as much information about him as we can get."

Jayfor nodded. "I have heard Ernest talk about someone called the Mentor before, but I never asked him about it. I assume it's someone important if they don't even go by their real name?"

"Exactly. That's the problem. He is the head of authority for the Scorned; everyone in the group answers to him and calls him only by the title 'Mentor.' We haven't gathered much about this man, or woman, only that he has only been seen by a select few of the Scorned, and never by anyone outside of the group. There are rumors, of course, but nothing concrete."

"And that's what made Ernest accept the offer of meeting the contact? Promises of knowledge about the Mentor?"

"Pretty much. It's unlikely that a simple Scorned initiate would have any information about him, but it's a risk we're willing to take. The Willing have to be willing, you know." He chuckled at his own joke, which he had thought of on the spot.

Novak looked at Jayfor, hoping he would laugh too, but Jayfor only glared at him. "It would be more funny if you didn't find it so amusing," Jayfor said in an exasperated tone.

"Oh be quiet!" Novak defended. "Anyway, we're getting close to the meeting point, so from now on, act like you can't hear anything."

Not that I have anything worth saying, Jayfor mused.

The "meeting point" was simply an alley. There was something about it that gave Jayfor extra thrills. He always wondered what it was like to be a criminal. Not that he ever wanted to be one, but he was just curious as to how they operated and how they went about with life. It was common knowledge that alleys were where shady business was done.

Technically, this was shady business. So did that make Jayfor a criminal? Unfortunately, no. He was too good of a person and he was simply acquiring information – not mugging someone like a criminal would do.

As they turned into the alley, Jayfor noticed that someone was already standing there – a short man wearing a cloak. He was dressed in the same attire as everyone on the streets, woolen vest, gloves, hood covering most of his face, and insulated pants.

He was facing the opposite direction of Novak and Jayfor. After taking a few steps into the alley, Novak stopped, and Jayfor copied. Novak cleared his throat and said softly, "I assume you're the contact?"

The man didn't move at first. *He must not have heard.* Novak was about to speak again when the man slowly turned around, his cloak lifting and snapping in the breeze. Piercing eyes peered from beneath the hood. "Most likely."

Most likely? Odd response. "You have information that me and my men could benefit from?" Novak laid emphasis on *my men,* since it played along with his charade of being a leader of the Willing.

"Oh, definitely. There are things I know that you would beg for."

Novak was starting to catch a hint. He placed a hand on his swords grip. "Is this a trap?"

The man smiled. "No. It is your death!"

XXXII

B Y SOME SENSE OF clairvoyance – or perhaps it was sheer luck – both Novak and Jayfor looked up. It was the most logical place for an attacker to be. An assassin could fall upon them and put a knife in their back easiest that way.

Novak knew this. But Jayfor didn't. It was a stroke of luck that he happened to guess that danger might be coming from above.

And he was right. That danger was in the form of four men falling from the rooftops. Two of them dropped straight toward Jayfor and Novak, knives ready, seconds away from falling on top of the two men and moments from slicing their throats.

Jayfor's reflexes kicked in, and he half stumbled, half jumped backwards a few paces, just far enough. The assassin came down, but instead of landing on Jayfor, his boots hit the ground. Since the boots were designed for stealth, they hardly made a sound.

The assassin was skilled, however. Most men would have cursed themselves for missing such an easy kill. But experienced ones knew not to waste any time. Jayfor was off balance and hadn't even drawn his sword. Within a second, the assassin dashed forward and thrust the dagger at Jayfor.

Jayfor didn't have time to draw his sword. In desperation, he grabbed the wrist of the assassin to stop the thrust. He was slammed against the wall, his arms bulging from the strain of holding back the knife from sinking into his stomach.

The assassin drew another blade from his belt with his free hand, attempting to finally end Jayfor.

Jayfor kicked the man hard in the shin. Just as he expected, the assassin wore no armor. The silent assassin let out a yelp of pain as the boot cracked into the bone. He instantly recoiled, taking a second to recover. That second gave Jayfor enough time to draw his sword and take in what was happening.

Jayfor looked for Novak, trying to see if he was okay. When he saw the way Novak was fighting, he knew he was better than okay. He was absolutely flying. His swordwork was far quicker than Jayfor expected. Jayfor recognized the style of fighting, called *Trecarum.* It was a very fast and quick way of dispatching enemies that focused on creating weaknesses to exploit.

And it was working well for Novak. One man was on the ground, dead. It must have been the original assassin that tried to fall on him. Another assassin was slowly retreating, gripping his shoulder in pain, blood soaking through his fingers.

Novak was left facing two men at once; one was a rooftop assassin, and the other was the man who baited them into the ambush. It's extremely hard to face two opponents, especially when they are on opposite sides of you. Novak was smart, and with fluid footwork, managed to only engage one at a time. By the time the next assassin got close enough to attack him, Novak had already sidestepped and was engaging the other one.

Jayfor took a little too long watching the scene, giving the assassin enough time to recover and assume a ready position. Jayfor attacked, not noticing his sword was glowing faintly, much like it had in the previous battle with the Scorned captain. The short blades of the assassin were ineffective against the long blade of Jayfor's sword. Within a few powerful strokes, the short blades were knocked back, exposing the assassin for too long. With a quick motion, the sword went in and out, and the assassin fell to the ground, his knives clattering on the stone ground.

Jayfor rushed to help Novak. Novak was having a hard time maneuvering in the alley. It looked like the assassins finally had him pinned. One of them didn't notice as Jayfor slipped behind him until it was too late. He stopped short, mid attack, and looked down to see a sword through his stomach. Then everything went black and he fell to the ground.

While Jayfor and Novak fought the now one remaining assassin, the man who Jayfor fought first lay on the ground, dying, but not dead. He had only minutes left to live. He watched the fight go on in front of him, knowing that his last comrade would be overwhelmed and eventually fall.

Curse the Mentor for not sending more men! Five men weren't enough against two Willing, especially not these two.

But all was not lost. He could still fulfill the mission. His mind, while having trouble focusing, suddenly remembered the cross-bow on his back. It was already cocked and had an arrow in it, as assassins usually carried this weapon, ready to be pulled and used at a moment's notice.

None of the assassins of the Scorned used the crossbow unless in dire need. It was a last-resort weapon. They prided themselves on their skill at overcoming their opponent with melee weapons.

Killing someone with one was viewed as dishonorable, too easy. But what good was his honor now that he would die?

If he could manage it, he could kill one of them with a swift shot from his bow. He knew which one he would aim for.

He had one shot.

Fighting against the eternal slumber that threatened to overtake him, the assassin propped himself up on his elbows. He wasn't in as much pain as he was shock, his body malfunctioning and hard to control. He gritted his teeth, less he make any noise to alert his two enemies.

He saw his last comrade fall to the ground, dead, his neck sliced from one of the blades. He didn't have time for remorse, though. Reaching behind his back and unhitching the crossbow took so much effort that he nearly died, but he fought to remain conscious.

He used both hands to aim. He had to make it. One shot. He could die peacefully knowing that he had killed the man they were hunting, who, coincidentally, was the one who sprung their ambush.

"I knew it!" Novak said, sliding his blade into its sheath without wiping the blood off. This action made Jayfor frown. It would be messy cleaning the blood off both the blade and sheath.

Novak continued. "We're lucky there weren't more. Assassins are dangerous. The Scorned have many tools that they deploy." He looked at the dead bodies around them. "I have to give them credit for trying, though."

Something caught Novak's eye. One of the dead bodies didn't look quite right. It didn't look dead. Why was it propped on its elbows and... Oh no. Oh no.

Jayfor asked, "Novak? What is it?"

Novak's eyes widened, and he suddenly leaped at Jayfor. "Look out!"

Novak flew in front of Jayfor. There was a quick *twang*, and then a thud. Novak landed on his side on the ground and remained there.

Then Jayfor saw, a few yards in front of him, the assassin he thought was dead, propping himself on his elbows and pointing a crossbow at him. The crossbow was empty, and the string was still vibrating. Like it had just been fired.

With a sick feeling, Jayfor didn't have to look at Novak to know what had happened.

The assassin cursed. "You fool. Why won't you die?" He coughed, blood beginning to froth at the edges of his mouth. His elbows grew shaky. "I know exactly who you are. Son of Hailar, king of the once-proud kingdom of Faldon. You have no idea who hunts you!"

With that, the last of the assassin's strength gave out. He fell to the ground, the crossbow limp in his hands.

Jayfor stood for a second in shock, but only a second. He rushed to Novak, kneeling down by his side.

The arrow was just under the right side of his chest. A red spot, slowly growing, engulfed the entry of the arrow. Novak's breathing was shallow and fast. Jayfor opened his mouth to say something, but his throat was suddenly dry. He didn't have the words to speak, either.

Sweat dripping down his forehead, Novak's breath was shallow. Quick. Labored. "I did it, Jayfor. I saved you."

"Don't talk too much," Jayfor instructed. *What's the best way to treat this? I must remove the arrow, but that in itself might kill him.* Then suddenly, another thought occurred to him. "How... How do you know my name?"

Novak smiled and let out as much of a laugh as he could, though it sounded more like a gasp. "We knew all along."

Jayfor knew that he needed to act fast, but this information shocked him. "How?"

"Oh, it really wasn't difficult. We had someone watching you and Trenson – that was his name, wasn't it? I can't remember, everything is so clear and foggy all at once – we had someone watching you before the brigands attacked you. Your conversations with your friend were enough."

Jayfor clenched his jaw. "Why?

"We saw something was special about you. Your journey was different. You had... purpose." He wheezed, but never lost his smile. "You're also... a bad liar."

Jayfor's mind raced as he considered everything that had happened between him and Ernest. Ernest knew? This entire time? Why did he not say anything? There was so much he wanted to ask. But there was no time.

Jayfor finally found words. "Well... you have a lot to explain once we return to the hideout."

"Haha... I'm not returning, Jayfor. Not breathing, anyway."

"Stop saying that. Here, I'm going to take the arrow out. Don't struggle, or else it will be much more painful."

Jayfor reached behind Novak's back and gripped the shaft with one hand, and snapped the arrowhead off with the other. Novak gasped at this slight movement. "That hurt."

"This is going to hurt much more," Jayfor commented. Without giving Novak a warning, Jayfor grabbed the shaft and pulled. The arrow gave way and came out. Novak cried out in pain and his body shook. Blood and other things came out with the shaft.

"We need to staunch the wound on both ends, so you don't bleed out." Jayfor was thinking mechanically. He did this to focus on what he could do to fix things, rather than what was happening. If he tried to even grasp all the new information and emotions that surrounded him, it would crush him, and render him paralyzed.

Novak stopped shaking, but his breath remained ragged. "Why are you trying to save me, Jayfor? Is there a better death for a servant of Va'ar? To sacrifice himself for the king of Faldon, that is a death we dream of!"

"Faldon is gone. It's dream died under the ashes of Loronis."

"Ah, but you forget the Faldon was never a kingdom – it was a dream. An ideal. A vision. You still carry that, Jayfor! You still – carry..." Novak closed his eyes and stuttered as another wave of pain crashed over him.

"Don't give up on me, Novak. We need to get you back." Jayfor ripped a piece off his cloak and folded it, placing it under Novak's cloak and at the wound. The fold immediately soaked red as soon as applied to the wound. "I'll carry you. Walking will only stimulate the blood more."

"It won't help. I'm going to die, Jayfor."

"No, you won't. I'll stop it."

"You don't have a choice in the matter. It is something that I... know. It's strange. I have almost died before, in ways similar to this. But this one is different. I have – more – more clarity. I see now. It's... nice."

Novak coughed again, a dreadful sound that resembled choking.

Jayfor grabbed Novak's shoulder, sensing that Novak was drifting out of consciousness. "No, you're not!" Jayfor yelled, fighting back the tears that threatened to fill his eyes. He couldn't let his emotions take over.

Novak smiled, but this wasn't his usual good-natured, humorous smile. It was content. It was one that spoke of a life of good events, bad events, good deeds, bad deeds, but overall... a regretless life.

"Thank you for your time with me, Jayfor." Novak's blinks became longer, and his breathing slowed. "It was an honor... my king."

He closed his eyes and sighed.

"No!" Everything became blurry as Jayfor's eyes flooded with water. "NO!" He pounded the ground in anguish. "*NO!*" He kneeled over his friend.

And wept.

XXXIII

TRENSON KNEW WHAT WAS going to happen that day.

And it wasn't because of the rumors. The rumors came and spread quickly. First, it was the guards. Then the inmates caught wind of it, and with very little to do during the day, it was the talk of the mess hall.

Mess hall. Trenson had heard this term before when referring to a prison cafeteria, but never understood what it meant. Now he understood why it wasn't called a clean hall, given that it was anything but.

Anyway, Trenson knew what was going to happen to him that day. How? Because he had a dream.

Trenson had to shake his head and smile after he woke up and turned last night's dream over in his mind. *I didn't think You'd release me from here this soon.*

He wasn't complaining, though. The sooner he was out of the prison, the better.

Trenson held his head a little higher that morning when led out of his cell and into the mess hall. Of course, he didn't hold it that much higher. Even when he was in a good mood, Trenson sometimes forgot to smile. But on the inside, he was brimming with anticipation.

As he entered the hall, which was simply a long corridor with several long tables with benches as seats, Trenson picked a random seat and prepared to be served his meal. He looked down the length of the table. All the other inmates wore the same dull clothing he did, and by their bloodshot eyes, everyone looked like they got as much sleep as he did. Some of the men crossed their arms across the table and laid their heads down, sleeping while waiting for their meal.

Trenson noted that many of the men in these cells were much older than Trenson expected. In Loronis, most people convicted of crimes and sent to jail were young. But there were far more people with gray in their beards here than Trenson assumed. He wondered why that was the case.

No surprise, this morning's breakfast was the same as it had been every other morning for the past few days: soup. Trenson didn't have any grudge against soup, but he became fed up with eating it all the time. It was what he ate as a slave, and even when he moved up the ranks, it was still frequently served. Now he was a convicted felon, and he was served... soup once more.

At least it was warm.

Everyone ate in silence. There wasn't much to talk about. Correction: there was probably plenty to talk about, but nobody felt like talking. And this suited Trenson just fine.

After finishing the soup, which was mediocre, Trenson and all the other prisoners were led into another, much larger, hall. This was where the prisoners spent their time during the day, and it was simply a large room with multiple tables and chairs, and a few games, such as dice and darts.

The prisoners were split into two groups: those that came to this room before lunch, and those who came after. Each group was allowed to socialize for three hours before returning to their cell. Trenson was part of the morning group.

He didn't socialize with the other cellmates during these times. He would watch them play darts or dice – they were very competitive with their games, and it wasn't unusual for a fight to start, which had to be settled by the guards – or listen to bits and pieces of information from the other prisoners.

It's funny, the only conversations most of them are having are about the message on the king's wall. Trenson remembered a conversation he had heard a few days earlier. The conversation was in Faldian. Since he didn't speak the native language of Augustria, Trenson had a hard time understanding orders and announcements. But thanks to a few people who spoke both languages and gossiped about the news, Trenson was able to stay up to date.

"Well, what take you of it?"

"Of what?"

"Of what they just told us earlier in the mess hall! About the message on the wall and decipherin' it."

"Eh, I don't think much of it. That's been going on for a few days now."

"Why not? Don't you remember what the warden said? The king himself said that anyone who knows anything about codes or knows any old languages may come and try to interpret it."

"And?"

"And, well, don't you think we should at least try? A lot of men volunteered and claimed to be able to understand it. The king is offerin' a reward to anyone who can determine what it means. We could earn our freedom if we figure it out!"

"But what if we don't?! Nobody has solved it yet, or else we would have heard about it. But even then, nobody that has volunteered has returned here. What do you think happened to them? Nothing good, since they essentially lied to the king, which is punishable by death."

"I mean, I guess it's possible. But come on, we're going to spend so much time here it's worth the risk. In fact, I think I'll volunteer tomorrow."

"Please don't. What do you know about ancient writing systems?"

"Nothing, but it's worth a shot. I just want to get out of this place. Heck, I don't care if I make it or not, I'm sick of this!"

The conversation went on for a few more minutes, with one man trying to convince the other that it wasn't worth the risk and that he had no chance. Trenson had thought about the content of this exchange for some time.

So someone had broken into, not just the palace, but the king's bedroom, and instead of killing the king or holding him for ransom, the intruder leaves a note on the wall that no one can read? Not a smart decision. What were the motives behind doing this? And why leave a message no one could read? It didn't make sense.

In any case, the king was scrambling to find someone, anyone, to decipher it. That much was understandable. And since none of the regal translators could make anything of it, the king was allowing anyone that volunteered to have a shot at it, offering a reward to anyone who understood it.

A thousand people probably lined up for this "reward." I'm surprised someone hasn't made something up and told the king in order to get the reward. Of course, they probably have, but I'm sure they have methods for determining the truth.

He smiled. The king would have his answer tomorrow, if Trenson's dream was correct. Trenson only had to wait until this evening, when supper was being served in the mess hall, to announce that he volunteered to decipher what was on the king's wall.

I had a dream about it last night. It was so clear, so precise... As soon as I finish eating, I will announce it. A guard will approach me and check to see if what I said is correct. When I say yes, he will grumble about this being a sneaky ploy to get out for a few hours. The guard will order me to come with him, and I will get up from the table and follow him.

He'll bring me to the warden's office and tell him that, per king's orders, I need to be usurered to the palace immediately. The warden will consider it – and go on a rant about how everyone was treating this serious matter as a loophole – before telling the guard that they will take me to the king in the morning.

Before I leave the room, I will ask the warden for one request: that I need my sword in order to decipher the message. The warden will laugh and say that prisoners don't make requests. My guard will counter this by saying that one of the prisoners asked to be allowed tarot cards to help decode the message, and the king allowed it. The warden will give up and say fine, but that since my sword was currently the property of the captain of the guard, he would have to acquire his permission, and the chance of that happening were slim.

After this, I will be taken back to my cell, sleep, and in the morning, I will be taken to the palace. Once there, I will be led under heavy surveillance to the king's chambers. And then...

Trenson thought harder, trying to remember it more clearly. It became more fuzzy at this point. He had woken up from his dream right as he was being given his sword and using it to decode the message on the wall... he couldn't tell what happened after that.

Trenson went against his character and smiled, for no external reason. He knew that this was no ordinary dream. This was a vision. He had never had a vision before. But the dream invoked a certain feeling after he woke up that he had never felt before, a sense of knowing, a... *feeling* that transcended normal understanding.

He felt as though he had looked into the future, like he had cheated the rules of life and saw what would happen.

Trenson's faint smile slowly faded. Emotions change. Reason doesn't. Feelings serve no purpose but empathy, and even then, it's still dangerous. Just because he *felt* like he had seen the future, didn't necessarily mean he had.

Still...

Either way, he was going to do exactly what happened in this dream. It was his only shot out of this place.

***

The warden wasn't in a good mood. That brings up the question, was he ever in a good mood? Sometimes. He enjoyed drinking and making bets on the local gladiatorial fights and races. Not to say that he was always in a good mood when he did those things, but that he was less likely to punch you for talking to him during those times.

It was because all day, he was being pestered by prisoners requesting that, since the king issued a decree to allow *anyone* to attempt reading the mysterious code on his wall, they should be allowed to give it a try.

"What a wonderful loophole they've discovered," the warden mumbled under his breath. The king probably didn't consider this when he issued his statement. The word choice mattered. *Everyone* seriously meant *everyone*, even prisoners. Even the warden himself could take a shot at this.

"This whole affair is being treated like a luck game," the warden continued talking to himself. "Like a lottery! The king might as well said, 'Here ye, here ye, try your skill at this secret code! Come on now, don't be shy! Step right up and have a chance to win a prize!"

The warden laughed mirthlessly as he made decisive swipes with his pen across the papers.

Thankfully, the day was almost over. He could return to his warm bed that he had so painfully left that morning. His servant had probably already begun warming the bed in preparation for him. Elated at the thought, he quickly pushed the remaining papers on the desk to one side. He could deal with that tomorrow. He rose from the table.

Then the knock sounded on the door. "Sir, a volunteer?"

The warden was disgusted. In fact, he was more than disgusted. "Of course!" He said the words out loud, loud enough for the servant on the other side of the door to hear him. He meant to say the words in sarcasm about the irony of the timing. In fact, his next words were going to shoo the guard away. But the guard took the *Of course* to mean that, of course, he could enter.

The servant opened the door and timidly walked into the office, dragging a prisoner who was much younger than the usual cellmate. The guard cleared his throat. He knew that he was being aggravating to the warden today. It wasn't his fault. He was charged with reporting each time a slave volunteered.

Both the guard and the warden agreed: the prisoners were using a poorly planned decree from the king to get some free time outside of jail, and it was driving them crazy.

"Why did you come in?" The warden demanded. "I didn't even admit you!"

The guard was confused. "But sir, I told you I had a volunteer, and you said 'of course,' implying that I could come in?"

"That's *not* what I meant! I was being sarcastic. The day is over, I'm about to go home. No more volunteers for the day."

The warden stared at the prisoner and got a good look at him for the first time. Tall, with a skinny but strong frame, and dark hair that had gone too long without cutting. Not much emotion on the face.

The warden wasn't impressed. He pointed a finger at the prisoner, and said in a tart tone, "You know what you're doing. I know what you're doing. Hoping to get some exercise through this, are you? A little jog to and from the palace – after all, it is quite a walk. Or maybe you're trying to win some type of lottery. Somehow, against all odds, you'll decipher this magical code with your own ingenuity! It's like a lottery for you, and what is the harm in trying to win? You don't have anything to lose."

The prisoner made no response. He gave the warden a look that he hadn't seen in a long time: a look of boredom, as if the warden was wasting his time.

Wasting his time! The warden was even more disgusted at the collected demeanor of the prisoner than he was at being interrupted.

The guard was the first one to break the uneasy tension in the room. "Shall I bring him back to his cell until morning?"

"Yes, do that." The warden decided he wasn't going to let a prisoner ruin the last part of his day. "He'll be taken to the palace and given his proper turn when it comes. Is that all?"

"Yes, sir," the guard replied.

"Excellent! You're dismissed." The warden waved his hand in a shooing gesture.

The guard bowed, and then turned on his heel to the door. He grabbed the cuffed wrist of the prisoner and started to lead him out, but the prisoner resisted and raised his head. "I have a request."

The warden stopped short of organizing his papers and looked up. Many emotions showed on his face, but the most prominent was bewilderment. "What did you say?"

The prisoner didn't flinch. "I said I have a request."

The warden straightened and tilted his head at the prisoner. It took him a few moments, but slowly a grin spread across his face, and he started to chuckle. "A request." He laughed harder. "A request! How honored am I to grant a request to thy noble self!" The warden said between bursts of laughter.

The guard was uneasy. "Sir, I apologize. I will personally see that he is—"

"No, no, it's alright. Who knew he was a jester!" The warden took a few steps closer to the prisoner, who remained devoid of emotion. "Who are you, to think you can demand requests?"

The prisoner didn't respond or move a muscle.

The warden smiled. "I do believe you made my day. In fact, I'll not even punish you for your little skit. But, please, tell me, what is you request?"

The prisoner spoke calmly, as if he had rehearsed what he was going to say. "I used to be employed at the residence of the captain of the guard, Wulfric. In order to interpret the writing on the king's wall, I must have my sword with me in his chambers. My sword is currently still at the house of Wulfric. If you can't acquire it for me before my meeting, then our time will be wasted."

The warden seemed to ponder this and started pacing. He looked down at the ground. Such a request! This whole ordeal was making the warden's day much more interesting. This certainly was an intriguing prisoner. But there could only be one reason for wanting to bring a weapon in the presence of the king.

The warden spread his arms wide. "I see now I have misjudged you! I thought you were a simple man, hoping to make some profit off of this opportunity. But no! You attempt to assassinate the king! What aspirations!"

The warden smiled wide as he laughed. He really was having a good time.

The prisoner shook his head calmly. "Nothing like that. I need it in order to decipher the writing."

"How, hm? How is a *weapon* going to help you read?"

"Because it does," the prisoner replied, a small level of sarcasm underneath his tone.

The warden's smile diminished. "I'll think about it." He scratched his head for a few seconds and looked off into the distance. "OK, I have thought about it. *No.*" He put an enormous amount of emphasis on the last word.

The guard cleared his throat and said, "Actually sir... I believe you have to let him."

The warden shifted his glare to the guard. There was very little tolerance left in the warden. "And, pray, why is that?"

The guard's nervousness showed through his voice. He was regretting speaking up. "No disrespect, sir, but a few other prisoners have requested things to bring into the chamber as well. Of course, they weren't weapons, just religious pieces like tarot cards or something of that sort." The longer the warden stared at him, the more the guard backpedaled. "But I understand your judgement. It's dangerous to allow him a weapon, even if he somehow needs it. I didn't mean to disregard you, sir—"

"Shut up!" The warden snapped. "I get it."

The guard obeyed and shrank slightly in embarrassment.

The warden sighed and turned his attention back to the prisoner, who still hadn't changed his expression. It was little unsettling. "I'll see what I can do. Bear in mind that I will have to get permission from Wulfric to see if I can even get this 'sword' – let alone if he'll even know what your sword looks like. And then there's the issue with allowing a *criminal* to carry a weapon in the king's presence."

The warden shrugged. "Either way, I'm not going to try very hard, so don't expect much. You've already given me enough trouble. I'm not going out of my way." He snapped his fingers to get the guard's attention and directed his final words to him. "Get him out of here. I'm done with people today."

XXXIV

"**Y**OU'LL WAIT YOUR TURN here," the soldier barked.

Trenson wisely obeyed and waited calmly outside the door of Thrance's bedroom. The door was closed, but Trenson could hear voices coming from inside. Most likely the voices of the king and his guards, not to mention the latest volunteer.

Behind Trenson was a line of other people who decided to try their hand at this. Trenson now understood the sentiment of the warden: everyone was treating this like one big luck game. There was even a prize. It was even better than a luck game, however, since it was free to enter.

As a result, Trenson had waited a very long time in this line that stretched through the palace, winding through the long hallways almost to the entrance. Thankfully, Trenson got in line earlier than most people, which meant he only waited around thirty minutes to get to the spot he was at now. He could only imagine how long the line was now.

Good thing I'm used to standing for long periods of time.

The line behind Trenson was composed of all sorts of people. Most of them looked hungry and unemployed – explained why they were here. On either side of the line, there were guards stand-ing at intervals, keeping the line straight and orderly.

Trenson took this time to look around. As someone who had spent a great amount of time living in a palace, he was somewhat familiar with the décor and styles. He felt hurt as he realized what he had just inwardly said. *Décor and style?* What was he, a palace designer?

Anyway, this palace was a little under par for his tastes. He understood the aesthetic look they were trying to create; marble and quartz, very stone-oriented. It made sense, since there were mountains in the distance, which probably provided the ore.

However, the artwork on the walls didn't quite match. Paintings weren't uncommon to be on walls, especially in palaces, where with such long hallways, paintings were often used to break the monotony.

It wasn't just that there were lots of paintings on the wall. It was the fact that most of these – in fact, every single one – were pictures of flowers.

There were pictures of big flowers. Little flowers. Colorful flow-ers. Dull flowers. Flowers in fields. Flowers in gardens. Many flow-ers all in one picture. Only a single flower in another.

The last example was the one closest to Trenson. It was a large frame that took up much of the wall, and composed of a single blue flower with no background.

This is a little... strange.

Trenson shrugged. Everyone has different tastes, he guessed.

That didn't make those tastes good, however.

The door in front of Trenson suddenly opened. To Trenson's surprise, smoke rolled out of the room and into his face. He gagged and backed away as it stung his nose and eyes.

"What's going on in there?" one of guards beside Trenson mumbled to himself as he backed away from the doorway as well, holding his spear tighter.

The sound of several people coughing came from within. "Open the windows! Open the windows!" a voice said between gags.

This order must have been carried out, because within a few moments, the haze started to clear in the room, and Trenson started to see what was going on inside.

He could make out a few soldiers in the room, most of whom were still coughing. He could also see what must have been the king, judging by the expensive attire and the prominent cheekbones that every king seemed to have. He was also coughing, more violently than everyone else, in fact.

The king gave an order in the Kallarian language, waving his hands toward the doors. He ran to the window and leaned across the sill, taking deep breaths of the fresh but cold air. *Someone his age could choke to death easily,* Trenson mused.

Two guards shuffled out of the room, escorting a small man out with them. The man had a candle in one hand, and a bowl with ashes in the other. The candle still had wax rolling down the side of it, looking like it had been put out not long ago, and the contents of the small bowl were still smoldering, leaving a grey trail as they exited the room. It didn't take long for Trenson to deducted that the man must have tried to burn something in the bowl. Maybe as a ritual?

In any case, it didn't work, much to Trenson's satisfaction.

The smoke soon cleared out of the king's room, and after the man was escorted away – not without a few words in the foreign tongue that didn't sound nice – there was hardly a trace a smoke left.

The king, who was still having trouble catching his breath, was soon surrounded by a handful of advisors. The king accepted a glass of water, and after a few more moments, recovered himself. His advisors guided him to a chair in the room, and he slowly lowered himself into it. The king muttered a few words in a hoarse voice and placed his arms on the carved armrests, leaning back in the comfortable chair.

One of these advisors, who wore a long blue robe with long sleeves, turned to face Trenson. His face was pinched with wrinkles, and he looked like he didn't have much teeth left. He impatiently gestured that Trenson enter the room.

Trenson took a deep breath and entered the room. He took a few steps in, then stopped when everyone, including the king, rested his eyes on him. Trenson met eyes with each of the advisors – they all looked about the same – and let his gaze linger slightly with the king. The ruler of Augustria might have been old, but he was in no way timid. However, Thrance had no idea that the person who was in the room was already comfortable with kings.

The king said a few words that Trenson didn't understand. Trenson frowned. "I don't understand, my lord."

In a second, Thrance shifted languages like it was nothing. "You have your time, then." His voice was like an old sword, the tone slightly fragile but still full of authority. He pointed to the opposite wall, where written in black letters against the wall, was the message.

Trenson swallowed. This was his chance, just like in his dream. He had to play this right in order for this to work.

He glanced back through the door at the guard who had been ordered to accompany him. The soldier knew his role and stepped into the room, holding a sword in a simple sheath. The eyes of the king and his advisor immediately landed on this newcomer questioningly.

The guard was clearly uncomfortable. He bowed before the royals. "My lord, the volunteer made a request. He claimed to be able to interpret the words, if he had his sword."

The soldier wasn't finished, but one of the advisors cut him off. "A sword?! Preposterous, of course weapons aren't allowed in the presence of the king!"

The soldier bowed his head lower. "I understand, your highness. I expected this. I shall remove this man from here at once." The guard rose from his kneeling position and started walking towards Trenson.

No. This wasn't the way this was supposed to happen. Trenson started to back up. "I understand your apprehension," Trenson warned while glaring at the king, "but if you want to know what that writing means, if you want to sleep well at night, you will consider changing your mind."

The king looked mildly surprised. He wasn't expecting a cellmate to be so bold. Most people gave the writing on the wall a half-hearted attempt, and then left. But this man seemed convinced.

"You'll do exactly as you are told!" an advisor retorted, disgusted that this man would speak up against him.

The king raised one hand. "It's alright. Let him have his turn."

The guard stopped in mid-stride, glancing at the king with uncertainty. The advisors were shocked. "But, my lord, it's a weapon! We can't allow you to be in any situation that presents danger."

"I assure you, I am well protected," the king replied slowly. He waved a hand at Trenson. "Well, go on. Get on with it."

The advisor opened his mouth to say something, but decided against it, and sourly closed his mouth.

Trenson nodded his appreciation, and took his sword from the guard. The soldier was hesitant to let go of the weapon, but under the gaze of the king, he relented. Trenson took his sword and pulled it free from the scabbard, making a familiar hiss as the simple and plain metalwork reflected the light from the window. He turned it a few times in the light, glad to be with his weapon again. He was glad that his request had been made, and that the sword was found in the stockpile at Wulfric's barracks.

Promptly, Trenson approached the wall with the writing. It looked just like it did in his dream: a few sentences, written along a single line, in the strangest letters he had ever seen. The letters were about the size of his finger, but they were intertwined and flourished in such a way that it was hard to tell where one letter began and another ended. He noticed that the wall was covered in handprints and stains of dirt and ashes. Apparently people had been rough with their methods of interpretation. Not that he would be an exception.

"What exactly is he going to do?" One advisor whispered to another. "How can you use a weapon to interpret writing?"

Trenson took a deep breath. This was it. He closed his eyes and looked down at the ground, grasping the hilt of the sword with his right hand. *Va'ar... give me the strength. Let me be a vessel that accomplishes Your will.*

He opened his eyes, and his eyes immediately noticed his sword: it was beginning to glow. It was faint at first, but it slowly began to intensify in the familiar bluish-white.

He heard a few mumblings behind him. Obviously, this was something that caused a stir for people who had never seen such a thing. He didn't turn around to face them. He kept his eyes on the letter in front of him.

Stepping closer to the wall, Trenson placed the edge of the glowing blade against the wall. Then, very slowly, applying slight pressure to the blade, Trenson began scraping across the section of the wall that the words were embedded into.

And as he scraped the sword across the wall, the words changed.

The first letter was L. A single, bold L, emerging from the scramble of shapes as Trenson swiped over it. Everyone in the room gasped. Something was truly happening this time. The king rose from his chair so quickly that the chair fell backwards and clattered to the floor. Nobody paid it any mind.

The next letter was an A.

The king walked briskly to Trenson's side, his mouth agape as his watched this glowing sword running over the letters, interpreting them. Trenson felt the urge to rush through the process, but resisted it, and kept his pace slow.

The next letter was C. The advisors huddled around him, watching in awe.

Then K...

Then I...

Then N...

Then G.

The message was deciphered. And a single word was revealed. *Lacking.*

Trenson straightened and backed a few paces from the wall, letting his sword, still glowing, drop to his side. He surveyed the word before him, written boldly on the wall. Where there used to be a chaotic mess of lines, there was now order.

Nobody said anything for a few moments. Everyone stood in shock, from the advisors to the soldiers. The king stepped forward and ran his thin fingers across the letters, making sure it was real. He had to be sure. Many people in the past claimed to have interpreted this message, but the truth seekers – servants who were trained to tell if someone was lying or not – found them to have lied.

However, none of them had produced a glowing sword that actively changed the letters before his eyes.

"What does this mean?" Thrance muttered. *Lacking?* What could the word imply? He finished tracing the word with his hand and turned to Trenson, who was standing straight and had a different air about him than usual. "What does this mean?" he asked again.

Trenson opened his mouth to respond with *I don't know*, but something happened at that moment. He felt the grip of his sword grow warmer, almost as if his sword was fusing to him. This feeling shot from his hand to his heart, and like a tidal wave, it poured over him.

All at once, Trenson's mind seemed to lose control of his body. He suddenly felt detached from himself, as if his conscious was now outside himself. He was no longer in control of his actions. The sword was. Or rather, Va'ar was. The feeling was a combination of ecstasy and terror. But Trenson didn't even have the time to register these emotions.

The force of it overcame him. He was at its will now. Without control, he opened his mouth, and the words unleashed. "It means, Thrance, that a certain group of people have weighed you upon the scale, and found you wanting. These people are not simple peasants or street folk. Not anymore. These people have a deep hatred for anything that guards them from what they want. And what they want is the kingdom, Thrance. And what stands in their way? You. And to think you never did a notable thing in your life. But your neutrality will not save you, oh no, inaction is far worse than action of any kind. By simply existing, you pose a threat. What is the threat, you might ask? Your inheritance. These people want the throne, Thrance. And you stand in their way! And they hate you, how they hate you. The less you do – the more wine you drunken yourself with –the more fiery their ambitions become! These people are not lazy. They have fought tooth and claw for everything they have owned. And when they see you, sitting on your throne, having done *nothing* in your life to deserve such privileges, then a hatred awakens in them that only the oppressed know."

Like a war horn in the quiet before a battle, Trenson's words sparked awe in the eyes of everyone listening. His voice was deep and powerful, and yet slow and calm. It was a sea that seemed serene on the surface, but carried devastating power beneath. Nobody knew exactly what to make of Trenson's words. The guards were shocked, the advisor's were shocked, and even the king's eyes widened and he took a step back, his hands half-raised as if he was preparing to flee from the room.

Trenson wasn't finished. "I know the thoughts that run through your head. Va'ar also knows. You have heard that name before, correct? Va'ar knows you have. 'A foolish notion,' were your exact words about it." Trenson smiled grimly and chuckled, a chilling sound. "You think your unbelief will save you. You don't realize that by allying with no one, you have made an enemy of everyone. But you will learn, soon you will learn!"

The king managed to gather himself to some degree. Closing his gaping mouth and clearing his dry throat, he attempted to speak with equal authority, although the words came out hoarse. "Speak with some sense! You've deciphered the word, but your interpretation has been nothing but balderdash!"

Trenson chuckled again. The sword was still glowing, held firmly in his hand. "Like a river over the rocks, these words flow over you. If only you had the memory to remember these words. You could store them deep within your mind, and draw upon them in time of need. But it is not so! By next month my words will be forgotten!"

Trenson sighed and turned back toward the wall. He reached out his hand and ran his fingers across the letters. "I will give you the interpretation you so earnestly desire. In one week, there will be an attempt on your life." Trenson spoke more softly now. "Exactly four assassins will enter the palace. They will enter the palace through the gardens, taking down the guards placed there and wearing their armor to blend in. And they will murder you."

Trenson turned to face them again. Their faces seemed frozen in time, horror-stricken. The king's face was white, and he looked about to collapse.

"With you dead, it will be easy to eliminate the rest of the palace, or convince them to join. You're not well-received by your subjects, especially your slaves. Few will mourn your death. And just like that, the city will no longer be yours. Your name will be reduced to ash, all in one night."

Trenson took a step toward the king. Everyone, including the king and his guards, stumbled backwards a step as well, afraid of Trenson's piercing words.

"I act not of my own accord, however," Trenson said, the volume of his voice rising with each word. "I am simply a messenger. A messenger of Va'ar. And it was by Va'ar's order that this warning be placed on your wall, in order to give you a second chance."

Trenson felt the temperature of the sword rising in his hand. His entire body buzzed with this otherworldly feeling. Every second, when he felt like he couldn't feel any higher, the energy surged through him and pushed him farther. The energy was so overpowering that Trenson felt as if he might explode, that it might be too much for his body to handle.

Trenson pointed at Thrance, glaring at him through eyes of fire. "You walk a thin line, Thrance. Everything you do from this point forward, tips the scales in one way or another. And with the path you are currently walking, death is a much more probable fate. Va'ar doesn't wish to save you out of pity, oh no. You don't deserve such a thing. But you are the only thing stopping those *people*, The *Scorned*, from achieving further catastrophe." Trenson curled his hand into a fist. "You... are fortunate."

And then, suddenly, without a warning, Trenson felt the presence of Va'ar leave him. Without a warning it suddenly vanished. There was no longer a fierce messenger from Va'ar standing in the room, pointing at the distraught king. Now a simple man remained, a simple prisoner. Trenson took the place of the messenger.

Trenson felt empty, as if everything inside of him was suddenly gone. He was hollow. The power was gone. Trenson's body felt like a empty vase, with nothing left on the inside.

The last thing Trenson remembered before blacking out was the sword falling from his grip and landing with a clatter to the ground. After that, everything went black, and Trenson was too weary to resist it.

XXXV

Ernest heard the noise of the flap being opened and turned to see Jayfor walking quickly into the room. Ernest was immediately overjoyed. *At last! The two of them have finally returned from the mission. Maybe there will actually be some useful information this time.*

"Conrad! Glad you're back. That took you longer than I expected." Ernest suddenly noticed Jayfor's red eyes, raw and irritated. Jayfor glared at Ernest, the usual lighthearted expression all but gone, replaced by a cold gaze and a clenched jaw. Jayfor's tunic was torn, exposing part of his side just above the hip.

But what concerned Ernest the most was the dark, dried blood on Jayfor's face, hands and clothes.

And Novak wasn't behind him.

Jayfor didn't give an explanation. He stared at Ernest a few moments, his face void of emotion. Then he said in a hollow voice, "Tomorrow I'm leaving."

With that, he approached the fireplace, grabbed a bowl from the stack beside the fire, and methodically began ladling the contents into the bowl.

Ernest never took his eyes off Jayfor. He had so many questions. What had happened? Why wasn't Novak with him? Deep down, he feared he already knew the answers to these questions. He suppressed his assumptions. He decided that interrogating Jayfor immediately wasn't a good idea, seeing the state he was in.

Controlling himself, Ernest silently watched Jayfor fill the bowl almost to the brim, set the ladle back in the pot, and take a seat opposite of him – all of this Jayfor did with no emotion or sense of urgency. Ernest could see the weariness etched on Jayfor's face, the weight of whatever had transpired bearing down on him.

Once Jayfor had taken a seat, Ernest cleared his thought. "What happened?" he asked softly.

Jayfor glared at Ernest, his eyes barely visible as his face pointed down at his bowl. "It was an ambush."

Ernest nodded. He assumed as much. "And Novak?"

Silence. Jayfor took a small sip from the bowl in his hands. Ernest noticed he was gripping the bowl extremely tight.

After finishing half the bowl in one go, Jayfor leaned forward and placed his elbows on his knees. "He's dead."

Ernest had always mentally prepared himself for this. Before sending people on such dangerous missions – especially his friends – Ernest reminded himself that he needed to brace himself in case they didn't return. This saved him a lot of pain.

But Novak was closer to him than most people. And even though Ernest was used to losing friends, this time, it hit harder. Much harder. He recognized the pain he felt, as if part of his soul had caved in.

Neither man spoke for a few minutes. Ernest sat deep in thought, mourning his lost friend. His face showed no sign of expression as he thought about what would happen now, with such a powerful warrior lost.

After some time had passed, Ernest spoke. "I'm... sorry." He spoke as much to himself as he did Jayfor.

Jayfor suddenly stood. The bowl gripped in his right hand, Jayfor pulled back his arm and threw the bowl to the ground violently. The bowl hit the ground and smashed into countless pieces, exploding soup and ceramic across the floor. Shards of the dish scattered, with the soup splattering on the otherwise clean, wooden floor.

"To blazes with you, Ernest! Or is that even your real name?! Novak told me all about you, how you've been lying to me this entire time!" Jayfor roared.

Ernest's eyes went wide and he stood from his chair, backing away a few paces. He had never seen this side of Jayfor before, and it terrified him. "What are you talking about?"

"You knew who I was this entire time! You've been watching me and Trenson for weeks! Don't act so surprised, as if you didn't think I would figure out!"

"Conrad, I—"

"Shut up! That's not my name!"

"I—I'm sorry." For the first time, Ernest wasn't wearing the stoic expression. Now he showed emotion: shock. "I'm sorry, Jayfor."

Jayfor was breathing heavy and he looked like he wanted to tear Ernest to pieces.

Ernest ventured to ask, "Why are you mad?"

"Why?! *Why?!*" Jayfor took a step toward Ernest and pointed a finger at him. "Because you knew! You knew exactly what I'm doing, how dire my mission is, why I need to find Trenson! And if that wasn't enough, you didn't help us when we were on the road, traveling in the rain, in the cold, fighting for our lives! Do you know how much we suffered? Ah, that you do! You were spying on us this whole time, all for your amusement! And you did *absolutely nothing* when we were attacked on the bridge and I almost drowned! You did *nothing* to help Trenson!"

Jayfor faintly smiled and chuckled huskily. The blood on his face and clothes gave him a grotesque look. "Some sick game this is, huh? Baiting me into this group of yours with promises of helping me to free him. You let it happen."

"Jayfor, I didn't let it happen," Ernest tried to reason. "I had people watching you two, that's correct, but—"

"And so, you knew exactly what circumstances we were going through, what we were doing, how desperate we were," Jayfor said, his words coming out quickly. "And what did you do to help? Nothing. Not even when we were at death's door on the bridge."

"I only had one, perhaps two, people watching you at a time. Certainly not enough to help you in most circumstances." Ernest's voice was returning to normal as he began to gather himself. "I also instructed my men not to engage you in any way."

"Why?" Jayfor demanded.

"Because... I didn't want you to know about us."

"And why is that?"

"You had your mission. The last thing you needed was more interferences."

"Ha! True. But do you know what we did need? Help! Help that you never offered."

Ernest cleared his throat and stood straight. "I don't think you realize how much we have done for you. We took you in and gave you food and shelter. You never would have made it into the city without us."

"I disagree. I have made it through more dire situations without your help. Possibly, I might be able to forgive you for that. But let's put that to the side for now. The real question is, why would you pretend like you didn't know who I was? You know what I need to do. You should have doubled your efforts to find Trenson and free him. Instead you played a charade, pretending that finding Trenson was no big deal. And I have a theory on why."

Ernest raised an eyebrow.

Jayfor continued. "This sword?" Jayfor patted the sword at his hip. "It carries power. And only I can use this power. Knowing this, you convince me to join your little cult in order to use my abilities, promising that you'll help me find Trenson. It's been weeks, Ernest! *Where is Trenson?!*" Jayfor screamed the last three words, his fury resurfacing.

Ernest frowned and looked at the ground. "I... I don't know," he admitted.

Jayfor smiled, a terrifying smile smeared with dirt and filth. "I know. Remove the treat, and the dog will sit no longer. Find Trenson, and I have no need to do your housework."

Ernest shot a glare at Jayfor. "You helped innocent people and saved the lives of good people. I would hardly call that time wasted."

"I had no choice!" Jayfor roared. "I only helped you because I *thought* you were returning the favor! How was I supposed to know that you were dangling it in front of my face, making me jump through hoops for you?!"

Ernest took a step forward, his face stern. "I kept my promise," he said in a low voice. "I do have men searching for Trenson."

"Then where is he?" Jayfor demanded, taking a step forward as well. Both men were only a few feet from each other now.

"I don't know, Jayfor!"

"Liar! Either you know and won't tell me, or you haven't kept your promise at all. Either way works to your benefit!"

Suddenly, a smaller, softer voice spoke from behind them. "Ernest? What is going on?" It was Tindra. She had entered the room and was watching the scene before her with a furrowed brow.

Ernest turned to her. His expression and tone softened. "Just a simple disagreement. Can you give us some time alone, please?"

Jayfor turned to Tindra, bits of foam building at the edges of his mouth, adding to his wild appearance. "He's a liar, just like you! You're all a den of vipers!"

Ernest stepped inches from Jayfor's face, a dark glare in his eyes and ice in his voice. "Don't you dare speak to my wife like that." He looked on the verge of punching Jayfor in the face.

Tindra's eyes widened and her mouth formed an O. She quickly turned and left the room.

Jayfor wasn't finished. "You have no authority over me. I am a king!"

"Not anymore." Ernest said each word as if they were two different sentences.

Jayfor's breath was hot and heavy on Ernest's face. Jayfor opened his mouth to lash out again, but suddenly stopped. His eyebrows, once crossed, relaxed slightly. It wasn't much, but the temper that engulfed him seemed to have dissipated. Jayfor was beginning to realize what he had said and what he was doing. Clear thinking was beginning to replace wrath. Jayfor looked Ernest in the eyes. The captain was still fuming and ready to fight; his features pulled into a hard scowl.

Jayfor backed up a few paces, going from a mad fury into a daze. His mouth still hung open. He looked at the ground for a few moments, thinking hard. Then he looked up at Ernest, and tears began to well in his eyes. "Novak is dead…"

Ernest softened as he realized exactly what was happening. He had seen it before, and it had even happened to himself before. When a man was put through a crushing amount of tension and suffering, his mind would begin to work in overdrive, and he would become great at multitasking. His mind would lock away all the pain that had happened in the past, and start balancing the many calculations, assignments, and goals that it had set. It would become so good at its job that it would forget what had happened and push it to the side in a fight-or-flight instinct.

However, if something shocking were to happen, it would topple this finely set tower. Everything that was running through the mind, every emotion it was attempting to suppress, would explode out and wreak havoc on the person. The person would essentially go insane for a short amount of time as they had to re-experience everything they were pushing aside as well as the new pain.

Jayfor collapsed into a chair and put his head in his hands. Uncontrolled, heavy sobs escaped from his fingers, as well as tears. His body shook with each cry of pain. "He's really gone, he's gone!"

Ernest felt the cavern of remorse open in his heart, draining him, causing him to feel lifeless. He felt water start to build in the corners of his eyes. "I know..."

XXXVI

TRENSON WOKE UP IN a cold sweat and felt terrible. The first thing he noticed was the fact that everything was bright. Even though his eyes were closed, he could still tell that there was a fair amount of light in the room. If he was in a room. He kept his eyes closed, not ready to come face-to-face with the blinding light.

He could feel something soft and cushiony beneath him. It reminded him of his bed at Loronis, the bed he used to sleep in every night, all those months ago… In fact, it felt so similar to his old bed that he wondered if everything had just been a dream. Maybe he had finally woken up from that terrible dream and would be back at the palace, where a hearty breakfast awaited him every morning.

He slowly cracked open his left eye. Expecting to see the wooden rafters above him, instead he saw a simple, painted ceiling. Trenson sighed. Nope. This was all too real.

He opened both eyes and squinted. He propped himself up on his elbows. Light came from a window to his left, a window that looked out into a mountain range. In the distant rut formed by two peaks, the sun was starting to creep out, shooting its brilliant beams through the window and onto the foot of Trenson's bed.

He looked around. He was in a large, clean room. The only furniture in the room was a bookshelf half-stocked with books, a carved wooden chair and its counterpart, a desk with a few compartments. There was plenty of open space in the room. Trenson liked how spacious the room was.

Trenson laid his head back on his pillow. His whole body ached. The memory of what happened in the king's room came back to him. Translating the words on the wall, interpreting its meaning for Thrance, the sword taking control of him and causing words to flow from his lips... It came back to him now. He wondered if that's why he felt drained, because the sword seemed to draw upon his energy.

They must have put me here after I passed out.

The door to the room opened so quietly that Trenson didn't hear it, so he was startled when he heard a voice say softly, "Good morning, sir."

Trenson picked up his head from the pillow to see a young girl – likely a servant by her outfit – standing beside the recently opened door. She carried a few bundles in her arms which looked like clothes. Trenson was suddenly aware of the fact that he was wearing only a loincloth. He quickly pulled the covers higher over his chest when he realized this.

"Sir?" the girl said as she approached the bed, still unsure if Trenson was awake. When she was closer she realized he was. She set the bundle of clothes on the floor at the foot of the bed. "My lord wishes an audience with you within the next hour. I suggest you don't keep him waiting." She curtsied – a gesture that confused Trenson, having never seen it before – and then turned and left the room, closing the door quietly behind her.

She's right. I need to figure out where I stand with this, and what's going to happen now. As Trenson pushed the covers off him and swung his legs over the edge of the bed, standing up and immediately wincing as his aching calves and thighs protested, he wondered what would happen now. His dream didn't extend this far. He was in uncharted territory. Would Thrance be happy that the message was deciphered, or angry since the message wasn't favorable? Trenson did say some not-very-friendly things to him yesterday. Not that Trenson could control what he said in that moment, but Thrance didn't know that.

He held up the clothes that the servant set in his room. They were a simple tan color, both the trousers and the tunic. The sleeves were oversized and long to a degree that Trenson knew it had to be on purpose. He quickly donned the outfit. He was surprised at how comfortable it was. He was glad everything fit. It would be aggravating to complain to a servant that his clothes didn't fit.

There was a mirror on the wall next to the door that reached the roof. Trenson stood in front of it to check his appearance. When he saw himself, he was shocked. It had been months since he had seen himself, and it amazed him how much he had changed. His frame was more lanky than usual, which was probably because he had eaten nothing but thin soup for a month. His hair was much longer than he expected. He had used some scissors at Wulfric's barracks to cut the front, but since the place lacked any mirrors, he simply cut enough of it to keep it out of his face. It was a tangled mess in the back, falling over his ears and reaching almost to his shoulders now.

I look so... wild. Everything from his neck down looked formal, royal, even. Everything from the neck up looked like he was living in the woods.

He sighed. Nothing could be done about it at this point. Straightening his shoulders, he attempted to fix his bedhead before walking to the door and pushing it open.

As soon as he had opened the door, he came face-to-face with another servant. The man was a head shorter than Trenson and a good deal heavier. He was bald and almost had a double-chin. The servant nodded to Trenson. "Master Trenson, the king is waiting. Allow me to escort you to the dining hall. He has been eagerly awaiting your presence."

Trenson, who was used to fancy talk like this, was able to interpret it as, "You've kept the king waiting for too long. Come with me or else."

The servant turned to his right and started walking at a brisk pace. Trenson hurried to catch up to him. "How long have you been waiting?"

"Only an hour or so," the man replied evenly. Although the servant had gone through heavy training and was good at hiding his feelings, there was a sour note to his words that Trenson picked up on, hinting that the man wasn't very happy about waiting so long.

"I'm sorry," Trenson said, falling into tempo a few steps behind the servant. "I was exhausted."

"Indeed." Trenson knew this was servant talk for *I couldn't care less.*

Trenson decided to stay quiet and let his eyes soak in his surroundings as he followed the servant. Marble columns supported the high vaulted ceiling above, with windows decorating the walls in various places all the way to the roof, allowing the fresh morning light to spread to every corner of the hallway. There was plenty of open space, the lack of decorations giving it an airy feel.

It's definitely not nicer than Loronis, but the simplicity of it does add to it.

The only real decorations were portraits on the wall. And of course, all of these portraits were of flowers. Trenson considered asking the servant about them, and why Thrance had such an affinity towards them, but he decided against it.

Presently, they came to the end of the long hallway, where two large doors were propped open, revealing a long, wooden table covered in food inside. Trenson's stomach growled at the sight of food – real food like meat and bread, not soup.

They passed through the doors and stopped a few paces into the room. The room was fairly small but very long, much of its space taken by the table. Not just meat and bread, but potatoes, carrots, beans, and other fruits and vegetables made it seem more like a grand feast than a simple breakfast. *Seems a little excessive to me.*

The king, the only one sitting at the table, was busy cutting a slice of ham with his fork at the head of the table when he looked up and noticed his guests. He smiled, but didn't stop his hands from working. "Ah, thank you Clarence. You may be dismissed."

The servant quickly bowed and left the room.

Trenson stood uncertainly, unsure of what to do. Did the king need to tell him where to sit, or could he seat himself? Was there a formality that he was forgetting? He glanced at Thrance, hoping for an answer, but Thrance merely continued to smile. The king seemed to enjoy how uncomfortable he was making Trenson. He finished cutting the ham and placed it gingerly in his mouth using his fork, chewing it carefully.

After what felt like a lifetime, Thrance swallowed and gestured to the opposite end of the table. "Please, sit! You must be hungry."

Trenson was relieved and took his seat in the velvet chair opposite the king. The food on the table was arranged in such a way that Trenson had a clear view of Thrance. Trenson wasted no time as he started pilling food on his plate, putting more food than the plate was designed to hold.

Thrance chuckled and took a sip of wine from his cup. He looked down at the contents of the cup and swirled them around. "You slept far longer than I expected. The healers were fearing that you might die, given that your heart was barely beating. I had no doubt you'd revitalize."

Trenson didn't respond. He was too busy tearing into the meat, not bothering to use a fork or napkin.

Thrance continued. "Once you fainted, I was offered various suggestions on what to do with you." He set the cup down and begun cutting another piece of ham. "My advisors are wise men, and each had equally applicable ideas. But none of them suggested that I let you live and go unscathed. See, even though you made a mockery of me, I still concluded that you could be of help."

Trenson looked up and said with a mouth full of potatoes, "And what help is that?"

Thrance pushed his plate to the side. "You've demonstrated extraordinary abilities. You seem to be the only one capable of doing anything with that sword. I had a few men attempt to imitate your show, with little result. The staff requires his wizard, I suppose." Thrance narrowed his eyes. "Would you consider yourself a wizard?"

Trenson couldn't help but snicker. He finished the potatoes in his mouth and shook his head. "Not in the slightest. I am merely an instrument, of sorts."

Thrance cocked his head to the side. "Of sorts?" He prompted Trenson to elaborate.

Trenson wiped his hands on a napkin. "The sword takes control of me. I had no charge over what I was saying at that moment. I couldn't have resisted if I wanted to."

Thrance nodded. He didn't understand, but it would look immature for him to be overly curious. "So in effect, the sword is the wizard, and you are the staff?"

Trenson chuckled. "Into wizards are we?" Trenson was so used to talking to high officials as below him in Loronis that he had forgotten that in Kallary, he was a slave, and was supposed to act humbly before a king.

Thrance's smile faded slightly. "I merely attempt to understand what I don't."

Trenson took a sip of mead, which quickly turned into him draining the entire cup, as it was so good. "I am simply a vessel. Va'ar uses the sword to speak through me."

"Va'ar? Is this your... god?"

"No. It's the only God."

"You confuse me. We tolerate many different types of religion here. I worship any and all gods of the city."

"Then you waste your time, praying to statues and fantasies that have no ears."

Thrance scowled. "And you're one to talk?" His voice was firm and unfriendly.

Trenson wasn't fazed and shrugged. "Let's not forget that I alone was able to decipher the message when the rest of your *wizards* could do nothing."

Thrance balled his hands into fists. So, he was going to be the difficult type. This would not make things easier. But no matter. He had things set in place to counter it. "Don't abuse your position," he said evenly.

As you abuse yours? The response was on his tongue, but Trenson held back and said nothing. He reminded himself that he wasn't in any position to be acting snarky. He needed to find a way out of this, and curt remarks wouldn't help.

Thrance took a sip of wine to calm himself, clearing his throat before speaking again. "I don't believe I know your name."

Trenson replied quickly before stuffing his mouth with another roll. "Trenson."

"Trenson? That's an eastern name. I take it that's where you're from?"

Trenson nodded.

"I don't suppose you know any Kallarian, much less any of the smaller dialects?"

Trenson shook his head and swallowed. "Nothing besides a few simple words."

Thrance nodded. "We shall have to remedy that then."

This made Trenson stop. *We* will have to remedy that. This implied that Trenson was going to be staying. He had no intention of doing so. Now that he was no longer a slave, he needed to continue traveling north to find the tree of Ramadus. He didn't have time to stay. What did Thrance need him for?"

Trenson thought about his words carefully. "I appreciate the offer, but I really must be going soon. I have family to return to."

Thrance smiled. "Ah. That is something I can't allow you to do."

Trenson looked up and stared at Thrance across the table. "I'm sorry?"

"You've shown yourself to be unusual. That in itself is unusual and should be used. You no doubt have other skills, some of which could be put to good use."

Trenson huffed. He didn't like the direction the conversation was going. "You mean your use," he said. He meant to say it under his breath, but was a little too loud.

Thrance smiled and took another sip of wine. "My uses *are* good. But that's beside the point. You've successfully revealed an assassination plot against me. Whether you are correct or not, remains to be seen. But with what you've shown me, I have no doubt you can be trusted."

Trenson interrupted. "So, what do you need me for?"

"Well if you predicted it, then you should also know the best plan of action to thwart it. Furthermore, your sword – which only seems to respond to you – could be incredibly powerful in our hands. It would give us an edge."

Thrance calmly wiped his hands with a napkin and ignored Trenson's glare. He sniffed. "To put it simply, I would like for you to work with us and guide us in preparing for this assassination attempt."

Trenson narrowed his eyes. "You want me to remain here to help you repel the assassins?"

Thrance nodded. "Yes."

Trenson looked to the side for a few moments, appearing to be thinking deeply. Of course, in reality he already knew what his answer would be, but it would help if it looked like he had considered it. After a few moments he spoke, using a tone of regret. "I appreciate the offer. But I really need to return home. I have loved ones who haven't seen me in months, and I don't want to put off returning to them. I hope you understand."

Surprisingly, Thrance smiled. "I do understand. But unfortunately, for your health, I cannot allow you to leave."

Trenson raised an eyebrow. "For my health?"

Thrance pushed his plate to the side and crossed his arms. "Have you heard of the plasmeric herb, Trenson?"

Trenson shook his head slowly, having a feeling that it wasn't something good.

"It's a rare plant that's almost extinct. We grow it here, at the palace, to study it. It has a curious effect that is almost the opposite of poison, but equally lethal. When ground into powder and placed into food in large quantities, it has no immediate effect. The only way to tell if someone has taken it is that after an hour, their saliva will turn a yellow tint. However, once the victim has ingested enough of it, the body becomes addicted to it. The victim then must continue taking the herb daily, because if he withdraws at any point, he will die in the next forty-eight hours."

Thrance wiped his mouth with his napkin. "Think of it more as an addictive than a poison. It's an extremely interesting plant."

It didn't take a genius as to why Thrance was talking about this. Trenson immediately spat out the food in his mouth. He pushed his plate, still loaded with food, violently to the side, almost knocking it off the table. "You would stoop so low!" he yelled, standing up from the table.

Thrance smiled. "Like I said, it's rare. So finding other sources of it in order to stay alive are impossible. The only way to break the addiction is to slowly lower the concentration of the herb, and to do so with extreme skill and precision."

Trenson's eyes darted around at the food on the table. Suddenly, all the meat, bread, and fruits lost their luster. It was startling how quickly something could be viewed as lifesaving one moment to lethal the next. Dread came over him as he realized just how much he had eaten. "How much have I consumed?" he asked frantically.

Thrance was entertained at how upset Trenson was. "An enormous amount. Given how rare it is, you've likely digested the equivalent to several hundred pounds of celts. That's enough to feed a full household for months."

Trenson picked up his plate, still filled with food, and flung it across the table. The plate hit the table first, landing with a loud thud and skidding to a halt into glass pitcher of wine, resulting in a staccato *ping*. The food, from bread to gravy to ham to apple slices, soared across the table, landing in various places across the table.

A piece of bread landed into a bowl of potato soup. Meat became sprinkled everywhere in oval slices.

Trenson was aiming for Thrance's head, but the table was so long, neither the plate nor the various projectiles hit the king or even got near him.

The next thing Trenson knew, his head was slammed down into the table. He was momentarily stunned. He felt a heavy hand on the back of his head, pushing his face into the wood. Another pair of hands grabbed his wrists and pinned them behind his back. He tried to kick at his assailants, but missed, and received a swift strike in the shin as a reward.

"Enough!" Thrance's powerful voice commanded. Immediately the hands were removed from his wrists and head. Trenson remained slumped forward on the table for a few more seconds, then slowly stood upright. He rubbed his wrists and turned his head, seeing two guards standing behind him, glaring at him, ready to restrain him again.

Thrance directed his words to the guards. "There's nothing he can do. Even if he manages to kill all of us, he will meet the same fate within two days, anyway. If he is wise, he will cooperate with us, since it is the only way to ensure his survival."

Trenson turned to face the king, his eyes firing daggers at Thrance's smug smile. He balled his fists. "How do I know you're not bluffing?"

"Oh, the only way to find out for certain is to go without eating for two days. Or you could spit into that glass in another hour and see how your spit is already turning yellow. Either way, I think you know that now is not the time to be doing anything rash."

Trenson tried to think of some way out of this, but found none. He had been wrong that morning; he was not free. He was still a slave. And until he gave it time, he had no way of knowing that his body was not becoming a death clock. He had no choice but to go along and do Thrance's bidding, in case he was right.

"Rest assured, I don't intend any malice with you, Trenson. I ask you only to aid me in preventing this assassination attempt. After you successfully – and you will be successful – do, we can start the recovery process. But for now, it's necessary that you remain addicted."

Trenson searched for some witty comeback but found none. All that came to mind was, "May Va'ar deal with you."

Thrance put his hands under his chin. "He is trying. But you will help me to stop it."

XXXXVII

"Y OU'RE CERTAIN OF THIS?" Jayfor asked.

"Absolutely," Ernest replied. "I get my information from an inside source. He reports that the target frequently works with the Scorned and has been trading business with them, giving them money and protection in exchange for information."

Jayfor crossed his arms and leaned back in his chair. "How dangerous is he?"

"Very. But I'll explain more in our meeting."

Jayfor and Ernest were sitting in a small meeting room, with a square table in the center surrounded by seats. Ernest had called for a council this evening, summoning every member of the Willing within the area. When asked what this meeting was about, Ernest pushed the question away. "I don't like to explain things twice. It will be much easier to tell everyone at once."

If he's summoning every Willing in the area, it must be something big. This can't be one of the usual hit-and-run missions.

Jayfor and Ernest were the only ones in the room so far. It was expected that twenty or so more would arrive. Jayfor had never been told exactly how many Willing were in the city. He hoped there were more than twenty. Then again, the city was large, so when Ernest said *in the area,* he could be talking about only a small portion of the city.

It would be a while before anyone else arrived. While he had this moment of quiet, Jayfor mused over his decision to stay, and what he had decided to do after this mission.

Eventually, Jayfor was able to think clearly again. He saw with newfound clarity that he had wasted time here, and that finding Trenson had turned into him making commitments that he was regretting. It was true that the Willing could search for Trenson much more efficiently. But their help had led to nothing. Jayfor was helping them in exchange for... what? Nothing. He had helped good people, he had to admit. But that wasn't his goal. His goal was to reach the Tree of Ramadus.

As much as he hated to admit it, he was forced to confront the fact that he might have to take this mission alone. He had been in the city for months now. His progress was delayed severely. Not that there was any deadline to complete the mission, but... who's to say there was? What if Trenson was dead at this point? Or what if he had left the city?

Such questions made his head spin. Thinking about all the different possibilities wouldn't do anything. He had to make a decision. And so he did. He would leave the city, with, or without, Trenson. Trenson was resourceful; he could figure his way out of things if he was still alive. It wasn't an easy choice to make, but Jayfor had suffered enough. Another sacrifice wouldn't be difficult.

He told Ernest of his decision a few hours after their argument. Surprisingly, Ernest didn't seem upset or surprised. "I understand.

I think that is in your best interest. I will not stop you." However, he did have a request. "I know it's a lot to ask, seeing as I haven't been able to make a return on my previous promises. But there is a mission in the next few weeks that is our biggest and most important mission yet, and likely our most dangerous. I can't give you too many details, but it is one that will push all of us to our limits. I can understand your hurry. But if you would please, stay and help us one last time. Your help could be pivotal. In addition, I will provide you with two escorts and a blessing for your journey north. It's not a lot. But I am asking you as a fellow follower of Va'ar, Jayfor... and as a friend."

Jayfor didn't know if he would consider Ernest a friend. But that didn't matter. He couldn't say no. And so, without even knowing the full details of what he was signing up for, he agreed to help Ernest, one last time.

After that, he would hit the road again. With, or without, Trenson.

The sound of footsteps interrupted Jayfor's thinking. He looked to the doorway to see a short man, likely in his early twenties, with shaggy hair and wearing many layers of clothes, enter the room. He was shorter than Jayfor, but then again, Augustria was filled with people that were below average in height. He had light blue eyes and a good-natured face that looked... scared. He looked as though he once had an optimistic outlook on life, but then the world showed him how brutal it was, and it broke his innocence. He had remnants of optimism, and he still had a faint smile that was likely etched into his face because of habit. It was more of a sad smile now, though.

Ernest took notice of him and rose from his seat. "Ah, I don't believe you've met our new initiate, Conrad. This is Colly. One of our men overheard him spreading the story of Va'ar in a tavern a few days ago, and decided to trust him. He doesn't have any skills – yet – but he has a willing heart."

Colly smiled at Jayfor, then at Ernest. "Well, I kind of figured that was a requirement, especially since this group *is* called The Willing. By the way, how did you come up with that name?"

Another Novak, Jayfor thought to himself. Jayfor wondered if that was the reason Ernest let him into the ranks so quickly: since he had a similar demeanor as Novak, and that recruiting him would help to soften the blow. Although he knew Ernest would never admit it, he was sure he already knew the answer.

"I don't know," Ernest replied. "Given that we are willing to sacrifice everything to serve Va'ar, I think it is an appropriate name."

"But isn't everyone willing? Or every organization willing to put things on the line?" Colly asked for no reason.

Ernest couldn't help but let a hint of aggravation creep into his voice. "None of them took the name, however."

Colly nodded. "Ah. That does make sense."

Jayfor cleared his throat and addressed Colly. "A pleasure to meet you. My name is Conrad."

Jayfor didn't expect Colly to come around the table to shake his hand, but that's exactly what he did. "The pleasure is all mine! It's so reassuring to meet other people who have the same mindset. It's not easy to find. I can't wait to work with you and find out more about this!"

Jayfor simply smiled and waited for Colly to stop shaking his hand so enthusiastically.

Shortly after, the rest of the Willing trickled into the room. Some came in groups, others came by themselves. They all wore heavy coats or fur-lined tunics, appropriate for the weather outside. A lot of them were older men, and beards seemed to be a common trait among them. Jayfor felt like a child, being more skinny and without a beard in this group of men.

There was a pleasant hum of conversation as men and women were introduced to each other and old friends reunited. Most of these people were separated over long periods of time. They would take up missions, and by the time they finally rooted out the hideout or whatever their goal was, months would pass, and they wouldn't see their friends during that time. While obvious that they had been gathered here to discuss an important mission, that didn't prevent them from catching up.

Ernest separated himself from a conversation and stood at the head of the table. He scanned the room, mentally counting all the heads, to come up with a grand total of twenty-six. At least it was more than he anticipated. Still not a lot, but more than anticipated. He cleared his throat and, in a voice that wasn't loud, but the depth and power behind it reached everyone in the room, said, "If I could have everyone's attention, please."

The room fell silent almost immediately. Every eye turned to Ernest. Jayfor's conversation was stopped mid-sentence by the commanding voice. Ernest didn't look fazed in any way amid the fifty-two eyeballs staring at him.

"I have gathered you here today to give you an announcement. Along with the others in command, we have discovered that there is a powerful enemy against us, one who needs to be stopped if our efforts are to prosper. When I tell you of this person, and the mission it requires, many of you will be shocked. This is not an ordinary, hit-and-run objective such as you are used to. This will have to be a coordinated rush, one that is quick and with purpose."

Jayfor looked over to see Colly staring at Ernest with wide eyes and a starry expression. Jayfor couldn't help but smile. He could tell Colly was swept up in the excitement of being in a secret organization, designed to bring good into the world. That excitement would go away with time.

"Before I tell everyone gathered here of this mission, I would first like to commend our brethren in the northern hideout for rooting out and clearing the northern sector of the black market dealings. We have tried for months to put a stop to it, but it was your skill and tenacity that led to the capture of their leader. As a result, we have cut off a major supply of funds from the Scorned. Let's give them three cheers, shall we?"

Three cheers were promptly given, many people raising their fists in the air with each chant. Gathered in a group, a few members of the northern hideout smiled and nodded their appreciation.

Ernest continued. "Funds are a major part of what keeps us, and our enemies, afloat. In out fighting, we often neglect simple things, such a food and basic needs. Our enemies have retaliated to our victories over the last month by going after our beneficiaries. To counter this, I began tracking down the people who were offering aid to the Scorned. But the results were surprising. I found that everything seemed to trace back to a single source, and after much research, I discovered the shocking truth."

Ernest took a deep breath. "He is a man that wields great power. And he has been in league with the Scorned for a long time. He provides them with assistance and all the funds they need, pushing their agenda behind closed doors. If we were to take him out, we could achieve a significant victory, possibly great enough to rid all of Augustria of our enemies."

Ernest paused, letting the tension in the room grow taunt. Jayfor, Colly, and twenty-four other Willing looked Ernest in the eyes before he said the words that put everyone in shock.

"My friends, that person is none other than the king of Augustria himself."

XXXVIII

A FEW HOURS AFTER his breakfast with the king, Trenson went to his room, closed the door, and spit in his hand. His fears were validated at what he saw. There was no mistaking it. His saliva had turned a noticeable bright yellow color.

He scowled. How did he get into this mess? It was better than being in prison, no doubt. But being forced to protect the king from an assassination attempt wasn't exactly freedom either.

Trenson had a habit of tracing his footsteps whenever he did something wrong, or something bad happened. Whenever he did this, he usually found that his current situation was the result of some foolish action he made in the past.

He did this now, mentally going backward in time. Every time he thought he landed on what made him arrive at this point, he was always forced to admit that he had no way of doing better. He could have let Wulfric's son, Geoffrey, win the knife throwing contest. Geoffrey probably wouldn't have felt the need to frame Trenson if that were the case. But how was Trenson supposed to know that?

Ultimately it came down to the confrontation at the bridge, when the brigands killed Jayfor and sold Trenson into slavery. That was the turning point. The fatal mistake. If he had fought in sync with Jayfor more, if he had pushed himself a little harder, maybe he wouldn't be here. Maybe they would have defeated the bandits and continued forward, traveling north and eventually reaching their goal. They might have even found the tree of Ramadus by now.

No. Thinking of what might have been only distracts me from what can be. There's nothing I can do about my past decisions. All I can do now is figure out how to get out of this mess.

Trenson took a deep breath.

OK. So Thrance said he had infected him with a sort of reverse-poison. It would only kill him if he stopped taking it. According to Thrance, it was such a rare plant that it would be useless trying to find it anywhere else. If he wanted to survive, he would need to continue taking it. The king would continue to administer the poison to Trenson in his food, on one condition: do exactly as he said. And that was to help him prepare and repel the assassination.

It wasn't a terrible arrangement, Trenson had to admit. It wasn't like he was being forced to commit some atrocious act. He simply had to protect the king. After that, he could – *finally* – leave this city that couldn't seem to let him go.

Trenson had to chuckle. He had been in Augustria for months. It was about time he left.

Trenson was tired of being thrown from place to place, forced to be one slave after another. First it was the slave trader. Next it was Wulfric. Now it was the king of Augustria himself. Trenson kicked himself for not trying harder to escape in the past. It certainly wasn't becoming easier to get away.

Trenson wiped the spit off on his trousers and looked at himself again in the mirror. "I don't care if it kills me. This is the last master I'm serving."

***

Trenson was shown around the palace by the same chubby servant that lead him to breakfast that morning. He was slightly disappointed. He was secretly hoping that he would be shown around by the girl that woke him up that morning. She seemed much nicer – and cuter.

"I'm showing you the areas which you are allowed to go," the servant said as they descended a flight of stairs. "If you don't remember me showing you around an area, or you find yourself somewhere that I didn't show you, then you likely aren't supposed to be there."

Trenson didn't tell the servant that he had lived in a palace for five years, which meant he already knew what the inside of a palace looked like.

It was true, though: this palace had a very similar layout to the one in Loronis, the one that burned in front of his eyes. Was that a year ago? He couldn't remember. It had to be months. It felt like ages.

He was shown the dining hall – at least, the one dedicated to the lower class of staff – as well as the training yard, the library, the "commons" room – really a hall where they could spend their free time – and a few others.

If Trenson had been the common ex-prisoner that everyone thought he was, he would have been confused out of his mind. The sheer size of everything around him, from the size of the roof to the length of the halls, was bewildering. But Trenson was used to it. It had been a while, but the layout was surprisingly similar to his old home.

However, all the flower paintings on the wall did bring down the sophisticated factor the palace attempted to present.

The tour ended back in front of Trenson's room, the same one he had woken up in that morning. "That is all," the servant said. "You have no duties yet, but I am certain the king will find something for you to do in the next few days. Until then, spend the rest of the day familiarizing yourself with the place, and don't cause trouble. Dinner is served at six. Find me if you require any assistance."

Without waiting for Trenson's response, the servant turned and briskly walked down the hall.

Trenson wondered what he should spend the next few hours before supper doing. Then an idea struck him. In fact, it was such a good idea that he silently congratulated himself for thinking of it. He would take a nap.

XXXIX

THE ROOM FELL DEAD silent after the words left Ernest's lips. Nobody knew what to say. The fact that the king was in league with the Scorned wasn't a huge surprise. Most political leaders were. But Ernest's plan was to assassinate him? To take such a drastic action? That was what shocked everyone.

One of the men from the northern hideout was the first to speak up. Clearing his throat to break the awkward silence, he asked cautiously, "Isn't that a little extreme?"

Ernest was respected as a leader. He was always clear with his instructions and made sure the orders he gave were easy to understand. He wouldn't make someone do anything crazy – at least, not usually. So to hear him give such a decisive and dangerous command out of the blue was a shock.

Ernest didn't show any surprise at the reaction on everyone's faces – not that he showed much emotion anyway. "I understand it is sudden. I have done research for months and not told anyone. Everyone here knows that I wouldn't call for such a drastic action unless I thought it was necessary."

Another man spoke up. "You act like it's so simple!"

"No, I don't," Ernest responded calmly. "I know this will be dangerous and has a low chance of success. But I think it's a risk we should take if we are to end this conflict."

Jayfor raised his voice. "How will it end the conflict?"

"By depriving the Scorned of their funds and assistance. In the last few years, we have made significant progress. We have stormed their meeting places, reduced their numbers, and dramatically improved our presence. I believe we are on the verge of eradicating them permanently. This is the last thing holding them up. We can sever the final string, and they'll be forced to disband."

Ernest wasn't finished. "I know you have many questions. I understand. It would be one of the most prestigious tasks we attempt. I hesitated bringing you here today, because I knew how dangerous it was. But I believe this is our chance to strike the final blow!"

A Willing stood up from his chair. "It's not so simple as assassinating the king! You have to think of the consequences that it will bring. Who will replace him? What will this do to the city, to the people? Thrance isn't a great king, but it wouldn't be hard for a worse one to take his place. We don't know who his successor is, or if he even has one! You have to consider the ripple effect of this!"

Ernest frowned. "I don't think you understand how bad he truly is. Most of his work is done in the shadows. While not serving under them in any way, he provides a massive amount of supplies and information. Essentially, he is the backbone of the Scorned."

Ernest continued. "As for who will become king after him, that was more difficult to find out. While he doesn't have any immediate family, he does have a nephew, Duncan, seventeen years old, who holds a fief to the west. I've deduced that he would be next in line for the throne. He's a good chap, not quite old enough to be prepared for his role as future king, at least not by Kallarian standards, but he manages his fief well."

Jayfor was surprised. In Faldon, the king usually voluntarily stepped down from his throne to give it to the next-in-line, and would spend his last days mentoring the new king. He knew that it was different in some places, though: he had heard that sometimes the kingship would pass down only once the king died. That always seemed a little odd to him. It was safe to assume that Augustria took the latter option.

"More importantly, he has shown distaste for the Scorned. We captured multiple ambassadors of the Scorned, and all of them said the same thing: Duncan refused offers of working together, and hated the organization for its covert ways. I think this is assurance that once he becomes king, we won't have to worry about him helping our enemies."

This was a favorable response, as shown by the murmur of approval that ran through the room. There was still hesitation, though. The same man spoke up again, still not convinced. "Are you certain?"

Ernest nodded. "Yes."

There was a moment of silence. Seeing as no one else was going to ask, Jayfor raised his voice. "It's one thing for us to talk about it here; it's another to execute it. How are we supposed to assassinate him? I know how well a palace is guarded. It's designed to keep the king safe."

Ernest's response was quick and without hesitation, demonstrating how well he had thought this out. "One of our men once worked as a palace guard in the gardens. From his information and other intel, I believe I have found a route that almost guarantees success."

He continued, gesturing with his hands and pacing as he spoke. "There is a small canal that runs through the garden, serving as an artificial river. The canal is fed by underground, which connects the garden to the Indigo River. It is through this tunnel which we shall enter the palace."

He frowned, looking his audience dead in the eyes now. "Now comes the most difficult part. There are four guards in the gardens, two situated by the pipe's opening, and two more by the door leading out. The fact that they even post guards in a room like the garden shows how valuable they view their security."

Ernest nodded at a particular man in the crowd. "Weston, have you finished preparing the blow darts?"

Weston smiled. "Aye, finished them days ago. So that's what they're for?"

"Precisely. Using your tranquilized darts, it will be easy to render the guards unconscious. The canal flows in such a way that, if we only allow our head to show, we can be within range of all four guards to hit them."

"Just can't get the blowpipe or the darts wet," Weston added for everyone to hear. "It'll make them useless."

Ernest nodded. "Point taken."

"And then what?" another man asked.

"After the guards are dealt with, we shall steal their armor and outfits. I have been informed that the palace has a strict set of rules for the height and build of their guards. Because of this, I'm only taking men who are five feet, six inches."

Jayfor raised an eyebrow. That wasn't exactly tall. Then again, most people in Augustria were shorter than Jayfor. And Jayfor was already short.

"Aren't you taller than that?" another man asked Ernest.

Ernest shrugged. "Not by much. I should be able to wear the armor and not arouse suspicion. Anyway, after this, we will don their armor and take their places, hiding the bodies. The guards change every three hours. When the replacements come, we will enter the palace and act as though we are heading to our new posts.

"Once we're in the palace, we will locate the main stairwell. It's likely that the king's bed is on the higher floors. We should be able to go a few floors without anyone noticing, but since security is always tight around the king, it's likely we will have to blow our cover to get past his inner guard. It should be easy to find his room when we reach the highest floor. Once we're in, we find his room, and put him down quietly in his sleep."

Jayfor ran through the plan again in his mind. It was still risky. They could easily be caught at any point. But it was probably the safest way to do it. "What about the escape plan?" Jayfor asked. They needed a way to get out of it alive, even if they succeeded.

"After we finish the job, there are two ways to get out. If we haven't been spotted, we can quietly exit the room, and make our way back to the garden. There's almost a zero percent chance of that happening, and even if it did, it's unlikely we make it out without someone noticing. That's why there's always a backup plan..."

Ernest paused for a moment, letting the silence add emphasis. "As it turns out, the gardens are directly outside the window of the palace."

A surprised buzz rose from the crowd. "You're suggesting jumping out the window?! At that height?! Even if we manage to land in the canal, we could still get hurt! And if we miss the landing?!" These along with other objections were thrown at Ernest.

His powerful voice silencing the noise, Ernest spoke again. "I understand it's not safe. But none of this is!" He shook his head. "Listen. If we don't do this, this... this *war* we've been fighting could last two, three, even ten more years. I am tired of this." He raised a closed fist, his jaw clenched in passion. "I'm tired of us going nowhere in this fight! Here is our chance to end it. I don't care if you don't want to do this. I'll find others who do. Let the cowards speak up, or leave the room."

Nobody moved. Ernest's eyes scanned the room with a fire, daring them to leave. It was either the fear of being called out, or a genuine desire to fight, or both, that kept everyone standing in their spots.

After a few moments of silence, Ernest relaxed. "Very well. Either you are brave, or you are too stupid to understand the danger. Or both. In any case... it's time to get busy."

T HE NEXT FIVE DAYS were busy for Trenson. Very busy.

"I don't see why we don't just block off the pipe if that's the case," a secretary said to Trenson. "I mean, if that's how they're going to get in. A few iron bars, and our problem is solved."

Trenson shook his head and sighed. He was aggravated that he had to deal with people like this all day. He gestured to the pipe in question. "If we seal it off, they'll simply turn around, go back home, and think of another way to accomplish their goals. You think they're going to stop just because of a few bars? I don't think so. People that attempt these sorts of things are dangerous. They need to be caught."

The secretary shrugged. "Fair enough." His accent added a certain trill to his words. Faldian wasn't his first language, but the fact he could speak it was why he was assigned to Trenson. "But if that's the case, why don't we trap them in the pipe, or at least apprehend them once they get into the gardens? You talk about letting them get all the way to the king's bed before we catch them. Seems awfully dangerous to me."

"The king will have to spend that night somewhere else, in some other room, so they'll be no danger to him. Haven't I already explained this to you?"

The secretary nodded sheepishly. "Yes, but I don't quite understand, so please, if you wouldn't mind, uh, doing it again?"

Trenson pursed his lips. He hated explaining himself once, but twice was almost unbearable. "I've played these games before. These assassins, they know what they're doing, and they're great at escaping if things don't work out. My goal is to catch them, since I'm sure they're better use to you alive than dead. I've seen them turn tail, break windows, fall twenty feet out a broken window, sprain their ankle, and *still* manage to escape. We need to wait until they're so deep in the palace they can't run. Plus, waiting until they make it into the king's room makes sure that we don't accidentally apprehend the wrong people. Since the guards will be on high alert, they're likely going to act on the smallest suspicion. I've had cases where the guards were so jittery they mistaken each other for assassins, and the real assassins were almost successful."

The secretary raised an eyebrow. "You speak as though you have done this before."

Trenson's throat immediately tightened. He swallowed, thinking of an excuse. "I... used to serve a baron, a very prestigious one. There were a number of attempts on his life."

"You?" Surprise was evident in the secretary's voice. "I didn't realize you held such a... favorable position."

Trenson huffed. "You're surprised that I was in prison for holding a job like that."

"Well... yes."

Trenson smiled. "Honestly, I am too. Now, let's move on."

Over the next few hours, Trenson told the secretary everything that he knew about the assassination – which wasn't as much as Trenson wanted. Truth be told, when he had used the sword to decode the writing on the wall, he had seen a vision of how it would unfold, but it was unclear; blurry. It was like trying to watch your reflection in turbulent water. Certainly possible, but you can't focus on any single part of it.

Trenson knew they would enter through the pipe in the garden. He knew they would somehow make it past the guards and make their way upstairs, into the king's chamber. And he saw, clearly, how they would end the king's life: a knife to the throat.

Now he just had to stop it.

The plan was simple: allow the assassins to infiltrate the palace and make it into the king's bedchamber. Once there, they would be ambushed by the guards who were to be in hiding. "A simple plan," Trenson admitted. "But often, it's the simple things that work best."

The secretary glanced at the water clock on the wall of the library they were in, reading that it was a quarter 'til six, and took a deep breath. "I agree. Well Trenson, I think I know enough of this operation to say that your plan is a good one. I will inform his highness of it, and if you have his approval, you can head the operation." He gave a half smile. "I have many questions about your history, but I was told not to ask.

Trenson nodded. "Smart."

With that, the secretary stood up, bowed respectfully, and left the library, his footsteps echoing with each step and slowly growing quieter.

Trenson leaned back in his chair and sighed. *So now what?* He had days until the assassination attempt. He could read here, in the library. Or he could go to the training yard. That was the only time he was allowed to carry his sword; the king said it was a "safety measure." More like he was afraid of Trenson being armed.

Suddenly, a thought came to his head, an idea that was so good it made him bolt from his chair and chase the leaving secretary. "Hey, wait!"

The secretary turned with a puzzled expression.

Trenson cleared his throat, trying to figure out how best to phrase this. "I have a friend who works for Wulfric, the captain of the guard. Well, it's not really work, he's really a slave. Is there any way you can, say, purchase his freedom? Or is there something else I can do?"

The secretary clicked his tongue knowingly. "Using your fortunate situation for your personal benefit isn't a good idea. Regardless, I will see what I can do. But don't expect much."

Trenson relaxed. "Thank you."

It turned out the king approved of it, but it was purely out of the desire to strengthen Trenson's loyalty. He sent a message to Wulfric asking for the price. Wulfric responded with a much higher price than what was reasonable, which was to be expected. The king paid, and Aquila's freedom was bought that day. He was sent into the city with a loaded purse – per Thrance's orders – enough to pay for his meals for a week. Aquila found a job working at a blacksmith, where his large frame and strong arms came in handy. He slowly grew accustomed to the Augustrian language, and although he couldn't talk, he understood enough to get by. He worked happily at this job for the remainder of his life.

Aquila never knew who bought his freedom. And although he never saw Trenson again, he always had his suspicions, and he never forgot the broody man from Faldon.

XXXXI

J AYFOR WONDERED WHY HE had been looking forward to this. In the days leading up to the infiltration, Jayfor had grown more and more excited. Even though he didn't really want to do this, there was still a thrill to the idea of doing it.

Some of the thrill went away, however, when Jayfor saw that the entrance of the pipe was covered in algae and smelled like burned leather.

"This is disgusting," Jayfor remarked, wrinkling his nose.

Ernest glanced at Jayfor with a look that said, *what did you expect?* He was holding a torch, and the orange light illuminated his face sharply. The other two members of the team were standing in the pool of light as well. Jayfor wondered why nobody else thought of bringing torches, him included. They were lucky Ernest wasn't so unprepared.

"At least it's not as deep as we expected," one of the Willing said optimistically. The water was about waist deep if you stood up straight – and it was barely tall enough to do so.

"I thought you said it was a pipe?" Jayfor said.

"I did. And so it is."

"Well, I guess in a sense, but I was expecting something round and made out of metal. Like a real pipe. This is just a tunnel, a tunnel with a reinforced roof that goes under a hill."

Ernest laughed. "You think the crown wants to waste metal like that? By no means. I call it a pipe because it acts very much like the aqueducts in other regions."

Jayfor raised an eyebrow. "Aqueducts?"

"Never mind," Ernest said dismissively. "Anyway, let's get to work."

The four men made their way down the banks of the river. It was night, and the silver moon was a sickle in the sky, reflecting in the water before them. There wasn't a tree in sight. Empty plains filled with golden grass and rolling with hills were all to be seen besides the wide river before them. The gentle hum of waves filled the air. There was a faint breeze in the air, not strong, but just enough to push the freezing air into everyone's faces and make the night even more cold.

Jayfor pulled his cloak tighter around him, balling his fists to conserve warmth. "That water is going to be... cold."

Ernest didn't look in his direction, but merely said, "I'm glad you understand the principle of temperature, Conrad."

Conrad. He's using my alias as a way to preserve my identity from the others, like we agreed.

Jayfor huffed. "I'm just saying."

They reached the spot where the tunnel began, creating a channel of water that led under a hill and further underground. The echo of flowing water sounded within. Jayfor could see the timbers holding the roof up in the moonlight, creating a square tunnel, or pipe as Ernest misleadingly called it.

One of them men said, "We'll have to walk single file, but I'm sure we can fit through easy enough. Thankfully we're all short, so that helps."

"Another reason for everyone here to be a specific height," Ernest added.

There was a moment of silence. Everyone stared into the tunnel. They knew that the minute they stepped in, the icy water would reach their stomachs and suck every ounce of warmth from them. An awkward silence pervaded the air, everyone hoping someone else would volunteer.

Then one of the men, who went by the name Kurt, cleared his throat and turned to Ernest. "I think you ought to go in first. After all, you have the torch, and you know what they say: ladies first!"

This brought a chorus of laughter from everyone else. Ernest huffed without changing expression, and walked to the stream of water that led to the tunnel. Without breaking stride or slowing down in the slightest, he sloshed into the freezing water. His jaw-line tightened and he grunted, and he started taking quick, sharp breaths. The water reached just above his hips.

He stopped and turned to the group watching him. He held the torch high above the water. "Refreshing, lads. Now come on."

The only upside to the water freezing his legs off was that it took his mind off of how bad it smelled.

"It's sulfur that makes it smell bad," the man walking behind Jayfor, Quinn, whispered – Ernest told them to walk slowly and whisper so that their voices weren't carried to the other end of the tunnel. "It's in a lot of water that comes from the ground. There must be a spring somewhere nearby."

It made sense that Quinn knew about sulfur, Jayfor mused. He was the chemist that made the smoke bombs, so naturally he should know what it was.

The only source of light in the tunnel was Ernest, who led the way forward. He made sure to walk quietly, only allowing a little water to splash with each stride. If he felt like everyone behind him was being too loud, he would slow his pace even more. Ernest could hardly blame them, because he wanted to get out of this freezing water too.

Jayfor's teeth chattered uncontrollably. His stomach started to churn from the cramped walls and the rancid smell. He wondered how strong the rafters were to hold up the roof. They certainly didn't look very strong. Wouldn't that be wonderful, to have the roof come crashing down on him and bury him alive? It would be such a boring way to die, considering everything he had gone through.

They sloshed on, ignoring the crippling icy water that wanted to lock up their knees. Jayfor's boots started to fill with mud from beneath. He gritted his teeth. *It'll be over soon, it'll be over soon...*

Finally, after walking for what seemed like an eternity, they spotted a faint glimmer of light ahead. A joyful murmur ran across the group, but Ernest lifted a finger to silence them.

The light became brighter. Ernest dowsed his torch in the water, the orange pool of light instantly vanishing. Guided by the light ahead, everyone pressed forward.

Before long, they were a few feet in front of the exit, where the water flowed seamlessly into a canal that flowed through the garden. They stopped.

Ernest turned to the group, and motioning for them to copy his movements, pulled out the small, cylinder blowpipe that was in the front pocket of his cloak. Everyone else did the same thing and placed a dart in one end. Each person had two extra darts.

Jayfor remembered what Ernest had told them: *There are two guards stationed beside the pipe. Take them out first. After that, we'll have to make our way further down the river to get within sight of the guards at the doors, and then we will take them out as well.*

Ernest stood at the left side of the threshold of the exit. He motioned for Kurt to stand on the other side, which he quickly did. He held up three fingers, then two, then one.

They both stepped out of the threshold. Jayfor watched them point their blowpipes and then heard the sharp pop and they shot the darts. He heard two grunts, then the sound of armor clanking.

Ernest looked at Jayfor and Quinn and nodded. All clear.

Jayfor quietly exited the tunnel. He stopped for a moment and gazed around him, taking in the exotic foliage around him. There were more trees here than he had seen in all of Kallary.

Both guards were slumped on the ground, completely unconscious. Jayfor couldn't help but marvel at how fast it had taken effect. Within seconds, they were out. He had never seen such a powerful sedative before.

Ernest whispered, "Kurt, Quinn, stay here. Don't change into the armor yet, it'll be too loud and alert the other two guards. Wait until you hear me clear my throat loudly, that will be the signal. Hide the bodies."

Both men nodded. Ernest motioned for Jayfor to follow him, and both men slowly crept further down the river, following it as it twisted and turned through the garden forest.

The trees above obscured most of the moonlight, making it difficult to see. Jayfor held his loaded blowpipe in his hands, ready to use it. He couldn't even enjoy the landscape around him, his senses were so high, and the water was so cold.

After another twist in the river, both men froze and ducked behind the corner. The entrance to the palace was about ten yards away. Two guards were on either side of the large doors, holding spears in their hands and on the verge of sleep. Their armor glinted in the moonlight.

Ernest pulled out his blowpipe and took aim. Jayfor did the same, just as he had done the last few days, practicing for this moment. Ernest mouthed the words *three, two, one.*

Two darts flew towards the guards. But only one hit. Ernest's shot hit the target right in the neck, the only exposed part. He grimaced and felt the dart with his hand before falling over. Jayfor's dart was close, but not close enough. It whizzed past the guard's head and struck the hard wall behind him with a *ping.*

Come on! Jayfor was silently yelling. The guard immediately snapped to attention and saw his fallen comrade. "Hey!" He started to yell, but that was all he said. Jayfor loaded another dart and shot it, this time hitting his mark. The guard fell to the ground.

Ernest gave Jayfor an unamused look. Jayfor mouthed, *sorry.* Ernest ignored him and started towards the fallen guards, Jayfor following closely. It felt amazing to get out of the cold water, even though the air was equally cold. Ernest cleared his throat loudly to give the signal, not fearing anyone hearing him since the guards were taken out. There was no fear of anyone seeing them either, because there were no windows from the garden to the inside of the palace.

They changed armor quickly. Thankfully, it was light armor, only a thin chain mail under a shoulder plate. All they had to do was ditch their cloaks and the armor fit snuggly over. Jayfor took off the guard's boots and put them on his own feet. He wasn't about to take on the rest of the mission with squeaky boots – or cold feet.

After changing, they hid the bodies in the underbrush. They then took up the spears – although they still kept their swords at their hip – and took their posts beside the door.

Now all they had to do was wait.

XXXXII

Trenson had a hard time staying awake, but he was commanded to be a part of this. He tried to argue with the king, but it was useless.

"You warned me of this. Now you get to see it ended, to honor our agreement," Thrance had said.

So now, Trenson was hiding under the king's bed, laying flat on the ground, waiting for the assassins to come in.

Five other men were in the room as well, hiding in various places, waiting to ambush. Trenson wondered if they were about to fall asleep as well.

Come on, stay awake. All you have to do is capture or at worst kill them, and then you can finally leave this place.

XXXXIII

FINALLY, THE DOORS TO the palace opened. Four men came out, two ready to replace Jayfor and Ernest, while the other two to replace Kurt and Quinn.

Jayfor and Ernest briefly nodded to the replacements. Their helmets covered the front of their face, so there was no fear of them recognizing them. Jayfor's legs didn't want to move, stiff from cold and being drenched, but he willed them to carry him through the palace doors. Thankfully, it was a little warmer inside.

They waited until Quinn and Kurt came through the doors. They all nodded to each other, not daring to speak. Ernest closed the doors to the garden; they came together with a thud. Then he turned to Jayfor and nodded. *Lead the way.*

Jayfor nodded, and with Jayfor in the lead, started walking through the palace, heading towards the stairs up ahead that went to the higher floors, which led to the king's chamber, which led to the king, which led to the end of it all.

It had been decided beforehand that Jayfor would lead them in their quest to find the king's room. After all, he used to live in a palace, so he would be most familiar with the layout. Jayfor tried to explain to Ernest that not all palaces were the same.

"Well, you've lived in one. That's one more than everyone else. So you're leading us," Ernest said.

Jayfor couldn't argue with that. So here he was, having no idea where to go. Thankfully, there was a stairway further down the hallway, which made it much easier now.

They synchronized their footsteps, as real guards would do. Thud. Thud. Thud. Another group of four guards marched towards them. Jayfor couldn't help but fear that they might be recognized. *What if they try to speak to us?* That would certainly be the end. They couldn't hide their voices.

They passed by each other. Jayfor could feel their eyes on him. He tried not to look at them. It was best to take as few risks as possible. He must have done it right, because they passed each other without hinderance.

Jayfor breathed a sigh of relief, but it wasn't over yet. It was likely they would pass many more guards in their ascent. They needed to keep their guard up – literally.

The marching continued. Rhythmic. Synchronized. *They're doing a good job,* Jayfor had to admit.

They climbed the spiral stairway. Upon reaching the second floor, they saw another stairway at the opposite end leading to the next floor. *Why are the staircases for each floor on opposite ends? Wouldn't it be better to just have one for all the floors?*

They marched towards it, and climbed it with ease. The third floor was the same way: the next set of stairs was on the opposite end of the hall. And so was the fourth floor. And the fifth floor.

Good thing I'm used to walking, Jayfor thought to himself. They passed by a few more regiments, but thankfully, none of them took notice of them.

Why are there so many pictures of flowers on the walls?

As they ascended to the sixth floor, Jayfor immediately knew that this was it. The king slept here. It was evident by the change of layout, the cleaner floors and, most importantly, the increased number of guards. Up ahead were two large, wooden doors that reached halfway to the roof, adorned with carved images of dragons. These doors were open, and inside was a much larger hallway.

This is exactly how it was at Loronis. The king has his own, separate hallway with a private room, study, and washing room. We're almost there.

Jayfor wanted to look behind him to check on the team, but resisted the urge. Even the slightest suspicious movement could give them away.

There were so many guards here, twelve in total, lined up against the walls on either side. Holding their spears tightly in one hand and maintaining a rigid posture, they stood like statues. Jayfor wished they were. But no, they were men, men with eyes and ears, men who watched and would pick up the slightest inconsistency and recognize a faker.

Jayfor took a deep breath and continued walking, making for the king's hall at the end. He heard his comrades' footsteps behind him.

His goal was to get as close to the king's chambers as possible. There was no good excuse as to why they should be up here. All the guards were in place, and the king's inner security is extremely tight on schedule. As soon as they were noticed, they would be targeted, and at that point, all they could do was try to finish the job and hope to stick the water landing out the window.

Water landing is going to be difficult with all trees covering it. The fact dawned on Jayfor and made him even more uneasy.

Wait... Why weren't the guards acting? They had passed four already, and none of them had said a word, or made any move. Jayfor was confused. They were completely out of place here, and yet nobody was doing anything.

Jayfor wasn't complaining, but it seemed odd. He silently thanked Va'ar for this.

They made it halfway through the hallway. None of the guards stirred. They made it two-thirds of the way through. Still, none of them moved. They approached the large doors that led to the king's room. Again, none of them moved.

They passed through the doors and were ten yards from the room and the end, which had to be the king's room. And once again, none of them moved.

Something was off. There was no way that security was this loose. It was too easy. There were literally no guards in this part of the hallway, so it was obvious they weren't supposed to be here. But the guards didn't move or even show signs of seeing them.

It was concerning.

Regardless, it was too late to turn back now. They pressed on, finally ceasing their march in front of a normal-sized door. The king's chambers. This was it.

Jayfor took a deep breath and looked behind him. The rest of his men nodded. Then, he gently opened the door.

***

Trenson heard the footsteps before he saw them. From his hiding spot under the bed, he turned his head to see the door opening without a sound. Then a pair of boots entered the room. They hardly made a sound on the hard floor. These men were good.

Trenson was no longer sleepy. Every ounce of him was brimming for action. He had waited hours for this. He resisted the urge to call out immediately. They need to get further into the room if they were to trap them. And even if they escaped, the guards outside were ready to strike.

Trenson fingered the knife in his right hand. When they approached the bed and realized it was a bluff, he would yell to attack and stick the knife into the leg of the closest assassin before climbing out. The assassins were going to lose anyway, but adding an extra measure made it more exciting.

The door opened wider. More boots stepped in. It was a funny feeling, knowing exactly how many people were going to enter the room. His vision had allowed him to know that for a week. He wondered if this was how Va'ar felt, since he knew the destiny of everyone in the world.

Trenson watched as all four pairs of boots entered the room. They closed the door behind them. The boots made no movement. *They're surveying the room. They're bound to notice something is off.* It didn't take long for them to approach the bed. Trenson gripped the knife tighter.

They stopped in front of the bed. Trenson could have reached out and touched them if they liked, or lashed out with his knife. But he waited, just a little longer.

Then he heard the whisper. "It's just pillows! He's not here. It's a trap!"

"*Now!*" Trenson yelled. And with all his strength he drove his knife into the leg of the closest man standing to him.

XXXXIV

KURT SCREAMED. HE FELL to the floor, clutching his leg. Jayfor stumbled backward in shock.

Guards emerged from the shadows and behind furniture, swords drawn. "Drop your weapons! Get on the floor now!"

Jayfor gritted his teeth to prevent himself from cursing. So this was why it was so easy. They had been baited into a trap. How clever. But who ratted them out? Who was the spy?

It didn't matter right now. Jayfor held his sword before him, pointing it at the nearest guard. Ernest kneeled on the floor to help Kurt. Jayfor and Quinn stood on either side of them, guarding them.

A man appeared from behind the bed. He must have been the one hiding beneath it, the one that stabbed Kurt. He said in a loud voice, "Drop your weapons, and perhaps you'll be spared."

Suddenly, like the flash of a thunderbolt, Jayfor's mind stopped racing. Something had caught his attention, but even he wasn't sure what it was.

Then he realized: it was the voice of the guard behind the bed. He sounded a lot like Trenson. *Could it be?* Jayfor couldn't see very well in the dark, so he couldn't tell. He dismissed the idea. Trenson wouldn't be here.

Ernest pulled the knife from Kurt's leg. Kurt tried to stifle his scream, but it came out as a moan instead. Blood began to soak the carpet underneath. Ernest tore a piece from the tunic under his armor and began wrapping it around Kurt's wound. He looked up at Jayfor, and in his eyes was something Jayfor had never seen in them before: fear.

Jayfor gritted his teeth and didn't respond to the guard's threat. He instead held his sword before him and took a ready stance, a gesture of defiance.

The guard with Trenson's voice, who was obviously the leader, drew his own sword. "Very well, then. Disarm them!"

***

Trenson knew that the assassins would be extremely skilled. But it was entirely different to watch that skill in motion before his eyes.

With one assassin wounded and one attending to him, that left two men, who formed a wall around their comrades. The guards approached them with swords drawn, preparing to disarm or draw blood if needed.

The first guard attacked. With precision, the assassin parried the blade to the side and thrust into the shoulder of the guard. Although he was wearing armor, the force was enough to knock him backward. Another guard attacked the second assassin. The assassin fell back a step, but it was a feinted retreat. As soon as the soldier advanced, the assassin used the crossguard of his sword to push the sword away, get close to the guard, and plant a dagger in his side under the plate armor. Another guard fell to the ground, yelling in agony.

Drat! They're good. At least the noise will attract the other guards. Trenson leaped on the bed and, using the element of surprise, landed a hard kick into the face of the nearest assassin.

***

Jayfor didn't see the boot coming toward his face until he felt it slam into his helmet and felt himself falling to the ground. He landed on the carpet and rolled, seeing stars. By the time his eyes readjusted, he caught sight of the leader of the guards above him, preparing to deliver a boot to his throat and pin him to the ground.

Jayfor rolled to the side, feeling the vibration in the ground as the boot hit the carpet hard. He quickly rose to his feet and assumed a ready stance. He didn't notice, but his sword began to glow. It was barely enough to see, but in the heat of battle, nobody paid it any attention.

If Jayfor would have calmed his mind enough to get a good look at his opponent, he would have seen that his sword was glowing as well. This would have made him stop and wonder who he was fighting, and question what his true identity was.

But neither man noticed.

The guard held his guard, waiting for Jayfor to attack first. This was an advanced tactic, to allow your opponent to attack first in order to counterattack. Jayfor knew it was a trap but needed to finish this fight fast.

He attacked with a quick thrust. As expected, the guard countered and responded with his own thrust. Jayfor dodged to the side, making another lunge, but the guard saw it coming and stepped back. Both men disengaged for a brief second.

This man is good, Jayfor thought.

***

This man is good, Trenson thought. Fine then. He would just have to make his strokes more lethal and stop holding back.

He pointed his sword at his opponent in a ready position. Behind him the other assassin was engaged in a fierce fight against multiple guards, barely managing to hold them off. The sounds of footsteps echoed from the hallway. Trenson smiled. Even if they couldn't disarm the assassins, they had the numbers to overpower them.

He chanced a quick glance behind him. The wounded assassin was still on the ground, but his comrade was finishing wrapping the bandage around the wound. In a few seconds, he would join the fight as well.

Trenson wasn't worried, though. It wasn't possible for them to escape.

Trenson lunged forward, matching blades with the assassin, but he made the surprise move of sliding his blade close to the assassin's crossguard and pushing the edge of it away. Trenson grabbed his opponent's wrist and twisted it sharply. The assassin cried in pain and involuntarily dropped his sword, but immediately kicked Trenson in the stomach.

Trenson felt the air leave his lungs and stumbled backward, gasping for air. He didn't have much time to recover before his opponent lunged at him again.

This time, Trenson didn't hold back. His survival instincts had kicked in and he was no longer thinking about disarming his opponent, but killing him. His cuts and thrusts were quick and fast, but the assassin was so infuriatingly fast that he would parry and return with a slash of his own.

Trenson let down his guard and overextended his thrust. The consequences of this were quick. Now much closer to Trenson, the assassin slid his blade close to Trenson's and with an extremely quick flick, used the hilt of his sword to rip the blade from Trenson's hand.

Trenson tried to back up but found his back against the wall. The assassin held his blade against Trenson's throat, seconds away from slicing in his neck and ending his life immediately.

Trenson was powerless. The slightest movement would only end his life sooner. But in this moment, when time seemed to slow down and the world around him faded away, Trenson noticed something that stopped his mind dead.

The sword pressed against his neck – it was glowing.

And there was only one other man who wielded a sword like that.

Jayfor pressed his sword against the guard's throat. He was tired of this fight; it had taken far too long. Now to end this quickly, help his friends, and get out of this place.

Jayfor gripped the sword tighter, preparing to cut the guard's throat, when the guard whispered, "Wait."

Jayfor looked up at the man's face for the first time, the light from his sword illuminating his features. And that's when, for the first time in months, after weeks of toil and strife, hanging on to desperate hope or bitter remembrance, Jayfor and Trenson saw each other.

XXXXV

JAYFOR DROPPED HIS SWORD to the ground and took off his helmet, letting it fall to the ground as well. "Trenson?! Trenson, you're alive!"

Jayfor immediately forgot about the battle around him. Ecstasy flooded his senses. He rushed Trenson and wrapped him in a tight embrace. "I found you! I found you! Thank you Va'ar, oh thank you Va'ar!" Tears started to flow down his face.

"Jayfor?" Trenson was in a daze. "But you... You died! I saw it! What... How?" Trenson's voice was barely above a whisper.

Jayfor's voice was thick with sobs. "No! I've been looking for you for months now." Although the moment was euphoric, the sounds of fighting returned to Jayfor's ears. He released Trenson and took in the scene before him. More guards were entering the room. Ernest and Quinn were fighting them off, but they were overwhelming him. Kurt was on the ground, holding his wrapped shin in pain.

Jayfor took a deep breath and turned to Trenson, trying to gather his thoughts. "Listen, I... I don't know what you're doing here, why you're fighting against us, but that doesn't matter. I need help getting out of here."

Trenson looked at the room around him. Suddenly, his perspective of the "good guys" and "bad guys" shifted. The assassins were with Jayfor, which made them his friends. The guards – his guards! – were attacking them, so he had to help them! "Uh… Well, it's impossible! There are guards everywhere! And more are coming!"

A soldier who just entered the room attacked Jayfor, who was completely unprepared and saw the attack all too late. Trenson saw it and, quickly grabbing it from the ground, used his sword to deliver a fierce cut to the soldier's back, drawing the blood of his former comrade. The guard cried in pain and fell to the ground.

Jayfor looked at Trenson in relief. "Thanks." He grabbed his sword from the ground. "Listen, the window is our only way out. Come with us!"

"The window?! You're crazy, you'll break your legs from this height!"

"Not if we hit the water. Come on Trenson, help us!"

Trenson's mind was spinning. He had no idea who was the good guys or bad guys at this point, but one thing was certain: he had found Jayfor. And he would do anything to prevent losing him again. He nodded slowly. "Go. I'll cover you."

Jayfor breathed a sigh of relief. He then quickly appeared by Ernest's side to help him, engaging one of the guards attacking Ernest and taking some pressure off of him.

"What have you been doing?!" Ernests demanded after finishing off another guard. "This is no time to have a chat with one of our enemies!"

Jayfor blocked a cut. "He's a friend! It's Trenson, the one I've been looking for! He's coming with us!"

Ernest shot a quick glance of surprise at Jayfor, but there was no time for him to ask for more details. "Good. Listen, you carry Kurt; Quinn and I will break the glass and cover us. We need to get out of this alive!"

Jayfor nodded and rushed to Kurt, who was leaning against the bed, clutching his leg in pain. He looked up at Jayfor with red and watery eyes, through the holes in his helmet.

Jayfor said, "We're getting out of here. Come on!" With a grunt, he lifted Kurt off the ground, barely managing to keep his balance. Kurt gasped in pain and his eyes went out of focus. Jayfor could only imagine how painful this was.

He turned to Quinn. "Quinn, the window!"

Quinn turned to Jayfor, then the window, and nodded in understanding. However, he took his attention away from his opponent for a little too long. The guard attacked Quinn and he had just enough time to parry. Now off balance, he barely kept his defense against the numerous hacks and slices.

Luckily, Trenson took notice and delivered a decisive head blow to the guard attacking Quinn. When the guard fell to the ground, Quinn looked at Trenson with confusion, not understanding why he would help him. Trenson offered a faint smile. "Go, I'll cover you!"

Quinn nodded and lost no time getting to the window. Moonlight illuminated his face as he took a good look at the thick window. A sword would do little to shatter this. He looked around and spotted a small statue of a cat in the corner of the room. He grabbed it, feeling its hefty weight. Carrying statue above his head, he ran at the window and chucked it at the glass.

The sound of exploding glass caught everyone's attention. The fighting ceased for a few moments, everyone's attention focused on the glass-free window. Shards littered the ground. Freezing air instantly swirled into the room.

Quinn put one foot on the sill. "Come on!" He looked down below for a few moments, then jumped, disappearing from view.

More guards poured into the room. "They're getting away!" Ernest and Trenson edged their way to the window, locked in fights so fierce it would be a death wish to turn around. Sparks flew from the blades as they clashed. Trenson's blade glowed faintly, leaving streaks in the air with each swing.

Jayfor's arms started to shake from holding Kurt. "Come on, come on!" he yelled. He needed to make sure his friends made it out safe.

Ernest got close enough to his opponent to deliver a kick that ended his fight. He then turned and dashed to the window. He rushed to the edge and looked over. He couldn't hide the fear from his face as he looked down at the drop, but he didn't linger. He turned to Jayfor. "You're next!" Then he jumped.

Trenson and Jayfor were the only ones left now – besides Kurt, who was groaning in Jayfor's arms. Trenson was being swarmed. They were surrounding him from all sides. He couldn't stop fighting or they would strike him from behind. Jayfor knew he needed to go, but he wouldn't leave without Trenson. He wouldn't lose him again.

"Trenson, come one!" Jayfor yelled.

Trenson didn't turn to look at Jayfor. "Go! I'll be right behind you!"

"I'm not leaving you again!"

"You won't have to! Now go!"

Jayfor sighed. He had to trust him. He stepped onto the windowsill. Thankfully the sill was big enough for him to stand with both feet. He peered over the edge and felt his breath leave as fast as his courage. It was a long way down. He was five – or was it six? – stories high. He could see the garden directly below him, and the river that wasn't quite large enough to make him feel comfortable jumping. He could see Ernest and Quinn below, looking up at him.

Jayfor took a deep breath. He had to do this. They had made it, and so could he.

Kurt peered down and gulped, looking even more terrified than Jayfor was.

Jayfor turned. Trenson was continuing to back up and was only a few feet from the sill now. Jayfor wanted to wait a little longer, but he knew it was too dangerous. Taking one last look at the water below, Jayfor took a deep breath, and jumped.

***

Trenson was fighting for his life, but he wasn't fighting to win: he was fighting to get away. Desperately he wanted to disengage, if only for a second, so he could jump out of the window and leave this place. But he was blocking the blows of three men at once, and even if he managed to defeat one, two more would instantly take his place. Trenson was only a few feet from the window now. Just a little more.

He sensed that Jayfor had jumped, but didn't dare turn to look. He darted his sword left to right, blocking multiple blows and sidestepping thrust after thrust. He need to wait just a few more seconds for an opportunity to present itself.

At last! Trenson had a brief moment where none of the blades were attacking him and he had a free moment. Now was his chance. He spun around on his heel and darted for the window. It was only a few feet away.

He was inches away. He was about to lift his foot onto the sill when he felt a kick hit him in the back of the knee. He couldn't stop himself as he fell forward, his ribs slamming into the windowsill. He gasped, both in pain and at the drop in front of him. His face was hanging over the edge of the sill and he could see the sheer drop before him.

As he fell forward, his arms flew over the edge of the sill. His sword flew from his hand and out the window, falling far out of reach. "No!"

This delay was enough to allow his enemies to catch up to him. Trenson felt hands grabbing his legs from behind him. He kicked and tried to free himself. He needed to raise his legs above the sill so he could fall into the water below. But more hands grabbed his legs. He kicked harder but it was no use. They were pulling him back in.

He grabbed the edge of the sill and tried to pull himself over. He could hear Jayfor's voice below. "Trenson! Trenson, come on! No! No, no, no!"

Trenson was yanked viciously. He lost his grip and fell back into the room. He tried to lash out, but he felt a fist connect to his head, and then everything went black.

***

"NO!" Jayfor screamed.

Ernest, dripping wet with strands of hair hanging over his eyes, grabbed Jayfor's arm. "Conrad, they're coming! We're leaving now!"

Jayfor resisted. "I'm not leaving without him!"

"You saw them stop him, he's not making it out! We'll be next unless we leave now!"

Jayfor was on the verge of tears. To get *so close, so close* to freeing Trenson, only to have to leave without him, was so maddening that Jayfor wanted to scream into the sky, to go into the palace and end the life of everyone inside, to let everyone know the *pain,* the raw *pain* that consumed him.

But there was no point in any of it.

Jayfor noticed something falling out of the window, somersaulting before splashing into the water. As it started to sink, Jayfor rushed back into the freezing water and grabbed it, pulling it out of the water. It was Trenson's sword, his real sword, the one that was given to him by the Senver after the fall of Loronis.

"Conrad, come on!" Ernest yelled.

Jayfor gripped the sword in his hand and jogged with Ernest toward the pipe entrance. He heard the doors of the garden opening and the sound of voices mixed with clanging armor. They were coming.

"Go!" Ernest yelled. This time it was Quinn who carried Kurt, and he sloshed his way into the tunnel into the darkness. It was funny how this time, nobody noticed the cold water.

Jayfor looked up at the broken window one last time. He was on the verge of leaving everyone and rushing into the palace by himself. But he knew it was useless. He had his chance. Now that he had failed, he would suffer. He followed close behind Kurt.

Ernest was about to enter the tunnel when he heard the solid *thunk* of an arrow hitting the ground beside him. He turned to see four guards in view, two of them with bows. One was reloading while the other was taking aim. Ernest gritted his teeth. They couldn't outrun the bows; they would simply shoot them while they were in the tunnel.

Reaching into his tunic, Ernest pulled out the smoke bomb, then realized with a frown that it was soaking wet. So much for that idea. He placed it back in his tunic and dashed into the tunnel. "They have bows! Run!"

And run they did.

XXXXVI

TRENSON HAD PLENTY OF time to mull over his thoughts in his cell.

The dominant thought was of Jayfor. He was alive. He had been alive this entire time. Even if his circumstances were much worse than before, this one fact changed everything. Now he another reason to escape: to see Jayfor again.

Has he been trying to free me this entire time?

It still shocked Trenson that Jayfor was one of the assassins he had seen in his vision. He wondered what Jayfor had become tangled in. Hopefully nothing bad. Jayfor was gullible at times, which made it easy to take advantage of him. *No, he's smarter than that. If anything, I'm the one who was on the wrong side.*

Thrance's words echoed in his mind: *The only way to break the addiction is to slowly lower the concentration of the herb, and to do so with extreme skill and precision.* Trenson was still addicted to the poison. Unless he was given more of it in the next two days, he would die – at least, if Thrance was telling the truth.

But that wouldn't matter, since he would die tomorrow anyway.

Trenson glanced around the cell. A small, cramped space with a barred window and a pile of hay for a bed. There wasn't much to speak of.

He heard footsteps and looked up. Through the bars that served as his door, he saw two guards stop and stare at him curiously. "Who's that?" one asked.

The other said, "Oh, he's that 'prophet' that everyone was chattering about. Everyone treated him like he was angel, until he was caught helping the very assassins he warned us about. Not so prophetic anymore, is he?" He shot a dark glare at Trenson. "Anyway, he'll be hung tomorrow. And quite a show that will be!"

The other man nodded, and both of them walked away.

Trenson lay down on his straw bed. He wasn't scared of what would happen tomorrow. In fact, he wasn't downcast at all. Perhaps this was because he had found Jayfor, which lifted his spirits significantly. But that didn't seem to be the reason.

Trenson had been in many deadly situations, many of which offered no means of escape, but he managed to get away in the end. As such, the threat of death terrified him much less than it used to. Maybe that was why he wasn't worried.

Even though there was nothing *he* could do to save himself tomorrow, there was someone else who could. Jayfor was still out there. And he knew that if Jayfor was going to save him, he would put on a show in the process.

***

"Tomorrow is the long-awaited day! By midday, thieves, swindlers, and even an assassin are to be executed! His highness will attend himself, to watch the hanging of the man who attempted to take his life!"

The herald was obnoxiously loud, but he had drawn a crowd on the side of the street. In that crowd, concealed in long cloaks, were Ernest and Jayfor. Having heard enough, they slipped out of the group and began walking down the stone street.

"I didn't understand a word he said," Jayfor said.

"Oh right, you don't speak Kallarian. He said that there will be a hanging tomorrow, and that a certain enemy of the king would be executed."

"Rather quick for a hanging, don't you think?" Jayfor commented.

"That hanging has been planned for a week. Trenson will simply be the cherry on top."

Jayfor huffed. "Well, the people won't be able to enjoy that cherry if I do anything about it." As soon as it came out of his mouth, Jayfor realized how cringy it was.

Ernest slowly looked at Jayfor, unamused. "Was that supposed to be clever?"

Jayfor kept his eyes on the road in front of him. "It sounded better in my head."

"Undoubtably. I assume you have some sort of plan on getting Trenson out of this?"

Jayfor took a deep breath. "Well, in a way, but it all depends on one thing."

"And that is?"

"If you're going to help me do it."

Ernest was silent for a few moments. Jayfor shuddered from the cold and pulled his cloak tighter. He didn't know how Ernest would respond. It was a lot to risk, and Ernest wouldn't get anything out of it.

Just when Jayfor was going to tell Ernest to forget about it, the captain of the Willing spoke. "It would be dishonorable to not help you. You've helped us in so many ways and risked your life multiple times on our account. I've made you suffer, Jayfor. Of course I'll help. It's the least I can do."

That is true, Jayfor thought. He breathed a sigh of relief. "Thank you."

The side of Ernest's mouth turned up ever so slightly, which was about as much as he could smile. "Now then, I assume you have a plan to rescue this so-called cherry?"

Jayfor grinned. "Sort of. I was thinking of using smoke bombs to create a distraction and then rushing in and freeing Trenson in the confusion."

"Hmm... Well I'm sure we have a few extra bombs for the occasion. But executioners are trained to hang the victim as soon as there's any sign of trouble. Bombs will do little to stop that. Besides, bombs will restrict our visibility as much as it will theirs. They make good escape plans, but are little use for much else. You will have to be extremely fast."

"And then we'll use smoke bombs to cover our escape," Jayfor added.

Ernest chuckled. "You enjoy those bombs, don't you?"

"Well, no! They're just extremely useful!" Jayfor retorted.

Ernest gave a half-smile once again. "In any case, it seems we have a plan. But I must warn you, Jayfor, that this is a big event. The king himself will likely be in attendance, which will raise security even more. On top of that, this isn't the first time the Willing have rescued one of their own from a hanging. When the Scorned find out about this, they'll use it to their advantage."

Jayfor's spirit sank. "You mean the Scorned might be there?"

"I'm saying it's very likely. They know we rescue our own, and they use that knowledge to set up traps, exposing us in the open. We've failed these types of mission before for those reasons."

Jayfor thought about this. This would make things much more difficult. Not only would they have to contend with the guards, but the possibility of the Scorned was a much larger threat.

"I'm not trying to discourage you," Ernest added. "I'm just warning you."

"Oh, you're not going to discourage me," Jayfor replied. "At this point, nothing will."

XXXXVII

THIS WAS THE DAY. The day that Trenson would die.

The morning was a blur. He was given breakfast, although he didn't remember what it was now. The hours in his cell seemed to pass quickly.

He wasn't quite sure what to think. He was torn between despair and hope. Jayfor would rescue him. Or would he? His mind was numb. He was simply taking in what was around him, unable to do anything to affect his fate.

He had to leave it to Va'ar. If it was His will that he should die, so be it. If he should live, so be it. He wasn't sure if he had accepted this, but it didn't matter, because that was reality.

Now he was being led down the street. It was cold. It wouldn't be so unbearable if the wind wasn't blowing, whipping the air across his face and infiltrating what warm clothing he was wearing. He was at the tail end of a chained line, bound by their wrists to each other and being escorted by soldiers.

Trenson looked around. Crowds were gathering along the sides of the street, watching them pass by. Trenson couldn't help but chuckle. Even in Loronis, hangings were events that were looked forward to. Something about a human being strangled seemed to fascinate people. Trenson never understood it. He always thought it was strange how the ones being hanged were so always so stoic before death. Now he knew. There wasn't anything to do about it.

He continued walking. At least he was allowed to wear what he wore when at the palace, which was warmer than what most of the other prisoners were wearing. He could tell they were jealous by the way they looked at him – nobody spoke to each other.

Trenson heard insults thrown at him in Kallarian. He didn't understand the words, but that didn't make much of a difference. Yelling and spitting on those about to be hanged was common, even if the people didn't support the hanging. It was just something people did to add to flair to the event.

They exited the narrow street and came into the a large, open area, likely the city square. A crowd of people were already gathered here, all wearing fur coats and hats to shield them from the cold. In the center of the square was a wooden stage. It was poorly built, but that was to be expected, since it was put up and taken down frequently. Hanging from a raised post were nooses, hanging like carcasses in a butcher shop.

***

"My lord, it is dangerous for you to be here."

The king looked at the man who had spoken, a tall, muscular man wrapped in a dark cloak. "I understand the danger," Thrance replied, "but I fear nothing. You have your men at the ready, yes? They do not call you the Mentor for nothing."

The Mentor let out a husky sigh that clearly showed his annoyance. He hated playing the bodyguard, but the king requested. And if he wanted to maintain a positive relationship with the king, then he had to comply. "Yes, sir. My men are stationed upon the rooftops and within the crowds, ready at a moment's notice."

"Excellent. Then enjoy yourself, my good man." The king relaxed in his chair. He was given a slightly raised area to sit and watch, heavily guarded. For extra protection, he had three wooden walls placed around him and a roof.

But he wasn't worried. The Mentor had set a trap if –*when* – the Willing tried to make a move.

The Mentor leaned in closer to the king. "If it pleases his majesty, may I have a conversation with the assassin before the drop?"

The king shot him a questioning look. "A conversation? And what purpose does that serve?"

"In truth, I know this man. In fact, you might even say he is an old friend. I wish to speak to him one last time."

This surprised the king. To have a connection with an assassin was suspicious. "Are you sure that is wise?"

The Mentor spoke in an extremely polite tone. "Only if it pleases his majesty."

Thrance sighed. "Do what you will. But pray, don't take long."

The Mentor bowed. "Thank you."

***

Jayfor didn't know where Ernest was, but that didn't matter. He knew he was somewhere in the crowd, waiting, preparing for the moment that Jayfor made his move.

Through much pushing and shoving, Jayfor made his way to the front of the crowd and closest to the stage. There was a ring of guards keeping the people at bay. Jayfor tried to assume the same excitement as everyone else in the crowd to blend in.

Then he saw it: the prisoners. Even though he knew Trenson was among them, his heart still dropped when he saw him. Being led like animals to the slaughter. And that's exactly what would happen if he failed.

The air stunk. In winter, nobody wanted to bathe in freezing cold water. As a result, crowds didn't smell too great.

The people threw insults in a different language and spit at the prisoners as they walked. Trenson kept his head down and didn't make eye contact with anyone. A part of Jayfor wished he would look up and see him, but another part knew it was better that Trenson didn't know. It was better he not draw attention to himself.

An announcer in a colorful outfit stepped on the stage and said a few words to the crowd in Kallarian. Jayfor didn't understand what was said, but knew by the tone and hand gestures that this was designed to get the crowd excited. And excited it got them, for there was a cheer from the crowd.

As the announcer kept talking, the prisoners slowly ascended the stairs to the stage and approached their respective nooses. Jayfor heard their clanging of their chains stop as they took their places.

Jayfor knew how this would go. After the overseer was done speaking, he would leave the stage, and the executioner would set the nooses around the prisoner's necks. Then the lever would be pulled, and the victims would suffer "a short drop and a sudden stop," as the saying put it.

It was after the nooses were set that Jayfor would make his move.

The announcer finished his speech and left the stage as the crowd cheered and chanted, eager for what would happen next. The executioner, a burly man with a black mask around his head, approached Trenson, the first prisoner in line. Trenson didn't resist, his wrists tied behind his back and useless. He lifted his head, and the executioner slipped the noose around his neck, tightening it with a quick jerk. The executioner moved on to the next person.

It was almost time. Jayfor fingered the two swords at his side: his own, and Trenson's. He would give it a few more seconds. But just as he was about to charge the stage and dash through the circle of guards, he noticed a tall man slowly mounting the stairs of the stage, a hood thrown over his face. This man reached the top of the stairs and slowly approached Trenson.

***

"You don't remember me, do you?"

Trenson picked his eyes up from the ground to see a tall man standing before him. Trenson was confused. This wasn't the way executions were supposed to go. He wasn't sure who he was talking to. "What?"

The man chuckled, a deep sound that came from deep within his chest. Trenson could see little more than the man's half smile under the hood. "I thought not. But although I left your mind long ago, I've always remembered you, Trenson. You were never far from my mind. To be quite frank, I look up to you. Because of you, I have achieved what I never could before."

Trenson shook his head. He felt the noose scrape across his neck, forcing his head high. "Maybe if you would stop playing hide-and-seek under that hood, I could recognize you."

Another chuckle from the man. "Always quick with the tongue. You really haven't changed. Very well. We shall speak plainly, unguarded and without secrets..." he gripped the edge of the hood and slowly pulled it behind his head, the sunlight revealing his face. "...as equals."

For a few seconds, Trenson still had no idea who he was talking to. He didn't recognize the face as anyone he knew. Then he searched deep into his memory, and with brutal force, his mind matched the face with someone he knew. Someone he wished he wouldn't meet again.

The black hair.

The chiseled face.

The scar under his eye.

It was him.

Trenson involuntarily reeled back, but the noose kept him in place. His eyes widened and his mouth became dry. "No... not you! Not you!"

Xavson smiled, the same smile he had six years ago in Loronis. "I'm glad you remember me."

XXXXVIII

JAYFOR COULDN'T SEE THE man's face at first, since he was facing away from him. But he saw the shock on Trenson's face, the disbelief that struck him. Jayfor was confused. This man must have said something incredible to Trenson. But who was he?

Then the man slowly turned around, and, in an instant, his once-covered face was revealed.

No.

No.

It's him.

Jayfor's mind was dazed, shocked at what it was comprehending. It was him. The one who killed Annor. The one who took the throne. The one who tried to kill him. The one who slaughtered innocents to get what he wanted. The one who was banished from Faldon and never seen again.

My brother. But in title only.

***

"I wanted to see you one last time, before the drop," Xavson said, his voice smooth and good-natured. "Perhaps we could leave on better terms this time."

Trenson wasn't buying the easygoing attitude. "You came here to gloat," he said dryly.

"Gloat? About what? I am a humble man, Trenson. You humbled me six years ago. What point would I have to gloat?"

Trenson didn't respond.

Xavson turned to face the crowd. "These people came to watch the show. Funny how death and punishment is discussed as vile, but those same people rave to watch it. It reveals the true quality of people." He turned back to Trenson. "Unfortunately, you won't give them the show they want."

"What do you mean?" Trenson demanded.

"Oh, stop playing the fool! You know my little brother is going to rescue you. I would praise his tenacity if it wasn't so maddening. He's in the crowd, right now, watching, waiting, preparing to strike. That's why you show no fear. They think you're brave. But you know you have nothing to fear."

So Jayfor really was in the crowd? Trenson started searching the faces in the crowd. Xavson smiled. "Not only is he there, but so is his entire posse of do-gooders. They are here to rescue you. They outnumber the guards two to one. Not only will they rescue you, but they will re-attempt their attack on the king in the process."

Xavson huffed. "I couldn't care less about what happens to Thrance. He served his purpose. But you, you and Jayfor are the real prize."

Trenson looked Xavson dead in the eyes. "What are you here for?"

"It's quite simple, really. Jayfor has gathered most of The Willing here. It's much easier to catch fish when they are gathered together. My men are in the crowd as well, on the rooftops, waiting."

"Your men?" Trenson was trying to fit the pieces together.

"A counterforce to The Willing, to stop the propaganda and control they seek to enforce. My men are free and come from all walks of life. I taught most of them. They call me the Mentor for a reason."

Xavson looked at Trenson hard. "I know how Jayfor's mind works. I lived with him most of my life. Quick and simple, he will rush the guards, cut you loose, and create some sort of distraction for you to escape. His mind is so simple!" Xavson chuckled, a light chuckle that was too friendly for the person it belonged to.

Xavson glanced once more at the crowd. "But I overstay. See you when the battle unfolds, Trenson, and put on a good show!"

With that, he turned from the stage, his cloak whipping behind him as he quickly descended the stairs. Trenson was breathing heavily from his mouth. Xavson knew everything. He knew about Jayfor. There was nothing for him to do! Even if Jayfor *did* rescue him, he knew they would be ambushed. He had to warn Jayfor. But where was he?

***

Jayfor watched Xavson descend the stage. After six years, he saw what had become of his brother. Surprisingly, he wasn't the broken and bitter man he expected to see. Xavson looked incredibly decent, more so than when he was king of Faldon. The years had given him maturity in both his appearance and attitude.

Could this really be Xavson? Jayfor asked himself. But as much as he wished it wasn't, he couldn't deny the undeniable swagger, the hair, the eyes, the face. Those things didn't change with age.

Xavson here changed everything. There could only be one explanation for being allowed on stage: he was in league with the king, and held his respect.

Like a puzzle, the pieces clicked. Of course. The leader of the Scorned, the one they called the Mentor. It was Xavson.

So you have been productive, in all these long years...

That meant the Scorned were definitely here, and if Xavson was their leader, that meant the Scorned were even more dangerous now. If only he could find Ernest and warn him!

But there wasn't time. The drop was about to happen. He only had a few moments before he had to make his move.

The nooses were tightened around all of the prisoners. The executioner stood ready, his hand on the lever that would activate the swinging trapdoors that would turn the prisoners into corpses. The excitement of the crowd grew.

It was now or never. Catching the guards by surprise, Jayfor dashed forward and slipped past them. Panic immediately ensued. Jayfor drew his sword as he ran up the stairs. Voices shouted at him.

The executioner knew what Jayfor was doing and quickly pulled the lever. The trapdoors swung down. Trenson looked at Jayfor in panic as he started to fall, but the second the rope grew taunt, Jayfor slashed it in two with his sword.

Trenson fell to the ground and stumbled to his knees, gasping as the rope pulled tight around his neck but gave just enough slack to breathe. Jayfor dropped down beside him and quickly helped him untie the rope from his neck.

As soon as it was off, Trenson took a deep breath. "Thank you, thank you!" He couldn't relax now though. "Jayfor, Xavson, he's here!"

"I know, I know," Jayfor added breathlessly.

"He knows you're here, it's an ambush! He's going to kill us all!"

Just then, a horn blew.

Trenson and Jayfor looked at each other. It didn't take more than two seconds for them to mentally piece the information together and realize what was happening. The final battle was at hand.

***

The crowd was struck silent by the blare of the horn. The guards, once scrambling to apprehend Jayfor and Trenson, were now totally confused as to what to do. Everyone forgot about the festivities of the hanging. Nobody was cheering as the remaining five prisoners were hung. In fact, no one was even paying attention to them.

"My lord," one of the king's escorts said in shock, "what is happening?"

The king chuckled. "It's an ambush! But little do they know we have an ambush of our own planned."

Thrance turned to Xavson with a smile. "They are all yours. Put on a good show, please?"

Xavson smiled. "With pleasure."

***

The fighting broke out. The citizens were in a panic, especially when most of the people in the crowd revealed themselves to not be citizens at all.

Hoods were thrown back. The air filled with the drawing of dozens of swords from their scabbards. People screamed and scattered. Over half of the crowd remained, revealing hidden weapons, or removing their cloaks and letting them fall to the ground – an act that signified a readiness for combat.

Trenson and Jayfor emerged from under the stage with swords drawn. They took in their surroundings within a few seconds: confused guards, fleeing citizens, and many warriors. Many.

"We need to get out of here!" Jayfor yelled. "Let's find Ernest before they surround us!"

Trenson hesitated for a second at hearing the name. Ernest. It awoke a memory inside of him, but now wasn't a good time.

They rushed into the fray. The Willing were scattered among the crowd, distinguishable by their blue spaulders. Screams, clangs, shouts and sparks all filled the air as the battle reached its peak.

A Scorned attacked Jayfor, winding up his blade to deliver a vertical slice. Jayfor parried it and thrust, a quick and simple motion that left the man dead. Trenson engaged another attacker, shifting the momentum of the attack against the Scorned and ending with a slash across the chest.

Jayfor shook his head at Trenson with a smile. "You're rusty."

Trenson huffed. "At least I haven't gained weight like someone."

Jayfor frowned at looked down. "I have not!"

Trenson opened his mouth to throw another jab, but a different word came out. "Move!"

Jayfor felt the hairs on the back of his neck stand tall. He quickly sidestepped and watched a blade shoot past his side, where he was once standing. He rotated, using his momentum to deliver a hard blow that caught the attacker off guard. A few more thrusts, and the fight was over.

"Jayfor!" A deep voice called.

Jayfor turned to see Ernest running toward them, donned in light armor with sweat glistening from his forehead. Blood was on his sword. "It's worse than I feared. They're overrunning us!" He shot a brief nod of acknowledgement to Trenson, who returned it. "More are coming from the streets. Soon they'll have the exits filled with men and make it impossible to leave!"

Something whipped past Ernest's head, interrupting him as he ducked. An arrow landed in the ground not a yard from where Ernest was standing.

Trenson traced its path and found its source with a pit in his stomach. He yelled, loud enough for everyone to hear, "Archers!"

***

"Now *this* is entertainment!" Thrance said heartily. He was in an energetic mood, shifting in his chair and trying to watch the fight from different angles. "And to think I was once impressed by the arena shows Wulfric put on. You have outdone yourself, Xavson."

Xavson smiled. "It pleases me that such an event works to both of our advantages."

Xavson and Thrance were quite safe from the conflict inside the wooden booth, and since most of the remaining soldiers returned to it in order to guard the king, no one had attacked them. The Willing were too busy defending themselves to worry about the king.

The only two people in the booth, and with no eyes on them, Xavson knew this was his chance. "My lord, I must thank you again for naming me your heir. Truly, I did not ever hope to receive such an honor."

Thrance waved his hand dismissively. "I would rather it be a competent leader than that nephew of mine. He's as dull as the silver spoon. I want my lands to be held, and held fierce and tight at that."

"You need not worry, my lord," Xavson assured. He then approached the king from behind, pulled out a knife, placed his hands over the king's mouth and, in one fluid motion, cut his throat. "I will honor that promise."

***

A man fell beside Jayfor, screaming in agony as an arrow pierced his back. Trenson stumbled away from the man, wondering for a second if he should try to help him, then realized it was useless.

"Jayfor, come on!" Ernest grabbed Jayfor's arm. "We need to get out of here!"

It took Jayfor a few seconds before he could take his eyes off the dying man. He couldn't lose focus, he reminded himself. He made sure Trenson was beside him; he couldn't lose him again.

"*Retreat! Fall back!*" As loud as he could, Ernest yelled the order at the top of his lungs, over the clash of battle. He locked onto the closest Scorned and started attacking viciously as he echoed the command. "*Retreat! Fall back!*"

Jayfor followed his example. He didn't overthink; that would kill his instinct. Mind and instinct must work together. An enemy. Attack. Dodge the thrust. Attack. Parry. Prepare to attack again. Feint an attack at his legs, exposing his upper body. Successful. Slash. The fight is over. Another enemy. Engage. Combat.

The Willing were trying to retreat, but the Scorned pressed their advantage brutally. As soon as the Willing tried to disengage, the Scorned chased them with fury, overrunning them and cutting them down. Ironically, they were cut down even faster in fleeing than they were in combat.

Why don't they use their bombs? Jayfor wondered. His question was immediately answered.

BAM. A cloud of thick smoke exploded from the center of the conflict. Jayfor knew what was happening. He took a deep breath and closed his eyes tight. He heard yells of confusion. He felt the hot smoke consume him, swirling around him. Trenson coughed and wheezed beside him, completely taken by surprise. Jayfor wanted to open his eyes, to make sure Ernest and Trenson were still beside him, but the smoke stabbed his eyes when he cracked them open.

He felt a hand grab his left arm. It was Ernest, judging by where he was standing before the bomb was released. He reached out his hand for Trenson, but there was no one there. Jayfor panicked and resisted Ernest's pull. "Trenson!"

No answer. The sounds of running, of yelling, the aftermath of the explosion; it was all becoming harder and harder to distinguish in Jayfor's mind. Everything was starting to go out of focus. *No, no! Focus.* He was forced to take a breath. The smoke wasn't as dense now, the wind thinning it considerably, but it was enough to make him gag.

"Trenson! Trenson!" There was no answer.

A new voice spoke. "To think it was my name you called just as desperately when you were in need as a child."

The sounds faded. Jayfor's mind was ascending above the noise, tuning it out. That voice was the only sound he heard.

He shook off Ernest's grip and, dazed, started walking toward the source of the voice. He thought he heard Ernest calling for him behind him, but he couldn't tell. He kept walking forward. He sensed the smoke was thin enough for him to open his eyes.

At first, he didn't see anything. The smoke swirled around him, a mystic cloud hiding everything more than a few feet away.

Wait. There was a black shape, in front of him. It blended with the smoke at first, but it slowly took shape as it came closer. It was tall but broad. The figure of a man. A man holding two swords. A man wearing a black cloak that matched his hair and a scar that traced the outline of his chiseled, gently grinning, face.

Xavson.

"You left me!" Xavson said heavily, his smile fading slightly. "You banished me, out of Faldon, out of my home! Out of everything I loved!"

Jayfor gritted his teeth. Hate mixed with confusion mixed with sorrow for what his brother had become, put him in a volatile mindset. "You ruined everything I had!" Jayfor screamed, letting the words he had wanted to say to Xavson for six years pour out. "I was happy! You took all of that! *Everything!*"

Tears started to ebb around Jayfor's eyes. He couldn't control his emotions, his wrath. He wanted to beat the smiling face of Xavson, beat it until it couldn't smile at him anymore, couldn't hurt him anymore, couldn't haunt him anymore.

"I wanted a better life, Jayfor," Xavson said soothingly, taking a few steps closer to Jayfor. "Not just for me, but you as well! I admit that my methods were... callous, at the time. But I had good intentions. I didn't want to doom us to the cycle of ignorance and comfort our family has suffered for generations."

Jayfor gripped his sword tighter. "You can't excuse murder."

"Murder?" Xavson's voice grew harsher. "Tell me, how many people have you killed, *murdered*, thoughtlessly? How many people have you struck down in an instant, not thinking about their families or their motivation. They had lives, lives that you ended because they were in your way. You have spilled more blood in six years by your own hands than generations of kings!"

The tears were blinding Jayfor. His throat was too swollen to answer. Xavson was right. He knew he was right.

"What a narrow view of the world you have, Jayfor." Xavson didn't attempt to mask his raw hostility. "You think the world is two dimensional, good guys and bad guys. And what is the difference between them? Morality? Everybody thinks they are right. Everybody is standing alone against the world, clinging to rocks called worldviews to stabilize themselves in the storm of life. We are all trying to save the world, Jayfor. Stop thinking of yourself as some idiotic savior and face reality! You forced me to face that reality long ago."

Jayfor shook his head. No. He wouldn't let the lies overtake him. But it was true! His mind felt like it was turning against itself, everything he had fought for, every life he had taken, all for nothing. All for his own version of hope that every man clung to.

He felt a hand on his shoulder. "Jayfor!" It was Trenson. "Let's go, we can deal with him some other day!"

Jayfor shook his head. "I can't. He'll haunt me forever if I leave. I have to end this now!"

He heard Ernest's voice. "Jayfor, listen to yourself! He's using your anger against you. Don't let him control you!"

The words echoed in Jayfor's mind, taunting him: *control you.*

He had enough. Running away from the cries of Trenson and Ernest, away from every ounce of reason he had, he charged at his tormentor, his brother, with a drawn sword. He would end this — now.

***

Jayfor's gone mad! Trenson shook his head, gritted his teeth, tightened the grip on his sword, and followed him. If Jayfor was going all in, he had to protect him. Ernest followed suit beside him.

Three men against one. This wasn't even a fight: it was an execution. It was physically impossible to defend against three blades at the same time. Two opponents was pushing it, three took an impossible amount of skill.

But Xavson wasn't limited by physical boundaries. Trenson saw that there was a faint shadow wreathing itself around both of Xavson's blades. These were no ordinary swords. Like Trenson and Jayfor's, these blades had been made in an otherworldly forge. They were made from a metal that didn't exist.

As such, they gave their user incredible power, power that could defy odds.

The three blades attacked simultaneously. With inhuman speed, Xavson countered all three. He moved impossibly fast, the two swords leaving brief trails of shadows following their swings. Ernest thrust, Jayfor cut, and Trenson slashed, and all three of these met with an iron wall that knocked their attack to the side like it was nothing.

Xavson had the speed of three men in one. No matter how coordinated their attack, it was always stopped. Xavson was a blur, the darkness granting him inhuman speed. Sparks flew in the clash of light and darkness.

"You're reckless, Jayfor!" Xavson remarked casually, not breaking a sweat amidst the onslaught. "Sloppy. Years of easy living have made you soft."

As intended, this fueled Jayfor's rage and made his attacks even more careless. Sweat flew from Jayfor's hair in droplets as he violently swung, thrust, and slashed at the impenetrable wall.

Nothing was working. Xavson wasn't even trying. He was toying with them, simply blocking each attack with one of his two swords, the blade swirling around him at unnatural speed.

"You have some skill," Xavson said. "But you lack passion. And passion is best taught through pain!"

With that, Xavson was done playing defense. Instead of simply blocking each of their attacks, he suddenly countered them all and swept his swords around him at a defying speed. Ernest, Trenson and Jayfor all stumbled back, inches from death.

Xavson looked at each of them, all panting and out of breath, barely standing. Xavson smiled at Jayfor. "You have taught me about pain, Jayfor. You forced me to become stronger, to rebuild everything I lost."

A gust of wind started to blow, but this was no natural gust of wind. It slowly increased in force, whipping their cloaks in the air and making the windowpanes of the houses around them creak. The wind seemed to center itself around Xavson, the shadows swirling around Xavson spreading to his arms and the rest of his body. Jayfor shielded his eyes from the gale.

"That is why, before I kill you, I want to say thank you, brother!" Xavson shouted above the fury of the wind. "Thank you for making me who I am!"

Jayfor's mouth went dry. His rage cleared, replaced with... fear. He was afraid now. Xavson had more power than the three of them combined. There was nothing they could do.

They were alone this time.

Jayfor felt a hand on his shoulder and a voice. "No. You're not alone."

Jayfor turned to see a familiar face he hadn't seen in years.

XLIX

"**A**GROND!" TRENSON BREATHED.

The burly, bearded warrior smiled. "It's been a long time, hasn't it?"

The windstorm diminished. For the first time, Xavson looked doubtful – even fearful. But he immediately masked it, assuming a scowl. "This is not your fight, Senver!" he growled.

Agrond smiled and took a few steps forward, pulling a sword of pure light from his back sheath. "Oh, I think it is."

Xavson backed away a few paces, looking at a loss. The shadow power around him shrunk at the presence of this shining warrior in spotless armor. Xavson looked behind him, toward a dark alley, and paused. Then, turning back to the group, he grinned, a smile of sadistic joy.

"I think the odds deserve a little evening," he said slowly.

Ernest, Trenson, Jayfor, and Agrond watched and from the shadows of the alley, cloaked in bleak dark armor, a helmet with curved horns, a black cape flowing around a massive figure, a dark knight, a Krenor, emerged.

"Cosgroc," Agrond muttered dourly. He raised his powerful voice. "So, the puppet of Thrall himself has crawled from his pit!"

A hissing sound came from the helmet of the dark knight, a sound that pierced Jayfor's ears and rattled Jayfor's heart. "You have no idea what you're dealing with." Cosgroc stood beside Xavson, two dark lords, Cosgroc's size making Xavson seem like a child.

Agrond laughed and held his sword beside his head in a battle-ready stance. "Well then, allow me to be the fool who fights against it."

Then they charged.

Three men of light, one warrior of Va'ar.

United by a common strength, a common goal… and a common Lord.

Charging against the two forces of darkness with reckless courage.

A clash of light and dark.

Trenson, Jayfor, and Ernest targeted Xavson, while Agrond came for Cosgroc. Agrond's usual mirth was replaced by grim determination, a hard scowl. Cosgroc's face couldn't be seen under the dark helmet. The dark knight drew a heavy blade, made of obsidian and robed in shadows. The two blades clashed with a fiery explosion of sparks and fire.

Trenson, Jayfor and Ernest attacked Xavson with newfound vigor. No longer was there any hesitation, any doubt. They knew that Agrond was with them, that Va'ar was with them.

***

Xavson was hard pressed to repel all three blades. Now he was desperate, sometimes barely managing to deflect each attack. Jayfor thrust, and Xavson had just barely enough time to push it to the side, but Trenson delivered a horizontal slash. There was no time to parry it. Xavson ducked, the blade passing over his head, but he lost his balance. He fell to the ground on his back.

All three of the men brought their swords over their heads and, with tremendous combined force, swung down on Xavson. Xavson crossed his blades above his head to defend himself. The impact was enormous. The force of three blades was almost enough to cause Xavson's blades to cave in. The three men continued pressing down, slowly overpowering Xavson and forcing his blades closer and closer to his neck.

Xavson screamed in fury and found another burst of strength. He suddenly pushed all three blades off of him so hard that all three men stumbled back. Xavson rose to his feet, panting hard and soaked in sweat. Unstoppable anger rested in his eyes.

"Enough with this!" he spat. He didn't wait for them to attack him. Like a hurricane, he lashed out at the three men, attacking with a vengeance. Now it was Trenson, Jayfor, and Ernest who were in retreat. They defended themselves in unison, covering each others blind spots. If Xavson separated them, it was over.

Xavson suddenly unleashed a vicious kick at Trenson's knee. Trenson was caught off guard and could do nothing as the heavy boot slammed into his knees, knocking him backward on the ground.

"Trenson!" Jayfor shouted.

Now he was only fighting two men. Xavson feigned a thrust, but pulled his blade back mid-thrust and instead aimed a quick slash at Jayfor's head. Unfortunately, Jayfor fell for it. He couldn't guard it in time. The dark blade sliced across Jayfor's head, cutting horizontally just above his eyes. Jayfor stumbled backward, pain flooding his sense and blood cascading from the wound.

Ernest was standing alone. Before he could act, Xavson dropped a sword to the ground and grabbed him by the throat. The grip was so strong that Ernest was helpless, dropping his sword as he instinctively gripped the hand strangling him.

Xavson smiled and peered into the Ernest's eyes, wide with fear. He didn't hesitate for long. Trenson caught sight of what was happening and Jayfor cleared his eyes enough just in time to watch it happen. Both men screamed, "*NO!*"

It was one quick motion. The sword pierced Ernest's abdomen, just below his chest. Ernest gasped and his eyes seemed like they would pop from his head. Xavson smiled and held his sword in Ernest for a few more seconds, before pulling it out and releasing his grip on Ernest.

Ernest stood for a few seconds, breathing heavily. He looked around. He met eyes with Jayfor. Jayfor was stuck in place, help-less. Ernest held Jayfor's gaze for a few seconds. Then he smiled. A peaceful smile.

Then he fell.

"*NO!*" Jayfor screamed. He grabbed his sword and rushed at Xavson. Xavson was unprepared for the sudden onslaught, only holding one sword. Jayfor unleashed attack after attack, combination after combination, at such a speed that Trenson was left in awe.

Jayfor's sword began to glow brighter and brighter. His speed shocked Xavson. There was no weakness, no flaw. The sword was revealing its true power, and Jayfor was the master unleashing it. Xavson was being pushed back.

Another combination. And then another. Uppercut, slice, thrust. All in harmony. Each time Xavson met one attack, he barely managed to meet the next one. Both men moved at otherworldly speed. Nothing could hold Jayfor back.

Finally, the glow of the sword was so blinding that Xavson couldn't see. He cried out in pain and shielded his eyes from the searing light. But that was a mistake. With unstoppable force, Jayfor brought his sword back and thrust forward.

The blade pierced Xavson's armor like it was nothing, slicing through the metal going clean through his stomach.

Xavson gasped. Never did he anticipate defeat, and surely not death. He slowly looked down at the sword in him, then up at Jayfor's fiery eyes. Jayfor returned the stare, his breathing heavy, as his berserk attitude started to diminish.

Xavson let his dark sword fall to the ground. It clattered on the stone pavement. The blade became like dust, and the wind blew it away, leaving an empty hilt.

Xavson gritted his teeth. "I... I hate you, Jayfor."

Jayfor released his blade and stepped back. Xavson wobbled for a second, staring at Jayfor for a few moments. Then he fell to his knees. The light left his eyes. He fell to the ground.

Jayfor took a few steps back, his breathing ragged. His mind was spinning. He tried to comprehend what had happened, what he just done. He had done it. Xavson was dead. He had killed him, the one who had caused him so much pain, so much hurt.

And yet... he was sad. Remorse? Was that what he felt? His brother's blood was on his hands. He had killed him. The brother who was once his friend.

I... I did what I had to do. He's gone now. Now... I can be at peace.

***

Trenson watched the showdown happen with wide eyes, too stunned at Jayfor's power to move. When he saw Xavson fall, his heart leaped. A surge of relief filled him. Unlike Jayfor, he held no connection to Xavson. He was simply a murderer with dark intent. And now he was gone.

Trenson's ears perked up as he picked up on the sounds of a different battle. Agrond. He was locked in an intense battle with Cosgroc. Trenson grabbed his sword and rose to his feet, ignoring his aching body.

The forces of light and darkness couldn't be more obvious. Cosgroc's black sword cut through the air and smashed into Agrond's sword of light in a collision of sparks. Moving so fast they were nearly blurs, neither warrior could seem to get the upper hand. They were stalled, both looking for weakness, but finding none.

It was an unstoppable force meeting an unmovable object.

Cosgroc's back was turned to Trenson, which gave him an idea. He approached the two warriors, both of whom didn't notice him.

Gripping his sword tightly, he approached Cosgroc's back. Then, pulling his glowing sword back, he thrust his sword deep into the dark knight's back. He expected to meet resistance, but the blade cut like butter.

Cosgroc screeched, an inhuman sound so painful that Trenson let go of his sword and clutched his ears in pain. Trenson's sword started to glow brighter and brighter. Agrond stopped his attack, seeing the blade protruding from the front of Cosgroc's armor.

The light grew even brighter, so bright that nothing else could be seen. Trenson shielded his eyes, but the light still blinded him. Cosgroc's screams grew even louder.

Then they stopped. The blinding light lasted a few more seconds. Then it suddenly stopped. Trenson blinked and slowly uncovered his eyes.

Cosgroc was gone. His sword fell the to the stone, no longer glowing. Beside the sword, Cosgroc's empty helmet fell to the ground, clattering and rolling on the pavement before coming to a stop. The empty eye holes were no longer filled with darkness.

Trenson looked at Agrond in wonder. Agrond looked at the helmet for a seconds, then looked at Trenson. Then Agrond smiled, a broad, happy smile. He started to laugh. It was such a pure laugh that even Trenson smiled.

"Well done, Trenson! Well done." Agrond said.

Trenson grinned, but then he heard Jayfor's voice. He looked over to see Jayfor on his knees, holding Ernest's limp body.

Trenson quickly rushed over to Jayfor. "Jayfor! We won!" He couldn't contain his excitement. Jayfor looked bleakly at Trenson. There were tears in his eyes.

Trenson looked at Ernest's lifeless face and instantly knew. Ernest was dead. There was no life left in him, no breath. He had died by Xavson's hand.

Trenson turned to Agrond, who approached Jayfor slowly. "Is there anything you can do?"

Agrond shook his head, his smile gone. "He's in a better place now. I have neither the power nor the authority to bring him back."

Jayfor shook his head. "Can't you do something?!"

Agrond kneeled to the ground and looked at Jayfor at eye level with soft, compassionate eyes. "He died a hero's death. A warrior of Va'ar can ask for no more."

Trenson tried to hold back the tears. "I... I wish I could have known him better. I thought maybe, just maybe, he could have been..." he choked on his words.

Jayfor looked at Trenson questioningly. "What?"

Trenson looked down at Ernest. "I never told you this before, Jayfor, but... When I was child, when my house was destroyed and my mother and brother enslaved..."

Jayfor nodded.

"My brother's name... it was Ernest."

Agrond looked away and said nothing.

EPILOGUE

"THIS WAY." AGROND LED them through the gardens of the palace.

Jayfor looked around in wonder. "This place looks so much better during the day."

Agrond chuckled. He led them forward through the rows of trees and shrubs, which created an artificial forest around them. Jayfor and Trenson followed behind Agrond, carefully watching their steps over the uneven path. Behind them walked Reginold and Erador, both who had barely said a word to them the entire time. They were as stoic as ever.

To break the silence, Trenson cleared his throat and addressed Reginold, the closest of the Senver. "So... you two were in the city the entire time? And didn't think about helping us even once?"

"We were under order," Reginold replied, rather coldly. "We watched you from afar, but never interfered. Even at the execution, we were told not to. But it seems some of us can do whatever we please," Reginold shot a cold glare at Agrond.

"Oh please!" Agrond waved his hand in the air. "I was given permission, mind you, once it was found out that Cosgroc would be there. And it's a good thing I did."

Jayfor nodded. "We wouldn't have been able to hold our own against both of them."

They continued walking. The air was getting warmer. Spring was coming. While it was still cold, the biting wind was gone, replaced with a cool breeze. Soon the flowers would be blooming, and the winter that seemed to last forever would end.

The flora around them seemed to know this. Already, the winter plants were fading. The cycle of life would begin again.

A new season, Jayfor reminisced.

Agrond spoke. "I'm not ordering you to do anything at this point. You've already done enough, and let me tell you, Va'ar is very pleased with you. I would understand if you chose to live out your days in peace, find a pretty wife, and settle down."

Agrond cleared his throat. "That being said, since Xavson was named heir to the throne of Augustria, that essentially made him king the minute he killed Thrance. But since Xavson is now dead, the kingship falls on his closest relative." Agrond looked behind him. "That would be you, Jayfor."

Jayfor nodded. "I have thought about this myself as well."

"King?" Trenson asked, this being the first time he had heard this. "Jayfor, you could be a king once again! It will be like you never left home."

Jayfor smiled. "We can't, Trenson. We still have to find the Tree of Ramadus, remember? We still have our mission. This isn't the final victory."

"I'm not saying you have to take up the mantle," Agrond said. "You can always deny it. In that case, Thrance's nephew would be the next heir. He's a good person, and would rule Augustria with grace. You have nothing to fear if you decide to decline it."

Jayfor was confused. "But what about my mission? Don't we have to keep going north until we find the Tree of Ramadus?"

Agrond didn't respond.

It had been three days since the execution. The city was in shambles. Now that there was no king, and the latest successor was dead, who would take the crown? When word came that it was the successor's brother who had killed them, everyone knew what this meant: Jayfor was the new king, by law.

The city was holding its breath. There had been no ceremony or coronation. Jayfor was legally the new king, and as so he was given access to the palace and treated like a king.

But there were rumors that he was considering denying his position, that he would defer it to the original heir to the throne: Thrance's nephew. Would that be an improvement or not? Nobody knew.

In this state of confusion, everyone looked to Jayfor, waiting to see what he would do.

"How has the rehabilitation process been, Trenson?" Agrond asked out of the blue.

Trenson was confused. "What?"

"The addictive poison that Thrance gave you. You've been slowly getting off that, correct?"

"Oh right! Yes, we're putting lower concentrations of it in my food daily. It shouldn't be long before I can get off of it completely."

Agrond nodded. "Good."

"Agrond, where are you taking us?" Jayfor asked.

"To see something that will lift your spirits," Agrond replied mystically. "Ah, we're here!"

The dense foliage gave way to an open patch of grass. The forest was open here, and the grass gave way to stone pavement. It was a small courtyard, surrounded by the forest.

The only thing in this courtyard, however, was one thing, a single object in it's center that made Jayfor and Trenson stop dead in their tracks and stare, wondering if this was truly what they thought it was.

A tree.

"Your journey is over," Agrond said with a smile.

"Wait!" Trenson said incredulously. He turned to Erador and Reginold. "You're saying that everything that happened to us – becoming a slave, Jayfor joining the Willing, the execution – you knew it was going to happen? You knew it would lead us here?"

Erador shook his head. "Of course not. I knew that this was the tree we spoke of, but we weren't told why, or how, you would end up here. We were simply told what to tell you, and that was it."

Jayfor still was confused. "Why not just tell us to go to Augustria? Why not spare us all the trouble and keep it simple?"

"Because you would have died," Reginold said, his voice brutally blunt. "We were shown the possible future if we used a more direct approach. All of them resulted in you failing. We told you exactly what was needed, in order to survive, and to stop Xavson and the Scorned."

Jayfor had plenty more questions, but he decided not to think about them now. He turned his focus once again to the tree. It was old. Very old. Only eight feet high, it was gnarly and gray from top to bottom. It was thick at the ground, twisting itself into branches as it rose, the truck extending up to a pointy tip.

Jayfor approached it. A bed of dirt surrounded by cut stone encircled the tree. The tree was cracked in numerous places. Of all the words that could describe this short and ugly tree, *old* was the best. And yet, there was a single, white flower on the tip of one of its branches, small and tender.

Jayfor gently touched the small flower. "Is this truly it?" He whispered.

Agrond stepped beside him and placed a hand on his shoulder. "Yes. Your quest... is over."

Jayfor closed his eyes and breathed a heavy sigh. It was over now. He could rest. The pain, the journey, everything that was depending on them... it was all over.

Peace.

Trenson stood beside Jayfor. When Jayfor opened his eyes, he saw Trenson smiling at him. "We did it," he said softly.

Jayfor nodded, returning the smile. "Yes... we did."

Agrond let the moment hang in the air for a few moments, then he backed up and stood beside Reginold and Erador. "Well, my friends, this is where we take our leave."

Jayfor turned. "You're leaving already?" he said reluctantly.

Agrond smiled. "We have shown you everything we were allowed to. You have exceeded my expectations enormously." He looked at Reingold and Erador. "I think I speak for all of us."

Reginold and Erador both nodded, but didn't smile. However, Erador couldn't hide the pride in his voice. "I... enjoyed it. Before

I was assigned to you, I had little faith in mortals. But you've set a fine example for all your kind. It has made me think."

"You have impressed us both," Reginold added.

Jayfor nodded and smiled. To receive such compliments from such stone-faced men was a high honor. "Thank you."

"We couldn't have done it without you," Trenson insisted.

Agrond chuckled. "We merely showed you the path. You did all the work yourself."

Jayfor asked one last question. "What do we do now, now that you're leaving us?"

"Oh, I'm not leaving you. I don't know if we'll ever meet in person again, but know this: even if I'm not watching over you, Va'ar is, and he protects those who honor Him. And you have both honored Him greatly. So what is there to fear? The future is in your hands now. If you decide to take up the mantel of king of Augustria, Jayfor, then rule with dignity and honor, and don't forget your past. You can rebuild a new Loronis, in the memory of Faldon. Or if you decide to deny it, to take a simple life and live in peace in quiet, remember what you sacrificed. Remember what we have shown you. If the need ever arises, use your sword in His Name."

Agrond faced Trenson. "As for you, Trenson, I have a feeling you'll follow Jayfor no matter what he does?"

Trenson grinned. "I've followed him this far; what's the point of leaving him now? Besides, we both know he can't manage himself."

Jayfor shot Trenson a rueful look.

Agrond chuckled. "I thought so. Thank you for your loyalty, Trenson. Even when you were a slave, you still honored Va'ar in your actions. And if you are ever looking for another adventure, well... The Willing are in need of a new leader. I'm sure you could fit the position well."

The new leader of the Willing? "I... I will have to think about it."

Agrond nodded. "Of course. It seems you both have an important decision to make."

Trenson and Jayfor both smiled. How far they had come! One a thirdborn heir, the other a simple vagabond. And yet they had accomplished more in six years than most men their entire lives. Through all their mistakes and suffering, they had seen the world, both the good and the bad. Like a boulder, time had rolled on, but through their actions, they had nudged it in a new direction. Although history would never mention them, they had shifted the flow of history. People wouldn't know their names. But history would honor them.

Before leaving with Reginold and Erador, Agrond smiled at them one last time. "Looking back, I see that Va'ar had quite the journey for you. But I wonder, where will His destiny take you now?"

Did you like this book?

THAT'S GREAT, THANK YOU! If you really want to help me, please leave a review for my book on Amazon or Goodreads. Those reviews really make a difference.

I also love to hear from readers and hear what they thought of my book! Reach out to me through my email, contact@gunnerl ong.com, and let me know what you thought!

If you want to stay updated on my books and learn more about my life as an author, follow me on Facebook or Instagram @Author Gunner Long.

OR: Subscribe to the email list for updates delivered straight to your inbox!

Also by Gunner Long

1. Insurrection

2. Endeavor

3. Destiny

About the author

GUNNER LONG ALWAYS READ the works of C.S. Lewis and J.R.R. Tolkien, and was moved by the stories and messages they conveyed. Dedicated to the Lord, he was always searching for age-appropriate books that offered the same thrilling tales and adventures, but without the immorality that seemed to plague modern action books. So he decided to change that. He created the world of Ralladin and started his first book, *Insurrection,* when he was just thirteen, driven to create something that not only kids, but people of all ages could enjoy. He hopes that people read his books and leave with not only a story, but a message. He lives with his family near Brunswick, Georgia.

www.ingramcontent.com/pod-product-compliance
Lightning Source LLC
Chambersburg PA
CBHW071739110726
47908CB00006B/1634